Praise for
Jezebel

"The story of Jezebel in the Bible deals with a religious woman who was smart, deceitful, and manipulative, and she used her ways to get what she wanted at the expense of others. Jacquelin Thomas takes this Bible story and reworks it for modern times, and her character is just as cunning. I highly recommend this book." —Rawsistaz

"Perhaps the question we should ask ourselves is, How do I fight jealousy and greed in my everyday life? This is a book to read. The lessons that can be learned from Jesse Belle will stay with the reader. Is there a happily-ever-after where all our worldly possessions are admired, or does our faith in God shine as we walk in His light? You decide." — Romance Reviews Today

. . . and for Jacquelin Thomas and Her Novels

"Absolutely beautiful . . . page-turning drama and wonderful, heartfelt characters . . . reminds us of the power of God's love." —ReShonda Tate Billingsley, *Essence* bestselling author of *Let the Church Say Amen*

"Jacquelin Thomas is masterful." —Shades of Romance Reviews

"[Thomas] brings an African-American perspective and . . . edgier tone into Christian fiction, while keeping the gospel message up front and center." —*Publishers Weekly*

continued . . .

"Jacquelin Thomas's novels are about heroines who survive seemingly insurmountable odds. [They] are also about self-love and being happy with the person you are."   —*The Romance Reader*

"Thought-provoking."
                                    —Victoria Christopher Murray, bestselling author of
                                    Truth Be Told

"Entertaining African-American Christian romance that will surprise readers . . . invigorating."   —*Midwest Book Review*

"[Thomas] shows readers that prayer, strength, and forgiveness have the power to change everything . . . inspiring . . . very realistic and very touching."   —Rawsistaz

"Thomas tackles the tough subject of grief and reconciliation with grace. This is a novel to savor."   —*Romantic Times*

JEZEBEL

JACQUELIN THOMAS

NAL
PRAISE

NAL Praise
Published by New American Library, a division of
Penguin Group (USA) Inc., 375 Hudson Street,
New York, New York 10014, USA
Penguin Group (Canada), 90 Eglinton Avenue East, Suite 700, Toronto,
Ontario M4P 2Y3, Canada (a division of Pearson Penguin Canada Inc.)
Penguin Books Ltd., 80 Strand, London WC2R 0RL, England
Penguin Ireland, 25 St. Stephen's Green, Dublin 2,
Ireland (a division of Penguin Books Ltd.)
Penguin Group (Australia), 250 Camberwell Road, Camberwell, Victoria 3124,
Australia (a division of Pearson Australia Group Pty. Ltd.)
Penguin Books India Pvt. Ltd., 11 Community Centre, Panchsheel Park,
New Delhi - 110 017, India
Penguin Group (NZ), 67 Apollo Drive, Rosedale, North Shore 0632,
New Zealand (a division of Pearson New Zealand Ltd.)
Penguin Books (South Africa) (Pty.) Ltd., 24 Sturdee Avenue,
Rosebank, Johannesburg 2196, South Africa

Penguin Books Ltd., Registered Offices:
80 Strand, London WC2R 0RL, England

Published by NAL Praise, an imprint of New American Library, a division of Penguin Group (USA) Inc.
Previously published in an NAL Praise hardcover.

First NAL Praise Trade Paperback Printing, March 2009
10 9 8 7 6 5 4 3 2 1

Copyright © Jacquelin Thomas, 2008
Readers Guide copyright © Penguin Group (USA) Inc., 2009
All rights reserved

Scripture taken from the *Holy Bible, New International Version*®. Copyright © 1973, 1978, 1984 International
Bible Society. Used by permission of Zondervan. All rights reserved. The "NIV" and "New International Version"
trademarks are registered in the United States Patent and Trademark Office by International Bible Society.
Use of either trademark requires the permission of International Bible Society.

NAL Praise and logo are trademarks of Penguin Group (USA) Inc.

NAL Praise Trade Paperback ISBN: 978-0-451-22464-4

The Library of Congress has cataloged the hardcover edition of this title as follows:

Thomas, Jacquelin.
Jezebel / Jacquelin Thomas.
p. cm.
ISBN 978-0-451-22310-4
1. African-American women—Fiction. 2. Spouses of clergy—Fiction. I. Title.
PS3570.H5637J47 2008
813'.54—dc22   2007035519

Set in Centaur MT
Designed by Elke Sigal

Printed in the United States of America

Without limiting the rights under copyright reserved above, no part of this publication may be reproduced, stored in or
introduced into a retrieval system, or transmitted, in any form, or by any means (electronic, mechanical, photocopying,
recording, or otherwise), without the prior written permission of both the copyright owner and the above publisher of
this book.

PUBLISHER'S NOTE
This is a work of fiction. Names, characters, places, and incidents either are the product of the author's imagination or
are used fictitiously, and any resemblance to actual persons, living or dead, business establishments, events, or locales is
entirely coincidental.
      The publisher does not have any control over and does not assume any responsibility for author or third-party Web
sites or their content.

The scanning, uploading, and distribution of this book via the Internet or via any other means without the permission of
the publisher is illegal and punishable by law. Please purchase only authorized electronic editions, and do not participate
in or encourage electronic piracy of copyrighted materials. Your support of the author's rights is appreciated.

To Courtney, Camille, Alyssa,
Larika, Mahalia and Angelica—

I love you all!

And also concerning Jezebel the LORD says:

"Dogs will devour Jezebel by the wall of Jezreel."

—1 KINGS 21:23
(NEW INTERNATIONAL VERSION)

PROLOGUE

Blinding tears rolled down her cheeks, but Jessie Belle Deveraux was unable to wipe them away because her lead-laden arms weren't any use to her. She continued to sink deeper into depression.

I'm paying dearly for my sins.

The thought reverberated through her mind over and over again, bringing on more tears.

I can't even wipe my own nose. Lord, please have mercy on my soul and take me out of my misery.

Jessie Belle would prefer to have died from the fall that left her completely paralyzed to being imprisoned in a wheelchair with her life slowly draining away. She'd thought she'd made peace with her situation, but feeling the way she did—she hadn't.

The nurse entered the bedroom carrying a stack of clean towels. She took one look at Jessie Belle and dropped them on a nearby chair, asking, "Mrs. Deveraux . . . what's wrong?"

Humiliated, Jessie Belle felt like a helpless babe while Helen gently wiped her face.

"I h-hate being like this, H-Helen. I c-can't even wipe m-my own nose," she managed between sobs. "There was a time when I was on the top of the world and now . . . now I'm nothing more than deadweight."

"Mrs. Deveraux, you can still have a full life."

Jessie Belle shook her head. "Helen, I chose to harden my heart and betray the people I loved the most, and now I have to suffer the consequences. Although nobody has said it—I know they feel the same way I do. They think I'm reaping exactly what I sowed."

"Nobody's thinking that, Mrs. Deveraux," Helen countered. "You are a real sweet lady. I can see that."

Shaking her head, Jessie Belle stated, "You didn't know me back then. I was a terrible person."

Helen raised her eyebrows in surprise. "Oh, Mrs. Deveraux, I can't believe that. You're just going through a little depression right now."

"It's true, Helen," she insisted. "Do you know what they used to call me? *Jezebel*. People called me a Jezebel."

"But why? I don't believe you'd ever cheat on your husband."

"Jezebel was a powerful queen when she was alive, but hardly anything remained of her after her death. It wasn't about sex for her—it was power and control. She was tossed over a balcony for her many sins, trampled by horses and eaten by dogs. Did you know that there's a Jezebel spirit?"

When Helen shook her head no, Jessie Belle continued. "There is. Anyone who worships money, earthly treasures or power is vulnerable to this spirit. I should know, because it consumed me and at the time I didn't care. It took nearly losing my husband and my son to motivate a change in me, but by then a lot of people had been hurt—a lot of damage done." She gulped hard, fighting back more tears.

"If I'm to be honest—Jezebel and I had a lot in common. Oh, I was really something—a force to be reckoned with, for sure. Helen, all I cared about was what I wanted. Back then, I didn't care who I stepped on," Jessie Belle murmured. She paused a moment before adding, "The person that pushed me over the balcony—I don't blame them."

Her nurse sat there, stunned by what Jessie Belle was saying.

"You wouldn't have liked me, Helen." Jessie Belle suddenly felt the urge to bare her soul. "My mama used to say all the time to tell the truth and shame the devil. That's what I'm about to do. It all started when I was eighteen years old. . . ."

Her Character

CHAPTER ONE

🌿 *June 1970* ——◦ *Mayville, Georgia*

Eighteen-year-old Jessie Belle Holt knew that her laughter sounded like sweet music to the ears of that ol' nasty Ezra Josiah Jones.

All she had to do was giggle at his stupid jokes, bend down low enough to give him a glimpse of her youthful, full, round breasts and show off her shapely legs to have the pervert exactly where she wanted him. He was a beady-eyed mouse of a man itching to sample her goods and was always trying to get her on that cot he kept in the storeroom of his dress shop.

"Deacon Jones, you so funny," Jessie Belle cooed, making a conscious effort to lick her full lips. She'd read in one of her many fashion magazines that men found the act sexy.

He wiped away beads of perspiration from his face with a dingy white handkerchief. Ezra Jones glanced quickly over his shoulder, then back at Jessie Belle, mumbling, "Gal . . . you do things to me. I could just sop you up with a biscuit."

She giggled. "What on earth are you talking about, Deacon? I'm not doing a thing."

"Why don't you come by the store tomorrow? Tell your parents that I need you to help out with the inventory," he suggested. "Let me show you. . . ."

Jessie Belle pretended to be coy. "Deacon Jones, you still have that cute lil' dress—the pink one with the green and white flowers? I sho' like that dress." If the dress was gone, there was no need for her to continue this disgusting ruse.

He nodded furiously. "Uh-huh. It's still there. Somethin' like that would sho' look mighty pretty on you."

Leaning forward so that her breast touched his arm, she whispered in his ear, "I *really* like that dress, Deacon Jones. That mean ol' wife of yours—she told me it was too expensive for the likes of me." She stuck out her lips in a pout. "She really hurt my feelings when she told me that."

At the mention of his wife, Ezra's expression soured. "You don't worry your pretty little head about Agnes. She always been a spiteful wench. I'll take care of everything. You just come by the store tomorrow." Grinning, he added, "Work a few hours doing some inventory for me."

"Will she be there?" Jessie Belle questioned. She and Mrs. Jones didn't care for each other. *She knows her man has the hots for me. Ain't no point in being mad with me, though. It's not my fault if she can't hold on to her man or keep him happy.*

"Naw. She gon' be visiting with her kin down in Albany for a couple of days. You come on by the store. Okay?"

Before Jessie Belle could respond, she heard a noise coming from behind Ezra. She peeked around the nasty-minded deacon to find her mother glaring at them.

Pushing him away, she straightened her dress and said, "Ma . . . Deacon Jones was just telling me another one of his jokes."

"The deacon needs to tend to his wife," her mother stated coldly. "Agnes is looking for you."

"Thank you, Miss Anabeth." He brushed past her, walking as fast as he could, but not before Jessie Belle's mother saw the evidence of his arousal.

Bristling, Anabeth walked up to Jessie Belle, pinching her hard on the arm. "What are you thinking, gal? Your daddy could've been the one walking back here instead of me."

Straightening her dress, Jessie Belle said, "I wasn't gon' do nothing with him. All we was doing is talking."

"Humph," Anabeth grunted. "I know what Ezra was after and it weren't no conversation. He used to try and get me into corners. Jessie Belle, you've got to be careful if you want to marry well. You're only eighteen years old and already been pregnant twice. No God-fearing man will want you. If you'd listen to me and keep those long legs of yours closed . . ."

Running her fingers through her naturally curly, medium brown hair, Jessie Belle responded, "I'm beautiful and I'm smart, Ma. I really don't think I'll ever have to worry about being without a man."

Anabeth Holt patted her own brown hair, which was lightly sprinkled with gray throughout. "Well, if it's a good husband you're wanting—we can only pray for some kind stranger to come to town and marry you. And we'll have to trick him on your wedding night, I'm ashamed to say. How many times do I have to tell you that you don't have to give up the goodies to get what you want?"

Practically dragging Jessie Belle along, Anabeth stated, "Your father's waiting for us. C'mon."

A couple of church members glanced in their direction and began whispering as they walked by.

Jessie Belle knew they were talking about her, but she didn't care. Anybody who couldn't do anything for her was nothing more than a blot occupying space needlessly as far as she was concerned.

"I wouldn't be looking so hard in this direction," Anabeth told the women. "You need to be watching your own fast-tail daughters. You so busy trying to stir my grits—your own pot boiling over."

Jessie Belle broke into a short laugh.

Pinching her arm, Anabeth uttered, "Shush, gal. It ain't funny. Hearing the things people saying about you nearly breaks your daddy heart. He don't like people gossiping about you like that."

"And you think I do?"

"Then stop giving them stuff to talk about," Anabeth advised. "Save yourself for somebody worth something and not just taking up space on God's green earth. Find a man worthy of you."

Slowing her pace, Anabeth asked, "Are you listening to me, Jessie Belle?"

"Yeah, Ma. I heard you."

"*I mean it.* We've already had to get rid of that one baby. . . . God, forgive me, but I couldn't let you keep shaming your daddy. At least the good Lawd took the second one naturally."

Her father never knew about her babies—her mother made sure of that. She took Jessie Belle to Atlanta, where some back-alley doctor eliminated her burden the first time. The second time, she miscarried. The father of both babies turned out to be a jerk, so everything happened for the best.

Living the rest of her life in Mayville, Georgia, was not on Jessie Belle Holt's agenda. She felt she deserved better—that's what her mother always told her.

"Marry a man that's got something, Jessie Belle, even if you don't love him." Anabeth pulled a thin compact mirror out of her purse and checked her face. "Love will come later, if he a good man."

Satisfied with her appearance, she put it away. "You know I coulda married a doctor. He came through town when your daddy was courting me. He came from a wealthy family and was a real handsome man. Had a nice big car. All your daddy had was that old truck—the same one rusting in the backyard now. That doctor sho' nuff wanted me, but instead I married for love and look where it got me."

"Aren't you happy with Papa?" Jessie Belle wanted to know.

Anabeth nodded. "I love your daddy, but the truth of it is that I could've been just as happy if we'd lived in a nice big house somewhere in a big city or had some money." Anabeth's gaze met her daughter's. "Never settle for less than what you deserve."

A flash of regret shone brightly in Anabeth's eyes, but was gone.

"I won't," Jessie Belle vowed.

Jessie Belle hid in her bedroom from the moment they arrived home. She didn't feel like helping her mother with the cooking. Normally she loved being in the kitchen, but today Jessie Belle just wanted to relax and fantasize about her future.

She primped and posed in front of the full-length mirror in the corner of her bedroom, studying her reflection, mimicking the models in the latest fashion magazine.

Jessie Belle was extremely proud of her tawny skin color, her dark gray eyes and her full lips, but hated the tiny mole painted in the corner of her top lip. To Jessie Belle, it marred her otherwise perfect complexion.

Smiling, Jessie Belle ran her fingers through her warm chocolate curls. She heard her father calling her name and sighed.

"Gal, c'mon out that room. Help your ma in the kitchen."

She groaned. *Once I'm gone—I'm never coming back here to this old shack of a house.*

Jessie Belle couldn't stand the smell of her home. It smelled old and no amount of air fresheners or deodorizers could rid the house of its natural odor.

Jessie Belle muttered a curse, strolled out of her room and headed down the hall to the kitchen. Her mother didn't glance up from what she was doing, but said, "You make the potato salad, gal. Your daddy likes the way you make it. He thinks I put way too much mustard in it."

Jessie Belle bit back a smile. She could tell from her mother's tone that she felt more than a little put off.

"Anabeth, you're a wonderful cook, sugar," her father stated. "I just don't have the stomach I used to have. I—"

"Elias, just quit while you're ahead," Anabeth interjected. "Your daughter's making the potato salad, so just leave it be."

Chuckling, Jessie Belle washed her hands in the sink and immediately set out to peel the potatoes.

Seated at the small dining table off the kitchen, her father said, "Your mama was just telling me that Ezra Jones has been sniffing around you a lot lately."

She sat down across from her father. "He wants me to come by the store tomorrow to help with some inventory."

Jessie Belle picked up a raw potato.

"Why he need you to help?" her father asked. "Agnes is his wife. Don't she help him out in the store? What he need you for?"

"I don't think she's all that good with math, Papa," Jessie Belle uttered. She sliced off the skin and tossed the potato back into the bowl. "Deacon Jones called her a dumb cluck."

"He shouldn't be confiding in you," her mother stated with a frown. "He don't need to be involving you in married-folk business. It's not right."

Jessie Belle finished her task and she rose to her feet. "It was a chance to make some money. That's all."

She carried the potatoes over to the kitchen sink and washed them once more before placing them into a large pot of boiling water. "I didn't think it would become a federal case."

Her father shook his head. "I don't want you working there."

Anabeth agreed as she dropped a drumstick into a pan of hot grease, then another and another.

"You were the one that said I needed to get a job, Papa. You told me that if I wasn't gonna go to college, I had to work." Pointing to the bowl of cooked macaroni, Jessie Belle asked, "Do you want me to make the macaroni and cheese?"

Anabeth nodded. "Thanks."

Jessie Belle glanced over to where her father sat, and said, "Papa, I'm just trying to make a few dollars. There's a dress that I want and Deacon Jones said I could get it by doing the inventory and being a salesgirl, since his wife is gonna be gone for a few days."

"Oh no . . . ," Anabeth uttered. "His wife ain't gon' be there. I don't know about you, Elias, but I don't like the smell of this. Humph. I sho' don't like the smell of this."

Jessie Belle continued to plead her case. "Papa, I promise you that if Deacon Jones gets fresh with me, I'll come straight home and tell you."

"Jessie Belle, your mama and I both have had some concerns about you and some of the men in this town. I hear all the rumors about you. I'll not have a child of mine walking around giving her goods to Tom, Dick and Harry."

"People have nothing better to do than to stay in folks' business. They tell a lot of lies just to have something to talk about," she uttered. "I'm your daughter—Papa, you should know me better than that."

"I *do* know you, Jessie Belle," he stated. "And if you don't change your ways, I'm afraid they gon' lead you straight to trouble. Mark my words. . . ."

Elias stood up slowly. "I think I'ma go take a little nap until supper's ready."

When he walked out of the kitchen, Anabeth turned to face her daughter. "You lie so easy—it's scary."

"I'm not gon' be the one to break my daddy's heart," Jessie Belle responded as she shredded two cups of sharp cheddar cheese. "I'm just trying to protect him."

Anabeth woke Jessie Belle up at the crack of dawn the next day. "C'mon, gal. We need to get a head start on the chores."

Pulling the covers over her head, she complained, "Ma . . . I didn't get to bed until one. I'm tired."

"I didn't tell you to stay up half the night on the telephone. Your daddy's expecting that guest preacher this afternoon. The one who's preaching during tent revival. We got to get this house in order, so get on up. The day is passing us by."

Jessie Belle had planned on sneaking down to the store to see Deacon Jones and get the dress she wanted so badly. She didn't care what her parents said when it came to something she desired. She searched through the fog clouding her memory. "I forgot all about Reverend Deveraux coming. He the one y'all so excited about."

Anabeth nodded. "Reverend Deveraux is a for-sho' man on fire for the Lawd. Jessie Belle, that man can preach. We heard him when we went to Waynesville a couple months back, and your daddy told me right then and there—we had to get him to come preach for revival."

"Let's hope he don't fall asleep in the middle of his sermon like ol' Reverend Douglas did." Jessie Belle laughed. "That was so funny."

Anabeth chuckled at the memory. "Well, I don't think this one will be putting anybody to sleep. Just you wait and see."

"Listening to an old geezer is not my idea of a good time," Jessie Belle uttered. "Tent revival is always so boring, Ma. Why do I have to be there every single night?"

"Because you are the daughter of Reverend Elias Holt. Besides, if you want the truth—you need every night of that tent revival, Jessie Belle, because you on the wrong road."

She groaned. "Ma, don't start. . . . It's too early in the morning."

"It ain't never too early to get right with God."

"Why are we cleaning up the house? It ain't dirty, and besides, he's staying at the rooming house."

"We can't have Reverend Deveraux coming here for dinner and the house looking a mess. He won't be going back to Baton Rouge talking about how I keep a dirty house. No sirree . . . I can't have that. . . ."

Jessie Belle crawled out of bed and brushed past her mother. She padded barefoot to the bathroom across the hall. It provided a brief but peaceful escape from the high-pitched tone of Anabeth's voice.

Inside the cramped room, Jessie Belle stripped out of her pajamas and turned on the shower.

Half an hour later, Jessie Belle was dressed and seated at her vanity. She pulled her hair into a ponytail, tucked her T-shirt into her bell-bottom jeans and headed to the kitchen.

"I made some grits and eggs," Anabeth announced. "You want some?"

"I'll eat later," Jessie Belle responded. "What do you want me to do?"

"Make sure that you mop the kitchen floor and be sure to dust real good, Jessie Belle. We don't want the reverend thinking we keep a nasty house. Clean the windows inside and out and vacuum."

Jessie Belle rolled her eyes heavenward. *I'm not the maid,* she wanted to say, but knew that her mother would surely backhand her for being flip.

"When you get done back there, you can get started on the living and dining rooms. I'll never have it said that I don't keep a clean house."

"I'd better get started," Jessie Belle said quietly.

She pulled a set of sheets from the chifforobe and changed all the beds. Her mother insisted on having the bed linens changed three times a week. While Jessie Belle worked on the bedrooms, her mother was busy cleaning the bathrooms.

Jessie Belle sent up a quick prayer of gratitude. She hated that particular task, but like her mother, she couldn't stand a nasty house. While she cleaned, Jessie Belle fantasized about the grand estate home she'd have one day along with a maid to keep it clean.

She'd pinned her hopes on Kenneth Walker, her boyfriend of two years, marrying her. He'd promised to marry her before he left to play professional football for a team in California. But when he found out she was pregnant the second time and wouldn't have an abortion, he left town without so much as a goodbye, and Jessie Belle hadn't heard from him since.

Her mother was right. Jessie Belle held the power to control her destiny. She just had to find a suitable husband.

CHAPTER TWO

Traynor Deveraux Jr.'s car felt like a furnace.

The brand-new 1970 Ford Thunderbird felt more like an oven than a car. He wiped the sweat from his forehead with a perspiration-stained washcloth. If the heat was this miserable and smoldering now, Traynor never wanted to go to hell.

He read the sign welcoming him into the tiny community of Mayville and sent up a quick prayer of thanksgiving for arriving safely. He followed the directions he'd been given and paid close attention to the signs along the route.

Traynor really wasn't worried about getting lost in a town that was basically one exit in and one exit out.

He made the first left on Apple Road, noting the Cotton Patch Rooming House on the corner, where he would be staying during his visit. He continued driving down the dusty dirt road until he saw the sign for Strawberry Lane. He turned right and immediately began looking for the fourth house on the left.

He parked his car in front of the wooden house and got out.

Traynor's eyes surveyed the area, taking in his surroundings. No wonder his father had to back out of coming. It was a dusty town and would wreak havoc on his father's lungs. His father suffered from a condition known as sarcoidosis, which caused inflammation of the body tissues. His lungs were affected.

Reverend Holt pastored a small church in the farming community. He'd already forewarned Traynor's father that the love offering would not be much. The townsfolk were a poor lot but hardworking and had a heart for the good Lord.

That's all that mattered to Traynor. Born into a family of preachers, he had always known that he'd end up in a pulpit. Traynor preached his first sermon at the tender age of seven. His goal in life was to serve God with his whole heart. Traynor never worried about money. He fully believed that the Lord would provide him with everything he needed.

Traynor wiped his face with the washcloth, and then tossed it back into the open window of the passenger side of his car. He wanted to make a good first impression, so despite the hot, humid June weather, Traynor slipped on his blazer before strolling up the rickety steps to the porch.

He knocked softly on the front door.

The girl that suddenly appeared at the door looked like an angel—innocent, her loveliness breathtaking and ethereal. His father had mentioned in passing that Reverend Holt had a daughter, but he never expected to see such a vision of beauty standing before him. His attention was drawn to the tiny mole on her top lip.

"Can I help you?" she asked sweetly.

A vaguely sensuous light passed between them. Clearing his throat, Traynor managed to respond, "I came to speak with your father . . . Reverend Holt."

Her eyes never left his face as she asked, "May I have your name, sir?"

Traynor savored her deep Southern accent. "Traynor Deveraux," he replied. "Pastor Traynor Deveraux Jr. My father is ill and sent me in his stead."

She seemed surprised at first but, after a moment, broke into a tiny smile. "Please come inside, Pastor." She moved to the side to let him enter.

An older version of the girl standing before him appeared in the room. She eyed him from head to toe before asking, "Who is this?"

Traynor introduced himself again.

"Pastor Deveraux, we so glad you could make it," Anabeth said with a big grin on her chubby face. "My husband will be out shortly. He worked in the vegetable garden most of the morning. Soon as he get hisself all washed up, he'll be right out here to greet you." She gestured toward the multicolored sofa. "Make yourself comfortable."

She pointed to her daughter. "This here is Jessie Belle, our daughter."

Traynor smiled. "It's a pleasure to meet you, Miss Holt."

"Would you like somethin' cool to drink, sir?" Jessie Belle asked.

He smiled in gratitude. "Just a glass of ice water, if it's not too much bother." Traynor was mindful not to stare at her. He didn't want to give Jessie Belle or her parents the wrong idea.

"It's no bother at all."

Jessie Belle left for a few minutes but soon strolled back into the living room carrying a glass of ice water.

She held it out to Traynor, her eyes meeting his gaze.

"Thank you, Miss Holt."

She grinned, showing off a perfect set of white teeth. "Just call me Jessie Belle."

Anabeth sent a sharp look to her daughter, sparking Traynor's curiosity. As far as he could tell, the young woman hadn't done a thing. Perhaps her mother desired a more formal relationship between her daughter and strangers. It didn't offend him at all. Traynor admired the fact that Mrs. Holt was very protective of such a beautiful blessing.

Elias Holt joined him ten minutes later.

"Hey, young Deveraux. Welcome to Mayville," he greeted while shaking Traynor's hand. "I see you met the family. I hope they gave you a proper welcome."

"Yes, sir," Traynor responded. "My father sends his regards. He's sorry that he was unable to come. He was recently diagnosed with sarcoidosis and the doctor advised him to stay put for a while until he's feeling stronger."

"Well, we blessed that he sent you in his stead." Surveying Traynor from head to toe, Elias said, "I heard nothing but good stuff about you, young man. We all looking forward to hearing what you got to say tonight at the tent revival. We sho' glad you here."

He glanced over his shoulder. "Anabeth, the food 'bout ready?"

"We just waiting on the biscuits," she responded. "Everything else ready."

Traynor's eyes strayed to Jessie Belle, who was standing beside her mother. He'd caught her staring at him before she turned away.

Elias followed his gaze and said, "Jessie Belle . . . she plays the piano for the church."

She gave Traynor a shy smile before dropping her eyes. He reluctantly tore his gaze away from her, despite the way she radiated a vitality that drew him like a magnet.

Anabeth Holt walked out of the room, but a few minutes later, she called out for her daughter. "Jessie Belle, come in here and help me."

"Is there someplace I can wash up a bit?" Traynor inquired.

"Sure," Elias answered. "The first door on your left is the bathroom."

Traynor walked down the narrow hallway painted in a dull-looking beige color and stopped at a white door. Stepping inside, he turned on the water at the small sink and quickly washed his face and his hands.

He heard footsteps.

"Daddy wanted me to give these to you," Jessie Belle stated softly, offering a towel and washrag to him.

"Thank you," Traynor uttered with a smile. He couldn't get over how beautiful she was. Jessie Belle looked like a fashion model in her lavender and white T-shirt with the butterfly on it and the hip-hugging bell-bottom jeans. He noted the butterfly embroidered on the pants along her left thigh.

He wondered briefly if she had a boyfriend. Of course he didn't expect her to have a casual relationship of any kind—she wasn't the type—he could see that clear as day.

After freshening up, Traynor felt much better and went to join the Holt family at the dinner table.

Elias gave the blessing.

Without preamble, Traynor dug in, enjoying the delicious meal that had been prepared by the women. He hadn't eaten since breakfast and the simple fare at a roadside diner didn't taste as good as the food in front of him.

The sensation that he was being watched came over him. Traynor glanced in Jessie Belle's direction and found her eyeing him intently.

Their gazes met and held.

The moment passed and Traynor reluctantly returned his attention to his plate.

Jessie Belle couldn't take her eyes off the handsome pastor. She'd been expecting an old fart but found herself pleasantly surprised to see Traynor standing at the door instead. She didn't know how her parents felt about it, but Jessie Belle was ecstatic that his father couldn't come.

She estimated him to be around the same age as she or in his early twenties at the most.

Jessie Belle loved his deep, dark-colored eyes and quick smile. He wore his hair in a neat well-shaped Afro and his mustache was neatly trimmed. She couldn't help but wonder how much time he spent in the mirror working to get it perfect like that. He was tall and muscular, and his clothes fit him well, like they were made just for him.

Normally, the ministers that came through Mayville were a bunch of old fogies with an eye for the ladies. There had been a few of the rigid Bible-toting ones as well—they were the ones offering to pray for her lost soul.

But what could they possibly know about her?

Jessie Belle searched for something to say. "I can't believe you drove all the way here from Louisiana. Did you drive straight through?"

"I didn't drive from Baton Rouge," he responded. "My drive was only about three hours total."

"Oh, you were preaching at another revival or something?"

"I pastor a church in Atlanta. I moved there about three months ago."

"Your church mustn't be too small," Jessie Belle said. "That sure is a real nice car you driving. I bet you live in a pretty house filled with fancy furniture, don't you?"

Anabeth sent her a sharp look, but Jessie Belle ignored her mother.

"My father and my aunt thought that a pastor should have a decent home, so they purchased one for me when I took the preaching job in Atlanta. He bought me the car, too."

"Wow. Your family must be rich," Jessie Belle murmured softly. "How fortunate for you that your parents are so supportive."

"My mother passed a couple of years ago," Traynor told her. "Basically, it's just my father and Aunt Eleanor—she's his sister. We're all that's left now of the Deveraux family."

He seemed pleased that she was so interested in him, so Jessie Belle continued her line of questioning. "How old are you?"

"Jessie Belle . . . you can't go around asking our guests questions like that," Anabeth admonished.

"It's fine," Traynor stated. "I'm twenty-two."

Jessie Belle smiled and announced, "I'm eighteen. Graduated high school a couple of weeks ago."

"Are you going off to college somewhere?"

She shook her head no and quickly changed the subject by asking, "What made you become a preacher?"

"God called me to it," he responded. "Quite young. I was seven years old."

She pasted a pretty smile on her face. "How very interesting," Jessie Belle murmured. "I can't imagine being called at such a young age."

"It happens all the time," her father interjected. "I weren't that much older when God called me to spread the Gospel."

Jessie Belle wasn't interested in hearing her father's story again. She was more interested in learning about Traynor Deveraux and his family. He was cute and, from the looks of it, pretty well-off. He was the kind of man she'd been waiting for. "I know you said that you don't have much family left, so I'm guessing you're an only child like me."

"I had a sister," Traynor replied. "She died five years ago."

"Reverend, you don't have to go telling your life story to my nosy chile," Anabeth stated. "She's always been curious."

Jessie Belle knew her mother was only saying that to show good manners. She was just as curious about Traynor as Jessie Belle was. "I apologize if I've offended you, Pastor Deveraux. I was only trying to make conversation."

His gaze met hers. "You haven't offended me at all," he assured her. "I'm actually enjoying our conversation. Most people forget that we're also human—not just messengers for the Lord."

Jessie Belle and her mother shared a secret smile. She returned her attention to Traynor and said, "Please continue. . . . I want to know everything."

"That boy is the kind of man you need," Anabeth whispered when they were in the kitchen afterward. She glanced over her shoulder before whispering, "We've never heard him preach—your daddy's a little worried. The boy's daddy say he can really preach, but we don't know for sure."

"Hopefully he'll bring some life to revival. Those old ministers Papa always brings to town—they are so boring. *Ma, you know I'm telling the truth.*"

"Some have nearly put me to sleep," Anabeth admitted with a laugh. "Your daddy don't like putting someone in the pulpit without having

heard them first give a sermon, but he trusts and respects Reverend Deveraux, so he's gon' give his son a chance."

"Pastor Deveraux seems like a nice man," Jessie Belle murmured. "I
plan on really getting to know him."

"If you play this hand right—you just may end up with a husband."

"Don't worry, Ma. I'm not messing this up. I don't think this is going
to be hard at all. I believe Pastor Traynor Deveraux has some interest in
me already. The man can barely keep his eyes off me."

Traynor stood in the pulpit preaching from deep within his soul. He had
a gift—Jessie Belle could tell it right off. He wasn't one of those fire-and-
brimstone, doomsday preachers screaming and jumping around. Instead,
Traynor stood rooted in place, his sermon intelligent and eloquent.

"Think about the gifts the Queen of Sheba lavished on King Solomon," he was saying. "The perfume, spices, gold and precious stones. She
did all this to acknowledge his greatness—however, Solomon was only a
man. Think about the many ways we can acknowledge the greatness of
the Lord. I'm not talking about money. I'm speaking of worship, trust-
ing Him . . . praying."

Toward the end of his sermon, Traynor called a young man up to the
front, saying, "God just told me to anoint your hands. He has given you
a gift and God wants you to use it for His glory." The boy began sobbing
like a baby.

Traynor Deveraux was a truly anointed pastor. Jessie Belle could definitely see herself married to him. He was rich and he wasn't at all hard
on the eyes. He was intelligent and well-spoken. She was pretty sure that
Traynor had absolutely no idea of the power he held. *He needs a woman
like me by his side*, Jessie Belle silently considered. Together, they could ac-
complish great things.

Traynor's words commanded the attention of everyone in the tent.
People were wiping away tears and some were standing up, giving God
praise.

Jessie Belle watched as fourteen people walked down to the front to
give their lives to Christ. Even her own father didn't yield these kinds of
results.

Traynor had a gift for sure.

"Oh my goodness, did you see what happened in there?" Anabeth gushed when service concluded for the evening. "People didn't want to leave. There was just a different feeling about tonight. The Holy Spirit was sho moving."

Jessie Belle had to agree. "I kept saying to myself the whole time he was preaching, 'That ain't no man up there talking'—it was God speaking through him."

"The Lord walked into that tent tonight," Anabeth stated. "Yeah . . . he sho did."

"It's usually pretty quiet during tent-revival services, but not this time. People couldn't seem to stop all the crying, yelling and shouting."

"We didn't need all that, Jessie Belle. I know for myself that God really dealt with me about some things," Anabeth responded. "He wants me to be bolder when it comes to sharing my faith. I felt this sense of a divine presence—I've never felt this way before. I'm telling you—the Lord was here tonight."

"Pastor Deveraux is gifted, that's for sure," Jessie Belle murmured. She peeked inside. "What's taking so long? These mosquitoes are gonna eat us alive out here if they don't hurry up. I shoulda got the keys from Papa."

Traynor was slowly making his way toward the opening, but he was being mobbed by some of the people, seeking prayer or just wanting to share their testimony.

"He's so handsome," Jessie Belle whispered.

"He'd make a good husband for you."

She looked over at her mother. "I know. I really like him, too."

"I kinda figured you did. So do a lot of these gals around here. Look at that. . . . The poor man can't even get to the car." Anabeth wore a look of disgust.

"At least you're the prettiest girl in Mayville, Jessie Belle. If the pastor is looking for beauty in a wife—he's sure to pick you. If he's looking for something more . . . well, we'll just have to make sure you have everything he's wanting in a woman. With him staying over at the Cotton Patch Rooming House, there's no telling what he'll hear about you. You know how much Mabel loves to gossip and I got a feeling she's gonna want him for that sour-faced daughter of hers."

"He won't believe them, Ma. Traynor thinks I'm very innocent and probably even a little naive."

"Traynor Deveraux won't think so for long if he hangs around here. Jessie Belle, you need to reel this boy in quick-like. But you gotta do it without looking like you fast. That's the key."

"Ma, you taught me well. Traynor is mine for the taking."

The second night that Traynor preached, even Jessie Belle could feel a presence surrounding them. It was something she couldn't describe or give a name to—it brought tears to her eyes.

Traynor was eloquent in his speech, but it wasn't phony or for show. He spoke from the heart, his words stirring an unidentifiable emotion throughout the congregation.

Jessie Belle watched in awe as people went in droves down to the front of the makeshift sanctuary, crying out to God in repentance and pleading for forgiveness.

This is the kind of moment that only God could create, she thought to herself. A man destined to lead thousands to the Lord.

He's so amazing. I'd be a fool to let him get away, Jessie Belle decided. Her eyes traveled the tent, bouncing off the faces of the young women hoping to catch Traynor's attention.

None of you have a chance because he's mine, she wanted to shout. *Or he will be before he leaves Mayville.*

Jessie Belle escorted Traynor out of the tent.

"Look at that Jezebel," she heard someone say as she passed by. "Ought to be ashamed of herself . . ."

She tossed her long, flowing hair over her shoulders in defiance. "I really enjoyed the sermon tonight," she said loudly enough for the jealous crow to hear. "You're such a good preacher."

He smiled. "I actually had something totally different prepared, but when I walked into the tent, the Lord spoke to my heart and gave me the sermon tonight."

Jessie Belle was impressed. It must be something wonderful to have that kind of relationship with God. She'd never experienced anything like that in her life.

"Well, you did a wonderful job, Pastor."

"Be careful, Reverend," a young woman murmured as she strolled past Jessie Belle and Traynor. "You don't want to be catching nothing."

"What did she just say?" he asked.

"Doris is an idiot," Jessie Belle uttered. "I don't know why, but there are a lot of girls in this town who don't like me for whatever reason. I keep trying to figure out why."

Traynor met her gaze. "You're a very beautiful young woman. I suppose some would be threatened by your beauty."

"Oh, Pastor Deveraux, I sho appreciate you saying that. I kept thinking I'd done something wrong."

"You've done nothing as far as I can tell," Traynor offered.

When her parents joined them, Jessie Belle couldn't stop grinning. That night Jessie Belle dreamed of Traynor. She dreamed that when he left Mayville, he took her with him.

The next morning, Jessie Belle couldn't wait to share her dream with Anabeth.

"Ma, I dreamed that I married Traynor Deveraux. We had a small wedding right here and then he took me with him to Atlanta. *He's the one.*" Placing a hand over her heart, Jessie Belle said, "I feel it in here."

Jessie Belle left the house an hour later to run some errands. She headed straight to the Mayville Diner, where Doris worked—she hadn't forgotten what the cow had said last night when she was leaving revival.

There were only two customers in the restaurant when Jessie Belle arrived. She sat down in the booth closest to the door.

"Good morning, Doris," she greeted warmly when the woman approached.

"I'm surprised to see you up so early, Jessie Belle. I always figured you for the sleeping-until-noon type." Doris pulled out her pad and asked, "So what can I get for you?"

"What I want is really something simple." Jessie Belle's smile disappeared. "Doris, I can't help it if Kenny didn't want to be with you. People can't help who they fall in love with."

"Considering Kenny left you behind and is engaged to marry somebody else, he must not have loved you as much as you think he did."

Jessie Belle stiffened. "What are you talking about, now?"

"You mean you haven't heard? Kenny's marrying some model—gave her a huge rock. I think it was almost six or seven carats. It was on the news last night and this morning."

Her words stabbed at Jessie Belle, but she refused to show her pain. "I didn't come here to discuss Kenny," she stated without emotion. "I came to tell you to back off. Pastor Deveraux and I are getting to know each other, and I don't need you going around here trying to make me look bad."

Doris had the nerve to laugh. "I don't have to try to make you look bad. You do well enough on your own."

"I'm warning you, Doris. Another comment like the one you made last night, and stuffing your head down a toilet will not compare to what I'll do to you this time. You say another word about me around Pastor Deveraux, and I'll cut your throat without even blinking." Jessie Belle eased out of the booth. *"I mean it."*

She strolled out of the restaurant, leaving Doris visibly shaken.

CHAPTER THREE

Jessie Belle worked her feminine wiles on Traynor and had him so smitten that when Elias invited him to stay on for another week, he jumped at the chance, saying, "It would be my pleasure."

She was waiting for her daddy at the end of the hall. Jessie Belle's steady gaze bored into him in silent expectation.

He gave her an amused look. "Pastor Deveraux has agreed to stay one more week. People from surrounding communities are traveling here every night to listen to him preach. We had over a hundred last night."

"Thank you, Papa," Jessie Belle gushed, embracing her father. "The people all love him. Did you see all the folks that came to the Lord last night after his sermon? Pastor Deveraux is gifted. He seems able to reach even the most stubborn of folks."

Elias nodded in agreement. "I suspect you've taken a strong liking to him," he stated with a huge grin.

"I have," Jessie Belle confirmed.

Gesturing toward the front of the house, her father stated, "I think he's outside sitting in the swing. Getting a breath of fresh air. Why don't you go keep him company? But you sit in the rocking chair—you never know who might be watching."

"Thanks, Papa."

Grinning, Jessie Belle rushed past her mother, wanting to get to Traynor. She needed to spend every available moment with him in order for her plan to work.

"Papa just told me the good news," Jessie Belle announced when she saw him in the swing, floating back and forth. "I'm so glad you're not gonna be leaving just yet."

She dropped her eyes and said, "I hope I'm not being too forward, Pastor Deveraux."

"Not at all, Miss Holt," he assured her.

"Please call me Jessie Belle." She glanced over her shoulder, checking to see if her mother was lurking around somewhere, trying to listen to what they were saying. Her mother was nosy like that.

"Only if you call me Traynor."

Recalling her mother's words to not behave brazenly, Jessie Belle uttered, "I can't. My parents would want me to show you proper respect—you being a pastor and all. They would allow me to call you by your birth name only if we were dating."

Elias walked outside, joining them on the porch.

Traynor rose to his feet. "Reverend Holt, if it's alright with you—I'd like to take Jessie Belle on a walk. It's real nice outside. I thought we might have a picnic."

Jessie Belle eyed her father, silently pleading with him to give his approval.

"There's some fried chicken, potato salad and biscuits in the refrigerator," Anabeth stated from the doorway.

Jessie Belle had no idea how long she'd been standing there. Normally, it irritated her when her mother tried to keep close tabs on her, but not this time. She was in too good a mood. "Thanks, Ma," she told her.

"I'll make y'all a nice basket of food. Jessie Belle, you go and grab a blanket."

She did as she was told.

Jessie Belle returned to the porch, blanket in hand, to find Traynor standing on the bottom step with the picnic basket, waiting for her.

"I'm surprised that you're not dating anyone," Traynor stated as they began their walk. "A woman as beautiful as you . . ."

"I'm very picky," Jessie Belle responded. "I'm not the type of girl to mess around, so I'm looking for someone ready to settle down. And of course, he has to love the Lord."

She wasn't completely lying. Jessie Belle truly wanted to be married—she wanted to be the wife of a man financially secure and very successful. Deep down, she believed she'd found that in Traynor. He already seemed devoted to her and he came from a well-to-do family.

Jessie Belle was enjoying their conversation immensely. She and Traynor discussed what they considered to be great literature, music and the current happenings in the Eastern Christian Convention. She hoped to impress him with her knowledge of church politics. Jessie Belle wanted to show Traynor how much of an asset she would be.

"My daddy was a big fan of Sam McCall until all this stuff came out about him stealing money," Jessie Belle stated. "Papa admired the fact that Reverend McCall left Virginia and moved to Atlanta after becoming president. He felt like it showed dedication to the organization. He was so disappointed when all this stuff came out about Reverend McCall and that secretary and then that he'd stolen money from ECC."

"My father was never a fan of McCall's," Traynor responded. "I have to admit I had some questions about him myself. I've been in his presence only a couple of times and I can't explain it, but my spirit was grieved whenever I was around him. My father was one of the first to say that we shouldn't judge but offer to minister to McCall. 'Hate the sin but love the sinner' is what he says."

"Papa feels the same way. He even went down to the prison to meet with McCall and to pray with him," Jessie Belle stated. Giving him a sideways look, she asked, "How is your spirit when you're around me?"

Traynor broke into a grin. "There's nothing to worry about. I enjoy your company, Jessie Belle. I enjoyed listening to you play the piano. You could be a concert pianist—you're that good."

She was touched by the compliment. "You really think so?"

The smile in his eyes contained a sensuous flame. "I do."

They found a spot beneath a huge shade tree and spread out the blanket. Jessie Belle and Traynor sat down. "I like playing the piano, but it's not something I want to make a career out of, Traynor. I enjoy using my gift for the Lord."

"What do you want to do with your life?"

"I want a husband and a family," Jessie Belle answered. "I don't mind working, but I feel in my heart that God has called me to be a helpmate to the man I marry." Holding up the Ziploc bag of crispy fried chicken, she asked sweetly, "Would you like a piece of chicken?"

"Yes, please."

Jessie Belle placed a drumstick on his plate. "Ma makes the best fried chicken in Mayville. She's even won a couple of medals at the county fair.

She's taught me everything that I know about cooking. Matter of fact, I made the potato salad."

Traynor finished off his soda. "I haven't met a lot of women who enjoy cooking the way you seem to," he stated. "In fact, a couple of them didn't even know how to boil water."

Jessie Belle handed him another. "I guess you could say that I'm very domesticated for my age. Most girls are thinking about parties and I'm thinking about making a red velvet cake or a lemon pound cake—I really love to cook." She wasn't lying. Jessie Belle really did enjoy cooking—baking especially.

He smiled.

"Tell me about your church in Atlanta. Is it a big church like the ones I see on television?"

"Oh no, it's nothing like that, but it is a nice size. We have a membership of about five hundred."

"Our church only holds maybe a hundred folk. Papa likes it that way, though."

"I've never met a girl interested in the church like you are," Traynor confessed. "You seem to know a lot about the inner workings."

"You mean church politics?" Jessie Belle's mouth curved into a smile. "Church is all I know. I help out with the administrative duties and I play for the choir. I even help out in the kitchen. I'm there to serve."

Traynor awarded her an irresistibly devastating grin. "You and I are a lot alike, I see. While my friends were going to parties, I was at the church with my father. When I was in college, my friends were hanging out in clubs, and me—I was either home studying the Word or in church."

"The price for being a PK," Jessie Belle murmured with a laugh.

Traynor enjoyed Jessie Belle's company immensely. Just the mere thought of leaving her behind saddened him. He considered traveling back and forth to Atlanta—the three-hour drive wouldn't be too bad, he rationalized silently. However, his father had often warned him that long-distance relationships never worked out.

"You're so quiet," Jessie Belle said, cutting into his thoughts. "What are you thinking so hard about?"

"You," he confessed. "Jessie Belle, I've become quite fond of you. I . . . I don't want to leave."

Her gaze was as soft as a caress. "I feel the same way, Traynor."

He reached over, taking her by the hand. "The truth is . . . I've fallen in love with you. You're everything I've ever wanted in a woman. You're very mature for eighteen, Jessie Belle. You have such a warm spirit and you love the Lord—I can tell. I love that you don't mind being a woman and you're not out there trying to wear the pants."

She looked surprised by his admission. "Ooooh, Traynor, I had no idea you felt this way about me. You've made me so happy." She paused a moment before saying, "But you live in Atlanta and I'm here in Mayville. I don't really see the relationship working out."

"I've thought about that. I'm willing to drive down here to see you."

"But with your responsibilities at the church . . . Traynor, you just started pastoring there. That has to come first." Folding her hands in her lap, Jessie Belle added, "My parents won't let me come to visit you— they'd feel it was improper, you know. They're very strict."

He was touched by her concern for his calling. "I don't want to lose you, Jessie Belle."

"It's obvious that we both have deep feelings for each other. The challenge is gonna be in finding out how we can make this work."

Traynor had to fight his overwhelming need to be close to her. It seemed like each day he spent with her, his feelings deepened and intensified.

Traynor silently considered his options. He was in love and there was only one thing to do.

Kissing the back of her hand, he said, "I'll speak with your father later."

Her heart danced with excitement. Things were going according to plan.

"You want to tell me about that little secret smile you have on your face?"

Her eyes met his. "I'm just happy, Traynor. Happier than I've ever been. I've never felt so in love. I think I can truly say that you're my first real love."

"It's the same for me."

After they finished eating, Jessie Belle took Traynor over to the stables to meet her horse, Diamond. "I've had her a long time—since she was a pony."

"I've never ridden a horse."

"Really?" she asked. "I love it. One day I'd like to own a couple of horses. I've always had this dream that me and my husband will go riding in the mornings after breakfast and maybe in the evening right after dinner."

Happiness filled Traynor as he listened to Jessie Belle talk about her dreams. He wanted nothing more than to make them come true.

"Would you like me to teach you to ride?" Jessie Belle asked him.

"One day," he replied.

They walked back over to the huge oak tree to gather up the picnic basket and the discarded paper plates.

"I guess we'd better get back up to the house," Jessie Belle announced. "I promised to help Ma with the washing."

They walked hand in hand until they were within a few yards of the house.

Traynor summoned up his nerve and went in to speak with her father while Jessie Belle and her mother were out in the back of the house hanging the wash.

"Sir, I love your daughter."

Elias removed his glasses, and then proceeded to clean them. "You hardly know Jessie Belle."

Traynor became increasingly uneasy under his scrutiny. "I know enough about her that I want to make her my wife, sir. The truth is that I don't want to leave Mayville without her and we want to do it the right way. I'd like to marry her."

"Does Jessie Belle feel the same way?"

"Yes, sir. I believe she does. Reverend Holt, we would like your blessing."

Before Elias could respond, the door blew open and in rushed Jessie Belle.

"Papa, please say yes." She squealed with delight and rushed over to wrap her arms around Traynor. "I can't believe this. I'm so happy we're getting married."

He laughed. "I haven't formally asked you yet."

"I don't care. The answer is yes."

Anabeth rushed in behind Jessie Belle, grabbing her by the arm. "C'mon. We have more washing to do. Let the men finish their discussion."

Shaking her head, Jessie Belle snatched her arm away. "No, this concerns me and my future. Traynor and I love each other and we want to get married."

"How soon?" her father asked.

"As soon as possible," they answered in unison, then burst into laughter.

"When Traynor leaves, I want to go with him, Papa."

"What about Sunday?" Anabeth suggested. "Right after service?"

Traynor walked over to Jessie Belle. "Would you do me the honor of becoming my wife on Sunday?"

"Yes." She wrapped her arms around him.

Her mother cleared her throat noisily. "We have a lot to do in a short amount of time. Jessie Belle, let's get busy."

When they were alone in her parent's bedroom, Anabeth hugged her daughter. "You did it, Jessie Belle."

"I told you that Traynor would be mine. We're gonna be man and wife."

The week passed by in a blur as preparations for the wedding took place.

"I can't believe it," Jessie Belle murmured. "I'm getting married tomorrow. And did you see Traynor's father? He's so rich-looking."

"Hold still," Anabeth fussed. "I'm trying to pin your dress for hemming."

She glanced down at her mother. "Aren't you happy for me, Ma? I'm marrying into a powerful Louisiana family."

Anabeth didn't respond.

"Ma?"

"What, chile?"

"Aren't you happy for me?" Jessie Belle asked. "I've found a good husband. He comes from a very wealthy family and he's handsome. We're gonna make some pretty babies."

"Yep, he sho' is a good man. I just hope you ain't so on fire to up to marry him just because you think he got a whole lot of money. Reverend Deveraux is well-off but he ain't what you'd call rich."

"He might not be rich right now, but Traynor's got a lot of potential. With me by his side he's gon' do some great things. We're gonna have a great big house and drive nice cars. We're gonna have horses, anything we want. But to answer your question—I'm marrying Traynor because he loves me and he wants me to be his wife, Ma. *He picked me.*"

"Do you think he'd still want you if he knew you weren't as pure as you've been pretending?"

Her smile faded a little. "I haven't really figured out what to do about that yet."

"I told you never to give away your goodies until you got a ring on your finger."

"I thought he was gonna marry me, Ma."

"Well, you thought wrong. You're beautiful, gal. Use your looks and not your body. Just the promise of something more is enough for most men," Anabeth advised.

"I remember how the butcher would give you extra meat from time to time or that Deacon Jones used to give you more fabric than you asked for."

"And I never had to defile my marriage bed. *Remember that.* I let them assume whatever they wanted to—had nothing to do with me."

"I will," Jessie Belle vowed. "I won't forget it."

"I gotta get busy on the hem. You getting married tomorrow—we don't have a minute to waste."

"Ma, I don't love Traynor," Jessie Belle confessed.

"You'll learn to love him. You can't help but love a man who puts your needs before his own."

"Do you take this woman to be your wife. . . . ?" Jessie Belle's father said.

When it was his cue to respond, Traynor answered, "I do."

Jessie Belle couldn't stop smiling. Her dream of becoming a fine lady was finally coming true. She'd studied Jacqueline Kennedy—her role model—and fantasized about dressing like her, talking like her and being rich like her. In a few minutes she would be a first lady just like Jacqueline—only she would help her husband lead his church and not a country.

She was so caught up in her thoughts that Jessie Belle almost missed her father's question.

"I do," she stated. "I do."

Jessie Belle was not at all pleased with the simple wedding band Traynor placed on her finger, but he promised to buy her a diamond soon.

His daddy could've given me the one he'd given his late wife. Traynor told her that his father kept it in her jewelry box. The woman was dead—she wouldn't be needing any of her jewelry, so why was he being so stingy with it? That ring would've been a nice wedding present.

For the past couple of days, Jessie Belle had tried being friendly to her father-in-law, but while he was polite, she had a strong suspicion that he didn't care much for her.

Traynor's aunt threw away all pretenses. She couldn't stand Jessie Belle and didn't bother to hide her dislike.

After the ceremony, Jessie Belle walked over to Eleanor Deveraux-Barrett and said, "I'm so happy to be married to Traynor. We're family now."

Traynor's aunt walked off without a response.

"Your aunt hates me," Jessie Belle later confided in Traynor while they were seated at the head table, waiting to be served.

"Aunt Eleanor doesn't hate you," he stated. "She's still in a little bit of a shock over the news of our getting married. It happened rather quickly. I came to Mayville to preach in place of my father, and now I have a wife. They're just worried that we're moving too fast. Give them some time to get used to the idea of us being married."

"Do you have any regrets?"

Traynor shook his head no. "I've never been this happy before, Jessie Belle."

"Neither have I," she replied. Her heart danced with excitement. She was Mrs. Traynor Deveraux.

Her gaze traveled the room, eyeing the expressions on some of the girls' faces. Jessie Belle gloried in their heartache and disappointment.

She'd won.

When her mother could get her alone, Anabeth pulled Jessie Belle into one of the tiny rooms in the back of the church hall.

"Here, take this," she said, handing Jessie Belle a tiny pack of blood. "Now, remember what I said."

Skeptical, Jessie Belle questioned, "You really think this is gonna fool Traynor?"

She nodded. "Mamie Ella did it for her daughter when she married Saul Tinsdale. He never knew a thing. Traynor will think he married a virgin. Now, remember to cry a little and for goodness' sake, don't act like you're enjoying it. And now that you're a married woman—you need to start talking real proper-like." Anabeth broke into a grin. "You gon' be living in Atlanta."

Jessie Belle smiled. "I love you, Ma."

"I love you, too."

Her eyes traveled the reception hall, searching for her husband. Jessie Belle found Traynor talking to her father.

Their eyes met and held.

It was too easy to get lost in the way Traynor looked at her. Jessie Belle planned on being the perfect wife in every way, and she prayed that she'd be able to return his love. She didn't want to hurt Traynor ever.

CHAPTER FOUR

Jessie Belle couldn't believe how easily Traynor was fooled. Her mother's scheme had actually worked.

He pulled her perspiration-damp body into the crook of his arm. "I hope I didn't hurt you too bad," he murmured. "There's so much blood."

She moved away from him to get out of bed.

When he protested, she said, "Sweetie, I need to take a bath. Ma says that soaking in a tub of hot water will ease some of the soreness. Maybe you can get some fresh sheets out and put them on the bed?" she suggested.

Her parents stayed with an aunt down the road so that she and Traynor could enjoy their wedding night. Jessie Belle didn't want to stay at the rooming house, although it had occurred to her to rub Miss Mabel's and her daughter's faces in her newfound happiness.

In the bathroom, she ran a tub full of scented water, then climbed inside. Jessie Belle hummed softly to herself as she bathed. She was finally getting out of Mayville. She and Traynor were leaving first thing in the morning.

I can't wait.

Jessie Belle lay back in the tub, smiling. All her dreams were about to come true.

She finished her bath and got out.

Jessie Belle headed back to the bedroom wearing a towel. She loved sex, so it wasn't long before she started to crave the feel of her new husband. Traynor was inexperienced and a bit awkward at first, but he was definitely a quick learner.

Strolling into the bedroom, she let the towel drop to the floor.

Traynor's eyes lit up like firecrackers. "Are you still sore?"

"Huh?"

It took her a few seconds to remember that this was supposed to be her *first time*. "Just a little," Jessie Belle lied.

"I don't want to hurt you, sweetheart. Maybe we should wait and try again tomorrow."

It was so sweet to see Traynor so concerned about her, but she was growing weary of the charade.

"No," Jessie Belle uttered. "I want you now. I'm your wife, Traynor. Baby, we can have all the sex we want."

Jessie Belle woke up early the next morning feeling happier than she'd ever been in her entire life. She held up her left hand to admire the tiny gold band on her ring finger.

Freedom.

She was finally getting away from Mayville, Georgia, and not a moment too soon as far as Jessie Belle was concerned. She turned to face her sleeping husband and gently nudged him. "Honey, we should be getting up. We got to get dressed and get on the road. I can't wait to see our home."

He was sluggish, drunk with sleep. "Huh . . ."

"It's time to get up," Jessie Belle whispered. Maybe she shouldn't have kept Traynor up most of the night making love.

When he still didn't move, she covered him in soft kisses beginning with his ear and neck, and traveling to his cheek.

He moaned, then began to stir.

Traynor reached for her.

"C'mon, honey. We need to get up and get on the road. There'll be plenty of lovemaking when we get to our house in Atlanta."

"I want you . . . ," Traynor pleaded.

"I have to finish up my packing. The sooner you get up, the sooner we'll be home."

Jessie Belle jumped out of bed and began to get ready to leave. She couldn't wait to get to Atlanta and see her new house. Traynor had told her that it was two stories and had three bedrooms and two baths. He told her that she could change anything in the house she didn't like. She imagined herself getting out of the Thunderbird and walking up to a huge brick mansion.

Her parents arrived home just as they were putting the suitcases into the trunk of the car.

"Y'all gon' stay for breakfast?" her mother asked.

Jessie Belle shook her head no before Traynor could open his mouth to utter a response. "Ma, we need to get on the road. We're gonna stop along the way. Thank you, though."

Traynor and her father walked over to the porch and talked.

"You married now, gal. It's time for you to act like a proper lady. Be careful not to ruin Traynor's good name. He don't deserve that."

"I'm not gon' do anything to ruin my marriage, Ma. I feel like a rich lady now." Tossing her curly hair over her shoulders, Jessie Belle added with a chuckle, "I might not even know who you are the next time you see me."

"You might be on your high horse right now, Jessie Belle Holt, but it's still a pony to me. Mind your horse don't throw you, gal."

"It's Mrs. Traynor Deveraux," she shot back. "And don't you go forgetting it."

Grinning, Anabeth hugged her daughter. "My sharp-tongued chile. I wish you all the happiness in the world. Call me regular, now. I don't want to be worrying about you up there in Atlanta."

"We're only three hours away, Ma. I'ma be just fine."

"Stop talking like a country gal. You a big-city gal now."

"I'll be fine."

"That's much better. If you want money—you got to walk around like you already got it."

She blew Jessie Belle a kiss before turning around and walking up the steps to the porch, where Elias pulled her into his arms.

Jessie Belle had already said her goodbyes, so she stood beside the car while Traynor hugged her parents.

She was ready to leave.

Jessie Belle nearly cheered when she saw the sign bidding them farewell from the city of Mayville. She vowed to never return to this dying town of her birth—except to bury her parents. Now that she was free, she never wanted to look back.

"Think you gonna miss Mayville?" Traynor asked.

Jessie Belle shook her head no. "Not hardly. I've been wanting to leave this place since forever."

He glanced over at her. "I know you're gonna miss your parents."

"Yeah," Jessie Belle murmured. "But we're a family now. Besides, I'm sure they're happy to finally have the house to themselves." She was more than ready to get away from Mayville and her parents.

It was the first day of the rest of her life.

Jessie Belle swallowed her disappointment when Traynor pulled into the driveway of a redbrick two-story house that had clearly seen better days. "Is this the house?"

"Yeah, sweetheart. This is our house. Our home."

He seemed so proud and excited about it, but Jessie Belle just couldn't summon up the enthusiasm. It was bigger than the house she'd grown up in, but not by much. This was *not* the house she'd dreamed about or the house that he'd described as elegant. It wasn't even pretty—just functional.

Traynor insisted on carrying her over the threshold.

Jessie Belle didn't think much of the idea but kept quiet. She didn't want to hurt Traynor's feelings when her husband was trying to be romantic.

He gave her a tour of *his* house. She wasn't ready to call it her home.

The rooms weren't very large, Jessie Belle noted sadly. This was definitely not the grand house she'd imagined they would be living in.

"What's wrong, sweetheart?" Traynor inquired. "You look upset."

"Your father bought this house for you?"

He nodded.

"I thought he'd bought you a new house. This place needs a lot of work."

Traynor glanced around. "It's a very nice house, I think. We can fix it up together."

Jessie Belle nodded. She didn't trust herself to speak right now—she was so disappointed. This was definitely not how she'd envisioned her new life beginning.

That night, she pleaded a headache. She wasn't in the mood for making love. Jessie Belle felt like she'd been the one tricked.

She was in better spirits a week later after painting all the bedrooms in the house and putting up new curtains. Jessie Belle had even coerced Traynor into buying a brand-new sofa for the living room and a dining room table.

Later that afternoon, a couple from one of the neighboring houses came by to formally welcome them into the neighborhood.

"Hello, my name is Richard Reed and this is my wife, Mary Ellen. We live in the house next door. The one with the green shutters."

Traynor introduced himself, then Jessie Belle. "This is my new wife, Jessie Belle."

Richard held on to her hand a little longer than necessary, she noted silently. Jessie Belle broke the hold. "It's very nice to meet you both."

They settled down in the living room.

Jessie Belle was so grateful that the new sofa had been delivered the day before. She would've been horrified if they'd seen the worn brown leather couch that was there before.

While they talked, Jessie Belle's eyes traveled the room—she was relieved that the deep burgundy curtains matched the burgundy in the striped sofa and in the floral patterned rug.

They hadn't put up any pictures yet, so the bare walls bothered her, but there wasn't much Jessie Belle could do about it right now.

"You've done a beautiful job with the house," Mary Ellen complimented.

"We still have a long ways to go," she replied. "But we've only been working on it for a week."

"It looks real nice." Lowering her voice to a whisper, Mary Ellen said, "You should have seen it when the last owner had it. These walls were orange."

"Uggh . . . are you serious? I didn't like the pea green color Traynor had painted it, so we changed it to sage. I think it looks so much better."

Mary Ellen nodded. "It really looks nice. The old owners had some ugly green chairs in here, too. They were leather, but I didn't like the look. Every time I came over here, I felt like I was in a pumpkin patch."

They cracked up with laughter.

"You actually made me feel better," Jessie Belle murmured. She liked Mary Ellen a lot.

Smiling, Mary Ellen responded, "I'm glad I could help. By the way, we'd like to host a dinner party for you and Traynor tomorrow night. It'll be a nice way for you to meet your neighbors."

"Thank you so much, Mary Ellen. We'd be honored."

The Reeds stayed for about an hour before going back over to their house.

"I guess they're curious about you," Traynor said to her after their visitors left. "They never bothered to come over before today."

"Probably just wanting to make sure the good preacher isn't shacking up," Jessie Belle responded.

They chuckled.

Jessie Belle was looking forward to the dinner party tomorrow.

"You sure you want to go?" Traynor inquired as they were preparing for bed later that evening.

"Yeah," Jessie Belle answered as she examined her skin in the mirror for flaws. "I want to see if Mary Ellen's house looks better than ours. And I'd like to meet the people living around us."

"What does it matter how her house looks?" Traynor asked. "I love our house."

Jessie Belle picked up her brush and began brushing her hair. "It's a woman thing. You'd never understand."

Mary Ellen had apparently decided to invite everyone in the neighborhood, from what Jessie Belle could tell.

The women circled around Jessie Belle, while the men had Traynor cornered.

"Where are you from?" a woman who introduced herself as Nan asked.

"I'm from a small town called Mayville. It's about three hours from here."

"Welcome to the neighborhood, Jessie Belle. We hope you and the pastor will be very happy here."

"We will," she stated.

Jessie Belle was like a sponge. She soaked up every piece of information about the women in her presence. Nan lived in the largest house on the street, a two-story brick house with huge white columns. Hers was the type of house Jessie Belle thought she'd be coming to live in. Nan's husband worked at the Atlanta Bank and Savings.

Mary Ellen worked at one of the local radio stations as a program manager and her husband, Richard, was a history professor at Morehouse College. Lucille Beckham worked for Coca-Cola as a department manager. Her husband owned several laundry facilities in the area.

Cynthia Hargrove was divorced but had come with a date, whom she introduced as Atkinson Bradford. Jessie Belle was acutely aware of him watching her intently. He was a handsome man and dressed well.

When they were introduced, he reached out, taking her hand in his. When Atkinson didn't release it right away, Jessie Belle pulled away and excused herself.

Moments later, Atkinson appeared by her side. "I heard that you're from Mayville. I have some family in the next town. We used to go to Mayville quite a bit to the farmers' market."

Jessie Belle smiled politely. "Everybody used to come for the vegetables and fruits."

"My cousin used to tell me that Mayville had some beautiful women there, but I never saw anyone who looked quite like you in that town."

Atkinson was clearly flirting with her. Jessie Belle scanned the room, looking for her husband.

He was talking to Cynthia.

Jessie Belle didn't miss the way she kept eyeing Traynor like he was her favorite dessert. Nor the way Cynthia kept touching his arm when she laughed.

That tramp thinks she's slick, but I'm on to her game.

"You should probably join your date," Jessie Belle told Atkinson.

He followed her gaze. Grinning, he asked, "You're not jealous, are you?"

Jessie Belle didn't change her expression. "I have no reason to be jealous. When I get ready to leave this house, my husband will be with me."

Chuckling, Atkinson made his way across the room to where Traynor was held captive.

Atkinson leaned down to whisper something in Cynthia's ear.

Jessie Belle smiled when she glanced in Cynthia's direction, clearly surprising the woman. Taking a sip of her lemonade, she strolled over to where they were standing.

"Your husband is *soo* funny," Cynthia murmured when Jessie Belle joined them.

"My husband is a lot of things," she responded. "But what I admire most about him is that he's like David, a man after God's own heart. He's a good man and I feel very blessed because this handsome man is mine." Jessie Belle slipped her arm around Traynor's waist.

She ignored the look of amusement in Atkinson's eyes.

"Honey, I'm feeling kind of tired. Why don't we go home?" Jessie Belle suggested. She boldly gave him a wink.

Traynor's eyebrows rose in mild surprise. Breaking into a smile, he said, "Maybe we should call it a night."

Stealing a peek at Cynthia, she said, "After all, we're still on our honeymoon."

Jessie Belle almost laughed at the flash of anger displayed briefly in Cynthia's eyes.

She and Cynthia would never be friends. That much was clear to Jessie Belle. She couldn't have a relationship with someone she didn't trust.

Jessie Belle didn't care, because she didn't want a man-hungry tramp in her life. This woman would try to steal her husband as soon as look at her and Jessie Belle wasn't having any of that.

"I was wondering when you were gonna get your husband away from Cynthia," Mary Ellen whispered when Jessie Belle went to say goodbye. "I didn't invite her—another one of the neighbors mentioned the dinner to her. I'm so sorry."

"Oh, no . . . you don't have to apologize. I can handle women like Cynthia. She doesn't bother me—I'll never have to worry about another woman when it comes to Traynor."

"I'm not so sure I could say that about Richard. Don't get me wrong— he's a good guy and our marriage is good—but he is a *man*."

"Traynor would never betray me," Jessie Belle insisted. "It's not in his blood."

CHAPTER FIVE

Although they didn't have a whole lot in common, Jessie Belle and Mary Ellen became fast friends and began spending time together.

Traynor was at the church Monday through Friday, so Jessie Belle spent most of her days decorating, keeping the house clean and planning delicious meals for her husband.

When she tried new recipes, Jessie Belle would call Mary Ellen to come over and sample them before she served the dishes to Traynor.

"Hey, are you busy?" she asked as soon as her friend answered the telephone.

"No," Mary Ellen responded. "I just finished the last load of laundry and it's in the dryer. What's going on?"

"If you haven't had lunch, come over. I made lasagna."

Mary Ellen squealed with delight. "Girl, I love me some lasagna."

"This is my first time ever making it, so I hope it turned out okay. I usually do baked spaghetti or ziti—never tried lasagna until now."

"I'll be over there shortly," Mary Ellen said before hanging up.

Smiling, Jessie Belle took two plates down and set them on the counter. She then warmed up a couple of slices of garlic bread.

Twenty minutes later, Mary Ellen was knocking on the door.

Jessie Belle stepped aside to let her in.

Making small talk, they headed straight to the kitchen, located in the back of the house.

"How was your workday?" Jessie Belle inquired.

"Okay. I'm only there part-time right now. I've been looking for a job with another station—hopefully something will come through soon."

Jessie Belle and Mary Ellen sat down at the dining room table to eat lunch.

"This looks delicious, Jessie Belle."

"I really hope it tastes as good as it looks. I tried to follow my mother's directions, but I couldn't read some of her handwriting."

Picking up her fork, Mary Ellen uttered, "Well, I love me some lasagna, so I'll let you know if you did it right. I'm the lasagna queen. . . . Vegetarian, meat, chicken lasagna—I've had it all."

Jessie Belle responded, "That's why I invited you over for lunch. I wanted to do a test run."

Mary Ellen sampled the pasta dish.

While Jessie Belle waited for a response, she tapped her foot rhythmically on the linoleum floor.

Mary Ellen released her from her misery. "Ooh, this is delicious."

"Really?"

"Yeah. Jessie Belle, you did a good job, but I'm not surprised. You're a wonderful cook. Everything I've tasted is good. In fact, I want your mother's recipe for this lasagna."

Jessie Belle grinned with pleasure. "I hope Traynor's reaction is the same as yours. I want him to be proud of my cooking skills. That's one way to keep your man, you know?"

"It's so refreshing to see someone so happy and in love," Mary Ellen stated with a laugh. "You and Traynor remind me of Richard and me when we first got married."

"You and Richard aren't having problems, are you?"

Mary Ellen shook her head no. "We're fine. Our marriage is good, but Richard—he's a smart man, but he isn't what I call a go-getter. He settles and it drives me up the wall sometimes."

Jessie Belle wiped her mouth with the edge of her napkin. "Have you talked to him about it?"

"I've tried, but Richard's not a man you can just push around. I have to let him move to his own beat."

"I don't know if I could be satisfied with that," Jessie Belle admitted. "Traynor is a gifted pastor and I refuse to let him settle for anything less than he deserves." She changed the subject. "Mary Ellen, what is there to do around this town? Traynor and I haven't done anything or gone anywhere since we got married."

"Richard and I go to this little jazz club in Buckhead called LaBelle's Jazz and Supper Club. As a matter of fact, we're going there tonight. Why don't you and Traynor come with us?"

"That would be great. We need a night out."

"You'll enjoy it. They have a live band and everything."

"I've never seen a live band," Jessie Belle stated. "Where I come from, they had little holes-in-the-wall where they played records. There was this one place, Sugar's Spot—that was the hangout, but my daddy didn't like me going there. He called it a place of ill repute. I used to sneak out at night and go there sometimes."

"I was a party animal, girl," Mary Ellen said with a laugh. "My parents were always throwing parties, so I guess I got it honest."

Jessie Belle sipped some of her iced tea and finished off her food. "I know what I wanted to tell you. You wouldn't believe what Cynthia tried to pull yesterday. She ran across the street as soon as Traynor's car pulled into the driveway. She wanted him to hang some light fixtures."

Her mouth dropped open. "She what?" Mary Ellen asked. "Why didn't she ask her boyfriend?"

"That's what I went out there and suggested. I told her that the only lights my husband's changing is his own."

"That woman is something else," Mary Ellen uttered.

"I may be married to a preacher and be the daughter of one, but I've never been much into sharing. That girl will get hurt if she's trying to mess with my husband."

"Girl, I know what you mean. I already done told Cynthia—I will beat her down if she comes near Richard. He don't do lights either."

The sound of the telephone ringing cut through their conversation.

Laughing, Jessie Belle answered the phone on the third ring. "Hey, honey."

"What's so funny?" Traynor questioned.

"Mary Ellen and I are sitting here talking. We just had lunch together."

"Sounds like you two are having a good time."

"We are," Jessie Belle confirmed. "How's your day going?"

"Good."

Mary Ellen eased up from the table and carried the plates to the kitchen. "I'll let myself out," she whispered.

Nodding, Jessie Belle waved. She followed her friend to the front door to make sure it was locked behind her.

"Traynor, let's go out tonight. I'm tired of sitting in this house," she complained. "We've been here in Atlanta for three weeks now. I want to do something besides church activities."

"Like what, sweetheart? What would you like to do?"

"Mary Ellen was telling me about this jazz club on Peachtree. We could go there and listen to a live band. I've never heard a real band before. She and Richard are going there tonight."

Shaking his head, Traynor told her, "I'm a man of God, Jessie Belle. I can't be seen in places like that."

"You don't have to drink anything, for goodness' sake. We're just going to listen to the music."

"Sweetheart, I can't even let the appearance of sin taint my ministry. I could order a Coke or even a glass of water, but from a distance—it would look like rum and Coke, or gin and tonic. . . ."

"But it won't be alcohol," Jessie Belle argued. "Traynor, this is crazy. You can't go out and listen to a live band because somebody might think you're in there drinking—that's what you're telling me."

"I'm sorry."

Jessie Belle was furious. "I never cared what people thought of me. As long as I know what I'm doing and God knows—it doesn't matter about a bunch of judgmental hypocrites. People are going to think whatever they choose."

Traynor tried to explain his position, but she wouldn't listen. "I don't want to hear it. All I wanted to do was spend a nice evening out with you and our friends. . . ."

"Why don't we just go to dinner?"

Ignoring his suggestion, Jessie sighed. "I cooked dinner," she replied stiffly. "I spent all morning making this lasagna for you."

"I'll make it up to you," he promised.

"Whatever . . ."

Jessie Belle slammed down the telephone.

She was still angry with Traynor when he got home three hours later. He'd probably come home early just to make up with her, but Jessie Belle wasn't interested.

"I was thinking that maybe we could catch a movie later after we eat," he said.

"I've already eaten," Jessie Belle snapped. "I left a plate of lasagna on the stove for you. I'm not interested in seeing a movie. I'm going to take a nice long bath and go to bed."

"Sweetheart . . ."

"No, Traynor. I'm not in the mood to hear about the rules and regulations of a preacher. I grew up with a preacher, remember? Only my daddy appreciated good music from time to time. He didn't worry about the musings of other folk."

"Your daddy is a good man, Jessie Belle. I know that, but he lives in a small town—a place where everybody knows each other. Atlanta is a big city—it's different here and I'm new at this church. I have to live a lifestyle beyond reproach, sweetheart. So do you."

"What are you trying to say?" Jessie Belle demanded. "Are you saying that I don't?"

Traynor sighed. "Honey, I don't want to fight with you. I really didn't mean to upset you."

He looked so sad at the moment that Jessie Belle regretted her anger. "Traynor, I'm the one who should be apologizing. I shouldn't be carrying on so about a jazz club. It's not that important."

"If it wasn't a place where drinking was going on—Jessie Belle, I wouldn't have a problem taking you there."

"I know, baby," she murmured.

Jessie Belle walked over to Traynor and embraced him. "I love you."

He kissed her. "I love you, too."

"Since you won't take me to a jazz club—will you at least sing to me?" Jessie Belle removed his jacket and his tie. She began to unbutton his shirt. "The catch is that you have to do it with your clothes off."

Singing softly, Traynor picked her up and carried her to their bedroom.

Jessie Belle was surprised to see Cynthia and Atkinson in church on Sunday morning.

"I didn't know you were members here at Ninth Street Baptist Church. You never mentioned it when we were at Mary Ellen's."

Jessie Belle couldn't help but wonder why Traynor never mentioned it. "Does my husband know?"

"He should," Cynthia answered. "I was one of the first people he met when he first got here."

"The truth is that we wanted to surprise you," Atkinson responded. "I have to tell you. Your husband has broken some hearts here—a lot of mothers had their eyes on him for a potential son-in-law."

Jessie Belle smiled. "Well, he's off the market now."

"From the looks of it, Pastor found a pot of gold." He stood there and stared with longing at her.

Cynthia bristled but said nothing.

Atkinson clearly had no respect for Traynor or for Cynthia, even with her by his side glaring holes into him.

He was a bold one for sure.

Jessie Belle excused herself and took a seat in the second pew off the center aisle. She wanted to sit right where Traynor could see her.

His sermon held her captive.

Traynor's topic this morning was "Free at Last."

"We as Christians are free," he began. "We became free when Jesus Christ died, but we had to accept it. . . ."

Jessie Belle cast her eyes around the sanctuary, noting the expressions on the faces of the church members. They were enthralled by Traynor.

She was so proud of him.

"I meant to tell you earlier that you sho' looking pretty today, Mrs. Deveraux," Atkinson Bradford complimented when she walked out of the church after Sunday morning service ended.

Jessie Belle gave him a big smile. "Why, thank you, Deacon Bradford. I'm so glad to see that someone notices my efforts, although I truly doubt the sincerity of your words. You never intended to compliment me in front of your girlfriend."

"Oh, I notice," he responded. "A gorgeous woman like you is hard to miss. And as for me and Cynthia, she and I don't use words like that to define our relationship."

"Right." Jessie Belle felt the tiny hairs on the back of her neck stand to attention. Her eyes quickly took in her surroundings.

Standing a few yards away was Cynthia, and from the looks of it, she'd been watching her exchange with the handsome deacon. She was practically green with envy.

Loud enough for Cynthia to hear, Jessie Belle said, "Deacon, it was nice talking to you. I'll have to share this with Traynor."

"Huh?"

"Your girlfriend's right over there," Jessie Belle muttered in a low voice before moving on. "I can't imagine you with someone so insecure. She's been following you around and watching you like a hawk." Pulling at her own collar, she added, "It must be so stifling for you. Are you allowed to even breathe on your own?"

"You're a funny lady."

She walked past Cynthia, pausing long enough to say, "It's so good to see you this morning, Miss Hargrove."

"I saw you over there talking to Atkinson. Don't think I was fooled for a minute. I see the way he looks at you. But in case you don't know—Atkinson is my man. You just better watch yourself, Jessie Belle. You don't know who you messing with."

Jessie Belle met Cynthia's hard gaze with her own. In a low voice, she uttered, "Neither do you."

Traynor came up behind them. "Hello, ladies."

"Hey, honey," Jessie Belle greeted. "You ready to go home?"

Cynthia excused herself, but not before sending Jessie Belle a sharp glance.

Traynor looked after her. "Is everything okay between you and Cynthia?"

Jessie Belle nodded. "Of course. We're great."

He took her by the hand and they headed to the car.

She spotted Cynthia over by Atkinson's car. The woman glanced over at them but turned away when she saw Jessie Belle eyeing her.

She smiled.

Jessie Belle decided she'd gotten her point across to Cynthia and wouldn't have to worry about her anymore.

Traynor hung up the telephone with a sigh.

His father and aunt were still upset with him for marrying Jessie Belle, but Traynor knew in his heart that he'd made the right choice. Besides, he'd prayed about it before making his decision, and God had given him such peace about the marriage.

Jessie Belle was a good wife. She kept a clean, tidy house and food on the table. A couple of people had tried to tell him things about Jessie Belle before they left Mayville, but Traynor refused to listen. He didn't like gossip.

Traynor straightened and moved to make room for his wife.

"Sweetheart, I have to tell you . . . that roast was delicious," he stated. "You're a wonderful cook."

"Ma used to tell me all the time that I had to know how to take care of my husband." Smiling, Jessie Belle added, "She was right, too. The way to your heart is through your stomach."

He laughed.

"I was listening to you earlier," she began. "You're really a gifted speaker. I can see you in one of the large churches here just preaching away. People lined up all over the place . . . Traynor, you could be the next Billy Graham. We drove up to Atlanta a couple of years ago to hear him preach. He's good. But you're even better than him."

Traynor broke into a grin. "That's quite a compliment."

Jessie Belle was his biggest cheerleader and he loved her for that. She made him feel as if he could do anything.

"It's the truth, honey."

"If I never have a big church—that's okay with me," Traynor stated. "Wherever God sees fit to send me—that's where I'll go. I'm about His business."

"I'm all for God's business, but you need to take care of your own business, too."

"What do you mean by that?" Traynor asked.

"It's not just your calling, honey. It's your job as well. You need to treat it as a business."

"I do," he countered.

Traynor wasn't sure exactly where Jessie Belle was going with this. He glanced over at her. "You don't think I am?"

"I'm not saying you're not, but it's very easy to get so caught up in your ministry that you forget about home. I know because my daddy did it until Ma set him straight."

Traynor kissed her. "I won't ever forget about home—you're unforgettable."

Jessie Belle stood up and began removing her clothes. "You haven't even seen unforgettable yet."

He felt a wave of desire ignite in the pit of his belly.

"I thought maybe we could have dessert upstairs," Jessie Belle murmured. She licked her full lips.

Traynor stood up.

Laughing, Jessie Belle led the way up the stairs.

CHAPTER SIX

Jessie Belle finished up the last of the laundry. She put away the towels and changed the bed linens in the master bedroom.

The telephone rang.

Walking over to the nightstand, Jessie Belle answered it on the third ring. "Hello."

"Hey, beautiful . . ."

"Who is this?" she asked with a frown.

"It's your secret admirer," the voice on the other end answered.

Jessie Belle didn't recognize the voice, although it had a familiar tone. Not in the mood to play games, she uttered, "I don't have time for this. I'm hanging up."

"Wait . . . ," he quickly interjected. "This is Atkinson Bradford."

"If you're calling for Traynor, he's at the church," Jessie Belle stated. "You can reach him there."

"I was calling to talk to you."

Jessie Belle dropped down in a nearby chair. "Why?"

He laughed. "I thought maybe we could be friends."

"Why?" she asked a second time. Jessie Belle knew that Atkinson had more on his mind than friendship.

"You don't want to be my friend?"

"I don't need any more friends," Jessie Belle stated. "I have more than enough. Atkinson, I have to get back to my housekeep—"

He cut her off by saying, "I thought we could meet at this little jazz club I know. Around eight o'clock. I know your husband will be in a meeting at the church at that time. It'll be two friends getting out for a couple of hours. That's all."

The jazz club. She'd wanted to go there so badly.

Traynor will never take me.

"Hey, Jessie Belle . . . you still there?"

"I'm here," she stated. "Where is this club located?"

"Peachtree Street. It's called LaBelle's Jazz and Supper Club."

"I've heard of it," Jessie Belle responded. "Thanks for the invitation, but, Atkinson, I have to go. I need to prepare lunch for my husband."

"Are you going to meet me there or not?"

Jessie Belle hung up the telephone without giving Atkinson an answer. She wanted nothing to do with the man.

"I wasn't sure you'd actually show up," Atkinson stated when Jessie Belle sat down across from him. "Especially after the way you slammed down the phone on me when I called you earlier. But I guess I wasn't wrong about you after all."

Jessie Belle sat down at the table in the dimly lit club. "I've never heard a live band before, so I thought I'd check them out for a couple of hours and then I have to go pick up my husband. So that we're clear, I didn't come here to see you."

His eyebrows rose in surprise. "Never heard a live band . . . wow."

"My daddy is a preacher," Jessie Belle explained. "He didn't let me go out to clubs or anything like that."

"That's too bad," Atkinson uttered.

"It's not a big deal. He was preparing me for my role as Traynor's wife."

"So you were raised to be a preacher's bride, huh?"

"I was raised to be the wife of a great man," Jessie Belle countered with a slight tilt of her chin.

After a moment, she asked, "Were you born and raised here in Atlanta?"

He shook his head no. "I'm from Savannah originally. Came up here for a visit and never left." Atkinson leaned forward in his chair. "But I don't want to talk about me. I want to know all about you."

Jessie Belle boldly met his gaze. "You mean more than the fact that I'm happily married to the pastor of the church both you and your girlfriend attend?"

Atkinson laughed. "Then why are you here with me, pretty lady?"

"I told you. I came out to enjoy the music. *That's all.*"

"Liar."

Jessie Belle stiffened. "What did you just say?"

"You're just as interested in me as I am in you. *Admit it.*"

"I'll be honest. . . . you piqued a certain curiosity," Jessie Belle stated after a moment.

He grinned. "I knew it."

"But it doesn't mean a thing," she interjected. "I'm not here to cheat on my husband. Traynor doesn't deserve that."

Atkinson leaned forward. "I want to get to know you better, Jessie Belle. I have a feeling that you and I have a lot in common."

She wasn't flattered by his attention at all. In fact, he was getting on her nerves. "Atkinson, it's not going to happen. Give it up."

"Why don't you try and keep an open mind?"

"Not interested," Jessie Belle uttered. "I'm happy with my marriage and I have no intentions of having an affair with you. I just came here to listen to some music."

A waitress walked over to take their drink orders.

"Just water for me," Jessie Belle stated.

Atkinson ordered brandy. "Nobody orders water at a club," he said when the waitress left.

"I don't drink."

"Oh yeah . . . you're a preacher's kid. Sugar, one lil' drink won't hurt you."

Jessie Belle shrugged in nonchalance. "I don't want one. I've had every opportunity to drink, Atkinson. I simply choose not to."

When the band began to play, Jessie Belle's body swayed to the music.

"Wanna dance?" Atkinson asked.

Jessie Belle shook her head no. "I just want to listen to the music."

"Chicken," he uttered.

She sent him a sharp glare.

When the band took a break, Jessie Belle asked, "So what do you do for a living? Do you have a job?"

"I'm a sales manager at a car dealership."

Jessie Belle perked up. "What type of cars do you sell?"

"Chevrolets."

"You have any Chevelles in the silver color?" she asked.

Atkinson nodded. "Two on the lot right now."

Jessie Belle filed that in the back of her mind. She really liked the new Chevelle.

She checked her watch, then shot up out of her seat. "I didn't realize it was so late. I have to go."

"Why you leaving so soon? The waitress hasn't even come back with your water."

"I wanted to see a live band and now I have. Now I'm going home."

"Are you sure you want to leave right now?"

Smiling, she nodded. "Absolutely. I miss my husband. He's the one I want to spend the evening with."

"When can I see you again?"

"Sunday," Jessie Belle answered with a smile. "At church."

She picked up her purse and walked out of the club, a big smile on her face.

Jessie Belle drove straight to the church to pick up Traynor.

"You didn't have to get all dressed up for me," he said when he saw her.

"I have to keep my man interested," she responded with a grin. "Did you get something to eat?"

Traynor nodded. "Martha picked up some dinner from the Deep South Restaurant down the street. They have some of the best soul food in the city."

Jessie Belle moved over so that Traynor could drive them home.

After they arrived home, they sat down and talked over slices of lemon pound cake.

They went to bed around eleven and made love.

When the clock struck midnight, Jessie Belle eased out of bed, careful not to wake a sleeping Traynor. She moved around the room quietly, picking up her clothes so there wouldn't be a mess when he woke up.

I love Traynor, so why did I meet Atkinson at that club?

Jessie Belle continued to ponder the question as she ventured into the sitting room. Atkinson was an extremely handsome man, but he had nothing else to offer. It would be pure stupidity to ruin her marriage over him.

Traynor was the man she chose. Jessie Belle envisioned him being bigger than Billy Graham. He had a lot of potential, whereas Atkinson—he was a car salesman by profession. There was nothing he could offer Jessie Belle outside of a good deal on the brand-new Chevrolet Chevelle convertible in silver.

The more Jessie Belle thought about it, the more she liked the idea. She wasn't going to cheat on Traynor; instead she'd just string Atkinson along until she got her car. She had her husband almost convinced that they needed a second car and since his was paid for by his father, they could easily afford the car payment.

When the clock displayed six a.m., Jessie Belle went downstairs and put on a pot of coffee. While she waited for it to be ready, she read from her daily devotional and spent ten minutes in prayer. After her first cup of coffee, Jessie Belle was ready to start her day.

She pulled out a bag of flour. Jessie Belle was going to make a big Southern breakfast for Traynor.

Jessie Belle had scrambled eggs, fluffy biscuits, thin slices of country ham, spiced apples and a pot of grits ready by the time Traynor walked into the kitchen. He was still dressed in his pajamas and matching robe.

"How long have you been up?" he asked.

"I couldn't sleep, so I decided to come down here and make you a nice breakfast. I'm sure you're tired of pancakes, cereal and oatmeal."

Traynor wrapped his arms around her. "Jessie Belle, I appreciate all of this, but understand me—you're not expected to cook meals like this every morning. I love oatmeal and I love pancakes. It doesn't take a whole lot to please me, sweetheart."

"I just wanted to do something special for you this morning. You're such a wonderful husband—I feel like I can't do enough to show my appreciation."

Traynor hugged her. "I feel like I'm the luckiest man alive to have a woman like you."

"Together, we'll rule the world," Jessie Belle whispered. "You have the brains and the personality. . . . I have brains and beauty—honey, we're a team."

He laughed.

"I'm serious," she stated. "If we just stick together, Traynor, we can go places. We can have whatever we want."

"I believe in teamwork," he responded. "And you're right—we make a great team."

"We're going to have a great life together." Jessie Belle kissed him.

She fixed Traynor's plate and placed it in front of him at the table. She carried her plate to the other side and sat down.

Traynor gave the blessing over the food.

"Jessie Belle, do you need the car today?" he inquired between bites.

She shook her head no while buttering a biscuit. "Honey, I was just thinking about how much easier it would be on you if we got me a car."

Traynor seemed to be considering her words.

Jessie Belle took a sip of her orange juice. "You wouldn't have to catch rides home with Deacon Smith. I know he talks you to death the whole way home."

Laughing, Traynor nodded. "He's never at a loss for words—that's for sure. But, sweetheart . . . maybe we should wait for a while."

"We don't have any real bills outside of the mortgage, Traynor. I don't have any credit cards and your car is already paid for. Deacon Bradford works at a dealership—I'm sure he'd be able to work out a deal for us."

"I'll take it to prayer, sweetheart."

Jessie Belle smiled and nodded. But deep down, she was ready to shake Traynor. *Take it to prayer. For what?* It was pretty clear that they needed two cars.

Traynor didn't mention it again and neither did Jessie Belle. She knew he'd come to her when he'd made a decision.

Half an hour later, Traynor headed out the house carrying his newspaper.

Jessie Belle walked him to the car. "Have a good day," she told him.

"Where did you go last night?" Mary Ellen asked when Jessie Belle walked next door. "I was getting worried when you didn't come home. I thought something happened at the supermarket."

"I . . . I didn't go to the store." Jessie Belle had forgotten about the lie she'd told her friend. "I went to visit one of our church members—she's going through a hard time right now. She was so upset. . . . I spent all evening with her."

Cynthia joined them. "Good afternoon, ladies."

Jessie Belle didn't respond, but Mary Ellen did. "Hey."

"You must have caught a sale somewhere, Jessie Belle," stated Cynthia. "I'm sorry. . . . I overheard Mary Ellen mention that you'd gone shopping yesterday."

"Ladies, I'd love to stand out here and talk, but I need to go home and start the laundry, clean the house and get dinner started for my husband. I don't want to be remiss in my wifely duties." Jessie Belle's eyes traveled to Cynthia. "Doing so can quickly put an end to a marriage, wouldn't you agree?"

She couldn't stand Cynthia. The woman's very presence irritated her to no end.

"Jessie Belle, I heard that you play the piano. I'm surprised that you're not playing for the church."

"We already have a pianist," Jessie Belle responded. "You do remember Brenda, don't you?"

Mary Ellen quickly interjected, "Girl, I'd like to stand out here all day, but I need to get in this house and get my work done. Before you know it, it'll be time for me to start dinner. Richard will have a fit if he comes home and I haven't done a thing."

Cynthia's expression turned ugly. "Y'all don't have to keep throwing it in my face that I don't have a husband. I'm well aware of the fact that I'm divorced."

"I didn't realize we were being insensitive," Mary Ellen stated. "Sorry."

"No, you're not," Cynthia countered. "I don't have time for this mess."

She stalked back across the street, uttering a few choice words.

"You should wash that mouth of yours out with soap," Jessie Belle hollered. "Along with your laundry."

Mary Ellen laughed. "That girl act like she was about to have a nervous breakdown."

"I guess Atkinson hasn't mentioned anything about marriage to her."

Mary Ellen chuckled. "Why bother?" she asked. "It's like he practically lives with her anyway. I don't know how she can show her face in church, living so close to y'all."

"That's probably the one thing I do respect about her," Jessie Belle stated. "She's not a hypocrite."

"Marriage certainly seems to agree with you," the assistant pastor said when he walked into Traynor's office. "Every time I see you, you're wearing this great big grin on your face."

"Don, you know the Bible says that he who finds a wife finds what is good and receives favor from the Lord."

"Amen, brother." Don sat down on the small sofa facing Traynor's desk. "I'm waiting on the good Lord to send me my mate. A couple of the mamas here in church don't like the fact that I don't have a wife, you know."

Traynor laughed. "Yeah, they weren't too fond of me before I married Jessie Belle."

"She seems like a nice lady."

"Jessie Belle is wonderful. She and I are on the same page when it comes to my ministry—you know that's very important. She's ready to jump right in and do whatever is needed. Jessie Belle just wants to serve."

"That's a blessing, brother."

"I'm glad to have her in my life."

Traynor worked at the church for another hour before leaving with Don to meet with other area pastors. They were preparing for an upcoming pastors' summit in August.

They returned to the church shortly after four. Men's Bible study was scheduled at six, so Traynor went home to have dinner with Jessie Belle.

As usual she had everything ready and on the table. Jessie Belle greeted him with a hug and a kiss.

"I missed you," she murmured.

"I missed you, too."

Traynor washed his hands in the kitchen sink before sitting down at the table.

"I cooked you a nice rib eye steak and baked potatoes. I didn't know we were out of ranch dressing, but we do have Italian. I'll pick up some more ranch tomorrow."

Jessie Belle was a good wife. And a phenomenal cook.

After Traynor blessed the food, they delved into their meals. She sliced off a piece of steak, and then asked, "How did your meeting with the other pastors go?"

"I was asked to speak at the leadership conference."

"That's wonderful," Jessie Belle murmured. "This is the perfect opportunity to get your name out there. Our membership will grow just from your speaking at other churches and conferences like this. Traynor, I'm so proud of you."

"I'm pretty excited about it myself. I figured they wanted me to ask my dad to speak. He gave the keynote a few years back."

"Is he planning to attend this year?" Jessie Belle inquired.

Shrugging, Traynor uttered, "I don't know. It's here in Atlanta. . . . I told him that if he decided to come, he should take a few days to spend with us. I want him to really get to know you."

Jessie Belle reached over and took him by the hand. "I'd like that."

Deep down, Traynor prayed his father would accept the invitation to come for a visit so that he could get to know Jessie Belle. Traynor Senior and his sister continued to express their doubt that the marriage would last. He wanted to prove them wrong.

Jessie Belle had baked a sour cream pound cake for dessert.

Traynor ate two slices before helping his wife clean the kitchen. At five thirty, he walked out of the house to leave for Bible study, while Jessie Belle settled down on the sofa to watch television.

Mary Ellen was on the porch when he opened the front door.

"I came to keep your wife company," she stated with a smile. "Richard's teaching a night class this evening."

He stepped aside to let her enter the house. "She's in the den."

Traynor was glad Jessie Belle had found a good friend in Mary Ellen. He liked her and Richard.

He drove to Ninth Street Baptist Church and parked in his designated space. Traynor got out of the car.

Bible study moved at a steady pace and within two hours, Traynor was back in his car and on his way home.

He turned down the street where his house was located at the end of the block. Out the corner of his eye, he caught sight of a long, tall shadow moving along the side of his house.

Is that a man leaving my house? he wondered.

Fearing for Jessie Belle's safety, Traynor parked the car in front of the house and jumped out, running toward the front door.

"Jessie Belle, where are you?" he called out.

"Traynor, for goodness' sake—what's wrong with you? You nearly scared me to death."

"I saw something outside. . . . Was someone here?"

Meeting his gaze, Jessie Belle shook her head no. "Of course not. I just got out of the tub. I was getting ready to welcome you home properly."

Traynor couldn't shake the feeling that someone had been lurking outside his home. While Jessie Belle dressed for bed, he went outside, checking to make sure his eyes hadn't been playing tricks on him.

They weren't, he realized when he saw footprints.

Some man had been here, and from the looks of things, he'd been looking through the window, spying on his wife.

He walked back into the house.

"I found footsteps," Traynor announced, his eyes never leaving Jessie Belle's face.

"The yardman was here earlier. It's probably his footprints that you saw out there."

"When I was coming down the street, I saw something—a man outside. Someone's been spying on you. Jessie Belle, I want you to keep the doors and windows locked at all times. You're not in Mayville anymore."

"Honey, I think you're making more out of this than necessary. Are you sure it wasn't Cynthia? You know she's been dying to kick me out of your life. Maybe she was over here trying to catch a look at you." Jessie Belle released a nervous chuckle. She didn't like the idea of someone spying on her.

"The footprints were those of a man."

"Well, the gardener was here today. Maybe you just saw something but thought it was a person. The streets are well lit up—anybody could easily get caught."

"I'm gonna speak to Mr. Gunther about it in the morning."

Jessie Belle nodded. She hoped that the footprints did indeed belong to the gardener. But if they didn't, then whom did they belong to? It was probably Cynthia being nosy, she decided. Jessie Belle didn't doubt for a minute that the witch would slip on a pair of men's shoes to throw off suspicions.

Traynor went through the house once more, making sure all the doors and windows were locked. He closed all the curtains.

"If anyone's trying to peek inside here tonight, they're gonna be disappointed."

Removing her robe, Jessie Belle whispered, "Enough of that—I've missed my husband and all I want to do right now is show you how much."

Jessie Belle kissed him with a hunger that belied her outward calm.

They fell back against the bed. She made love to her husband as if it were the last time.

Later in bed, she tossed and turned beside a sleeping Traynor. She couldn't sleep because she kept hearing strange night sounds. Jessie Belle hadn't realized just how spooked she was by the thought of someone spying on them.

A couple of times, she thought she heard footsteps outside her bedroom.

Jessie Belle retrieved her knife from its hiding place between the mattresses and walked through the house, searching. She checked each window. Jessie Belle went to her living room and peered out the huge picture window.

There were still lights on at Cynthia's house. Jessie Belle's breath caught when she glimpsed Cynthia sitting on the porch.

She's staring down here. I knew it had to be her.

Jessie Belle was tempted to walk down to Cynthia's house and confront her. She wasn't gonna allow anyone to destroy her happy home.

Just as she headed to the door, the knife still in her hand, Jessie Belle heard Traynor call out her name.

Jessie Belle eyed the front door for a moment before yelling out, "Honey, I'm coming. I just came downstairs to get something to drink."

CHAPTER SEVEN

Seated in the rocking chair on her porch, Jessie Belle glimpsed Atkinson's car parked in front of Cynthia's house. She toyed with the idea of walking over there just to get on the witch's nerves, but changed her mind. Cynthia wasn't worth the energy it would take.

Atkinson and Cynthia walked out of the house all hugged up. It was obvious they'd just had a midafternoon tryst. Cynthia hadn't even bothered to comb her messed up 'fro and Jessie Belle was pretty sure she hadn't had that granny-looking housedress on when Atkinson arrived. The frock was just something to cover up her nakedness.

Every now and then, Atkinson would look in her direction. Jessie Belle pretended to be engrossed in her reading.

She spied him when he strolled off Cynthia's porch toward his car a few minutes later.

Atkinson climbed inside.

"Good afternoon, Mrs. Deveraux," Atkinson called out as he pulled his car to a halt in front of her house. "We just got in a fully loaded silver Chevelle. You and your husband should come down to the lot and check it out."

Jessie Belle got up and strolled down the steps. "What kind of a deal can you offer my husband?" she asked, well aware that Cynthia was watching them from her porch.

When she reached the car, Atkinson said, "I wish you hadn't left the other night. I wanted to spend more time with you."

"Your girlfriend lives right across the street, in case you've forgotten that little fact. Also you can't seem to remember that I'm married."

"She's not my girlfriend."

"Does she know that?" Jessie Belle asked. "I don't think she does, Atkinson. If looks could kill, I'd be keeling over right about now."

He laughed. "You don't have to worry about Cynthia. She ain't gonna do nothing to nobody. That girl all talk."

"I'm not worried about her doing anything to me, Atkinson. I just don't want any scandal tainting my husband's ministry."

"Traynor Deveraux is a man," Atkinson stated drily. "He ain't nothing but a man, Jessie Belle."

"I know that."

"Then stop trying to make him into more. He just like the rest of us—trying to make our way in an evil world." Atkinson checked out himself in the rearview mirror. "I came over here last night to talk to you, but then I saw your husband driving up the street, so I left. Girl, you got me parking my car on the street behind your house and cutting through folks' yards and bushes to see you. That ought to tell you something. I don't do no mess like that for a woman."

"You were outside my house? Traynor almost caught you." Her lips puckered with annoyance. "Atkinson, that can't happen again."

"Why don't you leave him?" Atkinson asked. "You don't love him. I can see it in your eyes that you want me."

Jessie Belle laughed. "Oh, really. You can see all that?"

"You're saying it's not true?"

"That's exactly what I'm saying. Besides, I don't think that Cynthia will really be thrilled about that."

"I'll leave her. From the moment I saw you, I knew."

"You knew what?" Jessie Belle demanded, her arms folded across her chest.

"That you're the only woman I want to be with. I'm falling in love with you."

Jessie Belle laughed to hide her irritation. She had no intention of leaving Traynor, so Jessie Belle said, "Atkinson, you're confusing love with lust. You don't even know anything about me—how can you have such strong feelings for me?"

"Jessie Belle, let's stop playing games."

"I'm not playing any games, Atkinson. The only thing you can do for me right now is give me and Traynor a deal on a car. That's it."

"You keep talking about this car—you really want it?"

"Of course."

"So if I cut you a deal on the Chevelle—you and me—we can spend some time together?" Atkinson's eyes traveled downward from her face to her neck and chest. " 'Cause I can get you a deal."

She smiled. "Well, that'll depend on how much of a deal you offer."

Cynthia left her porch and was headed across the street to where they were talking.

"I thought you had to rush back to the lot," she uttered loud enough for the entire block to hear. "At least that's what you told me."

Atkinson muttered a curse. "Sorry about that," he said.

Jessie Belle laughed. "I guess you'd better be going."

"Give me a chance," Atkinson pleaded.

"Goodbye."

Cynthia walked toward them fast. "I know you hear me talking to you, Atkinson."

He drove off before she reached the car.

Cynthia glared at Jessie Belle. "What do y'all have so much to talk about?"

"Ask him," she responded before walking away.

Mary Ellen rushed over to the house fifteen minutes later.

"Girl, I thought you and Cynthia was about to have words. What happened? I'm driving to the house and I see you two in the street all up in each other's face. What is going on?"

Jessie Belle shrugged in nonchalance. "I can't believe she's so upset. Atkinson stopped by here after he left her house. He and I were just talking about a car. I didn't know she was so insecure."

"Y'all buying a new car?"

"We're thinking about it," she confirmed.

"From Atkinson?" Mary Ellen wanted to know.

Jessie Belle nodded. "He's a car salesman, isn't he?"

"Yeah, but I think he's attracted to you. You don't want to go giving him the wrong idea."

"It doesn't matter, Mary Ellen. I just want that new Chevelle in silver and with a discount. If I can get it by flirting a little, what harm is done? I love Traynor, and Atkinson isn't worth losing him over."

"Then don't play this game with him," Mary Ellen advised. "Atkinson

Bradford is a player. He's been stringing Cynthia around for the past three years I've lived in this house. He started coming around about a week or two after her husband moved out."

"I wonder if they were having an affair."

Shrugging, Mary Ellen responded, "I heard they were, but I don't know if it's true or not."

Jessie Belle shrugged. "It doesn't matter to me. I just want him to give me a deal on the car I want—then Atkinson can go to Timbuktu."

She and Jessie Belle laughed.

"Girl, you are something else," Mary Ellen stated. "I'm glad we're friends. But seriously, be careful. Traynor was telling Richard this morning that he thought someone was peeping in your house last night."

"I told him the gardener from the church was over here yesterday."

"Richard told him the same thing."

Jessie Belle stole a peek out her window. "Cynthia's still sitting on her porch looking down this way. Don't that chick have something better to do?"

Traynor pulled into the driveway.

Jessie Belle glanced over at Mary Ellen. "My man's home. She'd better not run over here getting all in his face. I'll cut her up now and repent later."

"Remind me not to get on your bad side," Mary Ellen said with a chuckle. "You talking about cutting people and stuff."

"I'm not about to let that tramp mess up what I have with my husband. I'll fight for mine. That's just the way it is."

Mary Ellen eyed her for a moment. "Okay . . . I hear you. Let's talk about something else. I can see you all frowned up and looking like you ready to just walk across the street."

"I don't like that girl, and she better stay out of my way."

They heard Traynor enter the house and put an end to their discussion. Mary Ellen made a quick exit.

"Hey, honey," she greeted. "How was your day?"

"Great," he replied. "And yours?"

"Pretty good." Jessie Belle took him by the hand. "Dinner's almost ready. By the time you get settled, I'll have everything on the table."

"You're a good wife, Jessie Belle. And because of that, I'm going to get you that car. You deserve it."

"Thank You, Lord," she uttered. "Oh, honey . . . I'm so happy. Just talk to Deacon Bradford—he'll give us a good deal. I'm sure of it." Jessie Belle embraced him. "Thank you."

They shared a tender kiss.

"Oh, I spoke to the gardener," Traynor announced when they separated. "He said it was most likely his footsteps on the side of the house. He planted the perennials you wanted over there."

"I didn't even notice them," Jessie Belle murmured.

"Why don't we check them out now?" Traynor suggested. "He wants to know if you want more."

Jessie Belle's mind wasn't on flowers. She was getting a new car.

"I just got off the phone with Atkinson," Traynor announced the next day when Jessie Belle walked back inside the house. She'd spent the morning working on the flower bed. She'd decided to add more flowers and didn't want to wait on the gardener.

"I told him we'd drive out to the lot this weekend."

Jessie Belle couldn't stop grinning. "Really?"

She washed her hands in the kitchen sink and dried them with a paper towel.

He smiled and nodded. "We're getting you a car."

"I'm so excited," Jessie Belle squealed. "My first car . . ."

"I didn't know it meant that much to you."

"Traynor, all I've ever wanted was a loving husband, a beautiful house and a new car," Jessie Belle stated. "But I don't just think about me. Traynor, I want you to have a big church and be on television. The world needs to hear you preach, honey. I can see it now . . . you on the radio and on television just saving souls—bringing them to the Lord. Just think how many people you'll reach."

Traynor gave her an indulgent smile.

"We can have those things, Traynor. I just know it—we just have to step out on faith."

"If it's God's will . . ."

"God doesn't just want us waiting around on Him. Sometimes He requires that we step out of our comfort zones and just trust Him. You said this last Sunday when you preached."

Traynor grinned. "So you were listening."

She smiled in return. "Of course. You're my husband."

"I thank God for you, Jessie Belle. It means a lot to me that you are so supportive. You make me feel as if I can do anything."

"Traynor, you can. I don't believe God just called you to pastor a little church like Ninth Street Baptist. He's called you for greater opportunities—you just have to recognize them."

They spent a couple of hours together before Traynor left to run errands.

Jessie Belle could hardly wait for the weekend to arrive. She was excited about getting her very first car.

On Saturday afternoon, Traynor and Jessie Belle met with Atkinson at the Chevrolet dealership.

Three hours later Jessie Belle drove her car home.

When they ventured into the house, Jessie Belle noted Traynor seemed troubled by something.

"What's wrong, honey? Are you worried about the car payment?"

"No," Traynor responded.

"What is it, then?" Jessie Belle sat down beside her husband. "I can tell something's bothering you."

"I appreciate everything Atkinson did for us today, but I have to be honest. I don't like the way the man looks at you. I was watching him today—he can't seem to take his eyes off you."

"Honey, what are you talking about?" Jessie Belle laughed. "That man probably watches every woman in the church. I can tell just by looking at him that he's a ladies' man."

Traynor eyed her. "Just be careful around him. We don't want him misconstruing your kindness for something more."

"Honey, you can trust me," Jessie Belle assured him. "I thought you knew that, but I guess I was wrong. Traynor, I'm not some fragile little girl. I can handle these guys around here—I've been doing that since I got my first period."

"Jessie Belle . . ."

"For goodness' sake, Traynor, you're only twenty-two years old. Don't be such a prude."

———

Jessie Belle avoided any contact with Atkinson on Sunday morning before service began. She could tell he was trying to steal a few minutes with her.

After church, she was not so lucky.

He crept up behind her. "Baby, I held up my end of the bargain. Now it's your turn."

Jessie Belle pushed away from him. "Have you lost your mind, Atkinson?" she asked in anger. "Keep your hands off me! For goodness' sake, my husband is right down the hall."

Atkinson shrugged in nonchalance. "I don't care. I want you for myself. Leave Traynor. He's not man enough for you."

She turned to face him. "And you think you are?" Jessie Belle laughed. "You're kidding, right?"

"I'm dead serious."

Jessie Belle sighed in frustration. "Atkinson, for the last time, I'm not leaving my husband."

"You love me, Jessie Belle. I can see it in your eyes."

"This was kind of cute in the beginning, but now it's annoying, Atkinson. *I love Traynor.* Go find Cynthia and just leave me alone."

"No," he responded. "I don't love her. It's you I want."

Jessie Belle felt a tremor of fear after noting the crazed look in his eyes.

This fool is out of his mind. He's insane.

Not wanting to set Atkinson off, Jessie Belle softened her tone. "Listen to me, please. Atkinson, we can't do this. Not here."

"Meet me tomorrow at the Holiday Inn on Peachtree. The one by McDonald's . . . three blocks from the dealership. You owe me, Jessie Belle."

"I can't." She stepped around him. "I'm not gonna cheat on my husband. You received a nice commission when you sold us the car. Let that be enough." Jessie Belle made a move toward the door. "I'm sure Traynor's wondering where I am. I need to go."

Atkinson grabbed her, pulling Jessie Belle to him. "C'mon . . . just one kiss for now, baby. I can hardly wait to be with you tomorrow."

Before she could utter another word, his mouth covered hers.

CHAPTER EIGHT

S he'd known Atkinson was attracted to Jessie Belle, but Cynthia had no idea he'd acted on those feelings. And Jessie Belle . . .

The hussy.

Jessie Belle was going around acting like she so in love with her husband. . . . The tramp was sneaking around and sleeping with Atkinson. Cynthia was still having trouble believing what she'd just seen with her own eyes.

Jessie Belle and Atkinson all hugged up in the choir room kissing. She heard Atkinson talking about their plans to meet tomorrow at a hotel.

Blinded by tears, Cynthia brushed past one of the ushers, nearly knocking her down.

"I'm s-so s-sorry," she stammered. "I should've been l-looking where I was g-going."

"What's wrong, Cynthia? Did something happen?"

Her eyes filled with tears. "Angie, I can't talk right now."

She wrapped an arm around Cynthia. "Come over here and sit down. I've never seen you this upset."

"How could he do this to me?" Cynthia whispered as she glanced around the room. "And right here in the church . . ."

Angie was confused. "Cynthia, what in the world are you talking about? What happened?"

Instead of answering, she burst into another round of tears.

Cynthia kept telling herself that she shouldn't be so surprised. Atkinson was a player—he loved women. All women.

Her ex-husband was just like Atkinson—didn't know a thing about being faithful. But he wasn't as good-looking as Atkinson and he couldn't keep a job. Cynthia divorced him.

As for Atkinson, she liked him a lot—enjoyed his sexual prowess and loved spending his money. They'd been together for the past couple of years and until now, Cynthia had never felt threatened by another woman.

Jessie Belle Deveraux was evil.

Traynor Deveraux was a good man and she'd hoped to garner his attention, but then he left town for a couple of weeks and came back with a wife. Cynthia was on the verge of breaking up with Atkinson before she heard.

She dried her eyes.

Maybe there was still a chance with Traynor. If Jessie Belle and Atkinson got together . . .

"I need to see Reverend Deveraux," Cynthia stated.

"You want me to go with you?"

She shook her head no. "I'll be okay, Angie. Thanks."

Filled with jealousy and anger, Cynthia burned with the memory of listening to Atkinson make plans to meet Jessie Belle for a lovers' tryst. They were going to pay for their betrayal and in the end she would have Traynor. It really wasn't a bad trade-off.

Traynor was a much better catch than Atkinson. With that in mind, Cynthia walked as fast as she could to his office.

Cynthia knocked, and then opened the door without waiting for a response.

"Your wife is having an affair with Atkinson," she announced without preamble. "I just overheard them making plans to meet tomorrow."

Traynor didn't respond for a moment. When he did, he said, "You most likely misunderstood them."

"I heard them as clear as day," Cynthia countered, taking a seat in one of the visitor chairs facing his desk. "I'm sure you don't want to believe this about your wife, but it's true."

"What exactly did you hear?"

"They were planning to meet tomorrow."

"Where?"

"I didn't hang around long enough to hear that part. I was too upset."

"I hope you aren't in my husband's office bothering him with nonsense," Jessie Belle stated from behind them. "If you need to talk to someone, I'm available."

Cynthia stood up. "I was actually just leaving."

She made her way to the door, pausing long enough to eye Jessie Belle from head to toe.

"Why are you looking me up and down like that?"

Cynthia uttered, "Just seeing what a real *lady* looks like. You try and have a good day, Mrs. Deveraux."

Jessie Belle followed her down the hall and grabbed Cynthia by the arm. "You don't fool me. You're up to something. I can smell it all over you."

Snatching her arm away, Cynthia responded, "I'm not trying to do anything to you, Jessie Belle. I don't have to—you've done enough to yourself." Wearing a smug expression, she announced, "I told your husband about you and Atkinson. You know, I never thought you'd be so stupid."

Jessie Belle looked angry enough to physically attack her, prompting Cynthia to take a step backward.

"There's nothing going on between me and Atkinson." Lowering her voice, she added, "If you've done anything to cause problems in my marriage—I intend to make sure you regret it for the rest of your boring life. You better pray I can fix this mess."

Cynthia was still shaking when Jessie Belle turned and headed back to Traynor's office.

Jessie Belle chewed on her bottom lip as she made her way down the hallway to her husband's office.

That witch! If Traynor believes her . . . I'm gonna make her wish she'd never been born. He won't believe her. Traynor knows Cynthia is a lonely woman with no life. He knows how much she loves to gossip. He won't believe her.

Jessie Belle sent up a quick prayer. *Lord, I need You to help me with this mess Cynthia created. I'm innocent. Please don't let Traynor believe a word she says. I don't want to lose my husband. I haven't been unfaithful to him. Please get me out of this mess.*

Standing outside his office, Jessie Belle felt a little better.

I haven't done anything wrong. Cynthia's just jealous of me and she's afraid of losing Atkinson. Goodness knows . . . she can have the man—I certainly don't want him.

Jessie Belle decided feigning ignorance was the way to go. She would just wait and see if Traynor mentioned anything. Surely he wouldn't believe anything coming out of Cynthia's mouth.

She headed for the nearest exit door and walked outside. She'd wait for Traynor by the car.

Jessie Belle didn't have to wait long. He walked out a few minutes later, his expression grim.

She made small talk while they rode the short distance home. Jessie Belle couldn't help but notice that Traynor wasn't saying much.

"You were so quiet on the drive home," she began. "Is everything okay?"

"Why don't you tell me?" Traynor responded.

"I'm not sure what you mean. Is something wrong?"

He didn't say another word until they were inside the house. "Cynthia came to my office after service to tell me about an interesting conversation she overheard between you and Atkinson."

"Okay. Is there a problem with my speaking to Deacon Bradford? We've spoken on several occasions. He is a deacon at our church and he did sell us a car."

"Cynthia said you and Atkinson were making plans to meet tomorrow. Jessie Belle, I need to know the truth. Are you having an affair with him?"

"I can't believe you'd listen to lies about me and Atkinson. Especially when they're coming from Cynthia, of all people."

"I want the truth, Jessie Belle," Traynor insisted. "Are you and Atkinson having an affair?"

"No, we're not," Jessie Belle responded. "Cynthia's just an insecure and jealous witch." She stepped around him. "I'm not gonna entertain this foolishness any longer. I haven't done anything wrong. I bet she——"

Traynor interrupted her by saying, "Jessie Belle, I've seen the way Atkinson looks at you and the way he acts around you. I'm not stupid. And in my spirit I feel like there's something more going on between the two of you."

He walked over to the front door, opening it. "If you're sleeping with him, then, Jessie Belle, I think it's best that you just leave. Go to your lover."

Her mouth opened in shock. Jessie Belle could hardly believe her ears. *"You want me to leave?"*

"I'll not stand for you to carry on under my nose like that. If I can't trust you, then I don't see how we can have a marriage."

She'd never seen him look so angry and hurt. "Traynor, honey, I'm telling you the truth." Jessie Belle's words came out in a rush. "I've never had an affair with Atkinson. Look, you don't have to worry about him— it's Cynthia that's the problem. I didn't want to bother you with this, but she's made it perfectly clear that she's interested in you."

This time it was Traynor who was stunned. "Jessie Belle, what are you talking about?"

"She's attracted to you, Traynor. Haven't you noticed the way she hangs on your every word and how she follows you around the room whenever we're all together? As for Atkinson, I made it clear how much I loved you. He knows that I'm not interested in him. Honey, there's no affair."

"You think Cynthia made this up because she's after me?"

"What else could it be, Traynor? I mean, Atkinson has flirted with me, but it's nothing like what she's saying. If you picked up on his attraction to me, I'm sure she did, too, but Cynthia's using this to cause problems between us."

"She seemed really upset. I don't believe she was faking."

"I guess you'd rather think that I'm the one having an affair, then," Jessie Belle said over her choking, beating heart.

How could Traynor accuse her of betraying him?

"No, that's not it."

"Traynor, Cynthia's been after you from the moment she met you," Jessie Belle stated with staid calmness. "I even think she's been pushing Atkinson toward me, so that she can kill two birds with one stone— causing problems in my marriage and getting rid of Atkinson. I'm sure Cynthia's hoping you will leave me so that she can be with you. Women can be so manipulative, Traynor."

"Jessie Belle, I had no idea."

"I know you didn't. Men don't seem to notice these kinds of things, but women do. Ma used to tell me all the time about the different women trying to capture my father's attention."

Jessie Belle led Traynor over toward the window. "I bet she's sitting on her porch right now, waiting to see if one of us storms out of here. She's counting on your kicking me out of the house, I'm sure."

"She *is* on the porch," Traynor stated. "She keeps looking over here."

"I told you. She's waiting to see if one of us is leaving—mostly me."

Jessie Belle suddenly felt nauseous. She placed a hand to her mouth.

"Sweetheart . . . you okay?"

"I don't know what happened. I just suddenly feel sick to my stomach."

Traynor took her hand and led her over to a nearby chair. "Why don't you sit down for a minute and see if it passes," he suggested.

Jessie Belle searched her memory, trying to remember when she last had her period. She'd stopped taking birth control the moment she and Traynor decided they wanted to get married. She made a mental note to schedule a doctor's appointment.

If her suspicions were right and she was indeed pregnant . . . Traynor would forget all about Cynthia and her foolishness.

Please let me be pregnant, she prayed silently.

Some of Jessie Belle's color returned to her face, but Traynor was still worried about her. He felt guilty for accusing her of being unfaithful when he should have known better. She had never given him cause to make such an accusation.

"I'm sorry for accusing you of cheating on me," he told her. "I hope you can forgive me."

She nodded. "I probably would've reacted the same way if someone had come to me like that."

Traynor didn't believe her. "I think you would've come to me like a mature person and ask—not accuse me outright. I was wrong for the way that I treated you, sweetheart, and I'm really sorry."

Another wave of nausea hit Jessie Belle. This one sent her running off to the nearest bathroom with Traynor following close behind. He wet a washcloth and gently wiped her forehead as she emptied the contents of her stomach.

When she could vomit no more, Traynor picked her up and carried her up the stairs to their bedroom.

"I need to brush my teeth," she whispered.

"Just lay down for a little while, sweetheart. I don't want you passing out—you look a little weak."

Traynor was worried that he'd upset Jessie Belle to the point of making her sick. He sat beside her on the bed, holding her hand. Guilt seeped from his pores. "Are you feeling a little better?" he asked after several minutes passed.

She nodded. "Some."

Jessie Belle slowly swung her legs to the edge of the bed and climbed out. "I need to brush my teeth."

Traynor helped her to the bathroom.

"I'm sorry for upsetting you like this," he said.

Jessie Belle eyed his reflection in the mirror. "Honey, you didn't do this."

"Is there something going on with you?"

"Could be stomach flu. There's some kind of virus going around, you know."

"Are you sure that's what it is?" Traynor asked.

Jessie Belle gave a slight shrug. "I don't know, but I'm going to see the doctor tomorrow if I can get an appointment. Whatever it is, I intend to nip it in the bud."

She walked back into the room and removed her clothes. "I'm just gonna get into bed if you don't mind. I don't feel well at all."

Traynor stayed upstairs with her until she fell asleep.

As he watched her sleeping form, Traynor couldn't believe how close he'd come to ruining his marriage by listening to the lies of another woman. Still Traynor wondered at the reason why Cynthia would try to break up him and Jessie Belle.

Sure, she'd flirted with him from time to time, but Traynor had simply ignored it. He figured that she was just naturally flirtatious. It had never occurred to him that Cynthia would have other motives.

He felt like a fool.

CHAPTER NINE

Two days later, Jessie Belle's prayers were answered. She and Traynor were going to have a baby.

The doctor confirmed it that morning. Jessie Belle was six weeks pregnant. According to her calculations, she'd conceived on her wedding night.

Thank You, God.

A baby was just what she needed to put an end to this mess Cynthia stirred up.

She resisted the urge to pay the troublemaker a visit when she left the doctor's office. Jessie Belle decided to bide her time for now, but she wasn't about to forget what Cynthia had done.

The witch was gonna pay.

Jessie Belle cooked a special dinner, set the table and changed into a beautiful silk nightgown. Mary Ellen had helped her arrange several elegant floral displays around the living room and dining room. The scented candles emitted a soft ethereal glow, adding to the romantic ambiance.

Everything has to be perfect.

She checked the clock. Traynor was due home any moment. Jessie Belle couldn't wait to see the look on his face. Her husband would be thrilled to know of his impending fatherhood. He wanted children.

She stole a peek outside the huge picture window in the living room. Traynor had just pulled into the driveway.

He's home.

Jessie Belle checked her reflection in the mirror. "I look stunning," she whispered. "I just hope that Traynor thinks so."

He has to be happy about the baby.

She said a quick prayer before opening the front door to greet him.

Traynor did a double take when he walked into the house. "What's going on?" he asked. "Are we having company for dinner?"

Smiling, Jessie Belle responded, "Honey, do I look like I'm hosting a dinner party?"

His eyes traveled up and down her silk-draped body. She was wearing the black gown he loved with the matching robe. "You look beautiful, Jessie Belle. I guess you're feeling much better."

"I am," she responded. "Honey, why don't you go get comfortable? When you come out, I'll have dinner on the table ready and waiting for you." Jessie Belle planted a kiss on his lips.

Traynor went upstairs to their bedroom.

Humming softly, Jessie Belle navigated to the kitchen to prepare their plates.

"Did you do all this for me?" Traynor asked when he strolled into the dining room ten minutes later.

He sat down at the head of the table.

"Of course I did," Jessie Belle responded. "You're my husband and I thought we deserved an evening of romance." She walked over to the cassette player on top of the sideboard and pressed a button. "I figured I'd bring the jazz to us."

Traynor smiled. "Everything looks real nice, Jessie Belle."

"I made stuffed pork chops for dinner," she announced. "I know how much you like them."

Jessie Belle smiled as she watched Traynor enjoy his meal.

He glanced up. "Aren't you going to eat your dinner?"

"My appetite is still a little iffy, but don't worry about me," she responded. "I'll make some soup in a few minutes for me."

Traynor looked concerned. "Did you get a chance to see the doctor?"

"I did," Jessie Belle confirmed. "And there's definitely something going on."

"What is it?" He laid his fork down and wiped his mouth with the edge of his napkin.

"Honey . . ." Jessie Belle paused for a moment. "I'm going to have a baby."

"What did you say?"

She smiled. "I'm pregnant, Traynor."

Traynor looked as if he didn't know whether to jump for joy or cry.

"Did you hear me?" Jessie Belle asked. "We're going to have a baby. Aren't you happy about it? It's what we both wanted."

"Are you sure?" Traynor asked quietly.

"The doctor confirmed it this morning." Jessie Belle met his gaze. "I thought you'd be a little more excited about the news that we're going to be parents."

Traynor broke into a smile. "I'm very happy. I guess I'm a little in shock, too."

"We're gonna have a little baby."

His gaze met hers. "Wow . . ."

"I'm glad it wasn't the stomach flu," Jessie Belle said with a chuckle.

"So it's been morning sickness, then?"

She nodded. "Hopefully, it'll go away in a couple of months. I can barely keep anything down."

After dinner, Traynor sent Jessie Belle upstairs with a promise to join her as soon as he cleaned up the kitchen.

When he came up twenty minutes later, Jessie Belle was in bed naked.

"Make love to me."

Traynor did as she requested.

He fell asleep in her arms afterward.

Jessie Belle listened to Traynor's soft snoring for a few minutes before easing out of bed.

She was still seething over the fact that Cynthia had tried to destroy her marriage. Jessie Belle decided that she needed to settle this mess with Cynthia once and for all.

She slipped on a pair of black pants and a black shirt. Jessie Belle pulled her shoulder-length hair up into a ponytail.

Jessie Belle left home under the cover of darkness and walked across the street. Cynthia wasn't going to get away with this.

She ran up the steps to the porch and rang the doorbell.

"Cynthia, I want to have a little talk with you," Jessie Belle stated when the front door swung open.

"Do you know what time it is?" Cynthia demanded. "What do you want?"

Jessie Belle pushed past her. "I want you to stay as far away from me and my husband as possible. I think you should find another church."

Folding her arms across her chest, Cynthia asked, "What does Traynor have to say about this?"

Jessie Belle met her gaze straight on. "He knows you're nothing but a troublemaker."

"I haven't done a thing. Can you say the same?"

"Cynthia—you're messing with the wrong woman."

Jessie Belle smiled when she glimpsed fear in Cynthia's eyes. "I hope we understand one another."

"I know what I heard."

"Like I said, you don't know what you're talking about. I want you to stay out of my business. Stay away from my husband, Cynthia. This is my only warning." Jessie Belle headed to the door.

Glancing around, she added, "It doesn't take much to break in here. I hope you're not a heavy sleeper."

"Hey, what's with all the attitude lately?" Atkinson demanded.

Cynthia sent him a sharp look. "How could you do this to me?"

"Do what?" he asked. "What did I do?"

"I can't believe you're having an affair with Jessie Belle Deveraux right in my face like this." Cynthia wiped away a tear.

"I ain't having no affair with nobody."

"I saw you, Atkinson. You kissed her in the choir room and I heard what you said. Y'all was all hugged up and making plans to meet some-where on Monday."

"I was with you all day Monday," he stated. "I didn't leave your house until late, remember?"

"I know that, but what did you do when you left me?"

"It was after ten. I went home."

"Any other time you would've spent the night with me."

"You weren't doing nothing but being mean—I got tired of it, so I went to my own place."

"Okay, but I saw you kiss Jessie Belle. You can't deny that."

"I kissed her, but she pushed me away. Did you see that?"

"No," Cynthia said quietly.

"I'm not having an affair with Jessie Belle. She ain't nothing but a big user. She just wanted to get that car. That's why she even started talking to me at all. She think she better than us."

"That woman is evil," Cynthia spit out. "I'm telling you the truth. . . . She came over here last night and threatened me."

He cracked up.

Angry, Cynthia elbowed him. "It's not funny."

She stood up and started pacing the floor.

"Why you wearing out the rug?" Atkinson questioned. "You acting like you all scared and stuff. Jessie Belle wouldn't harm a fly."

"She really got you fooled, don't she? I'm not stupid, Atkinson. I know you're attracted to her. That woman ain't nothing but trouble. You better listen to me. I don't know what Traynor Deveraux sees in her. He's such a nice man. He don't deserve a woman like that in his life—she's gonna mess up his ministry."

Shaking her head sadly, Cynthia added, "I just hate it for him."

"Wait a minute. . . . You getting on me for being attracted to Jessie Belle and look at you. You after her husband."

"Boy, you crazy."

Atkinson shook his head. "Naw . . . *I know you*. You want Traynor Deveraux."

"And you want Jessie Belle," Cynthia countered.

Atkinson settled back against the cushions of the couch. "So what we gon' do about it?"

Cynthia smiled. "I told Traynor about you and Jessie Belle."

"So what happened?"

"I don't know. I thought he'd throw her out, but she's still over there acting like she the queen. *I can't stand that woman.* Traynor deserves so much better."

"She a pretty girl," Atkinson interjected. "That pretty skin and that long curly hair . . . men like that."

Cynthia gave him a punch in the arm. "I don't want to hear that mess."

"You pretty, too."

"I wonder what he sees in her."

"She's gorgeous, smart and sexy. . . . Jessie Belle has a lot to offer a man."

"You saying I don't?" Cynthia asked. "You think that witch look better than me?"

"I ain't saying that at all, girl. Stop trying to make this about you."

Cynthia laughed. "Oh my goodness . . . Atkinson, you got it bad."

"What are you talking about?"

"You're in love with her," Cynthia accused. "I never thought I'd see the day when a woman captured your heart."

"I spoke to a pastor in Raleigh, North Carolina, this morning," Traynor told Jessie Belle during lunch a few days later.

"He wants me to take over his church there. He called me because he's retiring and moving to Florida. Donald Thasher is a longtime friend of my father."

"So what did you tell him?" Jessie Belle wanted to know.

"I told him I'd pray about it and get back to him. I want to discuss this with you first."

"So how are you feeling about it?" Jessie Belle hoped that Traynor would jump at an opportunity to leave Atlanta since the incident with Cynthia. She thought it best to get far away from Atkinson, too. Now when he figured Traynor wasn't home, he was calling the house and just breathing on the line, or he would try to engage her in sex talk.

Jessie Belle decided not to tell her husband about the calls because she wanted them to move past all the trouble Cynthia tried to cause, but Atkinson was beginning to stress her out.

"I don't have a problem leaving Atlanta, honey." She nibbled on a saltine cracker, hoping it would help to settle her stomach.

"I thought about it, but to be honest, I feel in my heart that we're supposed to stay here in Atlanta," Traynor stated.

Jessie Belle couldn't believe what she was hearing. As far as she was concerned, it was long past time for a change. "But it's a great opportunity, Traynor. A bigger church, nice salary increase . . . you really think we should stay here?"

She had to find a way to convince Traynor to leave Atlanta.

Moving to North Carolina opened a world of new opportunities. They could sell this house and find something much bigger and not quite so old in Raleigh. This time she would have a say in which house they purchased. But the best part of the deal was that there wouldn't be a Cynthia or an Atkinson.

She wanted to escape the mess they were trying to start. Jessie Belle wasn't about to let them break up her marriage. "I think we could do with a change, Traynor, if you want to know the truth," Jessie Belle stated. "I'm pregnant, and I don't need to be upset."

"I understand what you're saying, sweetheart. I just want to make sure this is what God wants us to do."

Jessie Belle held her tongue. She didn't want to fight with Traynor.

She walked over to Mary Ellen's house right after Traynor left to go back to the church.

"I can't stand your neighbor over there and if she don't get a life—I'ma have to teach that strumpet a lesson."

Mary Ellen laughed. "What did Cynthia do now?"

Jessie Belle gave her friend a revised version of what was going on between her and Cynthia.

"I'm shocked. I knew that Cynthia messed around with married men, but I didn't think she'd go this far," Mary Ellen stated. "She's really trying to mess you up, huh?"

Jessie Belle nodded. "I'm not the one, though."

"I don't blame you. She's gone way too far with this. That's so wrong of her to go to Traynor with a bunch of lies like that."

"I'ma trip her up in her own game," Jessie Belle stated.

"I know you mad 'cause you done stopped talking all proper."

She and Jessie Belle laughed.

"Cynthia's gonna wish she never met me, Mary Ellen, when I'm done with her."

"What are you gonna do?"

"I'ma make sure Traynor sees her for the strumpet that she is. Trust me on that."

CHAPTER TEN

Jessie Belle looked upset when Traynor arrived home.

Normally she greeted him with a kiss and a smile, but today was different. He didn't know if it was due to morning sickness or if she was just in one of her moods. Since the pregnancy, she went through bouts of moodiness.

He knew something wasn't right when he found that dinner hadn't been prepared.

Traynor wasn't bothered by it. This was the first time since their marriage that his wife hadn't bothered to cook a meal.

He strolled into the living room, where she lay on the sofa. "Sweetheart, would you like for me to fix something for you?"

Jessie Belle shook her head no. "I'm not hungry, Traynor."

He sat down beside her. "You okay?"

She nodded, then sat up slowly.

Putting her hands to her face, Jessie Belle wiped her eyes. "Actually, honey, I need to tell you something."

Her eyes met his. "Traynor, I really hate to bother you with this, but I've been receiving phone calls from Cynthia all day. She wants you for herself and she told me that she'll do anything to break us up. Cynthia was even bragging about how she was able to convince you that Atkinson and I were having an affair."

He was speechless. Traynor had trouble digesting what he was hearing. Cynthia had seemed like a nice enough girl. He couldn't believe that she was putting on an act the other day when she came to his office all upset.

Shaking her head, Jessie Belle added, "Traynor, we really need to pray for that woman. She's getting out of control."

Traynor was furious. "I can't believe she's being so immature."

"She wants you, honey. From the moment she laid eyes on you, Cynthia actually thought that she had a chance with you, but then you traveled to Mayville and met me. She told me all this. She said that I didn't figure in her plans."

He shook his head in disgust. "It's a shame before the Lord to act like this. I never gave her any indication or cause to think I'd be interested in her."

"Honey, it's not your fault. I told you, Traynor. She needs prayer."

"Jessie Belle, I'm so sorry you have to go through this."

"It'll be alright," she assured him. "If Cynthia continues the harassment, though—we should really try to find a new church."

Traynor had to consider that she might be right.

Jessie Belle was just a tiny bit surprised to see Cynthia at the church on Sunday. She'd hoped that she'd scared her away.

She found Cynthia in the choir room and confronted her.

"What are you doing here?" Jessie Belle demanded. "I can't believe you actually had the nerve to show your face around here after everything you've done."

"Why not?" Cynthia asked. "I'm still a member here and I haven't done anything wrong."

"I had hoped you'd have the good sense to find a new church home. We don't want people like you here at Ninth Street Baptist Church."

Cynthia's expression soured. "This was my church long before you ever set foot in Atlanta," she snapped. "I grew up in this church."

Jessie Belle dismissed her words with a wave of her hand. "I really don't care about all that. Cynthia, I don't think you're hearing me. I'm not going to let you or anyone ruin what I have with my husband. You crossed the line when you went to Traynor with your lies."

Folding her arms across her chest, Cynthia stated, "I'm not buying your innocent act, Jessie Belle. Besides, Atkinson and I had a nice long talk."

"I don't care who you talked to—Atkinson Bradford is a fool." Jessie Belle saw movement out of the corner of her eye.

It was Traynor.

She decided to take this a step further. If Cynthia wanted a war—she just got one. Speaking loud, Jessie Belle stated, "I know you're after my husband, but you're not going to get him, Cynthia."

"He deserves better than you, that's for sure."

"And you think it's you?"

"Yeah . . . I do," Cynthia confessed. "I don't know where he found you, but he should've left you there. You're nothing but trash."

Now for the finale.

Jessie Belle suddenly doubled over, moaning.

"What's wrong with you?" Cynthia asked.

Traynor blew past her, reaching for Jessie Belle. "Cynthia, that's enough," he said. "You're out of line speaking to my wife this way."

"The baby . . . ," Jessie Belle said between gasps. She took pleasure in Cynthia's ashen pallor.

"Baby? *She's pregnant?*"

He ignored Cynthia, much to Jessie Belle's delight.

"Let's get you to the hospital," Traynor stated.

"Honey, it hurts so b-bad."

Church members were beginning to gather around them, trying to find out what was going on. Jessie Belle hid her face in Traynor's blazer to keep from laughing; the look on Cynthia's face was so comical.

"I didn't know," she kept muttering over and over. "Oh Lord, I had no idea she was pregnant. I didn't know."

"Would it have mattered?" he demanded. "Why are you trying to hurt my wife with your lies? What did Jessie Belle ever do to you?"

Tears swelled up in Cynthia's eyes and spilled. "Pastor Deveraux, I . . ."

"I really don't care to hear anything you have to say right now. Just leave us alone."

Jessie Belle would've cheered if she weren't pretending to be in pain. The church members were gonna have a field day with this. Surely her husband would be ready to leave Atlanta now.

Traynor picked her up and carried her to the car.

She could see Cynthia watching them from one of the windows in the church hall.

The fool.

Jessie Belle continued her ruse through the examination. The doctor assured her that the baby was healthy and he could find nothing wrong. He did, however, caution Traynor to keep the pregnancy as stress free as possible.

They left the hospital two hours later.

"I'm so glad the baby's okay," Jessie Belle stated. "I was so scared. I guess the doctor was right—I'm under a lot of stress."

"I can't believe that woman . . . ," Traynor uttered. "Because of her, we could've lost our child."

"I don't know how I can show my face at church again. I'm so embarrassed. You know they're talking about what happened. I just know it. Honey, you don't need this type of scandal. This is just wrong."

"I'll figure something out," he assured her. "But, Jessie Belle, remember . . . we did nothing wrong. We shouldn't have to hang our heads in shame."

This was not the response she was after. Atkinson and Cynthia were trouble—she could smell it.

Jessie Belle wanted to leave Atlanta.

She just had to find a way to convince Traynor.

Traynor walked out of the bathroom wearing a robe over a pair of silk pajamas. "I was thinking that maybe I should try and talk some sense into Cynthia."

"Talk to her about what?" Jessie Belle questioned, irked by Traynor's calm manner. "She's going to deny it, Traynor. I don't want you talking to that woman—Cynthia's crazy."

He sat down on the edge of the king-sized bed. "Ninth Street Baptist really doesn't need anything like this, Jessie Belle. Stuff like this can tear down a church."

Jessie Belle's lips puckered in annoyance. "*We* don't need this, Traynor," she interjected. "All this foolishness is wearing on my nerves."

Placing a hand on her stomach, Jessie Belle said, "I'm pregnant—I don't need Cynthia running around town trying to ruin my life just because she can't keep a rein on Atkinson or these feelings she has for you."

She doubled over in pain.

Only this time, it was for real. Sheer fright swept through Jessie Belle.

Traynor was instantly at her side, asking, "Honey, what's wrong?"

"I don't know," she uttered between gasps of pain. "I guess it's all this stress I've been under. Traynor, something's wrong—I can feel it. Take me to the hospital right now. . . . Please hurry."

He helped her down the stairs, out of the house and into the car.

Traynor broke the speed limit, rushing to get her to the hospital. He could hear Jessie Belle praying for the life of their child.

"Dear Lord, please let my baby be okay," she kept saying over and over.

Traynor sent up prayers of his own during the drive to the hospital.

She was wheeled to an empty room in emergency, but by then it was too late.

Jessie Belle started to bleed and she knew then that her baby was gone.

The doctor confirmed their fears. She'd suffered a miscarriage.

"I'm so sorry, honey," Traynor whispered, taking her hand in his.

Angry, Jessie Belle turned her face away from him. "If you'd listened to me and got us away from here . . . maybe our baby would still be alive."

She knew that her words cut into him like a knife.

He faltered into a silence that engulfed them.

"It's no one's fault," the doctor interjected. "It just wasn't a viable pregnancy."

"I really wanted this baby," Jessie Belle confessed.

The doctor nodded in understanding. "I'll leave you two alone."

"I wanted our baby, too," Traynor stated. "Jessie Belle, I wanted that baby more than anything. You have to know that."

Jessie Belle wouldn't look at him when she responded, "Not enough to leave this city."

She turned over, wincing from the pain. "I shouldn't have said that, Traynor. I know you're grieving, too. I'm just so angry right now." Tears filled her eyes. "I'm not going to ever get to hold my baby."

He sat down on the bed beside her, holding Jessie Belle in his arms. "God, give us strength," Traynor prayed. "We need You in our time of grief, Lord. Help us. . . ." His voice broke and he couldn't continue.

Traynor held Jessie Belle in his arms until she fell asleep, then eased her down gently.

CHAPTER ELEVEN

Traynor left the room to call his in-laws and his father to break the news to them. There were no words to describe the acute sense of loss he was feeling. The sympathetic words uttered by his father and Jessie Belle's father did nothing to soothe his grief.

He made his way back to the hospital room to check on his wife.

Jessie Belle was still sleeping.

Traynor sat down in the visitor chair. Closing his eyes, he prayed.

Father God, I come before You brokenhearted and disappointed. Lord, I need You to bring Your healing touch to us. We've suffered the loss of our unborn child through a miscarriage. Father, we believe that life begins at conception and that this baby is now with You. Still, the pain of our loss is a heavy burden. We loved this child from the moment we knew of the baby's existence.

Tears formed in his eyes. *Father God, we know that our unborn child will never experience the joys of life on this earth, but our hope in eternal life remains firm. Please help us to remember our baby in prayer often. Instill in us the joy that we will one day meet in heaven with You. Father, if we're blessed with more children, we will not forget this unborn child. This baby will always be special to us. Thank You, Father, for strengthening our faith and remind us that our joy comes from You, who are the source of all goodness and love. Amen.*

Traynor heard the *McCloud* theme music and his eyes traveled to the television. This was one of his favorite TV shows, but today his mind was elsewhere.

He played with the zipper on the jacket of his navy blue jogging suit.

Jessie Belle stirred but didn't wake up.

Maybe she's right, Traynor thought. *If I'd listened to Jessie Belle and taken the job in North Carolina—perhaps this situation would've turned out differently.*

A somber Jessie Belle was released the next morning.

They drove home in silence.

Mary Ellen came over shortly after their arrival with a casserole. "If you need me to stay with Jessie Belle while you go down to the church, I don't mind," she told him.

"I do have a meeting, but I was considering canceling it."

She shook her head. "You don't have to cancel. Traynor, I really don't mind staying here with her. Go on to your meeting."

"I won't be gone long," Traynor promised.

"Take as much time as you need, Traynor. I'm off today."

"I really appreciate it, Mary Ellen."

She smiled. "Not a problem."

Things were tense between him and Jessie Belle. Traynor wasn't sure if they'd be able to get past the grief. It was painfully clear that she blamed Traynor.

He'd made two attempts to get Jessie Belle to discuss the miscarriage, but she refused. She just wanted to be alone.

She's angry and she blames me. Traynor understood his wife was grieving and she needed to lay blame on someone.

"When I checked on her earlier, she was sleeping," he told Mary Ellen. "I think she'll be waking up soon."

Traynor gave her a quick rundown of the antibiotics Jessie Belle had to take.

He walked out of the house and got into the car.

Traynor was relieved to get away, despite the guilt he was feeling over it. He just couldn't face Jessie Belle right now. She was ready to leave Atlanta behind, but he'd refused, and now their child was dead.

Lord, I have to find a way to make this up to my wife. She kept trying to tell me that it was time to move on, but I wouldn't listen. Jessie Belle had great instincts when it came to people and even their marriage. He should have trusted her gut instincts.

He vowed not to make the same mistake twice.

Jessie Belle tried to sit up until a wave of pain swept through her. "Where's Traynor?" she asked when she spied Mary Ellen sitting in the chair across from her.

"He went down to the church for a little while. He'll be back shortly. How you feeling, hon?"

"I feel like a part of me is missing." Although she didn't confide in Mary Ellen, she blamed herself for the miscarriage. God had punished her for using her unborn baby as a pawn in her scheme to get Traynor to leave Atlanta. "I wanted that baby more than anything."

Mary Ellen moved to sit beside her. "You're young, Jessie Belle. You'll have plenty of chances to have another baby."

She wasn't so sure God would entrust another child to her after her selfish behavior. Jessie Belle began to cry.

Embracing her, Mary Ellen said, "It's gonna be okay, hon. . . ."

I'm so sorry, Lord. Please forgive me for using my baby like that. If You bless me with another child, I promise I won't ever do it again. I won't, Lord. I promise.

Mary Ellen forced Jessie Belle to eat a little of the chicken casserole she brought over.

She fell asleep shortly after lunch.

When Jessie Belle opened her eyes, she found Traynor with her instead of Mary Ellen.

"You're back," she murmured.

"I didn't want to stay away too long. I was worried about you."

"I'm fine," she told him.

"During the drive back here, I had a little talk with God and I'm going to see if the job in Raleigh is still available. If it is, I'm going to take the job. I think you're right. Our season here is over."

"I really hope it's still available," she responded. Jessie Belle winced when she tried to shift her position.

"Are you still in pain?" he asked.

"Yeah, but it's not as bad as the others have been." She lay back on the sofa. "I'll lay here for a while and see how I feel. If the pain persists, we'll have to go back to the hospital."

"You let me know," he told her. "I don't want anything to happen to you."

"I feel so safe with you, Traynor."

He smiled. "You get some rest, sweetheart."

When he left the room, Jessie Belle tried to stretch and was rewarded with an attack of cramping.

She moaned.

Jessie Belle turned to her left side, staring out the window. "We're leaving this godforsaken place finally . . . ," she whispered. "I just hate that it was at the expense of my child's life."

Jessie Belle strolled out of the nail salon, smiling, a couple of weeks later. She and Traynor would be moving at the end of the month. Four days after the miscarriage, Traynor went to Raleigh to interview for the job with New Salem Baptist Church.

After his trial sermon, he was offered the job. She traveled with him back to Raleigh a week later to find a home. Jessie Belle found one the first day and convinced Traynor to write a contract on it.

Yesterday, someone made an offer on their Atlanta home and would be closing the day before they left. Things were going well for Jessie Belle.

"You think you can just leave me like this?"

At the sound of Atkinson's voice, she stopped walking and turned around. "What are you doing here?" Jessie Belle demanded. "Are you stalking me now?"

"You don't have to be so mean. I just want to talk to you. Jessie Belle, let's be honest. We want to be together."

"Atkinson, get over yourself," she snapped in frustration. "I've told you that I have no intentions of cheating on my husband. You and that psycho girlfriend are the very reasons we're leaving Atlanta."

He shook his head in disbelief. "You don't mean that. Your husband took that job to keep you from leaving him for me."

Jessie Belle bristled. "Actually, I do mean it, Atkinson. Because of y'all, I lost my baby. And I want you to know, I'll never forgive either one of you."

"I had no idea you were pregnant. I'm so sorry, sweetheart."

"You mean Cynthia didn't tell you? I guess I shouldn't be surprised. *That woman is a trip.*"

"She knew?"

Jessie Belle nodded. "I started having pains at the church during an argument with her."

"She didn't tell me nothing about that. I heard that you two were arguing, but that was all. Sweetheart . . ."

"I'm not your sweetheart," Jessie Belle quickly interjected. "Just leave me alone, Atkinson. Why can't you take a hint? I don't want nothing to do with you—never did. All I wanted was my car."

Atkinson's face turned ugly. "One day . . ."

"Don't you dare threaten me," Jessie Belle hissed. "You don't know me or what I can do. . . ."

"Cynthia's right about you," he uttered after a moment. "You are evil."

Jessie Belle shrugged in nonchalance. "Say what you want—just stay the hell out of my life."

Atkinson walked briskly to the door but not before leaving her with a prediction. "Jessie Belle, you can't keep going around here playing games with people like that. You're gonna pay for your sins one day. *Mark my words.*"

She gave him a big smile. "You have a wonderful day, Atkinson."

CHAPTER TWELVE

"Oh, Traynor, I'm so glad we moved here," Jessie Belle said as they removed the ornaments from the Christmas tree. "Raleigh is a beautiful city." She glanced out a nearby window. "I was hoping for a white Christmas, but it didn't happen."

"If the weatherman is correct, we should have a white New Year's, though." Traynor handed her a silver ornament. "I'm glad you like it here."

Jessie Belle put a handful of ornaments into a plastic container. "I love living here in Raleigh, Traynor. These last three months have been the best."

He agreed. "I think moving here was the best decision for us. Things have been peaceful. I'm glad that we're back on track. I felt like things were pretty shaky between us after the miscarriage."

"I was angry," Jessie Belle admitted. "I blamed you, but mostly, I blamed Cynthia and Atkinson. It really wasn't anybody's fault. I see that now."

She'd played the guilt card against Traynor for the first couple of months after their arrival in Raleigh. Jessie Belle used his own feelings of remorse to get new furniture and the three-quarter-carat diamond engagement ring she was now wearing with her wedding band.

Jessie Belle took Traynor by the hand and led him over to the sofa and sat down, saying, "Honey, there's something I want to talk to you about."

He sat down beside her. "What is it?"

"You know we've been thinking about trying to get pregnant again, but I wanted some time. . . ."

Traynor's eyes lit up with joy. "Are you ready to try?"

Smiling, Jessie Belle nodded. "I've been given a clean bill of health and a bottle of prenatal vitamins. I wanted to get our first Christmas out of the way. With this being New Year's Eve—I figured making a baby was a wonderful and romantic way to bring in a new year."

"Praise the Lord."

She laughed. "That's not quite the words I thought I'd hear from you."

Slowly and seductively, Traynor's gaze slid downward. "I can't wait to make a baby with you, Jessie Belle."

Her gaze met his. "Why wait?"

He stood up and said, "We'll finish taking down the tree later."

Jessie Belle and Traynor made their way quickly to their bedroom.

Later in bed, Jessie Belle counted her blessings while Traynor slept. She felt like her life was finally back to normal since they'd left Atlanta. Now they could focus on the future.

There would be no distractions this time, she vowed.

Traynor decided to surprise his wife by cooking and serving her breakfast in bed.

"Everything smells delicious," Jessie Belle murmured. "How long have you been up?"

"A couple of hours. I went downstairs to spend some quiet time with God and then I thought, why don't I make breakfast for my beautiful wife? So that's what I did."

He was such a thoughtful man and Traynor treated her like a queen. Jessie Belle didn't know exactly when it happened, but she'd fallen in love with her husband.

Truly loved him.

Smiling, Jessie Belle patted the empty space beside her. "Why don't you join me?"

Traynor carried the tray over to the bed and then climbed in, joining Jessie Belle. "This is the first time I've ever tried to make an omelet."

"Honey, it looks good. You did a wonderful job." She gave Traynor a sidelong glance. "Is there anything that you don't do well?"

He reached for a glass of orange juice. "There's a lot, I'm sure."

"I think you are possibly the most humble man I've ever met." Jessie

Belle sliced off a piece of the bacon, mushroom, tomato and cheese omelet. She stuck a forkful into her mouth.

"I hear from a lot of other pastors that their wives complain about how much time they spend at the church, but you're so different. You actually encourage me to make myself available to the members."

"Ministering is your passion, Traynor. It's your calling—I recognize that. And don't forget, my father is a pastor. This is the way I grew up. I'm not threatened by your calling—some pastors' wives are, I guess."

"I love that you trust me like this, Jessie Belle. You've taught me a lot on that subject." Traynor's mind traveled back to the night he listened to Cynthia and her lies. A wave of guilt washed over him.

"The past is the past," Jessie Belle murmured. "We have our entire future ahead of us, Traynor. I love you and I'm looking forward to having a baby with you."

"I'm a very lucky man to have a woman like you in my life."

Jessie Belle fed him some of the omelet. "I hope you'll always feel this way."

"I can't imagine why I wouldn't," Traynor responded. He finished off his orange juice.

The first weekend of the New Year, Mary Ellen Reed and her husband drove up to Raleigh for the weekend.

Jessie Belle greeted her friend with a big hug. "I'm so glad you finally made it here. I've missed you so much, Mary Ellen."

"I knew you were helping out at the church, and then Richard and I were going through our mess," Mary Ellen explained. "I just didn't want to be around anybody."

"So are things better now between you two?"

"They're better than they used to be. He just woke up one day and started acting a fool."

"Mary Ellen, leave him if you have to—you can always come up here to Raleigh."

"I appreciate that, but I'll be okay."

Mary Ellen hadn't been real forthcoming about her marital troubles, but Jessie Belle wasn't offended. She wanted to spend her energies on her own marriage. She and Traynor had a nice house, but she was already feeling crowded after seeing some of the grand homes the city had to offer, so they really didn't need another body in the house.

"Let's go into the kitchen," Jessie Belle suggested. "I'll fix us some lunch."

"So what's been going on back on Cable Lane?" she asked, handing Mary Ellen a glass of iced tea. "How do you like the new neighbors?"

"They're alright—nothing like you and Traynor." Mary Ellen sipped her drink. "Cynthia's still running around talking about how you threatened her."

"She'd better be glad this job came through for Traynor. Otherwise, I'd probably be stuffing her body somewhere."

Mary Ellen laughed.

"I'm serious," Jessie Belle said quietly. "If we'd stayed in Atlanta, she'd be dead and buried somewhere."

Mary Ellen didn't respond.

Jessie Belle made a stack of ham and cheese sandwiches, put them on a plate and carried it over to the table. She went back and grabbed the pitcher of iced tea, putting it on the table, too.

Mary Ellen walked over to the window and looked out. "I really like it up here."

"There are lots of colleges in Raleigh. You and Richard should consider moving up here."

"He actually mentioned that on the way up here," Mary Ellen responded. "He's ready to leave Morehouse."

"I hope y'all will do it—you're my only real friend, Mary Ellen. It'll be so nice to have you nearby." Placing her hand to her stomach, she added, "Especially when the baby comes."

Mary Ellen's eyebrows rose in surprise. "Oh my goodness! You're pregnant again?"

Jessie Belle laughed. "Not yet, but we've just started trying."

"That's wonderful."

"What about you and Richard? Are you two ready to become parents?"

Mary Ellen shook her head no. "We decided a long time ago that we weren't going to have children. Richard has one from a previous relationship and he doesn't get to see him much—too much mess with the mama."

Mary Ellen walked back to the table and sat down. "Besides, I'm not exactly maternal."

"So did you apply for the station manager position?" Jessie Belle inquired.

"No."

Jessie Belle wiped her mouth on the end of her napkin. "Mary Ellen, why not?"

"They're not gonna give me the job. I'm the wrong skin color for the position."

"Mary Ellen, sometimes you have to fight dirty for what you want. Do you know any of their dark secrets—something you can use against them?"

She gave Jessie Belle a confused look. "Like what?"

"Anything they wouldn't want anyone else to know."

Mary Ellen shook her head. "No. Jessie Belle, it's not that serious. They gave me a raise and I'm happy."

"You shouldn't sell yourself so short or so cheaply." Pushing away from the table, Jessie Belle rose to her feet. "When you want something—go after it with everything you have. That's the only way to succeed."

"I'll remember that," Mary Ellen uttered.

CHAPTER THIRTEEN

Jessie Belle rubbed her swollen belly. At seven months pregnant, she was finding it harder and harder to find a comfortable position in any chair.

She and her mother were in a store going through pattern book after pattern book, looking for the perfect wallpaper for the baby's room.

"I like this one."

"That is a nice one," Anabeth agreed. "But what about this one here? It has the same bold colors you're looking for."

Jessie Belle eyed the sample. "Oh, yeah . . . that's real nice, Ma. I think I actually like that one better."

"How are things between you and Traynor since leaving Atlanta?"

"Good," Jessie Belle answered. "It was the best decision for us. Thank the Lord we don't have any more crazy church members. Those two that we left in Atlanta . . ." She shook her head sadly. "Just pitiful."

Lowering her voice, Anabeth said, "I warned you to be careful. I told you a man like that don't like to take no for an answer. He and that girl was trying to break up you and Traynor for sure."

"I know, Ma. But it's over now. We're in Raleigh and my baby's healthy. I'll just be glad when it's here."

"I still say that baby is gonna be born on Christmas Day," Anabeth stated.

"You keep saying that, Ma, but I'm not due until December twenty-eighth. The baby might not come until January."

"I just believe it in my spirit. Don't go planning no big dinner or nothing for that day."

Jessie Belle laughed. "I wasn't. Traynor and I just want a quiet holiday.

We had a big Christmas last year. The next one will be after the baby comes."

After deciding on the wallpaper, Jessie Belle and her mother left and headed to Crabtree Valley Mall in search of crib bedding.

An hour later, Jessie Belle took her mother to lunch.

"I think we should check one more store before getting the comforter set we saw at JCPenney's," she told Anabeth.

"You don't like that one?"

"I like it, Ma. I'm not wild about it, though." Jessie Belle picked up her menu. "Do you know what you're going to order?"

"I think I want shrimp and grits. You've talked so much about it—I think I'ma try some."

Jessie Belle broke into a smile. "Ma, you're going to love it. It's addictive."

The waiter came and took their drink and food orders.

When he left, Anabeth eyed her daughter. "How are things between you and Traynor's folks?"

"They don't really talk to me and when Traynor asks them to come visit, they always say that his father isn't feeling well enough to travel. I don't think they're telling the truth. If they were—seems like he should be dead by now."

"Jessie Belle, that's not a nice thing to say," Anabeth admonished.

"Well, it's true. It's not like I'm wishing him dead. I'm just saying that if he's that sick, I'm surprised he's still alive."

"Maybe once you have this baby, things will change."

"I hope so. It bothers Traynor, I can tell. At least he knows it's not anything I'm doing. If they force him to choose—I know he'll choose me."

Anabeth smiled. "Good. That's what you want him to do."

"Ma, I have Traynor exactly where I want him. I followed your instructions to the tee. I am the never-ending supportive wife."

"Do you love him?"

Jessie Belle nodded. "I do, Ma. I didn't when we first got married—I liked him a lot, but he's such a good husband. I couldn't help but fall in love with Traynor. He treats me like a queen. I just wish he were a bit more ambitious, though."

"He'll come around," Anabeth assured her. "You just got to keep on pushing him forward. I had to push your daddy to run for ECC president. He's never been much into stuff like that, but I knew he was capable."

"I've been encouraging Traynor to align himself with some of Raleigh's more prominent pastors."

Anabeth nodded her approval. "They'll help groom him. And everybody trusts your daddy. Our church may not be as large as the ones in the city, but your daddy has power. When he talks—people listen. He been putting the word out about his son-in-law, so all Traynor has to do is step out."

"He will," Jessie Belle stated. "I'll see to it."

A sharp, knifelike pain sliced through Jessie Belle, jolting her awake. She glanced over at the clock on the nightstand.

Twelve fifteen a.m.

It's Christmas Day.

She sat up in bed for a moment, waiting. Jessie Belle had had Braxton-Hicks contractions from time to time over the past couple of weeks, but this one felt more intense.

She lay back down and waited to see if another would follow.

Nothing.

She drifted off to sleep.

Jessie Belle woke up two hours later when she felt a sharp contraction.

She had another one while showering, but assumed it was just another Braxton-Hicks contraction since she wasn't due for a few more days and the doctor had already told her she most likely would go past her due date.

Jessie Belle woke up her sleeping husband. "Traynor, I think I'm in labor," she announced.

"You're having contractions?"

"Yes."

"I thought the doctor said you'd go past your due date."

"Honey, I think our baby changed his or her mind." Jessie Belle braced herself for another contraction. She groaned. "I'm not liking this at all. *It hurts.*"

Traynor began tracking the time of her contractions: about twenty seconds every fifteen minutes.

Jessie Belle managed to make a cup of hot tea, put two slices of bread into the toaster, fry some bacon and scramble two eggs. She wanted to make sure Traynor had a full stomach. She figured she'd be needing him later on.

While he ate, Jessie Belle called her parents and Mary Ellen to tell them that she was in labor.

An hour later, her contractions were coming faster.

Traynor called the doctor.

"It's time for us to leave for the hospital," he announced.

"We're all set," Jessie Belle responded. "I want to freshen up before we leave, though. The suitcase is packed and already in the trunk of your car. It's a good thing you put it in there last week."

Jessie Belle went into her bedroom.

Ten minutes later, she walked out, having changed into a maternity dress. "I didn't feel right in my nightgown," she explained.

They headed out to the car.

Jessie Belle was hit with another contraction once they were on the road.

"I don't like pain," she complained. "You have to know I love you, Traynor. Going through labor is no joke."

Jessie Belle didn't like being so out of control.

Elias and Anabeth Holt arrived the day after Holt Jefferson Deveraux was born, to see their first grandchild.

While Traynor and his father-in-law were at the church, Jessie Belle watched her mother feed and change the baby before rocking him to sleep.

"I knew he was gonna be a Christmas baby. I told you."

"I know, Ma. You were right. What can I say?"

Admiring her grandson, Anabeth confessed, "I was a bit surprised that you didn't name him after Traynor."

"He didn't want me to," she responded from the bed. Traynor had insisted that she stay in bed for the next couple of days despite her pleas that she felt fine and could sit on the sofa.

"Besides, I like using Holt as a first name," Jessie Belle stated. "It's a strong name and in honor of Papa. It sounds very sophisticated and classy."

"Your daddy was happy when you told him." Anabeth returned her gaze to the sleeping newborn. "Traynor's a proud father," she uttered. "He can't take his eyes off that baby."

"Why shouldn't he be?" Jessie Belle questioned. "Ma, I've given him a beautiful and healthy son. Traynor has every right to be proud. Holt's going to attend prestigious private schools—he's going to have the best of everything. When he's older, he'll follow in Traynor's footsteps. We just got to get his daddy on the ball. Traynor's too content with where he is right now. He's not trying to do better."

Jessie Belle glanced over at her mother. "What is it, Ma? You look as if you want to say something. Just come out with it."

Anabeth moved her chair closer. "Jessie Belle, you have to be careful in the way you handle Traynor. You can't make him feel less of a man."

"That's why I've been biting my tongue, but I'm getting tired. We should be further than we are right now. Traynor acts like he's afraid to ask for a raise or something. We have a child to think of—I shouldn't have to tell him to ask for more money."

"Give yourself a chance to recover from childbirth and just wait and see what your husband's gonna do," Anabeth advised. "If he don't do nothing, then it's time to say something to him."

"Ma, I need to know something. Why did you accept those gifts from other men?"

"We needed stuff, and not enough money to get what we needed. If a man wanted to give me a token of his appreciation—I accepted, but I never slept with any of them."

"Did you ever tell Papa?"

Anabeth shook her head no. "No need to stir in a pot of trouble. He was my husband and Elias is proud and he's a jealous man. He once asked a man to leave church because he was trying to get familiar with me. Sometimes beauty can get you into trouble, gal. Men are drawn to you like honey, but if you don't stay in control . . . beauty can be a curse."

"Ma, I'm not gonna make the same mistake twice. I love my husband and I don't want to hurt him. I just want him to be the man I know he can be, though. I hate going behind his back to get what I want. *I just hate it.*"

"Secrets can be a burden at times," Anabeth stated. "Lawd, I know from firsthand experience."

Jessie Belle eyed her mother. "But they are sometimes necessary."

CHAPTER FOURTEEN

Six weeks later, Jessie Belle sat next to the first lady of New Bryant Baptist Church, listening to Traynor's sermon. This was baby Holt's first outing. She was thrilled to be back to her prepregnancy size and wore a formfitting dress to show off her figure.

The February weather was still chilly, so Jessie Belle made sure she'd bundled Holt enough to keep him nice and warm.

Pastor Rutherford Hamilton had invited Traynor to preach on Youth Sunday. Jessie Belle's eyes traveled around the sanctuary as she admired the larger and much nicer church.

While Traynor was in the pulpit preaching his heart out, all Jessie Belle could think about was that her husband should be leading a church like this. *He belongs in a beautiful sanctuary like this.*

After service ended, they joined the Hamiltons for dinner.

"Look at this house, Traynor . . . ," Jessie Belle said when they pulled up. "It's gorgeous and so big."

The two-story brick home sat on two acres of land. Vividly hued plants were nicely arranged in front of the house and along the sides despite the winter weather.

"It is nice," he agreed, parking the car.

Jessie Belle turned, looking up and down the street. "This is the way we should be living, honey. In a nice, big fine house like this and driving a Cadillac. You're a man of God, Traynor—one of His messengers. Who's going to want to follow a pastor if he looks as poor as they do?"

"That's not what it's all about."

"I've heard you say it a million times," Jessie Belle stated. " 'You have not because you ask not.' Traynor, it's time for you to practice what you're out there preaching."

Jessie Belle didn't want to get into an argument with him. She just wanted to indulge in this moment. She was in the lap of luxury.

When Traynor opened her door, she got out and walked briskly up the steps, following Sara into the house.

Her eyes bounced around, taking in her tastefully decorated surroundings. "Oh my . . . this is so beautiful."

Smiling and standing proud, Sara responded, "Why, thank you, Jessie Belle. I have to admit we've been blessed tremendously. God has truly been so good to us."

"I keep telling Traynor that it's time for him to seek a position in a larger church. His talents are being wasted and he's constantly challenged by some of the older members of the church. It's frustrating at times."

Sara gave Jessie Belle a knowing smile. "I understand. Rutherford and I went through a season similar to that. Just keep after him. Sometimes they have trouble understanding that while it's their ministry—this is also a business."

"Yes, they do." Jessie Belle glanced over her shoulder and found Traynor standing there with the baby.

Did he overhear our discussion? she wondered silently, noting the solemn expression on his face. It didn't matter anyway—she'd told Traynor the very same thing many times in the past. They had a son now, so things needed to change and soon.

Jessie Belle broached the subject once she and Traynor returned to their house.

"Traynor, we should be living like the Hamiltons live. You're a much better preacher than Rutherford is, and look at what his church is doing for him."

They were in Holt's room putting him to bed.

"Jessie Belle, I think our house is nice. I don't know about you, but I'm happy with what we have." Traynor planted a kiss on his sleeping son's forehead before laying him down.

"And you can't be happy with more?" Jessie Belle wanted to know. "Don't you think you deserve more?"

"I'm content in whatever way God blesses us, Jessie Belle."

She folded her arms across her chest. "Well, I'm not afraid to dream big."

"There's nothing wrong with that, sweetheart. All I'm saying is that I believe I'm exactly where God would have me be."

Traynor was touched by Jessie Belle's faith in him, but he was content with his life. He worried that his wife was becoming too materialistic. He kept his thoughts to himself for the moment to avoid a potential argument.

"I'd like a bigger house, Traynor," Jessie Belle was saying. "We have Holt now and we need more room."

"I think this house is plenty big," he argued. He didn't want to disappoint Jessie Belle, but Traynor didn't want to just go out and get into debt. He wanted to take some time and pray over any potential big decisions like buying a house. "Sweetheart, let's just take this slowly—buying a house is a huge decision."

"I know that," Jessie Belle replied. "And since we're on this subject, I'd really like some new furniture. Except for the sofa and a couple of other things, our stuff looks like it was handed down."

"Well, it was," Traynor stated. "It's the furniture my parents bought when they got married."

"It's old-fashioned. I want to pick out my own furniture. There's nothing wrong with having some nice stuff."

"I'm not saying there is anything wrong, Jessie Belle."

Her voice rose up an octave. "You're not *saying* anything, Traynor." Jessie Belle gestured for Traynor to follow her out of Holt's room.

"That's what bothers me," she continued. "You act like it's a sin or something to want a bigger house, a luxury car or even a raise. *It's not.* God wants to bless us and sometimes that means we have to step out on faith."

"Jessie Belle, I don't think you're listening to me. That's not what I'm saying at all."

Giving him a hard look, she asked, "Then what are you saying, Traynor?"

"Having a big house, new furniture or a new car—those things are temporary pleasures. I don't want to make them the center of my being."

"Nobody is asking you to," Jessie Belle shot back. She swallowed her disappointment in Traynor. It was becoming apparent that he wasn't the man she'd thought he was.

She was going to have to take matters into her own hands.

'The telephone rang.

Traynor answered it. "Hey, Aunt Eleanor. I was planning on calling y'all tonight bu——" He stopped short. "What did you say?"

Jessie Belle could tell from the look on his face that something terrible must have happened.

"But I just talked to him last night," she heard Traynor say. "When did he pass?"

His father's dead.

Jessie Belle's anger evaporated and her heart ached for her husband. She went over to Traynor, embracing him.

"I'll be there tomorrow, Aunt Eleanor. We'll be leaving out tomorrow morning."

They sat, holding each other.

"Baby, I'm so sorry about your daddy," Jessie Belle murmured. "Even though we never really got on——your daddy was a good man."

"He was sick," Traynor stated. "Real sick."

"I guess that's why he never came to visit us. How's Aunt Eleanor holding up?"

"She's distraught," he responded. "She and my dad were very close."

"That's usually the case with twins," Jessie Belle said matter-of-factly. "Traynor, what's gonna happen with your mother's jewelry?"

"He probably left it to Aunt Eleanor. She and my mother were close and they both loved jewelry."

Jessie Belle clenched and unclenched her fist. "It belonged to your mother, so I thought he'd pass it down to you."

I should be the one to get it.

Jessie Belle had admired all the exquisite pieces she'd seen in photographs of Traynor's mother——especially her sapphire and diamond engagement ring.

"He bought the stuff, so he could give it to whoever he wanted to give it to, sweetheart," Traynor told her. "Besides, we don't need it. You probably wouldn't have liked any of it anyway."

"I wasn't given the choice," she replied. "But I was thinking that it would be nice for Holt to have something from his grandmother. It's not like he'll ever get to meet her."

"I need to get the suitcases," Traynor uttered. "I don't care what my father left to whom. I'd rather have him back. Alive and well, Jessie Belle."

"I'm sorry. I didn't mean to—"

He was gone before she could finish her sentence.

The next morning they headed to Baton Rouge, Louisiana.

Traynor didn't say much during the first two hours of the drive and Jessie Belle didn't press him. Instead she focused her attention on Holt.

The baby was now sleeping in her arms.

"I'm really sorry about your daddy," Jessie Belle said. "I know how much you loved him."

Traynor stole a peek in her direction. "He was a good father to me."

She reached over and squeezed his hand. "I can tell because of the type of man you are, Traynor."

"I regret that Holt won't get to know his grandfather."

Jessie Belle nodded in understanding. "I regret that, too. Your father left behind a strong legacy, though. You should be proud."

Traynor glanced over at her. "I really wish he'd gotten to know you, Jessie Belle. But he was sicker than he allowed us to believe."

"He didn't want to worry you. I believe that's why he didn't tell us." Jessie Belle settled back in her seat. "I don't hold any ill will against your daddy."

"Aunt Eleanor's so upset—I'm worried about her."

"She won't have to go through this all alone, honey. Your aunt will have you. She'll also have me. Together as a family we'll get through this painful time."

Traynor reached over and took Jessie Belle's hand. "Thank you for being so sweet and thoughtful. I just know Aunt Eleanor's going to see you in a much different light now that she'll have a few days to get to know you."

Jessie Belle didn't respond.

Jessie Belle was ready to rip Eleanor Deveraux-Barrett's head right off her shoulders.

Since their arrival in Baton Rouge two days ago, the woman had been nothing less than rude to her. Jessie Belle cooked and cleaned the house, but all Eleanor could do was find fault with her.

She was careful not to do it in front of Traynor, Jessie Belle noted.

Just before eight a.m., Eleanor strolled into the bedroom without knocking. "You aren't up yet?" She pursed her thin lips in disapproval.

Jessie Belle rolled her eyes heavenward. "I've been up since six. Holt was cranky most of the night and I was up with him. Traynor suggested that I stay in bed and rest."

"The house will soon be overflowing with guests. You should be dressed and ready to receive our visitors."

"I'll get right up," Jessie Belle uttered.

There's just no pleasing this woman.

"Breakfast is ready," Eleanor announced. "Hopefully, it'll still be hot by the time you make it downstairs."

She walked out of the room, shaking her head.

Jessie Belle was glad the funeral was scheduled for tomorrow and that they would be leaving the day after. She couldn't wait to get back to Raleigh. Traynor had brought up the idea of Eleanor coming to live with them, but Jessie Belle quickly nixed the idea.

There was no way she'd have that bat from hell staying in her home.

Jessie Belle showered and dressed in a simple black pantsuit. She pulled her hair back into a bun.

Traynor came upstairs with Holt in his arms. "Did you get some rest?"

"Not really."

Jessie Belle didn't tell him about his aunt's treatment of her. It wouldn't do any good because Traynor wasn't going to say anything to Eleanor. He was blind when it came to his aunt.

"Aunt Eleanor made breakfast," he announced.

"She told me," Jessie Belle responded drily.

Traynor eyed her. "Everything okay between you two?"

She pasted on a fake smile. "Couldn't be better."

Jessie Belle stood up. "I guess we'd better get down to breakfast. I don't want to throw anything off schedule."

"Aunt Eleanor is grieving."

"Honey, you don't have to explain your aunt to me. I understand." Smiling, Jessie Belle planted a kiss on Traynor's cheek. "Everything is fine. I can take anything she dishes out."

CHAPTER FIFTEEN

Traynor was very exhausted after the long drive from Louisiana. He was glad to be home. His father's funeral had taken a lot out of him emotionally.

Jessie Belle put Holt to bed, and then came downstairs to join him.

"Honey, how are you feeling?" she asked. Jessie Belle began gently massaging his shoulders.

"I'm okay. I miss my dad, but I know he's in a much better place."

Jessie Belle agreed. "The pain will lessen a little as each day passes. At least that's what I used to hear Papa saying."

She was glad to be back in her own home. The past week with Traynor's aunt had been frustration for Jessie Belle. She bit back her words several times over the course of their stay.

Traynor's voice cut into her thoughts.

"I've said those same words so many times. I never really realized just how little comfort they actually offer until now."

Taking her hand into his, he continued. "I know my aunt Eleanor wasn't very nice to you. I want you to know that I had a long talk with her last night about it. I want her to be a part of our lives, but I won't have her disrespecting you."

"I know she was grieving," uttered Jessie Belle. "But she was working my nerves for sure."

Jessie Belle was so understanding—it was one of the qualities he loved about her. Traynor kissed her cheek. "You carried yourself well. I'm proud of you and I appreciate it."

"I would never shame you, Traynor."

"Aunt Eleanor gave me something right before we left," Traynor announced.

She broke into a smile. "She gave you your mother's jewelry."

Traynor shook his head no. "She kept the jewelry."

"Then what did she give you?"

He pulled something out of his pocket. "Dad instructed her to give me twenty-five thousand dollars."

Jessie Belle's eyes lit up at the news. "That's wonderful. But I can't believe she wouldn't give you any of your mother's jewelry."

"What am I going to do with it, sweetheart? Like I said, you wouldn't like any of it."

"You don't know that," Jessie Belle countered. "I liked the pieces I saw in the photographs. She had some nice jewelry."

Waving the check, Traynor said, "I think we should put this money aside for Holt's education."

"Oh, I agree that some of it should be put aside for Holt, but honey, we can use some of the money to get some things we need."

"Like what?"

Jessie Belle shrugged. "I can't think of anything right now. But at least we'll have the money if we need it. God bless your daddy's soul."

Twenty-five thousand dollars!

Jessie Belle danced around the living room while Traynor was upstairs checking on the baby.

"I can't believe it. That ol' hateful man actually left us twenty-five thousand dollars." Then another thought occurred to her. *He should've left us a whole lot more for the way he treated me. I bet he did——his sister probably has it stashed away somewhere.*

She dropped down on the sofa. "It don't really matter, though. She'll drop dead one day. Everything will go to Traynor and me."

While Traynor was in the bathroom taking a shower half an hour later, Jessie Belle got a chance to tell his aunt how she felt when Eleanor called.

"I was just calling to see if you-all made it back. Nobody called me to say if you did or not. I was worried."

"Yes, we made it home safe and sound," she replied to Eleanor's query. "Though I have to tell you that Traynor was a little upset over what his daddy did."

"Jessie Belle, what are you talking about?"

"He was hoping that his daddy would give him his mother's jewelry. He wanted to pass it down to Holt."

"Oh really? Well, Traynor never said anything to me about it. And what would a baby do with jewelry?"

"He didn't want to hurt your feelings, Aunt Eleanor. You know how much Traynor adores you. He just wanted his son to have something of his grandmother."

"His mother always wanted me to have her jewelry. I just wouldn't take it until Traynor Senior passed on. Tell my nephew to call me so that we can get this straight."

"Well, I was hoping that you'd just do the right thing and surprise him by sending the stuff to him."

"If Traynor wants his mama's jewelry—he can get it from me. So tell him to call me directly."

Jessie Belle stiffened. "What are you implying?"

"You just tell Traynor to give me a call. I want to hear this from his mouth."

Jessie Belle had to think quickly. "I already told you that he won't say nothing to you. He doesn't want to upset you."

"But you see fit to open your mouth. I'm on to you, Jessie Belle. See, I know my nephew. I helped to raise him. He's not upset about this jewelry. *You* the one who want it, but I'm here to tell you—you won't have it."

"You'll die one day."

Eleanor gasped in shock. "Get thee behind me, Sataaan. . . ."

"What did you just sa—"

Their connection was severed.

She considered calling Eleanor back and laying into her, but Traynor came downstairs.

"Was that the phone I heard?"

"Yes. It was a wrong number."

Traynor sat down on the sofa. "I need to call Aunt Eleanor and let her know that we made it home."

"I called her already," Jessie Belle blurted. "She wasn't feeling too well, so she told me that she was going to bed. Aunt Eleanor even apologized to me for the way she was acting. Like I thought, she was upset over your father's death."

"I'm glad you two were able to make up."

Traynor headed to the kitchen. "You want anything?"

"I'm fine, honey."

When he left the room, Jessie Belle reached over and picked up a magazine. "The first thing I'm gonna do is get me some nice clothes. If we want to have money—we need to act like we already have it. And I want one of those designer purses like Sara has."

We have money. Lots of it.

She jumped to her feet and walked over to the mirror, checking her reflection. Mrs. Traynor Deveraux . . .

Jessie Belle never tired of the sound of it. She was proud of being Traynor's wife.

"We're on our way, Traynor," she whispered. "Just don't blow it for us."

"Grandview Baptist Church is in need of a pastor," Jessie Belle announced when she came home from a lunch date with Sara and some of the other first ladies in the Raleigh area. She was a member of the Raleigh First Ladies' Ministry, and they met once a month to support and encourage one another. "Pastor Talbot's leaving."

Traynor laid down his newspaper. "I know. He told me when I saw him a couple of weeks ago."

"Well, did he suggest that you apply for the position?" she wanted to know.

"No, not really."

"I think you should," Jessie Belle stated. "They have over a thousand members and their church is beautiful. You can take your ministry to a higher level."

He sighed. "Honey, I'm so thankful for the faith you have in me, but I'm fine with where I am. I really enjoy preaching at New Salem Baptist. The members are great and they listen to me. It's not like it was in Atlanta. Some of the members thought I was way too young and they really didn't respect me."

"I'm just saying that with some effort and strategic planning, you could be the next Billy Graham."

"Bigger doesn't necessarily mean better, Jessie Belle," Traynor countered. "I'm not saying God can't use big churches, because He does. In the Bible, there were many times that Israel's armies overwhelmed their opponents with their numbers. But sometimes God chooses to use the small things, like small churches. In churches like New Salem, we all know each other. We are under no illusions that our members are perfect because we have seen their foibles. They know that I'm not perfect because they see me every day."

"But I bet the big churches don't have to deal with committees that don't function very well, people who are rude to one another or constant complainers you can never please."

"I'm sure they have their share of problems, sweetheart. All I know is that the small church has to depend on God. When I see lives transformed and courage in the face of great difficulties, Jessie Belle, I know that it is only through the power of God. I'm happy being exactly where I am and I have faith that God will move me when it's time."

"Sometimes you need to step out, Traynor," Jessie Belle pointed out. "You can't play it safe all the time."

"I know that," Traynor stated. "But sometimes you have to be still and wait for God's prompting. Remember, Jesus changed the world with twelve disciples—I'm sure He can still use our small church if we will let Him."

Irritated, Jessie Belle held her tongue. She didn't want their second wedding anniversary ruined by an argument. She had much to be thankful for—Traynor had used some of the money his father left him for furniture. Tonight they would be sleeping in their brand-new king-sized bed.

"I really appreciate your support and the faith you have in me, sweetheart," Traynor was saying. "I really do, but let's just wait and see what God will have me do."

"I'll leave it alone," she uttered. "Obviously, you refuse to look at this from my point of view."

"I hate seeing the disappointment in your eyes," Traynor said quietly.

"Then do something about it." Jessie Belle met his gaze. "I don't have much of an appetite, so let's just stay home."

"You don't want to go out to dinner?"

She shook her head no. "I'm not in the mood anymore."

"It's our wedding anniversary, Jessie Belle."

"I'm well aware of that."

"You're mad because I don't want to pastor a bigger church. Is this about money?"

Furious, Jessie Belle glared at him. "How dare you? This has nothing to do with money, Traynor. Excuse me for believing in you. Excuse me for wanting you to lead thousands to the Lord." Sighing loudly, she sat down on the love seat.

He tried to calm her.

"Excuse me for thinking that it was time for a larger flock. . . ."

"Sweetheart, I'm sorry."

Traynor sat down beside her. "I'm not discounting anything you say. Jessie Belle, I hear you, but I can't just move when you think I should. I've never been that type of man. I like to wait and hear from God."

"You think God only talks to you?" she asked him.

He shook his head no. "Why do you do that, Jessie Belle? Why do you always try to twist my words around?"

"Traynor, you've ruined this night for me already. Let's just not talk to each other right now. I don't want to make it worse."

"Jessie Belle . . ."

She rose to her feet. "I need to call and cancel the babysitter. Then I'm going to bed."

Jessie Belle fumed as she stormed out of the living room.

I can't believe I was wrong about Traynor. She'd assumed he'd be a bit more ambitious. She loved him, but she wanted more out of life.

I'm gonna have everything I want, Traynor.

With or without you.

CHAPTER SIXTEEN

Things had been tense between Traynor and Jessie Belle since their second anniversary a month ago. He'd done everything he could to try to get their marriage back on track, but Jessie Belle continued to keep him at a distance.

Why can't I make her understand that this isn't about money for me?

Although Jessie Belle kept denying that she was more concerned about his salary and expenses, Traynor knew that's exactly why she was so upset. Money and possessions seemed to be a big issue for her. She had even gone behind his back to Aunt Eleanor about the jewelry, although he hadn't mentioned knowing about it.

She constantly complained about not being able to drive a nicer car or buy expensive clothes. . . . Jessie Belle frequently compared their life with the lives of other couples in ministry. He couldn't help but wonder if that's how the first ladies spent their time together—comparing notes.

She was upstairs now with Holt.

Traynor suggested earlier that they go out for lunch as a family, but she refused. He'd never seen her behave this way and it bothered him. He loved Jessie Belle and enjoyed making her happy, but this time Traynor strongly believed he was right in this situation.

I'm not backing down.

He strolled outdoors to get the mail after seeing the postman drive away.

Back inside, Traynor spent the next five minutes going through the stack of envelopes.

He nearly choked when he saw the bank statement for their savings account. Traynor stormed into his son's bedroom waving the document.

"Jessie Belle, what in the world did you spend one thousand dollars on? I just got the statement for our savings account."

"Excuse me?" She held a hand over her son's ear. "Keep your voice down, please. You're going to scare the baby."

"What all did you buy at Dillard's department store?"

"I bought a purse," Jessie Belle stated in a loud whisper.

"A purse," Traynor repeated, his voice raising an octave. "*One* purse?"

She stood up. "I'm putting Holt in his crib and then we can go downstairs to talk. I don't want you waking him up with all of your yelling."

"I'm not yelling."

"Ssssh . . ."

Jessie Belle walked out of the nursery, carrying a baby monitor.

Traynor followed her to their bedroom.

Jessie Belle sat down on the love seat in their sitting room, her eyes trained on him. "You were saying," she prompted.

"You bought a pocketbook? One of them."

"Yes," Jessie Belle answered calmly. "Honey, I needed a nice handbag, so I bought one. It's a designer purse like the one Sara had."

"I can't believe you spent this much money on a purse. This is ridiculous."

Looking away, Jessie Belle dismissed his words with a wave of her hand. "You only feel that way because you're a man. Women understand these things. Half the first ladies in this city carry designer bags."

"You've been spending a lot of money on clothes, makeup and now this purse. Jessie Belle, we can't do this. I wanted to save most of the money I got from my father. We're down to half. This needs to stop."

She raised her eyes to his. "We could if you'd ask for a raise. Since you took over, New Salem's church membership has tripled. Honey, you should be getting paid a lot more money."

"Why? So you can waste it on shopping?"

"Traynor, that's not fair."

He shook his head. "Sweetheart, we're trying to save money, remember? You want a bigger house, a nicer car, and you want to send Holt to private school—we can't do any of that if we don't save money."

"I don't think I like your tone," Jessie Belle snapped.

"This has to stop," he said. "I mean it."

"You have some nerve, Traynor. You don't want to ask for a raise or get a job with a larger church, but you complain about money. Why do I have to suffer or Holt? You told me you wanted another child—can we afford one? Did you check your budget? Huh?"

"Don't try and make this my fault, Jessie Belle. You've been going into the savings and spending the money like water. I should have been consulted on this."

"Why?" Jessie Belle demanded. "The money is supposed to be *ours*."

"*Ours* is right. I wouldn't go around spending thousands of dollars like that without talking to you."

"Oh, that's right. You're a saint."

"Jessie Belle, I'm putting you on a budget. I'll give you four hundred dollars each month. That's all. Now, I'm doing this for your own good. You want nice stuff and the only way to get it is to save money."

"You ain't my daddy, Traynor. How dare you treat me like a child?"

"I love you, sweetheart. I know you're mad with me now, but one day when you're in your dream house . . . you're going to thank me."

Traynor reached out for her, but Jessie Belle slapped his hands away. She blew out of the house like a tornado. He hoped she would return in a better mood.

He went to one of the guest rooms upstairs and fell to his knees.

Father God, I'm worried about her, Lord. Jessie Belle's getting too caught up in material possessions. Guide her and show her Your way and teach her contentment. I love my wife and I want our marriage to flourish, but right now we're on two different paths. Help us find our way back to each other. In Jesus's name I pray. Amen.

Traynor felt a wave of peace flow through him. He'd done the right thing by placing Jessie Belle on a budget. She would understand after a while.

They were going to be okay.

He had to believe that, because the thought of losing Jessie Belle was too much to bear.

Jessie Belle met Sara Hamilton for lunch. They decided to do a little shopping afterward.

"This dress is gorgeous," Sara murmured, holding up a sleeveless lace sheath. "It'll look stunning on you. You have such a nice figure."

Jessie Belle was in love with the shimmery black dress. She normally wouldn't think anything about buying it, but since their last argument about money a few days ago, Traynor had placed her on a budget. He allowed her only four hundred dollars per month to take care of the utilities and miscellaneous expenses.

A four-hundred-dollar budget didn't leave much for her to shop with.

She was still furious with Traynor for treating her this way and hadn't spoken to him for the past two days.

The hair on the back of her neck stood up.

Jessie Belle glanced around the boutique, her eyes landing on a man standing in the back of the store.

For a moment she couldn't tear her gaze away from his profile.

She thought of Traynor and her vow to remain faithful.

"This dress is adorable," she murmured, and held it up in front of her. "What do you think, Sara?"

"It's lovely. Why don't you try it on?"

"I think I will," Jessie Belle stated.

She navigated through the store, making her way over to the dressing rooms. Jessie Belle slipped into the dress and walked out.

He was still there, eyeing her.

Jessie Belle met his gaze straight on. She couldn't help but notice the tingle of excitement inside her. Feeling bold, she stared back at him, willing him to say something.

The handsome man awarded her a tiny smile, then said, "I apologize for staring like that, but you're stunning."

A delicious shiver ran through Jessie Belle. "Thank you for the compliment."

She glanced around the store, looking for Sara.

"She's in the dressing room," the salesclerk told her.

"Thanks," she murmured.

Jessie Belle moved to the next rack of clothes. She selected a dress and held it against her, staring into the full-length mirror.

He appeared behind her. "That dress looks exquisite on you. It's as if it were made just for you."

She looked into the mirror. "I think so, too."

"You should buy it."

"I wish I could. It's not in my budget right now." Jessie Belle ran her hand down the side of the dress and sighed. "It's beautiful, though."

"I tell you what . . . why don't I give it to you . . . as a gift?"

Jessie Belle glanced over her shoulder to see if Sara was nearby. Turning her attention back to him, she said, "But you don't know me. Why would you be so kind to a stranger?"

"I am a great admirer of beauty. It would be my pleasure and my honor to gift you with such a beautiful dress."

"My goodness . . . ," Jessie Belle murmured. "I don't know about this. I'm married."

He leaned forward and whispered, "So am I. This is just a small token of my appreciation of such an exotic beauty. I don't think I've ever seen anyone as beautiful as you are."

"Perhaps you will allow me to pay you for the dress in installments," she suggested.

He shook his head no. "It's a gift."

"What is it you really want in return?" Jessie Belle asked. She knew this gorgeous dress didn't come without strings attached.

"The pleasure of your company from time to time would be nice. We will be very discreet. I give you my word."

"My time is much more valuable than this one dress is worth."

"You can have anything you want in the store. It'll be charged to my personal account."

"You must be a very rich man," Jessie Belle responded.

"I'm wealthy," he admitted. "Now that we have that settled, can I gift you with this dress?"

"I'm with a friend right now. . . ."

"It will be ready for you when you come back." Holding out his hand, he said, "My name is Samuel Hightower."

"Jessie Belle Deveraux."

"It's an honor to meet you, Jessie Belle."

She tingled as he said her name. Her heart fluttered wildly in her chest.

Jessie Belle heard the opening and closing of a dressing room door. "I need to get back to my friend," she told him.

"Your dress will be waiting here for you."

"Thank you," she murmured.

"Were you just talking to that man?" Sara inquired when Jessie Belle walked over to her.

"Yes, that's Mr. Samuel Hightower."

Sara seemed surprised. "You know him?"

Jessie Belle gave a slight nod.

"You certainly run in the right circles," she murmured. "The Hightowers are one of the wealthiest families in North Carolina. His poor wife has brain cancer. She's in the final stages, from what I understand. My heart just goes out to him."

"He's very loyal to her," Jessie Belle managed between stiff lips.

When they walked out of the store, Sara drove Jessie Belle back to the restaurant parking lot to pick up her car.

"Give Traynor my best," she said before driving off.

"Whatever," Jessie Belle muttered. She jumped into her car and headed back to the store to pick up her dress.

What if it was just a joke?

"Would he do that to me?" she whispered. "If I walk into that boutique and that dress hasn't been paid for—I'm gonna feel so stupid."

Jessie Belle sat in her car outside the store, trying to decide if she should go inside.

"If it's not there—no harm's been done." She got out of the car and went inside the boutique.

Before she could open her mouth, the young woman recognized her and said, "Mr. Hightower told me you'd be picking these up. I have everything ready for you."

Jessie Belle's mouth dropped open in surprise. Instead of just the one dress, there were four, along with shoes and other accessories. "Oh my goodness."

"He left this for you as well." She handed Jessie Belle an envelope.

She opened it to find a note and a key card.

Jessie Belle:
    I hope that I'll have the pleasure of seeing you in one of those lovely dresses one day soon. You are truly a vision of beauty. If interested, I would like to have lunch with you on Thursday afternoon. If you're able to make it, please

join me at penthouse suite 5108 at the Hightower Hotel. The enclosed key card will provide access via the private elevator. If you choose not to come, I will understand.
Samuel

"Hightower Hotel . . . of course." She hadn't made the connection until now. It was the only African-American-owned hotel in Raleigh. Jessie Belle had heard about it but had never been inside the hotel.

Jessie Belle eyed the clothing once more. "You know what . . . I've changed my mind. I can't accept these."

She turned and walked out of the store.

"I love my husband and I'm not going to cheat on him," she whispered. "I'll just have to find another way to make money."

"I'm meeting with the board this evening," Traynor announced when he met Jessie Belle for lunch at a deli near the church. "Don't wait to eat with me because I'm not sure how long I'll be."

Although she didn't show it, Traynor suspected his wife was still upset with him. They hadn't made love in a week, which was unusual for them, but he wasn't going to push—Jessie Belle would come around. She was smart and he was sure that once she thought things over, she would agree with him.

Jessie Belle took a sip of her iced tea. "That's great. I've actually been thinking about some things to take your ministry to the next level."

He finished off one-half of his roast beef sub. "Like what?"

"I think we should increase the tithes to a mandatory fifteen percent instead of ten. This way, no one should have a problem with giving you a better salary package. Lord knows you deserve it."

"Jessie Belle, I don't think the board will approve of these changes. To be completely honest, I'm not sure how I feel about them right now." Traynor wiped his mouth on a napkin.

"Just put it before the board, honey. That's all I'm asking you to do."

"I'll do that, but, Jessie Belle, the board isn't gonna approve it. They're very conservative."

"A lot of churches have instituted the mandatory increase in tithes. Sara was the one who told me about it. Everyone should be paying tithes anyway. But don't worry, Traynor. The board will see things our way," Jessie Belle murmured. "I'm sure of it."

Traynor found Jessie Belle waiting for him when he got home later that evening. He knew she wanted to find out whether her suggestion had been approved. He'd already forewarned her that it wouldn't go through, so she shouldn't be disappointed.

"They turned it down," she said. "I can tell from the look on your face."

"It's been tabled until the next meeting. We couldn't come to an agreement."

"Who opposed it?"

"Charles Maxwell, Tom Hopkins and Vernon Abbott. I expected it, though." Traynor sighed softly. "Charles practically accused me of being greedy. It got ugly tonight."

"That jerk," Jessie Belle uttered. "I never liked that man. It's just something about him."

"He's alright. Just a little power hungry, if you ask me. We butt heads sometimes but not like we did earlier."

"Just give them some more time to think it over. Who knows? . . . They might change their minds by the next meeting."

"I won't hold my breath."

She hugged him. "Honey, it's going to be fine. I can feel it in my bones that we're not going to have a problem with this."

Traynor wasn't convinced at all.

"Jessie Belle, don't go getting your hopes up, now. Like I told you before, a preacher is not the one in power. It's the board."

He could tell from her expression that it just wasn't acceptable to Jessie Belle.

But there was nothing that could be done to change what had been in place for years.

The next day Jessie Belle stopped at the restaurant around the corner from her house to pick up a pepperoni and sausage pizza per Traynor's request. They were going to eat junk food and watch a movie together before he had to leave for an appointment at the church.

Jessie Belle eyed the two women sitting in the booth across from her. They were looking around, watching every move of the restaurant employees. She was pretty sure they were planning to dart out without paying.

She got up and walked over to their table.

"Hello, ladies," she greeted. "My name is Jessie Belle Deveraux. May I sit down?"

"What do you want?" one of the women asked, spacing the words evenly.

Jessie Belle took a seat. "I'd like to pay for your meals," she announced. "I know what you were planning to do."

The two women exchanged looks.

"Lady, you don't know what you talking about," one huffed. "Just go back over to your table and leave us alone." Her tone was velvet, yet edged with steel.

"Do you have money?"

The two women glared at her in response.

"I didn't think so."

The one with the yellow tube top and Afro puffs asked, "What's it to you?"

Jessie Belle's voice dropped in volume. "I know you two were planning to run out of here without paying. Truth is that I'd rather not see you get arrested because you're hungry."

The other one in the red dress and the silver peace-sign necklace grunted, "I don't have no need for women."

Jessie Belle met her gaze. "What is your name?"

Folding her arms across her buxom chest, she said, "Sabrina . . . why?"

Jessie Belle ignored her. "And yours?"

"Karla."

"Ladies, I'm looking to hire a couple of girls to do some work for me. Interested?"

"What type of work?" Sabrina's voice faded, losing its steely edge.

"I guess you could call it acting."

Karla's eyes lit up. "How much does it pay?"

"A couple of hundred dollars each, but if you're any good—I could see you making a whole lot more."

Sabrina fingered her auburn-colored Afro. "We don't want no trouble."

"You won't have any," Jessie Belle assured them. "Unless you find some way to mess this up, this is not a difficult task."

"Why do you want us to do this job?" Karla inquired.

Jessie Belle smiled at them. "Because you're perfect for what I have in mind."

HER TRIUMPHS

CHAPTER SEVENTEEN

Jessie Belle met Sabrina and Karla at the same restaurant a few days later.

"So, how did it go?" she asked.

The two girls laughed.

"That well, huh?"

Sabrina handed her a thick envelope.

Jessie Belle scanned through the contents. She burst into a short laugh. "Oh my goodness, what a pervert!"

Karla chuckled. "The old fart has a fetish for toes. I thought he was gonna suck my nails off."

Jessie Belle frowned. "Not an image I want to savor."

Opening her purse, she pulled out two envelopes, each containing three hundred dollars.

Jessie Belle handed one to Sabrina and the other to Karla.

"You ladies did such a great job, I thought you deserved a little bonus."

"It was nice working with you," Sabrina stated with a grin. She wrote her number on a napkin and handed it to Jessie Belle. "Be sure and call me if you have any more *work*."

"Yeah," Karla agreed. "This is the easiest cash I ever made."

"You know . . . I'll definitely keep you both in mind. I may need your services again." Jessie Belle played with the idea of keeping Sabrina and Karla on her payroll. This way she didn't have to put her marriage in jeopardy.

She went home to relieve the babysitter.

After the girl left, Jessie Belle went upstairs to check on her son.

Holt was sound asleep in his crib.

He's such a good baby, she thought to herself. *And getting so big.* He was six months old and crawling around.

"We're on our way, Holt," she whispered. "Just wait until I see Charles Maxwell tonight. He'll be changing his tune pretty quick, won't he, sweetie? If he doesn't, the whole church will know about his little foot fetish. I wonder if he sucks Amy's toes? Uggh."

That evening, Jessie Belle went to the church. The first person she saw was Charles.

She broke into a smile. "Hello, Charles."

He walked over to her with a big grin on his face. Jessie Belle had deliberately worn sandals, and she bit back a grin when his eyes were drawn down to her feet.

"Mrs. Deveraux, it's good to see you."

"I was hoping to run into you," Jessie Belle stated. "Could I please have a word with you?"

Charles glanced around nervously. "Sure. What can I do for you?" he asked.

"Let's talk in here," she suggested, referring to the library. "When you hear what I have to say, you'll understand the need for privacy."

He gave her a puzzled look.

"You'll understand in a moment," she assured him.

As soon as Jessie Belle closed the door, she said, "I understand you and your cohorts are planning to vote against the mandatory fifteen percent tithe increase." The smile was gone. This was business.

His expression changed. "You heard right."

"I think I'll be able to change your mind." Jessie Belle sat down in a nearby chair.

A warning cloud settled on his features. "I doubt that, Mrs. Deveraux. There's no way I'd ever vote for something like that. This church was not built on greed. I thought you and your husband understood that."

Jessie Belle pulled the manila envelope from her tote bag. "Why don't you take a look at these before you make a decision?"

Charles glanced down at the photos. "What . . . where did you get these?"

"Does it really matter?" she asked. "I don't think your poor wife will care one way or the other. Do you?"

Charles gave her a look filled with venom.

Jessie Belle settled back in her seat. "Now, now . . . I wasn't the one being unfaithful, as you can tell from these pictures."

"You're supposed to be a Christian," he spit. "How can you do something like this? This is blackmail."

Jessie Belle's eyes narrowed. "You need to understand something, Charles. My husband is in charge of this church."

His dark face was set in a vicious expression. *"You're telling me that Traynor is behind this?"*

"Of course not," Jessie Belle responded. "Traynor is a saint. Look, Charles, none of these photos will ever see the light of day if you just do as I suggest. I want you to convince Tom Hopkins and Vernon Abbott to vote for the tithe increase. If you do—then all is well. If you don't . . . well, I don't see your marriage being happily ever after."

"They're not gonna listen to me."

"Yes, they will," Jessie Belle countered. "If not, just show them these. I have plenty of photos of each of you being naughty. And you have the nerve to accuse me of not being Christian."

"Does Traynor know about this?" Charles demanded. "That you're blackmailing me?"

"No. This is just between us and it'll stay that way as long as you leave my husband out of it and vote the way you should. My husband is the best pastor this church has seen and with your support, his ministry will grow and be prosperous."

"This is wrong what you're doing."

"And it wasn't wrong for you to cheat on your wife?"

"You are nothing but a Jezebel. As long as I got breath in my body— I'ma see that you pay for this."

"I can do without the threats and the name-calling," Jessie Belle stated. "I don't appreciate it. Charles, you really don't want to make an enemy out of me."

Jessie Belle pushed away from the desk and stood up. "I'm sure the meeting will be starting soon. I'll see you there."

"I still can't believe it," Traynor stated in the car on the drive home. "Jessie Belle, they all voted for mandatory fifteen percent tithing. I was prepared for Charles to come in there with his reasons to deny it. He was one of the main ones fighting against it."

"I'm not surprised," Jessie Belle murmured. "I told you that once they actually sat down and thought about it—they would go for it."

Traynor was still stunned by all that happened. "Wow . . . look at God. . . . I prayed over it and I asked for God's best in this situation." He glanced over and smiled at her. "You were right, as usual."

"Honey, isn't it time that you started listening to me?" Jessie Belle asked. "I haven't steered you wrong yet."

Traynor laughed. "I guess I should." Maybe Jessie Belle was right. It was time he really started listening to her. She truly had his best interests at heart and she believed in him.

She was a good wife.

His attention traveled back to the meeting. Charles and the other two had voted with him, although now that he thought about it . . . they didn't look too happy about it.

So why did they do it?

Traynor questioned Charles afterward about his sudden change of mind, but the man acted as if he was in a hurry.

He'd gotten what he wanted, but Traynor couldn't ignore the sensation that something didn't seem quite right about it.

"You really believe this is the right thing to do?" he asked Jessie Belle.
"Yes, I do."

Traynor gave a slight nod. "Then so do I."

He trusted his wife.

Jessie Belle decided to keep Sabrina and Karla on her payroll.

To keep them off the streets, she rented an apartment in Mary Ellen's name and moved them in. She didn't want anything traced back to her should they get into trouble.

Jessie Belle opened three other bank accounts to keep from drawing attention to large amounts of money being deposited. Right now there wasn't any real money coming in, but soon there would be.

She was just getting prepared. Traynor had preached recently on walking in your faith and Jessie Belle had taken the sermon to heart. She wanted to be the first lady of a grand church.

It was time to put her dreams into action.

But first she needed to make sure she covered her tracks. Jessie Belle's first stop was to visit her girls.

Jessie Belle walked into the apartment without knocking.

Sabrina was lounging on the sofa watching television, while Karla sat on the love seat polishing her nails.

"Jessie Belle, we didn't expect to see you," Sabrina said.

"I'm glad to see you're all moved in. Now that you're settled, I think it's important that we clear up some things. First being that you're not streetwalkers—don't charge like one and definitely don't act like one. Your services shouldn't come in less than two hundred dollars an hour."

Karla's mouth dropped open. "You want us to charge two hundred dollars for some sex."

Jessie Belle stood over by the fireplace. "I do. The type of men you'll be dealing with will pay that and more. The second thing is that no one is ever to know that you-all work for me," she stated. "This is not negotiable. If you tell anyone—I will deny it and I will be believed. After all, I'm the wife of a pastor and you two . . . well, you're hookers."

Karla bristled.

"I call a spade a spade, Karla. Now, I'm a fair woman. You can keep hooking, but you'll do it with class and you won't look like street hookers. You'll be given an allowance to buy new clothes, but understand that this is just an advance."

"So how are we supposed to pay you back for all this?" Karla wanted to know.

"By doing what you do best," Jessie Belle responded. "I'll allow you to keep fifty percent of your earnings—just don't try to cheat me. *Ever.* I will be good to you as long as you're good to me. Is that understood?"

"What happens if one of us is arrested?" asked Sabrina.

"Then you call Marcus Ackerman. I hear he's handled lots of cases like this. Sabrina, you meet with him and secure his services. You will be the main contact person. My name should never come up—I hope we're clear on this. I'm more of a silent partner."

"Why are you doing this?" Karla inquired. "I'm surprised, with you being a pastor's wife and all."

"I have certain aspirations for my husband, and you and Sabrina are going to help me achieve them."

CHAPTER EIGHTEEN

✿ *July 1975*

"I guess you were right again, sweetheart," Traynor stated as they walked along the sandy beach. They'd decided to drive to the Outer Banks for the Independence Day holiday.

"It's time for a bigger church. There was standing room only this morning."

Jessie Belle glanced up and asked, "I've been telling you this for how long now?" She wasn't surprised by his announcement. She'd put pressure on Charles to suggest it to the board just a few days ago.

She was enjoying life. Her girls were experts in their jobs and making good money for her, and Traynor was considered one of Raleigh's prominent pastors. He traveled more these days, but Jessie Belle didn't really mind.

It gave her time to handle the administrative tasks of her side business. She trusted Sabrina and Karla, but Jessie Belle's practice was to count her own money. Both women kept excellent records, but she couldn't say for sure whether they were stealing from her.

Holt was trying to climb down out of her arms, so she made her way over to where they'd placed their beach chairs and took a seat. Jessie Belle placed Holt on the beach towel beside her.

Traynor sat down in the empty beach chair on the other side. "I know you told me, Jessie Belle. The time just wasn't right before."

"You mean the time wasn't right until the board members suggested it," she responded. "And the only reason they came to this conclusion is because that woman passed out last Sunday. It was so crowded in church and it was hot. . . ."

"I'm sure that had something to do with it. That's why we had a meeting after church."

"Traynor, you're the pastor," she stated. "If that woman had a mind to sue, she'd be suing you—not the board members." Shaking her head sadly, Jessie Belle added, "Sometimes I wish you were more like Papa. One thing about my daddy . . . he runs his church."

"He still has to answer to the board, honey."

Jessie Belle shook her head. "He did whatever he wanted to do. He was in charge and people just didn't go up against him."

"What did he do if they did?" Traynor questioned.

"I don't think he ever had any of them ever disagree with him. Papa's a big man." Jessie Belle gave a slight shrug. "Maybe he intimidated them."

"Well, I don't want to use scare tactics just to get them to see things my way."

Holt picked up a rock and Jessie Belle took it from him. Ignoring his loud protest, she said, "I don't think my daddy did it intentionally—people were just scared of him. Papa was nothing but a big teddy bear deep down. I'm glad to hear that the board members have come to their senses, though. We've needed more space for a while now."

She handed Holt one of his toys. "Here you go, sweetie."

"I meet with some builders tomorrow afternoon," Traynor announced.

Jessie Belle was thrilled with the news of a new church building—it translated to more money. With the increase, they could demand a larger salary for Traynor.

"Honey, I'm so happy about this. I know we're definitely on our way."

Traynor broke into a grin. "I'm so fortunate to have you in my life, Jessie Belle. I love the way you take such an interest in my ministry."

"Honey, we're a team. I'm your helpmate and I intend to do everything in my power to fulfill my duties."

Traynor kissed her hand. "I think you should have a talk with some of the wives at church. Some members have complained about their personal lives being out of order."

"A couple of women approached me about having a marriage retreat—I think it's a great idea."

"Are you interested in heading up this project?"

Jessie Belle shook her head no. "I have someone in mind that I believe would be perfect—Deacon Daniel Patterson and his wife, Tamia."

Traynor agreed. "You're right."

"I'll give them a call to discuss it," she told him. "But I'll do that later. Traynor, honey, how do you feel about adding to our family?"

He blinked rapidly. "You're pregnant?"

"I think so," Jessie Belle responded. "How do you feel about it?"

"I'm happy. We've been wanting another child for so long. I just thought maybe it wasn't going to happen. How soon will we know for sure?"

"I can take a home pregnancy test today, but I need to call the doctor when we get back home for an appointment to confirm whether or not I'm really pregnant. When we stopped at the drugstore on the way here, I bought a test."

"Are you getting ready to take it?" Traynor asked.

Jessie Belle nodded. "I'm pretty sure I am, but I still want to take a test."

They gathered up all their stuff and headed back to the condo they were renting for the week.

Traynor sat on the bed with Holt while Jessie Belle went to take the pregnancy test.

Five minutes later, she strolled out of the bathroom, her expression blank.

Traynor rushed to his feet. "Are you?"

She broke into a grin. "We're going to have a baby. We're pregnant."

Jessie Belle's pregnancy ended in miscarriage eleven weeks later, breaking their hearts.

She and Traynor consoled themselves by concentrating on Holt and on the building of the new church.

Nine months later, Traynor surprised Jessie Belle with a romantic trip to Aruba to celebrate their sixth wedding anniversary.

They returned home a week later to prepare for the dedication ceremony of the new building.

The Saturday before the event, they walked through the huge sanctuary.

"It looks wonderful, Traynor," Jessie Belle murmured.

Traynor glanced around the sanctuary. "It's hard to believe this is New Salem Baptist Church. I'm so used to our little building."

"It won't be our little church any longer, honey. We're having it torn down and a recreation center built in its place."

He nodded. "I never thought I'd pastor a church this size. Do you think we'll ever have five thousand members?"

Jessie Belle embraced him. "Of course."

He laughed. "I don't know why I asked you that. You've always had this vision for us."

"Traynor, you've never been a small-time pastor. Why do you think people are always asking you to speak at their churches? You have the qualities of Billy Graham."

"I don't know about that."

"But I do," Jessie Belle responded. "Trust me, Traynor. You haven't seen nothing yet."

By the end of September, they were completely settled into the new building. Jessie Belle spent two days a week working at the church.

"You know, Traynor . . . ," Jessie Belle began as she dropped down into a nearby visitor chair facing his desk. She'd taken a break from the planning of the annual Fall Festival to come talk to her husband.

"The church is doing quite well. I think it's time for you to ask for an increase in your salary."

They had been in the new building for three months. She'd waited patiently for things to settle down before she brought up the subject of a raise.

"Holt's getting older and will be starting school soon. I want him to have a private-school education. He deserves the very best and so do we. Traynor, it's time for us to get a bigger house—a better house. We've been talking about trying again for another baby. We're going to need the room."

His eyes bouncing around the room, Traynor stated, "There's nothing wrong with our house."

"It's just not big enough," Jessie Belle retorted. "Traynor, I was talking with Patricia Lumley. I don't know if you remember, but her husband pastors over at Mount Sinai Baptist Church. Their house payment is included as part of their salary. We should have a similar benefit package. As far as I'm concerned, you're a much better pastor than he is."

"Jessie Belle, we aren't starving or anything. We live in a nice house now. . . . Why aren't you happy?"

"This has nothing to do with my being happy," Jessie Belle responded. "Why do you always just want to settle?" she asked him. "There's nothing wrong with living life more abundantly. I want to live my life to the fullest, Traynor. I want the good things in life—there's no reason why we can't have them."

"Why aren't you ever satisfied?"

"Excuse me?"

"You're never satisfied, it seems."

"This is the end of the discussion," Jessie Belle uttered. "I won't sit here and listen to you put me down."

"I'm not putting you down, sweetheart."

She rose up. "Don't you *sweetheart* me, Traynor. I'm pissed and right now, I just want you out of my face. I'm so tired of having this same argument with you over and over again. *Do whatever you want.*"

She walked over to a nearby window and peered out.

"Jessie Belle, if you want me to ask for more money—I will," Traynor stated with a sigh of resignation from behind her.

She glanced over her shoulder at him. "You don't have to say it like that. This isn't about me, Traynor. I just want you to get some of what you deserve. You have to treat your ministry as a business. Maybe I'd feel differently if we were a two-income family, but we're not. You have to consider the needs of your growing family."

After a moment, Traynor stated, "I guess you haven't been wrong yet."

Jessie Belle bit back her smile. She didn't want to appear too enthusiastic over her victory.

"And tell them that we're looking at buying a bigger house—we want the mortgage payment included as part of your salary. Better yet, I don't know if you should say anything about getting another house. Not yet anyway. Just don't let them put a cap on the mortgage payment."

She could see in Traynor's eyes how uncomfortable he felt about approaching the board, but Jessie Belle didn't care. They needed a house that was symbolic of their status in the church and community. He would appreciate it in time.

Jessie Belle was sure of it.

When Jessie Belle left his office, Traynor leaned back in his chair with his eyes closed.

Now she wants another house.

He put his hands over his face to drown out his sighs of frustration. "God, what am I supposed to do? I have a wonderful wife and I love her dearly, but she can be so irritating at times."

She only has my best interests at heart. No matter what field I worked in—I believe she'd still be the same way. What wife wouldn't want her husband to get a raise?

Truth be told, Traynor felt he deserved a raise as well. He was a devoted pastor and performed his job well. That's it. . . . It was his job and he should be compensated fairly.

Later at home, he sat Jessie Belle down.

"I thought about everything you told me and I want you to know that I agree with you, sweetheart."

"Traynor, I'm sorry if I pressured you into this. It's just that I—"

He cut her off by saying, "This is my decision, Jessie Belle. Sometimes I forget that this is a job."

"I know how you feel about your ministry," Jessie Belle stated. "Believe me, I do. But I believe God has so much more for you. Traynor, I listen to you preach on Sundays and you should see the impact you have on others. Your words—they move people. You have such a gift for ministering to the heartbroken and the wounded in spirit, honey. Embrace it, Traynor, and walk in it."

"I thought I was."

"You have been called to greatness. I can see our entire life in my mind. What Billy Graham has—God wants that for you, Traynor." Jessie Belle placed a hand over her heart. "I know it in here."

Deep down, Traynor didn't know if he was doing it for her or for himself, but he said, "Okay, Jessie Belle. You've convinced me. I trust you."

———

Jessie Belle woke up the next morning wanting to go house hunting.

"Sweetheart, I haven't had a chance to even talk to anybody yet," Traynor complained. "Why are you in such a hurry to go looking at houses?"

She sat down at the breakfast table with him. "Why should we wait till the last minute? We should go on and put this one on the market, too."

"Sweetheart, we don't have to move too fast. If we put this one on the market and it sells—where we gonna live if the board doesn't approve the salary increase?"

She didn't want to hear any negativity this morning. "We'll find a house—that's the easy part."

He eyed her for a moment before saying, "I don't understand you sometimes, Jessie Belle."

"Honey, all you need to do is love me. You don't need to worry about anything else."

Traynor smiled. "I do love you."

"And I you," she responded, removing her robe. "Right now, I need some loving before we go shopping for our new house."

She would give him what he needed and then Traynor would give her what she wanted.

They left the house two hours later.

"Jessie Belle, I don't know if we can afford this," Traynor whispered as they strolled through a six-bedroom house with a large gourmet kitchen, a media room, seven fireplaces, an Olympic-sized pool and a Jacuzzi.

Running her fingers across the delicate detailing of the custom cabinets in the kitchen, she responded, "We can afford it if the church is paying for it."

"Jessie Belle . . ."

Okay, he was starting to get on her last nerve.

Turning around to face him, Jessie Belle stated, "Traynor, the church is raking in thousands every single Sunday. The pews are filled and our members are generous. We can afford anything we want."

"You really like this house?" Traynor asked.

Jessie Belle nodded. "I love it. This house is perfect for us."

He turned to the real estate agent and said, "My wife has made a decision."

His words bothered Jessie Belle some, but she pushed it to the back of her mind. She wanted to relish her triumph.

She had found her dream house.

CHAPTER NINETEEN

Jessie Belle lost her father the day after Valentine's Day. Her mother had taken his passing well, but it was evident that she missed him dearly. Jessie Belle convinced her to sell the old house and move into one of the newly built apartment complexes right outside of Mayville. The house and the land were just too much for her aging mother to take care of on her own.

The weeks flew by, the months merging one into another. Without any real awareness, Jessie Belle found that it was April.

Traynor rushed into the house asking, "Whose car is that in the driveway?"

Jessie Belle met him in the foyer wearing a big grin. "It's *mine*. I bought it today."

He swallowed hard. "You did what?"

"I bought a new car," Jessie Belle said calmly. "My birthday is in two weeks and I've always wanted a Mercedes. I was thinking about getting one for you, too. I know how much you love that Cadillac, but honey . . . it's time for a change. We've got this big beautiful house—our cars need to match."

Traynor couldn't believe that Jessie Belle had gone out and purchased a car without consulting him. "These cars are not that old. But besides that, I thought it was understood that we'd discuss any large purchases from now on."

"What does that have to do with anything?" she wanted to know. "It's not like we can't afford it. You don't have to worry, Traynor. I used some of the money I got from Papa's insurance for the down payment. He left that money for me to do whatever I wanted with it."

Traynor tried to contain his anger. "I suppose you think the church should make the payments on this, too."

"What's wrong with that?" Jessie Belle asked. "There are church members buying cars for their pastors all the time."

"Those are gifts from the church body, Jessie Belle," he pointed out. "You went out and bought this car yourself."

"So what? It doesn't matter. We have to have a car to drive around town and to the church."

"There was nothing wrong with the other car."

"Traynor, I am the first lady. I should drive a car befitting the wife of a prominent pastor. How will people believe that they can ask God for anything and receive it if they don't see it happening in front of their faces?"

Jessie Belle walked over to where Traynor was standing. "Honey, God *wants* to bless us. What's wrong with that? You need to stop feeling guilty for reaping the benefits of what you've been sowing."

"Why are you being so materialistic?" he asked. "Are you trying to impress other people? You're certainly not doing this for God."

"I'm gonna pretend you didn't just say that to me, Traynor."

"No, I'd really like an answer, Jessie Belle."

"I like nice things and I think we deserve them. The Cadillac was showing its age."

"But you didn't decide this until Sara Hamilton got a new Mercedes. Jessie Belle, we can't keep up with the Hamiltons. I don't care about storing up earthly treasures. My focus is living my life according to God's Word and I thought you felt the same way."

"I've heard enough of your insults tonight, Traynor. I don't want to hear another word out of your mouth."

Jessie Belle rushed off to her bedroom, praying that Traynor wouldn't follow her. She was furious with him and if he kept after her—she feared saying something she could never apologize for.

Traynor was flabbergasted.

Jessie Belle was upset with him, but this time, she was definitely the one in the wrong. He should've been consulted before she went out and bought the car. Traynor didn't ask much from his wife.

"God, how do I get her to understand?" he whispered.

He couldn't figure out what was going on with Jessie Belle, but Traynor could feel in his spirit that she wasn't being completely straight with him. Clothes were still mysteriously appearing in her closet. Even Holt seemed to have new clothes he'd never seen before. Traynor even noticed a couple of pieces of jewelry. He hated going behind her back, but he needed to be sure.

Traynor checked their bank accounts and all moneys were accounted for less the ten thousand she put down on the Mercedes. Jessie Belle had told him that her father's insurance company paid out twenty thousand dollars. He never saw the check but saw no reason to doubt her.

Traynor checked their credit card balances, too, and found nothing out of the ordinary. He briefly wondered if Jessie Belle had gotten her own credit card, but no statements had come to the house.

He couldn't just accuse her outright of any wrongdoing without proof.

Maybe it's me, he reasoned.

But his gut instincts told him it was Jessie Belle.

Traynor rationalized that it was just one of Satan's tricks. He was not going to give in to his suspicions this time around. He would have to have solid proof before confronting Jessie Belle.

Jessie Belle was wrong in the way she treated Traynor the night before and she knew it.

Although she'd told him not to talk to her, it bothered Jessie Belle when he came to bed without so much as one word to her.

He was still angry.

In all the years of their marriage, Jessie Belle couldn't recall when she'd really seen Traynor furious with her. He was always so calm and even-tempered.

She'd overplayed her hand this time.

Jessie Belle tossed and turned most of the night. She couldn't stand the fact that Traynor was so angry with her.

When the clock struck six thirty a.m., Jessie Belle was up and on her way down to the kitchen.

She walked in and turned on the radio.

Humming to the music, Jessie Belle pulled out the ingredients necessary to make a healthy and delicious breakfast for Traynor. As she cooked, she listened to John Overton, a pastor they knew from the Atlanta area. His radio show was broadcast in over sixty cities.

"What makes you feel anxious? What do you worry about? Finances? Conflict with friends or family? Is it worrying whether you're going to make it to work on time? Perhaps it's your family or your health—anxiety seems to be everywhere these days. . . ."

Jessie Belle removed the sausages from the stove and paused. John Overton's radio show was a very popular broadcast and she could understand why. He was a very gifted speaker and his tone soothing. She was enjoying his words of hope and listened to him practically every morning.

She was seated at the breakfast table, deep in thought, when Traynor came downstairs.

"Good morning," he greeted.

No response.

"Jessie Belle . . . ," Traynor prompted.

"Huh?" She glanced over her shoulder. "Oh, honey . . . I didn't hear you come down."

"I can see that. What were you thinking about?" Traynor sat down at the table.

Pouring him a cup of orange juice, Jessie Belle answered, "I was listening to John Overton on the radio talking about his ministry, and I got to thinking—my Traynor would be good at something like that."

"Jessie Belle, sweetheart . . ."

"Honey, I know you're still upset with me, but I need you to just hear me out, please," she said, rising to her feet.

Jessie Belle walked across the room to where the toaster sat, and dropped in two slices of bread. "I really think you should have your own radio show. Just imagine how many people you'll be able to reach. People who won't walk into a church or can't because of illness or a disability."

"I'd never thought about that," Traynor confessed.

When the bread was toasted, she placed the slices on a small plate and strolled back over to the table, setting it down in front of Traynor. "Well, think about it now. This is something that's so perfect for you."

Jessie Belle sat down at the table. "Traynor, I owe you an apology. I was wrong for buying the Mercedes without consulting you. I couldn't sleep last night because it bothered me that you were angry with me."

He smiled. "I can never stay angry with you, sweetheart."

"I really am sorry, Traynor."

He kissed her. "Just promise me that you won't go making any other large purchases like that without discussing it with me first."

"I promise. Now back to this radio show. Honey, I think you should talk to the owner. Pitch him the idea of giving you a show."

"You really think I should do it?"

Jessie Belle took a small sip of her hot tea. "Yeah, I do. Traynor, you'd be so great on the radio. You could call it *Pearls of Wisdom* or *Wisdom from the Heart* or even *Daily Inspiration by Pastor Traynor Deveraux.*"

He laughed. "You got this all figured out, don't you?"

"I try to think out everything." She stuck a forkful of scrambled eggs in her mouth.

Jessie Belle and Traynor discussed her ideas for the show as they finished their breakfast.

Traynor left for the church around nine thirty.

As soon as he walked out the door, Jessie Belle made a phone call.

"This is Jessie Belle Deveraux—Pastor Traynor Deveraux's wife. I'd like to set up a meeting with Elton Newman, please. We have an idea for a show."

Jessie Belle dressed with care.

She wanted to look alluring and sexy, but didn't want to overdo it. She didn't want to give Elton Newman the wrong idea.

Two hours later, Jessie Belle pulled into the parking lot of the radio station. She was early for her appointment.

She glanced around the reception area, noting the outdated wallpaper and the boring color scheme. Jessie Belle had expected better.

They could definitely use the help of an interior decorator.

"Mr. Newman will see you now," the bubbly receptionist told her.

Jessie Belle rose to her feet and followed the woman to the administrative offices located in the back of the station.

"Mrs. Deveraux," Elton greeted her, holding on to her hand a little longer than necessary. "It's very nice to meet you. I met your husband a couple of months ago at a charity function."

"Yes, he told me," Jessie Belle replied.

Elton pulled out a chair for her.

Jessie Belle sat down, crossing her legs. "I'm thankful you were able to take some time to talk to me. I know how busy you must be."

"I was intrigued. We've never had a Christian talk show before."

"Have you ever heard my husband preach?"

"Can't say I have," Elton responded. "I have heard that he's a good speaker, though. A lot of people compare him to Martin Luther King Jr."

Jessie Belle smiled. "Traynor moves you to tears. He lives what he preaches about and when he gives a sermon—it's like he's having a one-on-one conversation with you."

"You're extremely proud of your husband, I see. And your unquestionable faith in him is admirable."

She met his gaze. "You must agree, or we wouldn't be having this meeting."

Elton broke into a grin. "Would you like something to drink?"

Jessie Belle shook her head no. "I'm fine, thank you."

"I hope you don't mind, but I ordered some lunch for us. I wasn't sure how long our meeting would take."

He was eyeing her like a piece of meat and Jessie Belle didn't like it, but this was for Traynor. She would do whatever she needed to do to help her husband. Pasting on a smile, Jessie Belle stated, "I'm starved."

He grinned and settled back against the cushions of his chair. "So you enjoy being the first lady of New Salem Baptist Church?"

"Of course I do," she responded. "My father was a pastor—it's the only life that I've ever known."

"I find that a little hard to believe. I can read people, Jessie Belle. You are an extremely beautiful woman and you know how to use that beauty."

"I go after what I want," Jessie Belle responded. "And I see nothing wrong with that."

Elton leered at her. "It works for me."

CHAPTER TWENTY

"Your husband has his radio program," Elton stated when they met two days later at an apartment he kept on the side. "I wanted you to be the first to know. I'll give him the good news later this evening."

"Thank you so much. I'm telling you—you won't regret it." Jessie Belle pulled an envelope out of her purse and offered it to him.

He looked puzzled. "What's this?"

"I told you that I'd make it worth your while," Jessie Belle stated. "I'm a lady of my word."

"I was thinking of something a little more intimate," Elton responded with a leer.

"I have a couple of girls working for me. You can take your pick. They are two of the most beautiful women in the world. You—"

Elton's voice was soothing but insistent. "I don't think you're hearing me. I want *you*, Jessie Belle."

Jessie Belle had known this was a possibility, so she'd had her detective check Elton's background. He owed some pretty scary people money. "I'm a married woman."

"Your husband doesn't have to know," Elton uttered with a chuckle. "It'll be our secret. Jessie Belle, we could be so good together."

Why does every man think he and I are so great together? she wondered silently.

"I'm sorry, Elton, but I'm not available for your pleasure."

He took a step toward her. "I want you, Jessie Belle. I haven't been able to get you out of my mind since that day you sashayed into my office looking all good and sexy."

"Elton, take the money. . . ."

"I don't need your money. Or your girls. A deal is a deal—if you want Traynor to have a radio show . . . well, I think you get the picture."

She'd totally misread Elton. Jessie Belle had been sure he would take the money and the girls. The last thing she wanted to do was bed him.

"Well . . ."

She swallowed hard, lifted her chin and boldly met his gaze. "I think I'll pass," Jessie Belle uttered. "If I were in your shoes, I'd take the girls and the money. You need money, don't you?"

Elton stared at her. "What do you mean by that?"

"Just that I know you need money."

He tried to kiss her.

Jessie Belle moved her head. "I said no, Elton, and I mean it."

"I've never met anyone like you," Elton uttered. "One day I'm going to warm that cold heart of yours."

He took the envelope out of her hands.

Jessie Belle released a low sigh of relief. "You won't regret this, Elton." She headed to the door.

"Why are you in such a hurry?"

"I have to get home to my family. In case you've forgotten, I do have a husband. It was nice doing business with you."

Elton followed her to the door. "You don't have to be so cool to me."

"Our business is done, Elton."

He reached for Jessie Belle, but she successfully stepped out of his reach.

"I'll expect to hear from you before the week is out regarding my husband's radio show. Elton, I caution you against reneging on our business arrangement."

"I'm a man of my word."

"See that you are."

"What! No good-bye kiss?" He laughed.

She threw open the front door and rushed out, practically running to her car. Jessie Belle wanted to get as far away from Elton Newman as possible.

As soon as she arrived home, Jessie Belle jumped into the shower.

After she toweled off and slipped on a pair of jeans and a T-shirt, she paid the babysitter and sent her home. Jessie Belle spent the rest of the afternoon with her son.

"Mommy just got Daddy a radio show," she whispered. "Isn't that wonderful? I almost had to pay a high price to get him that show and I would have. Because I know that in the end it'll pay off big. You see, I'm betting on your daddy."

Jessie Belle planted a kiss on his forehead. "You're just like him. I can see it already in your personality. Holt, you're gonna have a wonderful life. Mommy's gonna see to it."

Jessie Belle stormed out of her house muttering a string of curses.

That Elton Newman was a greedy ol' dog.

Not only did he order her to send the girls over to his apartment, but he wanted more money.

Fifty thousand dollars.

She didn't have that kind of money lying around, and even if she did, Jessie Belle wasn't about to give it to Elton. Something was going to have to be done about him, she decided. She wasn't going to continue to let him extort money from her.

She still had an ace up her sleeve. The detective had given her a complete dossier on Elton Newman. Jessie Belle knew, not only that he gambled away thousands of dollars, but also that he cheated on his wife, and that he'd been taking money from record companies to give their artists airtime.

"Is that illegal?" Jessie Belle had asked the detective, since it really didn't sound like a big deal to her.

"Payoffs like that violate state and federal law," he'd explained. "Songs selected for airplay aren't really based on artistic merit and popularity. Most times airtime is determined by undisclosed payoffs to radio stations and their employees. Record labels have offered a series of inducements known as payola to radio stations in the forms of outright bribes, expensive vacation packages, electronics, contest giveaways for stations' listening audiences and payments to cover operational expenses."

When Jessie Belle asked for proof of the transactions, she was told, "I have copies of everything. Apparently he's not paying his employees enough."

Elton Newman had taken steps to try to conceal most of the payments by using fictitious contest winners and making it appear as though the payments and gifts were going to radio listeners instead of him.

Promptly at one o'clock, Jessie Belle strolled into the apartment wearing a smile and feeling in control.

"It's nice to see that beautiful smile of yours again," Elton uttered. "I take it you're getting used to our little arrangement."

"Actually, no, I'm not," she responded. "I have no intentions of continuing *our little arrangement*, as you put it."

"Jessie Belle, I don't think you understand. I call all the shots here."

"Elton, darling, it's you who's confused." Jessie Belle tossed a thick manila envelope into his lap.

"What is this?" he questioned.

"Some lovely little pictures of you with a whore," Jessie Belle stated with a look of triumph. "Quite racy, don't you think? I thought your wife might want to know what you're doing when you're not home with her."

He had the nerve to give her a look of confusion. "Jessie Belle, what's this all about?"

"I want you to leave me alone."

Leaning back against the sofa, Elton shook his head no. "I'm not ready to do that just yet."

"If you don't, you might find yourself behind bars. I know all about the payouts you've been getting. I have copies of all of your little black books."

His expression turned ugly. "I don't believe you. Besides, I never figured you for stupid. You don't want to make an enemy out of me, Jessie Belle."

"Are you willing to test me?"

He held up the envelope. "Is this the only copy?"

Jessie Belle gave a short laugh. "Of course not. I have several copies— for insurance."

"I want all of it—the pictures, the records ... everything," he growled.

"So you can go to Traynor?" Jessie Belle shook her head. "*I don't think so.* This is my insurance. You leave me alone and I'll do the same for you."

"Nobody comes in here and tries to blackmail me," he yelled. "Especially if they have half a brain."

She refused to lower her gaze. Jessie Belle didn't want to give Elton the impression that he scared her. It would give him the upper hand.

"So you actually believe that you're the only one around here capable of blackmailing?" she chuckled. "You're the one who doesn't have a brain."

"You're making a huge mistake, Jessie Belle. I like you, so just hand over what you have and we'll just forget about this momentary loss of sanity."

"Elton, I'm dead serious. I'm holding on to my file—it'll be locked away in my safe-deposit box. If you agree to my simple terms, then you have nothing to worry about. Just stay away from me and let Traynor keep his show—the file never sees the light of day."

He spewed a string of curses at her.

She shrugged in nonchalance, unaffected by his profanity.

"Woman, you don't know who you messing with."

"Traynor's show is one of the highest-rated shows at your station. He's bringing in thousands of dollars in advertising. . . . Why would you want to take money out of your own pockets?" Jessie Belle paused for a moment before saying, "It's not about the money—it's control. You want to control me."

Blocking her path to the front door, he uttered, "I *do* control you."

Jessie Belle gave a firm shake of her head. "It ends tonight."

They faced off, each glaring at the other.

Finally, Elton moved away from the door. "Get out of here."

She gave him a tiny smile. "Gladly."

Jessie Belle walked past him, holding her breath. She wasn't entirely sure Elton was going to just let her leave like that. When she was in the elevator, she released a long sigh of relief.

"Thank You, Jesus," she murmured. However, Jessie Belle knew she wasn't entirely off the hook—she'd made an enemy out of Elton. There was no telling what he would do next.

Traynor was upstairs when Jessie Belle pulled her car up into the driveway. Even from his view upstairs, he could tell that she was upset about something. And she nearly jumped out of her skin when he made his presence known.

"You scared me," she told him. "I didn't expect you to be home so early."

"I thought I'd come home to surprise my wife—only you weren't here. The babysitter told me that you had a meeting."

"Sara and I have been trying to think of some new ways to get the children interested in attending Vacation Bible School. Numbers have been dwindling for the past couple of years, you know."

He nodded in agreement.

"Traynor, I thought you'd be at the church until after Bible study."

"I decided that I wanted to spend some quality time with you and Holt."

Jessie Belle's eyes watered. "You're so sweet to me, Traynor."

When she neared him, he could see her trembling. "You're shaking. Jessie Belle, what's wrong? Did something happen?"

"No honey, I'm fine," she lied. "I just want to take a hot shower and go to bed. It's been a long day."

Traynor wasn't convinced. "You sure you're okay?"

She nodded. "I'm sorry for being gone so long and for snapping at you—it's not been one of my better days."

"I made some dinner. Hungry?"

Jessie Belle shook her head no. "I'm not hungry. I just want a bath and a sleeping pill."

Traynor didn't push. She would confide in him whenever she was ready. Jessie Belle didn't like to be pushed when she was in a mood. He'd learned that a long time ago.

He watched her ascend the stairs.

Traynor had noticed that Jessie Belle hadn't quite been herself over the past month or so. Almost around the same time he'd gotten the radio show. If he didn't know better, he might assume that it was the reason for her recent mood swings.

I wouldn't have the show without her, so Jessie Belle can't be upset about that, he reasoned silently.

So what's going on with her?

CHAPTER TWENTY-ONE

"They found Elton Newman shot to death last night," Traynor announced when Jessie Belle came downstairs to fix breakfast.

"I just heard about it on the television," she responded. "I'm shocked."

His death was all over the news. Apparently one of his *dates* had gone to the apartment and found his body. She'd called the police to report the crime but ended up with a lot of explaining to do. Jessie Belle recalled her encounter with him a few days ago. "I guess he pissed off the wrong person," she stated. "I can't help thinking about his poor wife. . . . I feel so bad for Minnie. Losing her husband that way."

Traynor agreed.

"I'm just stunned by the news of Elton's death," Jessie Belle murmured. "I just can't believe it."

"They think he was murdered by one of the promoters he was taking money from or by a drug dealer," Traynor responded. "They found drugs in one of the drawers in the bedroom. They're saying it looks like a deal gone bad."

"What a shame." Deep down, Jessie Belle didn't really feel a thing.

When Traynor left to run some errands, she put on some praise music and danced around the house.

Now that Elton was out of her life permanently, Jessie Belle could proceed with her plans to elevate Traynor's ministry. The radio show was doing well and getting good response from the listeners.

It would be nice to have a show like that on the radio daily—not just once a week.

Suddenly another thought occurred to Jessie Belle, bringing a smile to her lips. She couldn't wait to share it with Traynor when he returned home three hours later.

"I was just thinking that we should buy the radio station." Jessie Belle scanned his face, trying to read his expression.

Traynor glanced over at his wife. "For what?"

"We could make it a Christian radio station—Lord knows this town needs one."

"Why don't we pray about it and let the Lord guide us," Traynor suggested.

"If that's what you want," Jessie Belle responded. "We'll pray about it."

While Traynor was praying, she would be taking the necessary steps to buy the radio station. Her husband would appreciate her efforts in the long run.

Jessie Belle decided it was in her best interest to spend some time with Elton Newman's widow. She would need a friend in her time of grief.

Minnie burst into a round of tears as soon as she opened her door and saw Jessie Belle standing there.

She immediately embraced the sobbing woman. "I'm so sorry about Elton. I can't believe he's gone."

Minnie wiped her face. "I don't know what he was doing at that apartment. . . . Drugs, a girlfriend . . . all the horrible things I'm hearing about my husband—it just doesn't sound like Elton. Jessie Belle, I feel like they're talking about a stranger. I keep telling myself that they can't be talking about my Elton."

The man was a greedy dog.

Jessie Belle followed her into the house. "Who knows what's really true, Minnie? But you shouldn't be worrying yourself with that mess. You've got enough to deal with."

"So many people have been over here. . . ." Minnie sighed softly. "I think mostly they just wanted details surrounding my husband's death. Elton did a lot for the people in this city, but all they want to remember is that he died in an apartment I didn't know he had and he was found by the woman he was having an affair with."

Jessie Belle shook her head in mock disgust. "Such a shame," she murmured.

"I don't even want to turn my television on. I just can't take anymore. This is such a mess."

"Minnie, why don't you let me help you? If you want, I'll deal with the media and anybody else. I'll be the family spokesperson."

She wiped away a tear. "Jessie Belle, thanks so much. I don't know what I'd do without you. I've got to deal with his family, legal matters and the funeral."

"I can help you with the funeral and probably the legal stuff, but Elton's family—I'm afraid you're on your own with that one."

Minnie smiled a real smile. "They're my biggest challenge. All his family wants is to know if Elton's left them any money. They don't like me much—never have."

"I have a bat at home if you need it," Jessie Belle teased.

"I may take you up on that offer," Minnie responded with a chuckle.

Jessie Belle spent most of the morning helping Elton's widow plan his Homegoing Celebration. When other relatives started to arrive, she decided that it was time to leave. She didn't want to get in the middle of family mess.

"Call me if you need me to come back over later."

Minnie nodded. "If you don't mind, please come back around three. I have to go to the funeral home and I'd like you to go with me."

Jessie Belle nodded. "I'll have my babysitter stay with Holt and I'll be back. He's with his father right now, but I'm on my way to pick him up."

"Thank you for all of your help."

"Minnie, it's no problem. Elton was a friend," Jessie Belle managed between stiff lips.

Traynor and Holt were out in the yard when she arrived.

"How's Minnie?"

"She's grieving," Jessie Belle answered. "Traynor, the poor woman doesn't know if she's coming or going. She wants me to go with her to the funeral home this afternoon. I'm going to have Carly come over and watch Holt."

"Just bring him by the church," Traynor suggested. "He can spend the rest of the day with me."

"Really?"

He nodded. "Sure. Holt and I have enjoyed our time together. Right, son?"

The little boy nodded.

"Thanks, honey," Jessie Belle said with a smile. She wanted to become Minnie's best friend so that she could subtly convince her to sell her the radio station.

Traynor and Jessie Belle attended Elton's funeral three days later.

They sat a few rows behind the Newman family. Jessie Belle noticed that there were a lot of female mourners in the congregation.

Apparently, Elton didn't have a faithful bone in his body.

She sat listening to all the wonderful accolades being tossed out. He sure had a lot of people fooled, Jessie Belle decided.

When it was time to pay respects, Jessie Belle and Traynor walked up to the open casket.

She stood there silently gloating.

That's what you get for trying to steal money from folk. What goes around, comes around.

Traynor took her hand and led her back to their seats.

They left the church when the service ended and went to the cemetery.

After witnessing several emotional goodbyes, Jessie Belle decided she'd had enough. She and Traynor got up to leave.

"I hate that I didn't have the chance to get to know Elton more," Traynor stated as they walked down the path toward the cars. "He sounded like a great man."

Jessie Belle wanted to gag. He was anything but great as far as she was concerned. "Don't forget that he was found in an apartment he was renting by a girl he was having an affair with. He wasn't faithful to his wife. And Minnie's so sweet."

"We really don't know what was going on."

"Traynor, why did Elton have a secret apartment? Because he needed somewhere to take his women. I know he's dead, but Elton Newman wasn't the saint everyone was trying to make him out to be."

"I'm sure they were just trying to be sensitive to his family's feelings. Despite what he did—Elton's family loved him."

"You're right," Jessie Belle murmured. "But I feel bad for Minnie. She didn't deserve to be married to a man like Elton. She's so heartbroken."

"With time, her pain is going to lessen," Traynor stated. "I hope she's forgiven him."

"She will," Jessie Belle replied. "Minnie loved that man. He was her whole life. I don't know how the woman is going to function. That's why I've been spending so much time with her. I feel it's my Christian duty."

Traynor assisted her into the car, then walked around to the other side and got in.

"Minnie is very lucky to have you, sweetheart."

Jessie Belle settled back in her seat. "I think so, too. She's got so many people coming out the woodwork wanting money. I don't want her money. Minnie trusts me."

CHAPTER TWENTY-TWO

Jessie Belle played the dutiful, concerned friend and checked on Minnie frequently after Elton's funeral.

"I brought you some of my famous mint chocolate-chip cookies," she told her when Minnie opened the door.

She stepped aside to let Jessie Belle enter the house.

They sat down in the dining room, where Minnie had obviously been going through a stack of paperwork.

"I don't understand what half of this stuff is," she said with a frown. "I never really concerned myself with Elton's business dealings. Maybe I should have. . . ." Her voice died. "I don't know how I could've lived all these years with a man I didn't know."

Jessie Belle reached over and squeezed Minnie's hand. "I'm so sorry."

"I've been thinking about what you suggested, Jessie Belle. I'm going to sell the radio station."

She swallowed her excitement. "Really? Minnie, are you sure you want to do that?"

"I don't know a thing about running a radio station. And right now, keeping it would only bring hurtful memories. I'd rather sell and just start fresh. I'm selling the house and moving back to Kansas. I want to be closer to my mother."

"Traynor and I were actually talking last night about buying it—if you'd planned on selling the station."

"I had no idea you were interested in owning the station, Jessie Belle. You never said a thing."

"It was my husband's idea and he only mentioned it to me last night," Jessie Belle lied. "I'm like you—I wouldn't know what to do with it—but Traynor, he really wants it."

"I'd be more than happy to sell it to Traynor. You two have been so good to me."

"Actually, I think I'd like to surprise him with the station, Minnie. His birthday's coming up in a couple of weeks—this is the perfect gift."

Minnie picked up one of the cookies and took a bite. "These are delicious," she murmured after swallowing. "Jessie Belle, if you want the radio station . . . it's yours, dear."

"Traynor will be so pleased. I can't wait to tell him."

"What is this?" Traynor stared down at the documents Jessie Belle thrust at him.

"You're the new owner of the radio station," she announced with a big grin. "The first thing we're going to do is change the name to WGOS—twenty-four hours of gospel music. Isn't that great?"

His eyebrows rose in surprise. "But how?"

Traynor couldn't imagine how Jessie Belle had come up with enough money to buy the station. "Where did you get the money?"

"Minnie made me an offer I simply couldn't turn down, so I sold off some stock," Jessie Belle answered. "She's letting me pay off the balance in installments. Traynor, this is such a good investment. Raleigh doesn't have a twenty-four-hour gospel station but it's sorely needed. What good is it just to have a show airing only on Sunday mornings?"

First the Mercedes and now the radio station.

"Jessie Belle, we should've discussed this first. I thought we agreed that you wouldn't go off on your own like that anymore."

"Honey, I had to jump on this as soon as Elton's widow was ready to sell," she explained. "If we'd waited, someone else would've snatched it up."

"I understand that, sweetheart." Traynor sat down on the sofa. "I do, but this is a major decision. We don't know a thing about running a radio station."

"I did this for you," Jessie Belle snapped in frustration. "A simple thank-you is enough."

She rushed off to their bedroom. He could hear the door slam shut all the way downstairs.

Traynor felt like punching his hand through a wall. What in the world was wrong with his wife?

Why won't Jessie Belle listen to me?

He was so tired of going through this with her. He'd dealt with her over spending money like it was going out of style and had assumed he'd gotten through to her, but now she'd gone out and bought the radio station. Sure, they'd discussed it briefly, but no definite decision had been made.

Traynor decided to take a walk around the neighborhood to clear his head.

When he returned twenty minutes later, Jessie Belle was seated in the living room as if she'd been waiting on him.

"I guess you're really mad with me, huh?" she asked.

Traynor answered truthfully. "After all the talks we've had, Jessie Belle, about this very thing—I guess I'm just disappointed."

"I was wrong, Traynor. I admit it, but it's because I got so excited and I didn't want you to miss out on the opportunity. We did talk about buying it at one time."

"But we never came to any decision," Traynor responded. "What am I supposed to do with a radio station, Jessie Belle? I'm not going to abandon my duties at the church."

"You don't have to," Jessie Belle replied. "All you have to do is hire a station manager to run it for you. Raleigh needs a twenty-four-hour gospel station. I think you should hire Mary Ellen. We trust her and she can do the job. You don't have to worry about anything, Traynor."

She rose to her feet and walked over to where he was standing. "Traynor, I promise you, I won't do anything like this again. I give you my word, honey. You can trust me."

He wasn't sure he agreed. What else would Jessie Belle take upon herself to do without talking to him first?

Late last night, Richard and Mary Ellen drove up to Raleigh to spend the weekend with them.

"Look at you and Traynor," Mary Ellen began. "Y'all got your own radio station. Wow."

Jessie Belle nodded. "A twenty-four-hour gospel station." She pulled out the frying pan and sat it on top of the stove.

"That's some birthday present."

"To tell the truth, Mary Ellen . . . my husband was a little upset at first, but he's come around." Jessie Belle laughed. "I don't know why it takes him so long to get it. It's my job as his wife to make sure he's on the right track. We're a team. If he would just listen to me—he'd be the next Billy Graham. Traynor is that powerful. I refuse to let him settle for anything less than what he deserves."

"He's lucky to have a woman like you in his corner," Richard said, entering the kitchen. He sat down beside Mary Ellen.

"Make sure you tell him that when he comes downstairs," Jessie Belle said with a short laugh. Her smile disappeared when she glimpsed the expression on her friend's face.

The tension was thick in the room. Jessie Belle felt like she could slice it with a knife.

A few minutes later, Richard got up to seek out Traynor.

"You and Richard okay?" Jessie Belle inquired.

She nodded. "He just thinks I'm a nag. Richard thinks I'm never satisfied. I just want him to be a little more aggressive when it comes to his career. He should have tenure by now."

"I understand," Jessie Belle murmured. "Traynor is the same way. He's not a go-getter. We wouldn't have any of this if I didn't just take charge every now and then."

"I'm tired of this," Mary Ellen complained. "I've been thinking a lot about my life and I've decided that it's time I make some changes."

Jessie Belle broke into a grin. "I'm so glad to hear this. Wow. This is perfect timing, too."

Confused, Mary Ellen asked, "Why? What's going on?"

"Mary Ellen, Traynor and I have a proposition for you."

"What is it?" She reached for her orange juice and took a sip.

"How would you like to be the radio-station manager?"

Mary Ellen put down her glass and eyed Jessie Belle. "Really?"

Jessie Belle nodded. "Of course. You'd be responsible for the day-to-day operation of the station, including managing the various departments, scheduling on- and off-air staff. You'd be dealing with promotions and any other advertising issues. You'd also be the liaison between us and the employees. Mary Ellen, I just know you're perfect for the job, but more than that—I trust you. How does thirty thousand to start sound?"

Mary Ellen beamed. "It sounds great! Wow!"

"How do you think Richard's going to feel about it?" Jessie Belle inquired.

"I really don't care," she responded. "He's held me back long enough. My husband can come with me or he can stay in Atlanta. I'm taking the job."

"What job?" Richard asked, walking into the kitchen.

Jessie Belle glanced up at Traynor, who said, "You told her already?"

She nodded. "Did you want me to wait for you?"

He laughed. "No, I'm actually surprised you waited this long."

The men joined them at the table.

"Somebody want to tell me what's going on?" Richard asked.

"You know about the radio station, right?" Traynor inquired. Without waiting on a response, he pushed ahead. "Well, we'd like for Mary Ellen to be the station manager."

Richard glanced from Traynor to Jessie Belle. "Seriously?"

"She's more than qualified," Jessie Belle contributed.

"What do you think, honey?" Mary Ellen wanted to know. "It's a great opportunity. Thirty thousand dollars a year."

Richard didn't look as happy about the offer, Jessie Belle noted.

He's jealous.

Traynor poured himself a glass of juice. "I guess you're going to have to start sending out your résumé to the colleges in this area, Richard."

The room was suddenly filled with tense silence.

"Let's eat," Jessie Belle suggested. "Cold eggs don't taste that great."

After breakfast, Mary Ellen and Richard went outside to talk.

"I don't think Richard's happy about the job offer," Traynor said to Jessie Belle. "Sweetheart, don't be disappointed if Mary Ellen turns us down."

"She won't. She wants the job and I think it's pretty selfish of Richard to not be happy for her."

"I don't want this to cause problems in their marriage."

"Honey, it's a job opportunity. Mary Ellen will be making more money—at least five thousand dollars more. Richard should be happy."

"It's for them to decide as a couple," Traynor advised. "We have to stay out of it."

"I would never interfere in somebody else's marriage. I wouldn't like if someone did that to me."

Traynor met her gaze. "I mean it, Jessie Belle. Don't get involved."

When he left the room, she whispered, "Is he kidding? Mary Ellen is the only person I'd trust the station with—I need her to take the job."

Mary Ellen and Richard returned.

Jessie Belle couldn't wait to get her alone.

"What did he say?"

"He thinks that I shouldn't take the job because we're friends. Richard feels like it could cause some problems down the line."

"Like what?" Jessie Belle wanted to know.

Mary Ellen shrugged. "I think he's just trying to find something wrong."

"It probably bothers him that you're going to be making more money than he is, but don't let that bother you, Mary Ellen—you deserve it."

Jessie Belle's friend started to pace the floor. "I can't believe Richard wouldn't be happy for me. If our roles were reversed, I'd be happy for him."

"Mary Ellen, you're a grown woman and you have your own dreams. Why not make them come true?" Jessie Belle asked. "You're in charge of your own destiny."

"I've been so supportive of him. Why can't he support me just this one time?"

Jessie Belle shook her head. "I don't know. It's not fair to you and I don't like seeing you so unhappy."

Their conversation came to a sudden halt when Traynor entered the room.

"So what are we doing today?" he asked.

"I was thinking about a day trip to the beach," Jessie Belle responded. "It's a beautiful day."

Mary Ellen agreed.

Jessie Belle excused herself when she spied Richard walking into the library.

She followed him and listened at the door while he made a quick phone call.

Richard nearly choked when Jessie Belle entered the room. He stuttered through his weak goodbye and got off the phone.

Her arms folded across her chest, Jessie Belle said, "I'm so surprised at you, Richard. When you're cheating on your wife—you should be a little more discreet."

"What are you talking about?"

"I just heard you talking to Amelia. That is her name, right? And if I remember correctly, that's the name of the financial aid manager at the school. Does Mary Ellen know you're sleeping with her?"

"You misunderstood the conversation. I'm not hav—"

Jessie Belle held up her hand. "I'm not stupid, Richard. I heard everything. You're planning to see her tomorrow night after you get home. You told her about Mary Ellen's job offer. . . . I also heard you say how excited you are about the *baby.*"

The color in Richard's face drained.

"A baby, Richard? You wouldn't let Mary Ellen have children with you, but you go and get your mistress pregnant. You're disgusting!"

"I don't want to hurt my wife."

"Too late," Jessie Belle uttered.

"What are you going to do now?" he asked.

"I'm not doing a thing. I think you should be honest with Mary Ellen. She deserves to know the truth. Richard, you don't have to worry about her. She has the job she's always wanted and she'll be here in Raleigh."

"I love my wife and I don't want to lose her. I'm trying to figure out a way to work all this out. I just need time."

Jessie Belle shook her head. "If you loved Mary Ellen, then you wouldn't have done all this to her. Let her go, Richard."

"Didn't you hear me? I don't want to lose my wife."

"Mary Ellen deserves to be happy. She can be happy here in Raleigh. She doesn't need to stay in Atlanta to have Amelia and your child thrown in her face at every turn."

"I can't just turn my back on my child, Jessie Belle. I messed up big-time. I know it. But I just need some time. Mary Ellen and I can work through this."

"You want both of them. . . . Richard, that's not the way it works. You can't have Mary Ellen and Amelia."

"Why not? It's not like it's your decision."

"Shall we go find out?" Jessie Belle headed to the door. "I'll go get Mary Ellen."

Richard jumped up. "No."

"Convince Mary Ellen that you're happy for her and that you want her to take the job, Richard. She can work up here in Raleigh while you remain in Atlanta. This way, you can have the best of both worlds. She'll never have to know about Amelia and your child."

"I used to think you and Traynor were good for each other, but now I see that I was wrong. Does your husband know that he has a snake in his Garden of Eden?"

CHAPTER TWENTY-THREE

"I guess with Mary Ellen moving up here in a couple of weeks, you're gonna be a happy woman," Traynor stated. "I know how much you miss having your best friend nearby."

Jessie Belle broke into a grin. "I'm glad she took the job. I trust Mary Ellen with my life. I can't say that about a lot of other people."

"She's good people. I hope that Richard will be able to find something at one of the colleges here. Being apart can cause problems in a marriage."

"They'll be fine," Jessie Belle replied. "Richard's just as excited as Mary Ellen is now. He loves her and he really wants her to be happy."

"I'm so glad they were able to come together on this. I didn't want it putting a strain on their marriage."

It won't. Richard's happy because he can have both women in his life. Mary Ellen's planning to drive down every other weekend and he'll come up the other times.

"What are you smiling about?" Traynor inquired.

"Just thinking how nice it's going to be with Mary Ellen here in Raleigh. We're going to have a blast." Jessie Belle gave Traynor a sidelong glance. "You sure you don't mind her staying with us until she finds her own place?"

"It's fine with me," he responded.

"I can hardly wait for her to get here. I really believe she's going to be very happy here. Getting away from Richard is what she needs."

Traynor glanced up. "Why do you say that?"

"I just mean that she and Richard need some space right now. I don't know what he's told you, but their marriage is on shaky ground. Don't get me wrong, Richard feels the same way she does—they think being apart is best right now. They haven't given up on their marriage, Traynor. They just want some time away from each other."

"I had a feeling something was going on between them," Traynor stated. "I don't know. . . . Maybe Mary Ellen should reconsider relocating."

"No, she shouldn't," Jessie Belle quickly interjected. "She's doing the right thing by coming to North Carolina."

"How can you be so sure?"

"I can feel it."

She could tell Traynor wasn't convinced, so Jessie Belle changed the conversation to a more neutral subject.

"Gladys Dunbar asked me to give her daughter piano lessons," she announced. "I'm thinking about doing it."

He smiled. "That's great. As much as you love playing the piano, why is it you never wanted to buy a new one?"

"I'd like to get one," she confessed. "A black baby grand. It's just not a priority for me right now. We have the one Mama gave us—it's fine for now."

Since Traynor was staying home today to take care of overdue home maintenance, he offered to watch Holt so that Jessie Belle could have some time for herself.

Jessie Belle left the house an hour later to meet Sara for lunch.

"It's so good to see you," she said when they met at the restaurant. "I'm sorry I wasn't at the last luncheon. We've been so busy with Traynor traveling and my volunteering at the preschool."

"I understand," Sara murmured with a smile. "Life happens."

Jessie Belle eyed Sara. She couldn't put a finger on it, but something just didn't seem right with her. "How have you been?"

Sara's smile disappeared. "I've been diagnosed with breast cancer, Jessie Belle."

"Oh my goodness . . ."

"Jessie Belle, I know what the doctors have told me, but as you know, God is the ultimate healer. I am going to believe His report."

She admired Sara's courage and told her so.

They talked about shopping, children and their husbands while they enjoyed their meals.

After lunch, they promised to keep in close contact.

"Jessie Belle, don't forget to do monthly breast exams," Sara advised. "Maybe if I'd done mine . . . who knows. . . ?"

She gave Sara a hug. "You call me if you need anything. Prayer, a shoulder—anything."

"Sara Hamilton has breast cancer," Jessie Belle told Traynor as soon as she walked into their house. "I can't believe it."

"Did they catch it in time?"

"She didn't say exactly, but I don't think so. Sara just seemed kind of resigned to whatever." Jessie Belle put a hand to her face, wiping away a tear. "I can't believe it. Life is too short."

Traynor agreed.

"That's why we have to make the most of whatever time we have on this earth. I don't plan on wasting a moment of it, Traynor. I'm getting everything I can before I die."

"Jessie Belle . . ."

She held up her hand to stop him. "No, Traynor. I mean it. I'm going after everything I want in life. When it's my time to die—I don't plan on having any regrets."

Traynor woke up ten minutes before the alarm went off.

He climbed out of bed and padded barefoot into the sitting room. Every morning he went there to spend some quiet time with the Lord before Jessie Belle and Holt got up.

Traynor wanted nothing more than to just preach the Gospel. Nothing else really mattered to him outside of his relationship with God, his family and his ministry. He was pretty content with his life.

He wished Jessie Belle could share in that contentment. It was his greatest desire.

Traynor was concerned about her reaction to Sara's bout with cancer. It seemed that Jessie Belle was determined more than ever to achieve her dreams that he become the superstar pastor. That wasn't his dream, but she didn't seem to understand that.

When Jessie Belle woke up an hour later, he was doing his Bible study. They were cordial, but Traynor felt like something had changed in their relationship.

He felt alone.

Before now, Traynor couldn't put a name to it. But the truth was that he and Jessie Belle were growing apart.

Over breakfast he tried to talk to his wife about their marriage. "Sweetheart, are you happy?" Traynor wanted to know.

Jessie Belle sipped her hot tea. "Of course I am. Why wouldn't I be?"

"I'm referring to our marriage."

She set down the cup and said, "So was I, Traynor."

"I feel like we've grown apart over the past few months."

She gazed at him. "I don't agree. Unless there's something you need to tell me. I take it you're not happy."

Jessie Belle was acting defensive. When she was like that, it was hard to talk to her, so he shut down.

"I don't think we can do this now," Traynor stated. "I need to get dressed, but let's talk tonight."

"You start this conversation and now you want to just walk out," Jessie Belle stated. "What's going on, Traynor?"

"There's nothing going on," he responded.

"Then why would you ask me if I'm happy?"

"I wanted to know," Traynor stated. "I need to get ready for work, Jessie Belle. We can finish this tonight."

"Whatever . . ."

Traynor went to work, his thoughts on his six-year-old marriage.

As soon as he walked into his office, fifteen minutes later, Traynor's thoughts shifted to his church administrative duties.

Traynor's attention was torn away from the sermon he was writing when his secretary knocked on the door. He glanced up and gestured for her to enter.

"I'm going out to get something to eat. Would you like me to pick up some food for you?"

He glanced up at the clock on the wall. It was half past noon. "Are you going by the deli?"

She smiled and nodded. "Their special today is the Reuben and a bowl of soup—I believe it's the broccoli and cheese."

Traynor broke into a grin. "I'll take the special." Serena knew that he loved Sanford Deli's Reuben sandwich and the broccoli and cheese soup.

Their eyes met and held.

Confused, Traynor dropped his eyes.

Lately, he'd been experiencing conflicting feelings for his secretary. Although he tried to dismiss it, Traynor had a strong suspicion that she felt the same way. He kept telling himself that he was happy in his marriage.

Wasn't he?

Truth be told, Traynor couldn't deny that if it weren't for Holt, his marriage probably would've ended a long time ago. He loved Jessie Belle, but there were times when he felt they had two different agendas.

An image of Serena formed in his mind. She paled in contrast to his wife, but he felt like he had a lot more in common with Serena.

Serena actually listened to him when he talked and she seemed to value his opinion. Once Jessie Belle made up her mind to do something—there was no stopping her.

Despite her faults, Jessie Belle is my wife.

Yet he had feelings for Serena.

Traynor tried to shake the thoughts of his secretary from his mind. He had no right to Serena.

She returned with the food.

They settled themselves in the conference room down the hall.

Traynor found himself enjoying his conversation with Serena more than he should. He bit into his sandwich.

"Pastor, is something troubling you?"

Swallowing, Traynor shook his head. "No. Everything's fine."

She smiled.

"I noticed that you're reading James Patterson's book *The Thomas Berryman Number*. How is it?" he asked.

"It's wonderful. It's been out for a few years, but I love his books. I'd never read it before."

"I'm a big fan of his work, too."

They finished their lunch.

Serena rose to her feet. "It's almost time for your appointment with Pastor Danforth. Do you want me to just send him in?"

"That'll be fine."

"The phone's ringing," she said. "I'd better go do my job."

"Thanks for lunch, Serena."

She turned and nearly ran into Jessie Belle, who was standing in the doorway.

"Mrs. D-Deveraux, I didn't see you s-standing there," Serena stammered. "I didn't mean to walk right into you like that."

Jessie Belle smiled and said, "It's okay, Serena. No harm done."

Serena left the conference room.

"I came by to see if you wanted to have lunch, but I guess you've already eaten."

Traynor felt a thread of guilt slide down his spine. "Serena was going out and she offered to pick up something for me."

"How sweet."

"It was just lunch," Traynor responded. "She picks food up for me from time to time."

"You don't have to be so defensive, Traynor. I guess I'll be seeing you at home, then," Jessie Belle responded. "You *will* be joining us for dinner, right?"

"Jessie Belle, don't start acting like a jealous wife. There's no need— Serena is my secretary."

"I'm not worried about her. I've never been an insecure woman, Traynor. I'm simply asking if you plan on eating dinner with me and your son."

Traynor hated when she talked to him this way. "I'll be home in time for dinner," he stated.

Jessie Belle eyed him for a moment before saying, "I'll let you get back to work. We'll talk when you get home."

Traynor gave a slight nod.

Although Jessie Belle denied it, she was jealous, but he didn't want her taking it out on Serena.

Jessie Belle was fit to be tied.

That little wench was after her husband. She wasn't a fool. Jessie Belle could see as clear as day that Serena had the hots for Traynor. What bothered her more was Traynor's attraction to his secretary.

It's not gonna happen, she vowed. *There's no way I'm gonna let that little plain Jane take Traynor from me. I'll see her dead before I let that happen.*

Jessie Belle climbed into her Mercedes and drove home.

She found Mary Ellen and Holt playing in the yard when she pulled up.

"What's wrong, Jessie Belle?"

"I think Traynor's thinking about having an affair."

Mary Ellen was shocked. "Thinking about having an affair . . . Jessie Belle, where in the world did you get that from?"

"I just caught him having lunch with his secretary."

"I don't think that's so unusual," Mary Ellen stated. "Richard and his assistant are always having lunch together. They work together. Sometimes they eat dinner together if they're working late."

Jessie Belle bit her bottom lip to keep from blurting out that Richard and his assistant were having a baby together.

"Honey, I really don't think you have anything to worry about," Mary Ellen said, trying to reassure her. "Traynor adores you."

There was a time when Jessie Belle would've agreed with Mary Ellen, but her relationship with Traynor had been pretty strained lately. Had been since she purchased the radio station without talking to him first.

"I saw the way they looked at each other. Traynor's attracted to her. I'm sure of it."

"Are you going to talk to him about it?"

"I don't know yet," Jessie Belle answered. "Mary Ellen, I don't know what I'm going to do right now. I have to do some thinking on it."

"Well, I think you're wrong about this. Look, I kinda noticed that things are a little off with you and Traynor. That's why I'm taking Holt to dinner and a movie tonight and I'm moving out this weekend."

"Mary Ellen, this doesn't have anything to do with you."

"I didn't think it did," she responded. "But I'm sure my being here isn't exactly helping either. It's time for me to get my own place anyway. Richard should be hearing something soon from one of the colleges up here. Hopefully, he'll be up here permanently in a couple of months."

Jessie Belle wanted to tell her friend that Richard had no intention of leaving Atlanta, but she didn't have the heart to do so.

"Traynor's not going to cheat on you. You do know that, right?"

"I'm not gonna let him cheat on me, Mary Ellen. I won't give up my marriage without a fight."

Jessie Belle took Holt inside the house for a nap.

Mary Ellen grabbed her purse. "I need to run some errands. I'll be back in a couple of hours."

"We'll be here," Jessie Belle murmured.

Holt was dressed and ready for his evening with his godmother when Mary Ellen returned.

"You look so cute," she told him. "Just give me a few minutes to shower and change and we'll be on our way."

Jessie Belle laughed. "He's so excited."

Grinning, Mary Ellen responded, "So am I. An evening out with my godson. What can be more exciting?"

Jessie Belle ran out and picked up a couple of lobsters, shrimp and scallops. She prepared each item with love, wanting to make the evening special for Traynor. He'd pretty much told her that they weren't as close as they used to be. She hadn't paid much attention to him until finding him and Serena being all friendly.

After dinner was prepared, Jessie Belle went upstairs to find something to wear.

Traynor arrived home promptly at six.

He did a double take when he laid eyes on Jessie Belle, dressed in a see-through negligee. "Where's Mary Ellen?"

"She took Holt to dinner and a movie." Jessie Belle strolled over to him. "I thought we could take this evening to get reacquainted again. Things have been crazy between us for months now. I miss the way we used to be, Traynor."

"Jessie Belle . . . we need to talk. Sex isn't always the answer."

"What's going on with you, Traynor?"

"Nothing. I just can't keep doing this over and over again. Jessie Belle, I'm tired."

"Tired of what? Me?"

"There you go again," he stated. "You don't listen to me."

"That's not true. I do listen to you. I know what's going on. You're still upset with me for buying the radio station. Why, I don't know. It's making us a lot of money. I could see if I did something to hurt you."

"Jessie Belle, you have gone behind my back too many times—I feel like I can't trust you."

"So this is about the Mercedes and the radio station."

"This is about the way you lied to my aunt," Traynor blurted. "You told her that I want my mother's jewelry. Why would you do that?"

"I never did any such thing," Jessie Belle lied.

"Aunt Eleanor wouldn't lie about that. I know you did it—I've known for a while, but I just didn't think it was something to dwell on. But now I see that it's the way you operate and I have to be honest with you, Jessie Belle. I don't care for it."

"Your aunt doesn't like me, Traynor, and you know it. She'd say anything to break us up."

"She's never once tried to break us up, Jessie Belle."

"We're never gonna agree on this," she murmured. "Traynor, I'm sorry for buying a car without your permission. I'm sorry for buying the radio station without your permission. I'm sorry for anything else I've ever done wrong in life."

"Jessie Belle . . ."

"No, Traynor. I'm sorry. I'm sorry for everything."

"I don't want your apologies, Jessie Belle. I want to be your partner. I want to be your husband. I am the head of this household and I want you to treat me as such."

"Is that it? I don't make you feel like a man?"

"I've had enough of this conversation," Traynor uttered.

"Honey, wait. . . ." Jessie Belle walked over to him and put her arms around his waist. "I'm sorry. I love you and I want us to get past whatever this is. If you need me to listen—I'm here."

He looked skeptical.

"I'm serious. I want to hear whatever you need to say to me."

They sat down in the living room.

"Jessie Belle, I love you more than my own life, but there are times I feel like I just don't know you."

He waited for her to respond, but she didn't.

"I really don't like the way you went behind my back with the jewelry, the car and the station. Jessie Belle, it's important to have trust in a marriage. I want to be able to trust my wife. If a marriage has no trust—what else is left?"

"I'm listening," was all she said.

"I want the woman I married, Jessie Belle. I want her back."

"Am I that bad?"

He shook his head no. "That's not what I'm saying. When I say that, I'm just talking about the girl that was up-front and honest. I don't like scheming, Jessie Belle, and I just want to make sure it's over."

"It's over, Traynor. I was wrong and I've apologized. I hope that after tonight we can just move on."

Traynor reached over and took her hand. "We can."

Jessie Belle gave him a sexy grin. "I've missed you. I was thinking we could skip dinner and go straight to dessert, if you catch my meaning."

"I'm right behind you."

CHAPTER TWENTY-FOUR

Traynor had to be in Wilson, North Carolina, the next day for a conference. He was the keynote speaker and wouldn't be home until after six p.m.

Jessie Belle decided that while he was away, this was the perfect time to confront his secretary. Serena was in her office talking on the telephone when she arrived.

She waved at Jessie Belle.

Taking a seat, Jessie Belle waited patiently for Serena to finish her call. There was no way this little snit of a girl was taking Traynor from her.

As soon as the secretary hung up, Jessie Belle went straight to the point. "I want you to leave my husband alone."

Serena gasped in surprise. "Mrs. Deveraux, I have no idea what you're talking about. I'm just the pastor's secretary."

Jessie Belle wasn't about to fall for her little innocent act. "Serena, I'm not stupid. I can look at you and tell that you want my husband, but you're not going to get him. Traynor Deveraux will never divorce me."

"He's a good man—a man of God," Serena uttered. "How can you treat him like this? He's not done a thing for you to not trust him."

"I'm not worried about Traynor—it's *you* that I don't trust. I know women like you. And for your information, Serena, I don't need you to tell me how wonderful my husband is. You just remember that he's a happily married man." Jessie Belle reached into her purse. "As a matter of fact, I think you should consider looking for another job."

"Excuse me?"

"I don't want you working with Traynor." Jessie Belle tossed an envelope containing cash on Serena's desk. "Here's some money—consider it your severance pay. Give your notice to my husband, effective immediately."

"I don't believe you. You're actually trying to pay me off? What kind of woman are you?"

Serena pushed the envelope back toward Jessie Belle. "Mrs. Deveraux, I don't want your money and I'm not leaving my job unless Pastor fires me. What I will do is pray for you and for Pastor Deveraux, because he doesn't deserve this foolishness. I can't believe I used to look up to you as a role model. I see now that I don't want to be anything like you."

Jessie Belle took a step closer, but the secretary didn't flinch. "You have no idea who you're messing with, Serena."

"Neither do you," she responded. "You don't scare me, Mrs. Deveraux. I've got the Lord on my side."

"You think so?" Jessie Belle chuckled. "We'll just see about this."

"I want you to know I'm gonna tell Pastor about this conversation."

"And if you do—it'll be the last thing you ever do in life," Jessie Belle warned. *"I mean it."*

Serena gasped. "I can't believe you just threatened me."

"It wasn't a threat, little girl. *It was a promise.*" Jessie Belle headed to the door but paused long enough to add, "Just remember what I said, Serena."

During the drive home, Traynor had a long conversation with God.

"What am I going to do with Jessie Belle?" he asked. "I do love her, but she infuriates me when she goes behind my back like that. We had a long talk last night and I believe that she's sincere."

He was met with dead silence.

"But even with all that, I'm not happy, Lord. I'm not happy with Jessie Belle. I just can't shake the feeling that I can't trust my wife."

More silence.

"I need Your help, Lord. Show me what to do to keep my marriage intact. I'm beginning to have feelings for another woman and I know it's wrong. I don't want to feel this way about Serena. Please help me."

Traynor revisited his earlier telephone conversation with Serena. She hadn't sounded like herself. He'd inquired if something was wrong, but she reassured him that she was fine.

He didn't believe her. She definitely sounded as if she was upset about something.

Traynor stopped at a pay phone and called Serena at the office because he wanted to check on her.

"Serena, when I spoke to you earlier—you didn't sound like yourself. I hope you know that you can talk to me about anything. If you're uncomfortable with me, then give Jessie Belle a call. I know she——"

She cut him off. "No . . . I'm fine, Pastor. Really, I am."

"I'm on my way to the house," Traynor told her. "I'll see you on Monday."

"Have a good weekend, Pastor."

"You too, Serena."

He ended the call.

There was something definitely wrong with Serena, but if she didn't want to confide in him, there was nothing he could do about it.

Jessie Belle wasn't perfect.

All her good qualities outweighed the negative—he couldn't deny that.

Maybe I'm being too hard on her and I haven't let go of the past. This is my issue. Not hers.

Traynor prayed for forgiveness and vowed to do better by Jessie Belle. She wasn't perfect and neither was he. He needed to remember that. She was worth her weight in gold, as his father used to say about Traynor's mother.

For the first time in a long time, he was actually looking forward to seeing his wife and spending time with her.

In the corner restaurant off Highway 98, seated in a booth near the kitchen, Jessie Belle paid off the two men.

"Did anybody see you leave her place?" she asked.

"No, lady," one answered. "We were real careful."

She smiled. "Thanks so much for your help."

"You need us to do anything else?" the one wearing the blue bandanna asked.

Jessie Belle shook her head. "Remember, you've never seen me before. *Ever.*"

"Got it," they said in unison.

Rising to her feet, Jessie Belle stated, "It was a pleasure doing business with you."

She left money on the table. "Don't forget to pay the check."

Walking out to her car, Jessie Belle broke into a grin. "That should teach that little troublemaker not to mess with me."

She rushed home, hoping to get there before Traynor did.

"Mary Ellen," Jessie Belle called out as she rushed through the door.

"I'm in the kitchen."

Jessie Belle cut through the dining room to get to the kitchen, where she found Mary Ellen preparing two steaks, baked potatoes and green beans. "We're going to need another steak. My man's on his way home."

"This is for you and Traynor. Holt and I have already eaten. I've given him a bath, and right now he's in his room playing."

"Mary Ellen, you didn't have to do this." Jessie Belle hugged her.

"You and Traynor have been way too good to me, and you two should at least have some quality time together without me underfoot, so I'm going to see a movie."

"Mary Ellen, you're always giving us time alone, and I appreciate it— especially since Traynor's been a little distracted."

"Distracted in what way?"

"You've met Serena—she's after him, and I can tell he's attracted to her, too."

Mary Ellen shook her head. "I don't think so, Jessie Belle. Traynor loves you."

"I know he loves me, but that doesn't make him immune to other women. Anyway, it's all over—I put an end to it already."

Folding her arms across her chest, Mary Ellen studied Jessie Belle. "What did you go and do?"

"I had a talk with Serena."

"Jessie Belle . . ."

"I'm not about to let that little tramp steal my husband. I've invested too much into Traynor."

"This is gonna blow up in your face. You do know that, don't you?"

Jessie Belle shook her head. "It won't, Mary Ellen. I paid a couple of guys to scare the heck out of Serena. Believe me, she won't be saying a word to anybody about our little conversation."

"I can't believe you'd do something like that." Mary Ellen peeked into the oven to check on the steaks.

"It's not like I told them to beat her up. I just told them to scare her, Mary Ellen. I want her to quit working for Traynor."

"Jessie Belle, you're wrong for this. I hope you know it."

"Mary Ellen, you're supposed to be my friend. What am I supposed to do? Just sit back and let her have Traynor?"

"You could've tried discussing this with your huband," she suggested.

Shrugging in nonchalance, Jessie Belle uttered, "Well, it's all done. I can't do anything about it now."

Mary Ellen eyed her for a moment before saying, "I found a place today. The realtor's putting in the offer tomorrow. Hopefully, in a couple of weeks, I'll be in my own place."

"I see. Congratulations."

"I'm happy about it. I've been here way too long."

"What is that supposed to mean?" Jessie Belle snapped.

"Just that it's time for me to get my own place. This has nothing to do with you, Jessie Belle. I need my own space."

"I'm sorry for snapping like that. Mary Ellen, I know what I did to Serena is wrong, but so is trying to steal my husband. I fight for what I want—it's who I am."

"I suppose it can be a good quality, but it's also a bad quality, Jessie Belle."

They finished preparing dinner in silence.

Mary Ellen left the house fifteen minutes before Traynor arrived home.

Jessie Belle greeted him with a hug and a kiss on the cheek. "How did everything go?"

"Fine," Traynor responded. "How was your day?"

Jessie Belle met his gaze and said, "Uneventful."

"Where's Holt?"

"In his room playing. Dinner's ready, and I was just about to fix our plates. Why don't you go up and spend some quality time with your son or just relax for a minute?"

He was watching her.

"Honey, what is it?" Jessie Belle questioned. "Why are you staring at me like that?"

"You are so amazing at times."

"What's this about?" she wanted to know. "You have this strange look on your face."

"I . . . we have not been as close as we used to be," Traynor stated. "There's been a lot of tension between us."

"I've made some bad choices, I know that. I'm sorry."

"I do love you, Jessie Belle, but I have to be honest with you—I'm not sure how much more I can take. I have to be able to trust you."

"Traynor, you can. . . ."

"I mean it, Jessie Belle. There are two people in this marriage and when it comes to major decisions—we need to be on one accord."

She nodded in agreement. "I understand."

Traynor went upstairs while Jessie Belle fixed their meals.

Apparently Serena decided to keep her mouth shut. *Wise girl,* she thought silently. Jessie Belle hoped that Serena would be smart and just quit her job, too. She didn't want the girl anywhere near Traynor. He was in a vulnerable state right now and probably too weak to resist Serena's seduction.

I'll never let her have my husband.

"Did you speak to Serena today?" Traynor asked when he and Holt entered the kitchen.

Jessie Belle turned around, facing him. "Why do you ask?"

"She didn't sound like herself when I spoke to her earlier. I think Serena was upset about something."

Shrugging, Jessie Belle responded, "Maybe she was having a bad day or something. I'm sure if it was anything serious, Serena would've told you about it."

"So you haven't talked to her, then?"

Jessie Belle shook her head. "No. Didn't speak to her today."

She picked up a plate laden with dinner rolls. "Could you put these on the table, please?"

CHAPTER TWENTY-FIVE

Monday morning, Serena marched into Traynor's office shortly after his arrival.

"Good morning, Serena," he greeted brightly. "I didn't see you in church yesterday."

Without a word, she handed him a piece of paper.

Curious, he asked, "What is this?"

Serena took a deep breath and said, "Pastor Deveraux, I'm . . . that's my letter of resignation. I'm leaving town."

Confused, Traynor asked, "When did you decide this?"

"It came about pretty sudden," Serena admitted. "But I prayed about it, and I know it's the right thing for me to do."

"Have I done something?"

Serena shook her head. "Oh no . . . Pastor, I've really enjoyed working for you. I really have—it's just that I've been offered a position with more money and it's in my career field." A lone tear fell from her right eye.

She hastily wiped it away.

"Really?" Traynor asked. "Is this the only reason that you're leaving, Serena? You can be honest with me."

She nodded. "I just came in to clear out my stuff. I appreciate you giving me a job when I really needed one, Pastor. You've been so kind to me, and I thank you for the opportunity. I pray that God will bless you and that . . ." Her voice died. "I'd better get back to my packing. I'm so sorry for leaving you in a lurch like this."

"I understand. Don't worry about it, Serena. I'm sure I'll be able to find someone to fill your position. I thank you for your time and your dedication."

She paused in the doorway. "I just want you to know that you're a good man, Pastor Deveraux." Serena looked like she wanted to say more, but changed her mind.

Traynor wasn't completely convinced that Serena was telling him everything, but he couldn't force it out of her. But something wasn't ringing quite true to him.

I need to stop reading so much into everything.

Traynor raised his eyes heavenward and whispered, "Lord, I guess this is Your way of working it out."

"Serena quit today," Traynor announced during dinner. "She said she received a job offer in her career field and she's moving away. I'm not sure I believe her. I could tell that she was afraid of something. But I can't figure out what's going on with her."

"I'm surprised," Jessie Belle murmured before taking a sip of her iced tea. "I didn't know she was planning to leave town."

Deep down, she was rejoicing that her scare tactic worked. She'd paid off two thugs to break in and vandalize Serena's apartment. Jessie Belle then called to let Serena know that that was just the beginning. Things would only get worse if she kept working for Traynor.

His words cut into her thoughts.

"Something happened," Traynor was saying. "She wouldn't tell me what, but I know that something happened to make her up and leave like that."

"Honey, don't fret over it. I'm sure we'll be able to find you another secretary. Perhaps Sister Blanche Stevens. I heard she's been looking for something part-time. She's pretty decent on the typewriter and she loves to talk, so I'm sure she'll be great on the phones."

"She's also about sixty years old."

"Is that a problem?" Jessie Belle wanted to know. "Are you more interested in young secretaries?"

Traynor chuckled. "Sweetheart, that's not it at all."

Folding her arms across her chest, she stated, "You should hire someone who will do the best job—not base it on age."

"Jessie Belle, you know me better than that. At least you should."

"I thought I did," she countered. "Until you made that stupid remark."

Traynor's eyes traveled to her face. "What's wrong, Jessie Belle? Are you jealous?"

She laughed. "Goodness, no. *Why in the world would I be jealous?*"

"There are women out there who might find me attractive."

"Honey, I know that, but they also know that you're mine. No one is gonna take my man away from me." Jessie Belle added, "Not and live to tell about it."

"But you're not jealous."

She shook her head. "No, I'm not."

Laughing, Traynor embraced her. "You are jealous, but I love it."

Jessie Belle met his gaze. "Really?"

He nodded.

She threw her arms around his neck. "I've missed you so much, Traynor. Things have been a little crazy between us, but I feel like we're finally getting back in line."

"We are," Traynor confirmed. "I really believe that we're finally on the same page. I want our marriage to work."

"Have you forgiven me, then, for buying the radio station without consulting you first?"

"Yes. In fact, I think it was a good decision. You were right yet again—the station is a wise investment."

Jessie Belle kissed him. "Thank you for saying that. I'm so glad you feel this way."

After putting Holt to bed, they spent the rest of the evening in their bedroom.

"Traynor, what are you going to do about a secretary?" Jessie Belle questioned as she undressed.

He gave a slight shrug. "I don't know. All I can do is post the opening in the bulletin."

"I can fill in until you find a replacement," Jessie Belle offered, climbing into bed. "Holt can go to the church with me or we can have the sitter watch him."

Removing his shirt, Traynor surveyed her face. "You sure you want to do that?"

Jessie Belle settled back against a stack of pillows and pulled the sheets up to cover her naked body. "It's only temporary, right? I can help you out."

"If you don't mind," Traynor responded, "it's fine with me."

"I think it's unfair the way Serena just up and left like that. She could've given a two-week notice or something."

"I guess they must have needed her to start work immediately."

"I still think it's pretty selfish."

Traynor reached for her. "Sweetheart, I don't want to talk about Serena or the church anymore tonight. I just want to concentrate on us."

Snuggling against her husband, Jessie Belle murmured, "I love the way you think, Traynor."

Sara's cancer was getting progressively worse, so Rutherford decided against running for president of the Eastern Christian Convention.

As she walked past Traynor's office, Jessie Belle could hear her husband and Paul Chambers, one of the deacons, discussing who should run in his place. She paused outside the door to listen.

"You should throw your hat in the ring for president," the man was saying.

She remained outside the door, listening.

"What about John Winters?" Traynor questioned. "I'd heard that he was thinking about running."

"You're the better man for the job, Pastor. You and Rutherford have some of the same thinking. He was the one who told me to ask you about running."

"I have to be honest, Paul. I don't believe in collecting campaign donations and flying across the country soliciting votes. I don't go for all that."

"Rutherford was critical of some of the methods candidates used, too. He always said that if you want the kind of leadership you have in the convention, then you need to change the method by which they are selected. That's what led to Sam McCall's downfall, you know. He got greedy."

Jessie Belle decided to make her presence known.

"Honey . . . oh, am I interrupting something?" she asked.

"I was just in here trying to convince your husband to run for president of the ECC," Paul responded.

"Honey, I think you should," Jessie Belle stated. "Papa is a past president, but that was a long time ago and before it became what it is now. Sam McCall and everything he did. Terrible scandal." She smiled. "I'd like to see it get back to the way it used to be, but with a few changes."

"Like what?" Paul inquired.

"Well, I'd like to see the convention promote women's rights within the church and the creation of an official Baptist doctrine for member churches."

"If I decide to run—and I'm not saying I am," Traynor stated. "But if I do, my reason for doing so is to restore God and accountability to the convention, contending that the potential of the convention to serve God has been overlooked by presidents hoping to make money off the membership rolls. I personally believe that any candidate should remember that power is best used when shared. If the convention elects a king wannabe and not a team player as its president, it will continue to lose members and credibility."

Paul broke into a grin. "Pastor Deveraux, I'm convinced. You should be running for president. I hope you'll seriously consider it."

"I'll get back to you in a few days with my answer," Traynor promised.

Traynor and Jessie Belle went into the conference room to have lunch. She pulled out paper plates, napkins, cold chicken, potato salad and rolls.

"There are some forks over in that drawer," Traynor stated.

He said the blessing over their meal.

Jessie Belle loaded Traynor's plate with chicken, potato salad and two rolls. "I really think you should do this, honey."

Traynor glanced over at his wife. "You do?"

She nodded. "They need someone like you after Sam."

"To be honest, Jessie Belle, I really think the convention is just on the wrong road. I'd prefer that the election be postponed until a mission plan is developed."

"You know they're not going to do that. They're not going to leave ECC without a president."

"I know. I think the organization needs to heal and turn our attention back to God."

"Put that in your campaign speech," Jessie Belle said with a smile. "The members will love it."

"I'm serious, Jessie Belle."

"I know that," she responded. "So am I."

Traynor met with Rutherford Hamilton the next day.

Jessie Belle tried to get him to open up about their meeting. "Well, what did you two talk about?"

"I think you already have an idea," he replied.

"Are you planning to run for ECC president or not?"

"Jessie Belle as soon as I know—I'll tell you. Sweetheart, relax. You'll be the first to know."

Two days later, Traynor rendered his decision.

"I'm going to run," he told her on the way to church. "I prayed about it and the Lord placed it on my spirit that ECC needs a leadership that is willing to submit to the authority of God. I'm not going to use this office to sell the Eastern Christian Convention to corporations, politicians or outside groups for personal enrichment or money or power."

"You're doing the right thing, Traynor."

"So you're really okay with this? With me running?"

Jessie Belle reached over and took Traynor's hand in hers. "Honey, I'm positive. I have this wonderful feeling that you're going to win."

He chuckled. "Here you go again . . . being my cheerleader."

"I have faith in you, Traynor. Don't you know that by now?"

CHAPTER TWENTY-SIX

The next day, Jessie Belle called her private detective, the same one she'd used in her dealings with Elton Newman.

They met at their usual place, Brown's Restaurant on Six Forks Road. She'd arrived ten minutes early only to find that he was already seated and waiting for her.

"I need information on the people listed here," she told him.

Jessie Belle wanted to find any dirt that she could use against the other candidates to increase Traynor's chances to win. "And make sure the trail doesn't lead back to me."

"The last person I investigated ended up dead," he uttered.

"I didn't have anything to do with that," Jessie Belle responded. "His death was drug related. It was unfortunate."

He eyed her a moment before uttering, "I'll let you know when I have something."

He left Jessie Belle to eat breakfast alone.

Afterward, she headed to the church to play secretary for Traynor. Jessie Belle was tired of the job but so far had found fault with everyone who'd applied for the position.

She didn't want another young girl working for her husband. They were nothing but trouble as far as she was concerned. Traynor was on the telephone when Jessie Belle arrived.

She waved at him and then strolled over to the receptionist desk and took a seat.

Traynor came out a few minutes later.

"How did your doctor's appointment go?" he inquired.

"Fine. It was just a routine visit, honey."

The telephone rang, interrupting their conversation.

Jessie Belle answered on the third ring. "New Salem Baptist Church . . . how can I help you?"

Traynor waited around to see if the call was for him. When it wasn't, he went back to his office, but not without blowing Jessie Belle a kiss.

When the clock struck one p.m., Traynor and Jessie Belle sat down to have lunch together.

"Have you received any more inquiries about the position?" he asked her.

Jessie Belle took a sip of her soda. "Tired of me already?" she teased.

Traynor broke into a smile. "No. I enjoy having you nearby."

She bit into her ham and cheese sub. "A couple of résumés came in the mail. One seems pretty interesting—I think you should set up an interview."

He blinked in surprise. "Really?"

Jessie Belle nodded. "If you like her, I think she'd make a great secretary for you, Traynor."

After lunch, she said, "I'm going to leave a couple of hours early today so that I can go by the hospital to check on Sara."

"Okay. Please give her and Rutherford my best."

"I will. I'll be home in time to make dinner."

When Jessie Belle arrived at the hospital shortly after three, she was told that Sara was too weak to have visitors.

She offered a few words of comfort to Rutherford and the children, then drove to Mary Ellen's apartment. "I just left the hospital. Sara's not doing too well. They're not sure she's going to last through the night."

"Oh nooo."

"Rutherford is so beside himself with grief. The poor man."

"Traynor's still going to run?" Mary Ellen inquired. "Everyone at church was saying that he's projected to be the winner now that Rutherford dropped out."

"He says he is," Jessie Belle murmured. "Hey, did you hear about the financial trouble that Pastor Danforth is in? Nobody is going to vote in a president with money troubles. It'll be Sam McCall all over again."

"I certainly wouldn't vote for him," Mary Ellen stated.

They sat down on the sofa.

"How are things between you and Richard?" she inquired. Jessie Belle worried that one day Richard was going to open his big mouth and tell Mary Ellen everything—especially her part in it.

"I don't know, Jessie Belle. Something's not right between us. I can feel it."

"Do you think he's cheating on you?" Jessie Belle asked.

She gave a slight nod. "I think it's Amelia." Mary Ellen's eyes grew bright with unshed tears. "I saw her last weekend when I was home. She was pregnant. She looked ready to drop any moment."

"Did you say anything to Richard?"

Mary Ellen shook her head no. "I'm not sure I really wanted to know. He never wanted kids. That's what he's always told me and then with not having a relationship with his son . . . I believed him."

"He doesn't deserve you. Mary Ellen, you're too good for him."

"Enough about me and my problems," Mary Ellen stated with a tiny smile. "Are you and Traynor set for the leadership conference? It's next week, you know."

Jessie Belle nodded. "Mary Ellen, I really appreciate you taking care of Holt while we're away."

"It's my pleasure. He's my godson. I love spending time with him."

The day before the Regional Leadership Conference arrived.

Jessie Belle hadn't attended the conference in years and was looking forward to going this year as Traynor's wife. She'd bought all new clothes because she wanted to outshine all the other first ladies in attendance. Especially John Winters's wife. Lorraine wasn't a beautiful woman, but she always managed to look like a million bucks.

She didn't care much for Lorraine because Jessie Belle envied her standing in the community and the fact that John Winters was rumored to be building the largest church in Raleigh.

That just meant that she and Traynor would have to build an even bigger church. She would never allow the mealymouthed Lorraine Winters to outdo her. At least they didn't own a radio station.

Jessie Belle spent most of the evening trying on clothes to see exactly what she wanted to take with her to the conference. For the past three months, she'd been on a diet and exercise program to ensure that her clothes complimented her figure.

Early the next morning, Jessie Belle and Traynor sat side by side on the airplane headed to sunny Miami, Florida.

She glanced over at the three women sitting across from her.

Sabrina met her gaze and smiled.

Jessie Belle dropped her head and pretended to be engrossed in the magazine on her lap.

Traynor had no idea that they worked for Jessie Belle and she intended to keep it that way. Sabrina had enlisted the aid of two more girls needing money. One of the girls, Chrissy, didn't sit right with her. Jessie Belle couldn't put her finger on anything in particular, but she just didn't trust the girl.

Jessie Belle had given the new girls money for clothing and makeup. It was time to stop looking like streetwalkers. She wanted them to look like ladies.

The girls had their instructions, but once they got to the hotel, Jessie Belle planned a meeting with them to reiterate the purpose of being at the conference. She wanted to remind them that business came before pleasure.

Her mother had once told Jessie Belle about the women who showed up at conferences peddling their bodies to the holier-than-thou group of men in attendance. Jessie Belle recognized that there was a lot of money to be made during events like the leadership conference and she intended to get her share.

Hopefully, she would get some damaging information on some of the candidates as well. Sabrina already had photographs of the candidates so that the girls would know whom to go after. Jessie Belle had hoped to have more to go on, but her private detective hadn't found anything super incriminating, so it was time to see just how faithful they were to their wives.

They went from the airport straight to the hotel on Key Biscayne. While Traynor was in the bathroom freshening up, Jessie Belle went two floors down to check on her girls.

"I trust the suite is to your liking," she stated when she entered the hotel room.

Sabrina and Karla nodded, but Chrissy just stared her up and down.

Ignoring her, Jessie Belle got down to business. "Remember what I told you? Carry yourself like ladies and don't forget that you're here to work for me."

Jessie Belle made sure they were dressed fashionably but more conservatively than they normally would have so that they blended in with the conference attendees. She didn't want them sticking out like sore thumbs.

"What's wrong with us making a little money of our own?" Chrissy asked.

"You're on my dime, so it's my time." Jessie Belle silently studied the full-busted girl with the long jet-black hair. "We're not gonna have a problem, are we?"

"Naw . . . I was just askin'. That's all."

"I hope I've made myself clear. You four are here to work for me. When you see me—don't acknowledge me in any way. I can't be associated with y'all."

"I guess you think you're too good for us, huh?"

Jessie Belle eyed Chrissy long and hard before saying, "I need to get back to my husband. And do nothing to bring attention to yourselves."

Sabrina walked her to the door. "You don't have to worry about us, Mrs. Deveraux. Everything is under control."

"See that it stays that way, Sabrina. The last thing we need is trouble."

Sabrina was standing at the door to Jessie Belle's hotel suite.

She glanced outside the room before pulling the girl inside. "I told you not to come to my room. We're not supposed to know one another, Sabrina."

"Chrissy just got arrested."

Jessie Belle felt a sense of dread wash over her. "What happened?"

"She wanted to make some extra money on her own, so she decided to pick up a couple of tricks in the hotel bar across the street. One was an undercover police officer. Mrs. Deveraux, I told her the rules. I never thought she'd do something like this."

"No better for her—trying to cheat me." Shrugging in nonchalance, Jessie Belle said, "Well, I certainly hope she made enough to bail herself out."

Sabrina's eyebrows raised in surprise. "You're not gonna help her?"

Jessie Belle shook her head no. "Chrissy's getting picked up for being a hooker has nothing to do with me. She was on her own time. This is her problem, the way I see it."

"Mrs. Deveraux . . ."

"Sabrina, I have nothing to do with her getting arrested. She was on her own time." Jessie Belle steered her toward the door. "Now get out of here before my husband comes back."

"Chrissy said that if you didn't help her—she'd call Pastor Deveraux and tell him what you've been up to."

"You tell her for me that if she wants to keep breathing, she'll forget she ever knew us. I have friends *everywhere*."

"Mrs. Deveraux, I didn't have nothing to do with this. I just want you to know that."

"I believe you. Now leave."

She was furious. *How dare that little snippet of a girl try to cheat me? That's the last time I'll take a recommendation from Sabrina. Her credibility is zero as far as I'm concerned.*

Traynor entered the bedroom.

"Hey," he greeted.

"How did the meeting go?"

"Great," Traynor answered. "So what have you been doing since I've been gone?"

"Just watching television."

Jessie Belle eyed her husband. "Why are you looking at me like that?"

"I'm remembering the first time I saw you. I thought you were an angel."

"And now?"

"I believe you're even lovelier. You are truly a vision to behold, Jessie Belle." Traynor sat down beside her. "I want to get to know you, sweetheart. Really get to know you. You've held back so much from me and I don't quite know why, but it has to stop."

"I don't know what you're talking about, Traynor. You should know me by now. We've been married for seven years."

"I feel so blessed to have you in my life."

"Despite all that I put you through?" Jessie Belle inquired.

"If that was your worst then I can handle it."

Jessie Belle wrapped her arms around him. "Traynor, I feel the same way about you. I'm extremely fortunate to have you in my life. I knew when I met you that we were destined to spend the rest of our lives to-gether. We're a team."

Later that evening, Jessie Belle ran into Chrissy down in the lobby. "I thought you were locked up."

One corner of the girl's mouth twisted upward. "Obviously, you not the only one with friends. Sabrina told me that you looked out for your girls. That sho' ain't true from where I'm standing."

"Keep your voice down."

"Why? You don't want people knowing that you ain't all you supposed to be?"

Jessie Belle tried to walk past her, but Chrissy blocked her path.

"Get out of my way," she uttered. "The last thing you want is to make an enemy of me."

"I came down here to help you out. This is how you show your gratitude?"

"You came down here to help yourself at my expense," Jessie Belle countered. "But you got caught. I wasn't about to assist you in any way."

"You're such a grand lady, huh? At least that's what these people think about you. How do you think they'd feel about you if they knew the truth?"

Jessie Belle didn't flinch. "Are you threatening me?"

"If you don't want people at this conference knowing your dirty little secret, then you need to give me ten thousand dollars and I'll disappear."

"I'm not giving you a penny," Jessie Belle retorted. "You stole from me. Why should I help you?"

"Suit yourself. I'll just have a nice lil' talk with your husband. I think he needs to know the kind of woman he's married to—you look like a high-class lady, but you're not."

Jessie Belle grabbed Chrissy roughly by the arm.

"Ow," she hissed. "You're hurting me."

"Chrissy, you don't even know the meaning of pain yet. I want you to be clear on this. I don't take kindly to threats."

"And neither do I," Chrissy stated, snatching her arm away. "If you want my silence, you'll have to buy it for ten thousand dollars."

"If you'd like to see another day, you'll walk away now. And I promise you it won't be a quick death. I have friends who will erase this life that you're wasting."

Her expression grew hard and resentful, but Chrissy walked away without another word.

Jessie Belle considered the matter settled.

She went back upstairs and sought out Sabrina. "I should have you thrown out of one of these windows," she threatened.

Taking a step backward, Sabrina looked perplexed. "For what? I didn't do anything."

"You brought that greedy whore into my life. Now, Sabrina, you need to fix it."

"What do you want me to do, Jessie Belle?"

"Find a way to shut her up," she ordered. "I mean it."

"I have a cousin here who could use some money," Karla interjected. "He . . . uh, likes to knock around women. He could scare her—you know?"

"I don't care what you do. I just want Chrissy out of my life *now*."

Sabrina nodded. "We'll take care of it, Jessie Belle. I'm sorry, Jessie Belle. I thought she was cool."

"Huh . . . I can't stand that girl," Karla uttered. "She needs to be taken down a peg or two."

Jessie Belle walked toward the door. "I don't want to know anything about it. Just arrange it and do yourselves a favor—leave town on the next available flight. I'll talk to you when I get back to Raleigh."

"Jessie Belle, I'm sorry," Sabrina stated. "I'll make sure she doesn't say anything."

"You'd better," she warned. "That piece of trash is not about to ruin my marriage."

CHAPTER TWENTY-SEVEN

"Did you read about the young woman that was beaten up behind the hotel last night?" Traynor questioned over breakfast.

"Oh my goodness," Jessie Belle uttered. Silently, she wondered if it was Chrissy.

If it was indeed the greedy little tramp, then no better for her. "What is this world coming to? She's alright, isn't she?"

"No. She was beaten pretty badly, from what I read. A couple of broken ribs and a broken leg."

Jessie Belle shook her head sadly. "It's such a shame. Probably a drug deal gone bad."

It was wrong of her to feel this way, but she truly hoped that it was Chrissy. The tramp had made a huge mistake trying to blackmail her. Jessie Belle hoped she now got the message that she was not to be trifled with.

Sabrina and Karla were good employees and never gave her an ounce of trouble. She trusted them. Chrissy, she never once trusted.

"Does it say if she's going to make it?"

"Not really. Just that she was badly beaten. The article talks about the irony that the leadership conference is being held at the same hotel and that she'd been arrested earlier for prostitution. They're speculating that she was beaten up by a john."

"I guess she didn't learn anything after the arrest, huh?" Jessie Belle shook her head sadly. "It's such a shame."

Traynor agreed.

While her husband was facilitating a workshop, Jessie Belle went to check on Sabrina and Karla, but they were gone. She found that they'd checked out shortly after her last conversation with them.

Good.

She called the hospital asking about Chrissy, but couldn't get any information.

Jessie Belle returned to the conference room where Traynor was finishing up. She sat in the back listening to and admiring her husband.

His eyes found her, and Jessie Belle winked.

A smile spread on his face. She was glad that they were on track once more in their marriage.

Jessie Belle intended to keep it that way. That's why it was so necessary to send the girls home and have Chrissy shut up. She didn't need any problems in her marriage.

Things were good between them, but the marriage was still fragile.

Traynor saw a group of his friends gathered in the lobby and made his way over to where they were standing. His footsteps slowed as he heard his name mentioned.

"I hear tell that it's Deveraux's wife that's in charge—she's the one those gals are working for. I heard it from the horse's mouth."

"No kidding? She's a madam?" asked the one named Sampson Taylor. "Man, are you sure about this?"

"If she's got herself a stable of girls working for her—that's for sho' what she is. That gal gon' bust hell wide open. Mark my words."

Traynor couldn't believe his ears. Surely they were talking about someone else—not his wife. Jessie Belle didn't have a stable of girls working for her. He'd know it if she did.

Wouldn't he?

"Who told you this?"

"A girl named Chrissy. She the one who got beat up last night. She approached me yesterday, but I turned her down. I sat down and tried to minister to her, but she just laughed and talked about all of us being hypocrites. She then told me that she worked for Jessie Belle. I heard her as plain as day."

"Does Deveraux know about all this?" Sampson questioned.

"He must—how could he not know?"

Furious, Traynor decided to make his presence known. "I know nothing of the kind because it's all a bunch of lies." He glanced over at Sampson. "I can't believe that you of all people are standing here listening to this mess. You know my wife—has she ever been unkind to you in any way?"

He shook his head no. "Hey, I'm just as shocked as you are, Traynor. But why would that woman lie?"

"I don't know, but I intend on finding out."

Traynor's eyes traveled to James Conway, one of the candidates for president. "Is this how you run your campaign? By trying to make my wife look bad? You're wrong for this."

James Conway stood in his path. "Look, Deveraux, I'm not trying to start any trouble here. I'm so sorry that you're gonna be hurt in all this, but I think it's time you know the truth. Your wife—Traynor, she's nothing but a Jezebel. I'm not talking rumors—I'm speaking what I know. That hooker clear as day say that she work for Jessie Belle Deveraux."

"I don't believe you."

"She's not who you think she is," James stated. "Open your eyes, Traynor. Didn't that girl fly on the same plane as you? She told me she and three other girls came down here with you and your wife."

Curling up his fists, Traynor declared, "I'll not have you talking about my wife like this."

Shrugging, James uttered, "I'm sorry you had to find out this way. I'm real sorry."

"Yeah, right . . . I don't believe that for a minute. You're enjoying this way too much." Traynor was ready to knock the fire out of the man standing in front of him. "If I hear you say anything against my wife . . ."

Sampson put himself between the two men. He reached over and placed a hand on Traynor's shoulder. "C'mon, let's go."

"Lies," Traynor uttered. "It's all lies. My wife a madam. It's crazy."

"I don't mean no harm by saying this, but do you think there's any truth to what they were saying?"

Traynor looked Sampson straight in the face. "Jessie Belle is nothing like that. She would never have a stable of prostitutes working for her."

They walked past the lounge.

Traynor stopped. "I need a drink."

"Not here," Sampson cautioned. "You can't be down here in plain sight drinking." He glanced over his shoulder to see if anyone was nearby. "Come up to my room."

Jessie Belle stopped her pacing back and forth long enough to check the time.

It was five minutes past the last time she looked.

Worried, she whispered, "Traynor, where are you?" She'd expected him back two hours ago.

Maybe his meeting ran later than he expected, she thought to herself. She felt a wave of irritation wash over her. He could've called to let her know. There were phones all over the place in the hotel.

Another ten minutes passed.

By this time, Jessie Belle was really getting worried. She picked up her purse and headed to the door.

Something was wrong. She could feel it deep in the pit of her stomach. She reached for the doorknob.

It turned.

Jessie Belle quickly opened the door. "I've been so worried about you," she stated.

Traynor practically fell into the suite.

Reaching for him, she asked, "Traynor, what's wrong with you?"

Jessie Belle caught a whiff of alcohol. "Have you been drinking? Traynor, what in the world. . . . ?"

She stared at him in disbelief. He was so drunk, he could barely stand on his own two feet. Traynor didn't drink, so what happened?

"Wh-who are you?" he hissed, slurring his words.

"What are you talking about? I'm your wife, silly."

Traynor shook his head. "No . . . naw . . . wh-who are you really? Are you J-Jezebel?"

She didn't know exactly why, but his question offended her. "My name is Jessie Belle."

"Do you know what people are saying about you? They're calling you a Jezebel. They say that you have women working for you. *Prostitutes.*" Traynor shook his head sadly. "Tell me it's not true."

"Honey, you know good and well that you're not a drinker," she admonished while silently trying to figure out how Traynor found out about the girls. Had he spoken to Chrissy?

"I don't know what you're talking about, Traynor. Honey, from now on, you need to stay away from alcohol."

Jessie Belle reached for him. "C'mon, let's get some coffee into you."

He pushed her hands away. "Are you . . . is it true? Are you a madam, Jessie Belle? Do you have girls working for you? I need to know the truth."

"What you need is a good night's sleep," she countered. Jessie Belle needed some time to figure a way out of this mess. "We'll talk about this in the morning, Traynor."

He shook his head no. "I want to t-talk to you n-now."

"Why?" Jessie Belle demanded. "You won't remember the conversation in the morning."

"It's true, isn't it?"

Before she could utter a response, Traynor looked like he was about to throw up. Jessie Belle rushed him to the bathroom, but not before vomit stained his clothes.

She wiped his head tenderly with a cool cloth—the same way he'd done when she was going through morning sickness—while he emptied the contents of his stomach.

When he was done, she helped him stand. "C'mon, I'll help you get out of these clothes."

Traynor pushed away from Jessie Belle. "Leave me alone. Don't y-you . . . don't touch me."

"I'm just trying to help you."

"I don't need your help. Just leave me alone." He staggered toward the bedroom. "Jezebel . . ."

Her back stiffened. "My name is Jessie Belle."

He muttered something she couldn't interpret before he slammed the bedroom door shut.

Jessie Belle began pacing back and forth across the floor, but this time it was because she worried what Traynor would do once he was sober. She prayed he wouldn't remember their conversation when he woke up tomorrow morning.

"I can't lose my husband," she whispered. "I've done all of this for him. Traynor just has to understand that I did it for him."

Jessie Belle peeked into the bedroom an hour later.

Traynor appeared to be sleeping.

She eased inside the room, removing her robe. Jessie Belle watched him for a few minutes before climbing into the bed.

He didn't stir.

Jessie Belle couldn't sleep. Her mind was troubled by the unknown.

After a restless night of tossing and turning, Jessie Belle climbed out of bed fifteen minutes after six. She was seated in the living room deep in thought when Traynor walked out of the bedroom two hours later.

"Good morning, honey," Jessie Belle greeted as brightly as she could manage. "How did you sleep?"

"Morning," he mumbled.

He remembers. I know because he's too angry to even look at me. Jessie Belle chewed nervously on her bottom lip. It wouldn't be so easy to get out of this fix. She wanted to strangle Chrissy for opening her big mouth.

"You really tied one on last night. What got into you?"

"You said we'd talk this morning," Traynor stated. "So talk."

"Do you have to sound so cold?" Jessie Belle questioned. "I've never done anything to hurt you. All I've wanted to do was to be a good wife to you and help you with your ministry."

His eyes traveled to hers. "Meaning what exactly?"

"Meaning that you are the man you are today because of my hard work. I found out things about people to help clear the path. That's all. Don't think they weren't researching your background for skeletons in the closet—I wasn't the only one, Traynor."

His eyes didn't leave her face. "So where do the prostitutes come in?"

Jessie Belle chewed on her bottom lip a moment before responding, "Traynor, it was their choice to commit adultery—I didn't hold a gun to anyone's head. All they had to do was say no, but they didn't."

"Jessie Belle, why?"

"What do you mean, why? Traynor, all I did was protect you so that you could take your rightful position. Those other men—they lied and cheated. These are not the men who should be in leadership. They're all hypocrites. I just didn't want another Sam McCall as president. The organization wouldn't survive and you know it."

"And you think we're not being hypocritical? None of us are without sin, Jessie Belle. *Sin is sin.* You deliberately set out to hurt those men and their ministry. I never wanted any of this."

"But you enjoyed the benefits nonetheless. *Didn't you?* So don't you dare try to act like you're better than me, because you're not."

"I feel like I don't even know you."

Traynor had never looked at her with such disgust and disappointment before and it stung. Jessie Belle fought back tears. She would not allow him to see her cry.

"I did all this for you."

"I didn't ask for any of this, Jessie Belle," he said a second time. "I didn't need this—any of it."

She continued to defend her actions to Traynor. "I didn't do anything that any of those hypocrites wouldn't have done to you. You don't think they were checking into your closet for skeletons—trying to discover your weaknesses?"

"And now you've given them all the ammunition they'll ever need, Jessie Belle. Because of you, I'll have to take myself out of the candidacy."

"No, you don't," she argued. "Traynor, you're still favored to win. Nobody will say anything. I'll make sure of it."

"Don't you get it, Jessie Belle?" His voice rose up an octave. "You've done enough. Just stop."

Traynor walked briskly into the bedroom with Jessie Belle on his heels. She watched as he pulled out a suitcase and laid it open on the bed.

"Where are you going?" Jessie Belle demanded.

"I'm not going anywhere," Traynor stated. *"You are."*

Her mouth dropped open in shock. What did he mean that she was leaving? "Excuse me?"

"Jessie Belle, I think we need some time apart. I'm staying here, but I want you to go home. I just can't be around you right now."

Her eyes filled with tears. "You're sending me away?"

He nodded. "It's for the best."

"I don't agree," she countered. "How do you think it's gonna look to everybody if I suddenly leave?"

"I really don't care," Traynor responded. "I don't want you here, Jessie Belle."

"How can you talk to me this way?"

"After everything you've done—it's through the grace of God that I'm even talking to you at all."

Traynor's words cut her like a knife.

"Tell me something. When you leave here . . . will you be coming home to me and Holt?"

"I don't know," Traynor responded. "I feel as if I don't know you, Jessie Belle. I don't think I can ever trust you again."

Wiping away her tears with her hands, Jessie Belle said, "I'm sorry, Traynor. Please don't do this to me."

"I'm not doing anything to you, Jessie Belle. I just want you out of my sight. Right now I can't stand to even look at you."

He was being so cold and distant toward her. Traynor didn't seem remotely like the man she'd been married to all these years. This man standing in front of her was a complete stranger. Her Traynor would never treat her like this.

"You're angry and you have every right to be, but, Traynor . . . honey, I'll be a better wife to you. I won't mess up again. Just give me another chance. Please."

"A car will be here to pick you up shortly. You don't want to miss your flight."

CHAPTER TWENTY-EIGHT

Traynor watched the shiny black Town Car pull off with Jessie Belle inside. She was on her way to the airport.

He was heartsick.

How could she be so manipulative? Girls . . . blackmail . . . I don't know this woman.

Traynor thought about all the things his father and aunt had told him about the woman he married. While he'd ignored the gossip during his visit to Mayville, they had not. They both tried to dissuade him from marrying Jessie Belle until he spent more time getting to know her. After all, she'd been a virgin when he married her, so Traynor knew for sure that some of the stuff said about her was false.

In the back of his mind, Traynor recalled the words his aunt had whispered in his ear, and shook his head. Jessie Belle couldn't have tricked him into believing that she'd been a virgin. He saw the blood.

His aunt told him about women using tiny packets of blood to conceal the truth of their promiscuity. He didn't want to believe that Jessie Belle had done something like that to him.

She might not be totally innocent, but she wouldn't do anything like that. She had no way of knowing that he would fall in love with her and want to marry her. He didn't doubt she'd been a flirt, but she wasn't as manipulative as all that.

Still, I should've listened to them and taken time to really get to know Jessie Belle.

It was too late now.

Lord, what do I do now? My wife is a madam. She runs a stable of girls. I'm a preacher—a man of God. How could I not know? Am I really that stupid?

Traynor felt the sting of betrayal. "How could You let me marry such a manipulative woman? Why didn't You give me some type of sign, Lord?" He instantly repented his words.

"Satan, get behind me," he uttered. "Forgive me, Heavenly Father. I rushed into a marriage with Jessie Belle. I should've taken time out to really get to know the person I was marrying."

Truth be told, Traynor hadn't taken time to consult the Lord when he proposed to Jessie Belle. Sure, he'd heard some of the rumors about her when he stayed at the rooming house, but he ignored them—he couldn't believe his wife capable of all they were saying.

Sampson stopped by his hotel room to check on him.

"You okay, Traynor?"

"As well as can be. I sent Jessie Belle home. I thought it best under the circumstances."

Sampson agreed.

"Did you talk to her about it?"

"It was a misunderstanding, but I still wanted her to go home," Traynor lied. "Sampson, I'm dropping out of the running for ECC president. I just think it's best."

"You don't have to do that, Traynor. Man, I got your back. James isn't gonna open his mouth about this."

"You didn't blackmail him, did you?" Traynor felt sick to his stomach.

"No, I just think he shouldn't go around making accusations without proof. I had a little talk with that girl Chrissy. She told me herself that she never told him that lie about Jessie Belle. She said she'd testify to that in a court of law."

"Really?" Traynor was surprised. He couldn't help but wonder why the sudden change of heart. Had Jessie Belle threatened her?

A sickening thought occurred to him. Surely his wife hadn't arranged for Chrissy to be beaten up.

In the morning session Traynor tried to focus on what John Winters was saying, but he couldn't. His mind was on his marital troubles and everything Jessie Belle had done during their marriage.

He put a hand to his forehead.

A tension headache was forming.

"You okay?" Sampson whispered.

Traynor nodded. "I think I'm going up to my room and lie down for a while."

Divorcing Jessie Belle was at the forefront of his mind. It was clear that she couldn't be trusted. But before he took steps toward divorce, Traynor had to consider what God would have him do.

Jesus was confronted one day about the question of divorce and re-marriage by the Pharisees and He told them God's original plan never included divorce, but He permitted it on the grounds of adultery.

Jessie Belle had not been unfaithful.

If she had, he didn't know anything about it.

So was divorce wrong in his situation?

It is, unless Jesus lied.

But Traynor had been at New Salem Baptist Church long enough to know that its members frowned upon a divorced pastor. He would be committing career suicide if he left Jessie Belle. No doubt he could pastor at another church, but Traynor felt at home at New Salem.

"Lord, what do You want me to do?" he whispered. "I need You to make it plain. Please tell me if I should walk away from my wife."

Jessie Belle sat in Mary Ellen's kitchen, wiping away her tears.

"So why did you do it?" She handed Jessie Belle a tissue.

"I was just trying to help Traynor win, Mary Ellen. You know how these things work. People are always looking for dirt on the candidates. I wanted my husband on even ground."

"It was wrong, Jessie Belle. You *do* know that?"

"He was so angry and disappointed with me."

"Jessie Belle, you can understand why, can't you?" Mary Ellen questioned. "You may have had good intentions, but it was wrong. I can't believe you actually have girls working for you."

"I was only trying to help him, Mary Ellen." She burst into another round of sobs. "I don't want to lose Traynor."

Mary Ellen embraced her. "I don't think you will, Jessie Belle. It may take some time, but he'll forgive you. Traynor loves you to death."

Wiping her face with a tissue, Jessie Belle asked, "You really think so?"

Mary Ellen nodded. "Unlike mine . . . your marriage can be saved."

"I'm so sorry for coming here with my mess and you're going through your own."

Mary Ellen gave a slight shrug. "It's alright. I'm getting a divorce and

I'm okay with it, Jessie Belle. I was the best wife I could be and Richard didn't appreciate me, so there it is."

"Traynor's supposed to be home tomorrow."

"He will be," Mary Ellen stated. "The man's got to come home, sweetie."

"I don't think he's coming home to me. He's too angry. Besides, I don't know what to say to him, Mary Ellen. I don't know if I'll ever be able to make Traynor understand that I was only trying to help him. Yeah, I went about it the wrong way. I admit that, but I know that those other candidates were doing the exact same thing."

"You're probably right, but I think that Traynor's platform was truth and honesty. The ECC has dealt with enough manipulations in the past with Sam McCall. Your husband wanted to separate himself from that type of reputation."

"He didn't do this. I did. And if Chrissy had kept her big mouth shut, nobody would've known. That's the way it should've been."

"Jessie Belle, what's done in the dark always comes to light. Didn't your mama ever teach you that?"

"I can't lose my husband, Mary Ellen."

"Sweetie, it's pretty much out of your hands now."

"Maybe not," Jessie Belle said. "New Salem frowns on pastors getting divorced. Traynor loves it there. He has to know that leaving me means he'll have to leave the church."

"Traynor would preach anywhere he wanted, Jessie Belle. One church won't stop him. What you have to do is be sincere in your apology to him. Sugar, you can't continue doing stuff like this or he will leave you. Traynor won't let you ruin his integrity."

"Are you divorcing me?" Jessie Belle demanded as soon as Traynor walked into the house. She'd spotted the taxi in the driveway and decided to wait for him at the bottom of the spiral staircase.

"I haven't really decided one way or the other."

His words wounded her.

"Is life with me so bad?" she wanted to know. "You have this big beautiful house, luxury cars. . . . You have me. Traynor, do you know how many men envy you? How many of them that would love to be in your shoes?"

"None of this stuff ever really mattered to me," he responded. "Jessie Belle, you wanted all this—that's a lot of our problem."

"I said I was wrong, Traynor, and I'm very sorry for what I did. I hope that you'll be able to forgive me."

"I don't know, Jessie Belle." Traynor sighed in resignation. "You have no idea how I felt hearing those men talk about you like that. I have never been so humiliated."

Tears filled her eyes and spilled down her face. "I'm so sorry."

"I'm going to take myself out of the running. I think it's best even though your secret is safe."

Jessie Belle blinked rapidly in her surprise. "Safe? What do you mean by that?"

"Chrissy told Sampson that it was all a lie. She claimed that she'd pointed out a woman standing near you as the person she was working for. You and I, however, know the truth."

"I don't want a divorce, Traynor," Jessie Belle blurted. "Honey, I love you and I enjoy being your wife, but I'm not going to beg you to stay with me."

"I'd be surprised if you did," Traynor responded. "It's beneath you to beg anyone for anything."

"Is that what you want me to do—beg?"

"All I've ever wanted from you, Jessie Belle, is to be my wife. Be my friend, my lover and my helpmate."

"I've done my best to do all of that, Traynor. Everything I've ever done is to help you. Traynor, I love you and I'm sorry if I went against you. I only wanted you to be the man I knew you could be. I admit, I went about it the wrong way, but I've learned my lesson. I really have."

"Jessie Belle, I don't trust you."

"I deserve that," she said quietly.

"I need time. I hope you understand."

She nodded. "I'll make this up to you, Traynor. If you'll give me another chance—I promise I'll behave."

Traynor didn't respond.

"I'm glad you're home safe and sound," she murmured.

"Where's Holt?" he asked. "I'd like to see my son."

"He's upstairs in his room," Jessie Belle responded. "He's really missed you."

"I missed him, too."

Traynor left her and went to spend time with their son.

Jessie Belle could still feel the chill that hung in the air from his words. She'd messed up big-time.

How am I gonna fix my marriage?

Traynor slept in one of the guest rooms.

The next morning, when she came downstairs to cook breakfast, he was dressed and on his way out of the house.

"You're not going to eat anything before you leave?" Jessie Belle asked.

"I'm not hungry."

"Traynor . . ."

"I won't be home until late."

Jessie Belle ran her fingers through her hair and fought back tears. She hated Traynor's being so upset with her.

"Please don't let him leave me," she whispered.

Jessie Belle spent most of the morning making sure the house was clean and the laundry done. She and Holt spent the early afternoon in the neighborhood park.

She toyed with the idea of surprising Traynor at the church for lunch but decided to give him space. Jessie Belle didn't want to further antagonize him.

He didn't come home until sometime after nine. Jessie Belle was in bed watching television. She heard him outside the room, but he didn't enter.

She climbed out of bed and slipped on her robe before strolling out of the bedroom. Jessie Belle caught him just as he was about to descend the stairs. "You could've come in and said hello."

"Yeah, I could have."

"Traynor, we have to talk. We can't live here in this house together and not talk to each other."

He walked back toward her and said, "I spent most of the day looking at apartments."

Jessie Belle gasped in surprise. "You're moving out?"

"I'm considering it."

"Traynor . . ."

"We can't live together, Jessie Belle. If I can't trust you—there is no marriage."

"I'll do whatever you want me to do. Please don't leave me, Traynor. I love you and all I was trying to do was help you." Jessie Belle burst into tears. "Please don't leave me."

"Do you think I'm happy about this?" he asked. "I'm not. I don't want my marriage in this kind of turmoil, but I didn't do this to us, Jessie Belle. *You did.*"

"You don't have to move out, Traynor. The only way we can work through this is if we stay here in this house together and try."

He seemed to be considering her words.

"You know how the members feel about divorced pastors," she murmured.

The look Traynor gave her was deadly. "Don't try to manipulate me, Jessie Belle. I'm tired of you doing that—I can't take it anymore."

Jessie Belle sighed in resignation. "All I'm asking for is another chance. Regardless of the mistakes I've made—we're a great team. Won't you at least admit that?"

"I can't really say that we were a team, Jessie Belle. That's a lot of our problem."

She didn't respond.

Traynor turned away from her and made his way downstairs.

Jessie Belle resisted the urge to follow him. Nothing would be accomplished tonight.

CHAPTER TWENTY-NINE

Jessie Belle was on her best behavior.

Traynor couldn't deny that he still loved his wife, but she infuriated him by being so deceitful. He resented the way she schemed and manipulated him—he felt betrayed.

My dad and Aunt Eleanor were right about Jessie Belle.

He wanted to confide in his aunt but was too embarrassed to do so—the last thing he wanted to hear was "I told you so." Traynor punched his pillow before tossing it across the room.

Traynor climbed out of bed and headed straight to the bathroom to shave and shower. He brushed his teeth, and then went back into the bedroom to find something to wear.

After getting dressed in a pair of khaki pants and a polo shirt, Traynor made his way towards the steps. He paused briefly outside the master bedroom, thinking of happier times.

How can we ever get past this?

They were still sleeping in separate bedrooms and hardly spoke to each other at home, but on Sundays and whenever they were at the church, they took great care to hide the fact that their marriage was in trouble, which made Traynor feel guilty.

Now we're deceiving the church members.

Traynor reasoned that it wasn't necessary to announce that they were going through a rough patch in their marriage. It wasn't anyone's business and he didn't want to give the church gossips something to talk about.

He heard Jessie Belle and Holt singing as they came downstairs. When they joined him in the kitchen, Traynor noted the dark circles under her eyes.

"Your breakfast is on the stove," she said.

"Thank you," he replied stiffly.

He and Jessie Belle tried to put on a cheerful facade for Holt.

She soon stood up, saying, "C'mon, sweetie. It's time we got you dressed. Let's go upstairs and find something for you to put on. Tell Daddy bye-bye."

" 'Bye, son," Traynor said. He was secretly relieved that Jessie Belle had decided to leave. As much as they tried to hide it, there was still too much tension between them.

Traynor left home nearly an hour later but found he couldn't really concentrate. His mind stayed on his marriage.

He spent the better of the morning behind closed doors in prayer. When Traynor emerged from his office shortly before noon, he felt better—more at peace.

Traynor didn't leave for lunch, instead working until three.

He stopped at his secretary's desk, saying, "I'm leaving for the day. I'll see you tomorrow."

Jessie Belle was lying on the couch when he arrived home.

Holt rushed into Traynor's arms.

As Traynor picked him up, his eyes strayed to Jessie Belle. "You okay? You don't look well."

"I didn't get much sleep last night," she murmured in response. "I had a lot on my mind."

"I'll make you a cup of tea," he offered. "I'll give this little guy his bath tonight and keep him occupied so that you can get to bed early."

Jessie Belle broke into a tiny smile. "Thank you, Traynor."

"Why don't we order out?" he suggested when she walked over to the refrigerator. "Don't worry about cooking."

"I don't mind—"

Traynor cut her off. "Jessie Belle, it's okay. Let's just order a pizza or some Chinese food for dinner."

Traynor rolled around on the floor with Holt while she called in their pizza order. Every now and then, he would catch Jessie Belle wiping her eyes.

She's crying.

Traynor struggled to rein in his emotions. He couldn't let Jessie Belle get to him—too much had happened and he was still wary of her. He needed space to think clearly about what he wanted—Traynor needed to receive direction from the Lord, but in order to hear Him, he had to be still.

The pizza was delivered and they sat down together at the dining table to eat dinner.

Jessie Belle was quiet throughout the meal.

Afterward, she helped him clean the kitchen despite his insistence that she go on up to bed.

Traynor took Holt upstairs and gave him a bath, although he ended up just as wet. Laughing, he managed to get his son all dried off and into a pair of pajamas.

Jessie Belle was in Holt's bedroom turning down his bed when they walked inside.

"I thought you were in bed by now," Traynor stated.

"I promised to finish the story I read Holt last night."

"I can do that."

Jessie Belle shook her head no. "Traynor, I'm trying to keep my word even with the small things." Lowering her voice, she added, "I really want to be the wife you deserve."

It hurt him to see her look so sad and forlorn, however. A part of him wanted to wrap his arms around her, but Traynor couldn't do that. He couldn't allow his emotions to take over.

He'd done that when they first met and look at all that happened.

Traynor stood in the doorway a few minutes listening to the story Jessie Belle was telling their son.

He eased away and went to the guest room where he'd been staying.

Traynor still loved her and he missed being with Jessie Belle. He hated this tension between them just as much as she did, but he couldn't just dismiss her schemes. She'd deliberately set out to hurt people and that was not something a Christian did.

Jezebel.

That's what James had called her. It was a name synonymous with wickedness. Although Traynor believed Sampson had defused the situation and proved the rumor false, he wasn't sure whether James wholeheartedly believed otherwise.

The two men had talked since then and James apologized for spreading gossip instead of coming to him directly, but Traynor knew the truth and it still sickened him.

Jessie Belle had him lying and covering for her.

Traynor was disgusted with himself.

He closed his eyes and began to pray. *Heavenly Father, I thank You for Your grace and for Your mercy. Help me live in a way that honors You. Help me find a way back to my wife. I pray that she will seek Your face and that she is truly repentant of her sins. If this marriage is to be saved, Father, we need You. . . .*

Jessie Belle didn't know how much more she could take.

The distance between her and Traynor hadn't lessened any in the past three weeks. Her hopes for reconciliation were slowly evaporating.

I'm losing him, she thought with growing dismay.

She confided her feelings to Mary Ellen during a phone conversation.

"I really think Traynor's gonna leave me. He's still sleeping in the other bedroom and he barely talks to me."

"Your husband loves you, Jessie Belle, but Traynor probably just needs some time to work all this stuff out."

"I've apologized to him, Mary Ellen. Over and over again. I've even worked hard to prove that I'm not the same person. What else do I have to do?"

Jessie Belle had done everything she could to prove to Traynor that she was trying to make a change in her life. She had even become more active in church.

"He's had a lot to deal with," Mary Ellen responded. "Just give him some time."

"I miss my husband."

"Jessie Belle, you're my friend and I thought we were close friends. Even I had no idea that you were running women. I have to be honest with you—I'm not so sure how I feel about that myself, so I can certainly understand your husband's hesitation. He's a man of God. What if your church members found out? Jessie Belle, something like this could ruin Traynor's career."

She was growing irritated. "Don't you think that I feel bad enough, Mary Ellen? *I was wrong.* I admit it."

Mary Ellen had no idea that Jessie Belle used her name to rent the apartment. She prayed that her friend would never find out. Their friendship would end—Jessie Belle was sure of it.

Jessie Belle felt like Mary Ellen was judging her and she didn't like it. "I can't undo the past, but I'm trying so hard to make up for what I've done. I just need a chance."

"We love you," Mary Ellen stated. "Jessie Belle, I hate what you've done, but I'm your friend for better or worse and Traynor is your husband. I'm sure everything will work itself out—at least that's my prayer."

Mary Ellen had to get off the phone because she had a meeting scheduled. Jessie Belle hung up and settled back on her sofa to watch television.

Traynor had to go out of town for a couple of days to preach. Jessie Belle was grateful for the time alone and she suspected her husband felt the same way.

She missed him, though, and looked forward to his return.

When that day finally arrived, Jessie Belle picked him up from the airport. They stopped and had dinner at a restaurant before going home.

Traynor seemed pretty happy to see her as well, so Jessie Belle felt encouraged.

Later at home, she and Traynor put their son to bed together. Afterward, they went downstairs to have some of the lemon pound cake Jessie Belle had baked earlier in the day.

"This is delicious," Traynor said between bites.

"Thank you." Jessie Belle longed to say more, but she didn't want to ruin the evening.

For now, she was content with the way things were.

July rolled into August and August into September.

Things were still tense between Jessie Belle and Traynor. They were barely talking to each other, leading her to worry whether her marriage would ever recover.

Traynor surprised her by sitting down beside her on the porch.

"The house was so quiet, I wondered where everybody was," he said.

"I was just about to take a walk with Holt around the neighborhood," she told him.

"I'd like to join you both—that's if you don't mind."

"I don't," she murmured, trying to disguise her surprise. "Holt and I would love it, actually."

They got up and walked down the steps with six-year-old Holt skipping around in front of them.

"I'm very happy with my life," Traynor blurted. "I need you to understand that, Jessie Belle. *I'm content.* I want you to raise our son and love me the way that I am—I'm a simple man and I won't apologize for that."

"I won't interfere, Traynor. I promise."

"I'm really struggling with whether or not to stay in this marriage. I'm so disappointed in you, Jessie Belle. I still haven't gotten over everything that's happened."

She nodded in understanding. "I'll never do anything like this again, Traynor. I promise."

He wrapped an arm around her. "I do love you, Jessie Belle."

"I love you, too."

They stopped for ice cream when Holt spotted the ice-cream truck.

"Holt's starting first grade tomorrow," Jessie Belle murmured. "Are you coming with me to take him to school?"

Traynor nodded. "I wouldn't miss it for anything in the world."

Jessie Belle sent up a quick prayer of thanks. Traynor wasn't going to divorce her. She vowed to be the type of woman that he wanted. She would be the perfect wife and mother.

The next day, Jessie Belle went to see Sabrina and Karla. She hadn't seen them since the conference fiasco. She had delayed this conversation with them pending the outcome of her marriage.

"I'm sorry this is short notice, but I need y'all to pack up and move out of here by the end of the month."

"Why?" Sabrina wanted to know. "What did we do? Are you still upset about Chrissy?"

"Because of that witch, my husband knows all about you and I want to save my marriage. I'm sorry, but it has to be this way."

Jessie Belle handed each of them an envelope. She didn't want to just leave them out in the cold, because they'd been very loyal to her. "Here's a little something extra to help you find suitable living arrangements."

"If I ever see Chrissy again, I'ma give her a serious beat-down," Karla uttered. "She really messed stuff up for us."

"I don't even want to hear that girl's name ever again in life," Jessie Belle uttered.

"We'll be out by the end of the week," Sabrina said quietly.

Jessie Belle embraced her. "Thank you for being so loyal to me. I want you to know that I really appreciate everything you've done. Because of your hard work, I have a nice little nest egg."

She hugged Karla next. "Thanks so much."

"I hope everything works out for you and your husband," Karla stated.

"Me, too," Sabrina contributed.

Jessie Belle didn't linger.

She returned home and spent the rest of the day with Holt. Jessie Belle felt like he'd grown up overnight.

Her Tragedy

CHAPTER THIRTY

April 1989

S he and Traynor were on their weekly lunch date. It had become routine for them to meet at Milton's Deli every Wednesday at noon.

"Holt is graduating high school in a month. I still can't believe it," Jessie Belle said. She took a sip of her iced tea. "It's gone by so fast. It seems like it was only yesterday when we took him to kindergarten. Do you remember that day?"

Smiling, he nodded. "It was also the day that our marriage got back on track."

Jessie Belle broke into a smile. "I'm so glad you didn't give up on me, Traynor. I will forever be sorry for hurting you back then—I can't believe I was so stupid."

Traynor reached over and took her hand. "We don't have to revisit the past, sweetheart. I love you more than my own life, Jessie Belle. You've made me so happy. I appreciate and admire the way you worked to become the person you are now. I'm very proud of you."

Jessie Belle bit into her sandwich.

"Has Holt decided where he's going to college?" Traynor inquired. "Every time I ask him about it, he gives me a vague response."

She wiped her mouth with the edge of her napkin. "He's received acceptance letters from UNC–Chapel Hill, Duke and NC State, but you know he wants to go to Los Angeles to be a musician. You know your son. . . ."

Traynor took a long sip of iced tea, then wiped his mouth with his napkin. "I'd hoped he would follow me in the ministry, but I guess it just isn't his calling."

"I wouldn't be so sure about that, Traynor," Jessie Belle responded. "He could be trying to run from it. Not everyone will embrace their calling like you did. He finally applied to a couple of Bible colleges after I nagged him about it, and we're still waiting to hear back."

"Jessie Belle, we can't force Holt into the ministry."

"I'm not trying to force my son into anything," she responded. "I can't help it if I want the best for him."

"Nothing wrong with that," Traynor stated. "But there comes a time to let go and let God."

"You're right," Jessie Belle stated. She finished off her baked-chicken sandwich.

"If Holt's been called to the pulpit, he won't be able to run from it. In the meantime getting a degree in music won't hurt. Maybe he'll step up one day as our minister of music."

Jessie Belle picked up her glass of water and took a sip.

Traynor reached over and covered her hand with his. "It's his life, sweetheart."

"I know. It's just that he's still young and a little naive. Holt thinks he knows everything, but he doesn't." She wiped her mouth with the edge of her napkin. "When he was born, my daddy said that God told him Holt would be traveling around the world preaching the Gospel. He didn't say anything about music."

Jessie Belle sighed. "I hate that Papa's not here to see his only grandchild graduate. Both of his grandfathers are gone."

Traynor nodded in understanding. "Aunt Eleanor, too. She loved herself some Holt. That was her only regret when she died. She hated that she wouldn't be here to see him get his diploma or graduate from college. You know how she was about education."

"Yeah, she sure did love my baby," Jessie Belle agreed. "She never could stand me, but she was crazy about Holt."

He finished the last of his fish. "We don't have much family left, outside of your mother, your aunt and her children. Now, me, I don't have anybody but some cousins left."

"We have each other, Traynor. For that, I'm so grateful and I thank God every single day."

He met her gaze. "I feel the same way, sweetheart."

"What in the world are we going to do when Holt leaves for school?" Jessie Belle asked. "We're gonna be in that big house all alone."

"I'm sure we can find ways to keep ourselves occupied."

Grinning, Jessie Belle responded, "As a matter of fact, I do have some ideas." She leaned forward in her chair. "C'mere and I'll share them with you."

Jessie Belle cornered her son outside his bedroom. "Holt, have you given any more thought to what we talked about yesterday?"

"I thought about it, Mother, but I can't. I can't be a minister."

"How can you disappoint your father like this, Holt? He really wanted you to join him in the pulpit."

Holt sighed in resignation. "Why can't you understand that it's not what I want to do? I'm a singer, Mother."

"I don't have a problem with that. Honey, you can still sing. I just don't believe it's your calling."

"Mother, I know Papa told you that I would be a minister, but he was wrong. I just don't feel it in my heart—not the way I do about music. I'm sorry. After I graduate, I'd like to move to Los Angeles so that I can explore my career. Mitch is moving out there, too. We plan on getting an apartment together."

"And if it doesn't work out?" Jessie Belle questioned. "What are you going to do then?"

He shrugged in nonchalance. "I don't know, but I'll figure out something. I might even change my mind about college."

"Why not get a degree in music, then?" she suggested. "You've already been accepted at several of the local schools—just go to college and major in music. You can do that."

"I want to move to Los Angeles, Mother. If I decide to go to school, I'll take classes out there."

"I think you're making a big mistake, Holt."

"I don't agree," he responded. "I wish I could make you understand."

"Honey, I do understand. Really, I do. Do you realize how hard it's going to be trying to break into the music industry? Thousands of kids move to Los Angeles for that same reason. The competition is stiff, and it's just crazy."

"Mother, you forgot who raised me. I have my faith and I know that I can do all things through Christ, who strengthens me. I am the head and not the tail. . . ."

Smiling, Jessie Belle hugged him. "What in the world am I supposed to say to that?"

"That you'll support me in whatever I do."

"That's a given, Holt. You know that I support you, but you're my only child. I can't help but worry."

Jessie Belle couldn't stand the little tramp Holt had insisted on escorting to the prom. Shannon Atwater had a reputation for putting out and that was not the type of girl she wanted Holt associating with.

"I don't know why he refused to take that Barton girl to the prom," Jessie Belle complained to Mary Ellen. "She's such a sweet girl."

"He doesn't like her. Holt says she's stuck up."

"At least she doesn't look like she's old enough to be his mother."

Mary Ellen hollered. "Now, you know that's not a nice thing to say, Jessie Belle."

"You know it's true. Shannon looks years older than she is. That's what being fast will do to you."

Mary Ellen looped her arm through Jessie Belle's as they descended the spiral staircase. "Holt's not trying to marry the girl. He's just taking her to the prom. It's not a big deal."

They settled down in the living room.

"I don't want her trying to seduce my son. She knows we have money and I'm sure the heifer wants some of it. She might even try to get pregnant." Jessie Belle clenched and unclenched her fists. "I'm not letting her ruin my son's future."

Mary Ellen laughed. "Sweetie, you're getting all worked up for nothing. Shannon is just his prom date. That's it."

Jessie Belle eyed her friend. "How do you know?"

"Because Holt talks to me," Mary Ellen stated. "He tells his godmother everything."

Jessie Belle folded her arms across her chest. "I think I'm jealous."

"He's not going to tell you stuff because you're his mother, Jessie Belle. Did you tell your mother everything that was going on in your life?"

Jessie Belle shook her head no. "Well, is there anything I should know about him?"

"Just that he really wants to go to Los Angeles. Jessie Belle, Holt really wants to try to get his music career off the ground."

"I know, Mary Ellen. It's all he talks about. I just don't believe that it's going to happen the way he thinks it is. I don't want to see Holt get hurt."

"You and Traynor raised a great son. He'll be fine."

"You're right." Jessie Belle stood up. "I need to see what Traynor and my son are up to—the limo will be here shortly."

She went back up to the second level.

Jessie Belle overheard Holt talking to his father.

"I'm sorry if I'm a big disappointment to you."

"You're not a disappointment, Holt," Traynor assured him. "All I ask is that you seek God's wisdom in all that you do. Pray about this and know that this is what God wants you to do. Just be sure."

"I have prayed and I truly believe God is leading me down this path."

Jessie Belle clenched her fists. Traynor was supposed to try to talk Holt into studying music at one of the colleges in the area. Instead, he was giving the boy his blessing.

"Obviously, Traynor's not going to do anything about this, so I'm going to have to," she whispered. "Holt's still too young to really know what he's been called to do. He needs our guidance."

If Traynor won't do his job as a parent, then he leaves me absolutely no choice. I have to protect Holt at all costs.

She knocked on the door before stepping inside the room. "The limo will be arriving shortly and we have to have pictures, so hurry up, you two."

"I'm ready," Holt stated. "Mother, you weren't serious about following the limo over to Shannon's house, were you?"

"Of course I was. Mary Ellen and I are going to take pictures of you and your date. It's your prom."

"Father . . ."

Traynor held up his hands. "Son, I don't have anything to do with it and I'm not about to come between your mother and godmother. Sorry."

"I can't believe you leaving me hanging like this," Holt complained. "That's not cool."

"Oh, so you want me to take on your mother?"

Jessie Belle smiled as she listened to the lighthearted bantering between father and son.

"And that godmother of yours . . . son, you on your own with those two."

She laughed. "Holt, stop complaining. We're just so proud of our handsome boy and we're doing what every mother in America's doing. We're capturing prom-night memories. My parents did it and I'm sure your father went through the same thing."

Traynor nodded. "I sure did. Son, I survived it, too."

Mary Ellen came up to the room and announced, "The limo's here." Holding up her camera, she added, "It's showtime."

CHAPTER THIRTY-ONE

With Holt at the prom and Mary Ellen gone, they had the house to themselves. Traynor led Jessie Belle upstairs to their bedroom.

They relieved themselves of clothes, lit candles and soaked in the large Jacuzzi bathtub.

"This feels good," Jessie Belle murmured.

Traynor agreed.

"Do you remember your prom?"

He glanced over at her. "Of course. I'm not that old."

Jessie Belle laughed. "I didn't mean it that way, honey. I remember mine, too. It was nice, but it wasn't great."

"My date ended up with chicken pox," Traynor stated. "I went to the prom alone."

"That's awful."

He nodded. "She was so upset about it. When she wasn't contagious, I told her to get all dressed up in her prom dress—we went and had pictures done and my dad reserved a table at one of the best restaurants. We had a nice dinner and went dancing afterwards."

"That's so sweet, Traynor. I'm not surprised, though. You're a good man and very romantic. That's one of the qualities I love about you. You inspire me to be a much better person."

"You have so much good in you, sweetheart. You are a phenomenal cook, a wonderful and devoted mother, and you are a good wife. There was a time I never thought I'd trust you again, but you changed that. You set out to prove you were trustworthy and you did. Jessie Belle, you are still as beautiful as the day I met you."

"You know exactly what to say to me."

"Everything I've said is true, sweetheart."

They got out of the tub.

Jessie Belle reached over, pulling her husband close. "I'm so happy, honey. I thank God for bringing you into my life even when I didn't deserve a good man like you."

Traynor dried her off tenderly, then led her over to the bed.

They made love and eventually fell asleep in each other's arms.

Holt came downstairs around ten a.m.

Traynor laid down his newspaper on the table and said, "Looks like you had a good time last night. You were supposed to be up an hour ago to unlock the church for the youth choir."

"Sorry, Dad . . . I forgot all about it."

"It's alright. I went down and did it." He pointed toward the kitchen. "There's a plate of pancakes, scrambled eggs and bacon on the stove for you. Just heat it up."

"Where's Mom?" Holt inquired.

"She had a hair appointment this morning. She should be back around eleven or so."

Over breakfast, Holt gave a brief recap of his evening. He and Traynor cleaned the kitchen afterward, and then walked outside to turn the sprinklers on.

Traynor enjoyed spending time with his son. They shared a close relationship and he hoped it would always be this way.

"I'm real proud of you," Traynor stated. "I just want you to know that, son."

"Even if I don't want to go to college right now?"

Traynor met Holt's gaze. "I can't see forcing you to go away to college, only to have you drop out later. You won't be focused."

Jessie Belle pulled up into the driveway.

Holt walked over to the car and opened the door for her.

"Thank you, son," she murmured. Jessie Belle kissed him on the cheek. "How was the prom? You got in pretty late."

He laughed. "How do you know? You and Dad were knocked out. I went to your room and y'all were sleeping like babies."

"I saw you peeking inside," Traynor stated. "It was almost three o'clock when you did that."

"I was home thirty minutes by then," Holt responded with a chuckle.

Traynor and Jessie Belle gave each other a knowing grin.

"Stop lying," she told her son. "Don't forget—all the games you try to run on us . . . we've already tried with our parents."

"Aunt Eleanor told me about you, Dad. She said you used to try and sneak out of your window until Granddad nailed it shut."

Traynor wrapped an arm around Jessie Belle. "I don't know what you're talking about, son."

They all laughed.

Inside the house, Traynor and his family sat down together in the family room. Jessie Belle snuggled up to him on the sofa.

"Holt, we're not going to fuss about your missing curfew last night, but understand this is a onetime pass," Jessie Belle stated. "Prom night is a special circumstance. I just hope you weren't doing something that may come back to haunt you."

"Mom, I know you not talking about what I think—"

"I'm talking about sex," she quickly interjected. "The last thing you need is a baby on the way."

Holt glanced over at his father. "Dad . . ."

"Your mother does have a point," Traynor responded. "I was young once and I know all about those raging hormones. Son . . ."

"Don't start preaching, please. I didn't do nothing. I don't want a baby either. I'm leaving town after graduation and I'm not gonna let anything get in the way of that." Holt stood up and said, "I need to get ready. I'm meeting Mitch down at the studio to go over a couple of songs."

"Make sure you're back here by dinnertime," Traynor instructed.

"I will."

Traynor eyed his wife when Holt left the room, and said, "I think our son has a good head on his shoulders."

"But how do we know that he'll always think with his head?"

Jessie Belle admired herself in the full-length mirror. She was wearing the triple-strand pearl necklace that once belonged to Traynor's mother.

After Eleanor's death, she was able to finally get her hands on the jewelry she felt should have been hers to begin with.

She never failed to thank God for saving her marriage, and Jessie Belle worked hard and diligently to be the type of wife Traynor could be proud of, but deep down she yearned for more. Each time ECC elections rolled around, she encouraged Traynor to run, but he refused.

"Why won't you run for ECC president, Traynor?" she'd asked him the night before. "Everybody thinks you should."

"I don't think the time is right," he responded.

"Traynor, it's been over thirteen years," Jessie Belle argued. "James died two years ago and Sampson, last month. Nobody is going to bring up a rumor that old—if they even remember it. I give you my word—I won't interfere."

He eyed her. "Why is this so important to you?"

"ECC needs a president they can trust, Traynor. That's you."

"You won't interfere?"

"Honey, I've learned from my mistakes. I promise you that you'll win fair and square."

"I'll pray about it."

Jessie Belle nodded in understanding. "Whatever you decide, honey— I'll support your decision."

"Thank you," Traynor murmured.

She drew her attention back to the present. Jessie Belle ran her fingers through her long curling tendrils. She gently patted the skin beneath her eyes and whispered, "I'm getting wrinkles."

Scrutinizing her appearance, Jessie Belle decided that she didn't look too bad for her age. Women in her family aged well, so she wasn't really worried about her looks, but she wanted Traynor to continue to find her attractive.

The church members seemed to be getting younger and younger and there were a few of them eyeing Traynor. Jessie Belle was cool about it, but she made it known that she wasn't about to put up with nonsense.

Traynor walked into the bedroom. "Sweetheart, it's almost time to lea—" He stopped short.

Jessie Belle turned around to face him. "What is it? Why are you staring at me like that?"

"You still take my breath away."

She smiled. "I feel the same way about you, Traynor. You are such a handsome man. You know I have to rein in some of those fast women at the church—always trying to sit on the front row with those short dresses on."

He chuckled. "I see you're still jealous."

"When it comes to you—yes, I am," Jessie Belle confessed. "You're the love of my life, and I'm not letting another woman take you away from me."

CHAPTER THIRTY-TWO

One week after Holt graduated from high school, Jessie Belle buried her mother. She died from complications due to diabetes.

"At least she lived long enough to see Holt graduate." Jessie Belle fingered the single strand of pearls around her neck. "She loved this necklace. It was the first gift my father ever gave her."

Holt entered his parents' bedroom.

"Mitch and I are leaving tomorrow," he announced. "He got the job as an intern with a record company, so we have to leave earlier than planned."

"You don't have to leave yet," Jessie Belle stated. "Honey, we can fly you there."

"I promised Mitch I'd help him drive."

"But—"

Traynor interrupted her. "Let him go, sweetheart."

Jessie Belle nodded. "The only way I'll support this venture of yours is that you give me something in return."

"What do you want, Mother?"

"That if this doesn't work out for you—you come home and go to seminary. I just know in my heart you have been called to follow in your father's footsteps. Son, you know it, too."

"Mother, I . . ." Holt paused for a moment before adding, "I haven't been honest with you. I know that I've been called to the ministry. I feel it, but I'm just not ready to accept it. This call on my gift is greater. Please understand that."

"I'm willing to try this your way, but I want your word, Holt. Promise me."

"Okay, Mother. You have my word. If I don't succeed as a musician— I'll come back and go to seminary."

She smiled. "You mean it?"

"Don't go getting your hopes up, though."

"I won't," Jessie Belle murmured. She leaned back against Traynor. "I'm going to do as your father suggested. Let go and let God."

Holt embraced her. "Thank you, Mother."

Jessie Belle held on to her son for dear life. The thought of Holt's leaving was breaking her heart. "I'm going to miss you so much."

"I'll miss you, too, but you and Father can come out to visit me."

"You better believe that we'll be out there," Jessie Belle stated. "You'll probably be begging us to stay home."

Deep down, Jessie Belle had a feeling Holt wouldn't last a year in Los Angeles. He'd be discouraged and come back home long before.

She would see to it that he was home in time to start college in the fall.

Traynor knew Jessie Belle's heart was breaking at the thought of Holt being away from her. She was already showing signs of separation anxiety.

"I'm very proud of you," Traynor told her later in bed. "I know how hard it was for you to give our son this opportunity."

"He'll be back, Traynor."

"Of course he'll be back. This will always be his home."

Jessie Belle sat up in bed. "That's not what I mean, honey. Holt will be back to accept the call on his life."

"Eventually," Traynor murmured.

"I have a feeling he'll be back before the year is out. It's not going to be as easy as he thinks in Los Angeles. The music industry can be cutthroat. Holt's going to find out the hard way. When he's had enough—he'll be back home where he belongs."

"I thought you were letting go and letting God."

"He's my only child, Traynor. Holt is the best part of me. You know, I really thought I was ready for this, but now I'm not so sure. He grew up way too fast."

Traynor pulled her into his arms. "I love our son, but I'm thrilled to have you to myself. This is our time, sweetheart."

He kissed her.

"Almost twenty years of marriage, and I still turn you on?" Jessie Belle asked. "I thought by now the passion would have evaporated, and we'd spend the rest of our marriage playing checkers."

"No way," he murmured. "Let me show you just how much I desire you."

Traynor surprised his wife with a romantic getaway to St. Simons Island.

Jessie Belle burst into laughter when she walked into their cozy suite at the King and Prince Hotel and saw that a table had been set up for a game of checkers.

"I figured it would give us something to do if we ran out of ideas."

She hugged him. "Traynor, you're a mess."

After getting settled, Jessie Belle and Traynor walked hand in hand along the beach.

"It's beautiful here," she murmured. "Have you ever been to St. Simons Island before?"

Traynor shook his head no. "One of the church members told me about it when I was looking for places to take you. I'm glad we came here."

Jessie Belle reveled in the nearness of her husband. With Holt gone, she and Traynor spent more time together. He wasn't traveling as much as before, although he still made a point of going to the church each weekday. Ministry was a full-time job for him.

He still made time to check in at the radio station, too. Mary Ellen was doing a wonderful job as manager, but Jessie Belle didn't believe in being absent owners. Besides, Traynor was still doing a weekly radio show.

"I've been thinking that maybe you should consider expanding your show," Jessie Belle stated.

Traynor surprised her when he said, "I've been thinking about the same thing, sweetheart."

While they walked, they discussed ways to expand the radio show. Jessie Belle was thrilled to find that they were finally on the same page. Expanding the show was something she'd felt strongly about for a while, but she hadn't wanted to seem as if she was trying to push Traynor into something he wasn't interested in. She'd tested the waters by mentioning it to him now.

He intruded upon her thoughts. "Ready to go inside?"

Jessie Belle nodded. "Yeah. What time are we having dinner?"

"Hungry?"

"I'm starved," Jessie Belle answered. "The salad I had for lunch wasn't filling at all."

"There's a restaurant downstairs. I hear that the seafood buffet is great."

"Let's go freshen up, then," Jessie Belle suggested. "We can have an early dinner and then take another stroll along the beaches tonight."

"I wouldn't mind living on an island like this," Traynor said. "It's really nice here."

"We could look into buying a condo in this area."

He embraced his wife. "It's just a thought, sweetheart."

"You don't think we could afford a place here? We don't need anything big, Traynor. A two-bedroom is fine."

"You're really serious about this, aren't you?"

Jessie Belle nodded. "Then we could come down for mini vacations. I think it would be nice to have a place to escape."

Traynor agreed.

She let the subject drop for now.

They walked up to the second floor, where their room was located.

Jessie Belle went straight to the bathroom to take a shower while Traynor selected a pair of shorts and a shirt.

She came out wearing a robe.

"I left the shower running for you," Jessie Belle announced.

She slipped into a navy-and-white-striped top and a navy skirt. For her feet, Jessie Belle chose a pair of navy and white sandals.

When Traynor walked out of the bathroom, Jessie Belle was in front of a mirror brushing her hair. She pulled it back into a ponytail.

After she applied the finishing touches to her face, Jessie Belle and Traynor walked over to the restaurant for dinner.

While they ate, they discussed the advantages of having an empty nest.

"I miss my son, but I am enjoying the time that I have with you," Jessie Belle was saying. "I want Holt in Raleigh or a little closer to us, but not necessarily in our house."

Traynor laughed. "I feel the same way. I'd like to have him closer, but he is an adult, Jessie Belle. This has to be his decision." He cracked open a crab leg.

"Holt and I have an agreement," she stated. "If things don't work out for him, then he's coming back home and going to college."

"Don't get your hopes up too high on that," Traynor advised.

"I know how much he loves music, but it's not his calling." Jessie Belle sliced into a shrimp. "I believe God's going to bring him home to us. Holt was called to the ministry—he knows it. He's just trying to run from it, but we both know that you can only run so far."

They continued their conversation as they finished their dinner.

Jessie Belle prayed that her son would come home soon. So far, he hadn't really gotten past the front door of record companies. It bothered her when he called her feeling discouraged. She didn't like hearing Holt sound so disappointed.

He wasn't ready to give up, however.

So she continued to ask God to bring her prodigal son home.

CHAPTER THIRTY-THREE

Holt had been in Los Angeles for seven months and while he hadn't gotten past a demo and several auditions, he wasn't ready to give up on a music career. Jessie Belle had expected him to be close to giving up by now.

She couldn't even convince him to come home for the holidays. He had joined them on a Thanksgiving cruise, but Jessie Belle and Traynor had gone out to Los Angeles to spend the week after Christmas with Holt because he couldn't take any extra time off from his job.

He called her three days before Valentine's Day.

"Mother, I have wonderful news," Holt told her. "God is so good!"

Jessie Belle felt a sense of dread. He was very excited about something and she prayed that it wasn't what she thought it was.

Clearing her throat, she asked, "What is it, sweetie?"

"I might have a record deal. I met with Peace Records and they love my demo."

Jessie Belle hid her true feelings and pretended to be happy for him. "That's wonderful, Holt."

After she hung up with Holt, Jessie Belle made a call to the radio station. "Mary Ellen, I need you to do me a favor. Contact Peace Records and tell them that if they sign my son—none of their artists will have any airtime on my station."

"Jessie Belle . . ."

"Holt's calling is in the ministry."

"But to do something like this . . . honey, you're gonna alienate him."

"He won't know about it, Mary Ellen. This is in his best interests, I assure you. I would never do anything to hurt my son."

Mary Ellen was quiet.

"If you're not comfortable with making the call, maybe you should reconsider your position as station manager."

"I'll make the call, Jessie Belle."

"Great. As a matter of fact, why don't you send that same message to anyone else who may be interested in signing Holt," she suggested. "I want my son to walk in his true calling—he doesn't need any other distractions."

"Whatever you say, boss," Mary Ellen uttered.

She hung up before Jessie Belle could reply.

Mary Ellen won't stay mad at me for long, she decided.

But just to be on the safe side, she picked up the phone and ordered a bouquet of roses to be sent to the station. Jessie Belle didn't want to lose her dearest friend in the world. The only other person she'd felt close to had been Sara, but she died thirteen years ago.

Traynor still talked to Rutherford every now and then. He'd remarried a year after Sara's death, and Jessie Belle never forgave him for that. She considered it a sign of disrespect to Sara.

Jessie Belle walked out into the hallway to find the housekeeper.

"Rosa, could you please make sure to put fresh linen on Holt's bed every week? I have a feeling he might be coming home any day now."

Jessie Belle waited a week before calling Mary Ellen.

"What do you want now?"

"Mary Ellen, I'm calling to say I'm sorry for what I said to you."

"No, you're not, Jessie Belle. You're not sorry at all."

It was clear that Mary Ellen was still upset.

"I don't want you to be mad with me," Jessie Belle stated. "Let me make it up to you."

"You can't."

"Mary Ellen, he's my son. I only want the best for him."

"Why is it that you think YOU know what's best for everyone, Jessie Belle? Tell me that."

"You'd do anything for your child, Mary Ellen, if you had one."

"Including break his heart?" she questioned. "I don't think so, Jessie Belle. I'm nothing like you. If people don't do what you think they should be doing, you will manipulate, blackmail—there's no telling what else you'd do to get what you want."

Jessie Belle was wounded. "I can't believe you said that to me."

"It's the truth. Jessie Belle, I pray for you constantly. I don't know what it is about you, but . . ."

"But what?"

"You want to control everyone. It's not right, Jessie Belle. I'm not trying to hurt you, but I'm your friend—I have to tell you the truth. What you did to your son was wrong on so many levels."

Jessie Belle was heated. "I can't believe you, Mary Ellen. How dare you come off like some kind of saint? You weren't even going to church when I met you—now you're all of a sudden such a Christian."

"Obviously, you can't handle the truth."

"It was a mistake to call you, I see," Jessie Belle uttered. "I'm sorry, Mary Ellen. I thought you'd understand how much I love Holt and want to protect him."

"I do understand," Mary Ellen stated. "Jessie Belle, I know how much you love your son. I know that you want the best for him, but what *you* need to understand is that you can't control his life. Holt is old enough to make his own choices—he should be allowed to do so."

"I don't want to lose you as a friend, Mary Ellen."

"Then don't ever use me in any of your schemes again. You can fire me—do whatever you want—but I won't be a part of it. Are we clear?"

"Yes, we're clear. Mary Ellen, I'm sorry. For the record, I would never have fired you."

"Jessie Belle, I think you should tell Holt the truth."

"I can't do that," she responded. "He'd never forgive me and neither would Traynor. Mary Ellen, please don't say anything about this," Jessie Belle pleaded. "I can't lose my husband or my son."

CHAPTER THIRTY-FOUR

🌿 *May 1996*

Six years later, Holt received his doctor of theology degree. Joy leaped in Jessie Belle's heart as she watched him walk across the stage to receive his degree.

Traynor and Jessie Belle hosted a dinner in his honor.

Shortly before dessert was served, Holt pulled her off to the side. "Mother, I have to tell you something."

Concerned, she asked, "What is it, Holt?"

"You were right. . . . This is my true calling. I realized it the first day I walked on Duke's campus. I just wasn't ready to admit it at the time. I was so discouraged when I came home from LA. I only decided to attend school because I knew it's what you and Dad wanted. But being here changed everything. I still love music."

"I love music, too, and at one time I considered being a concert pianist, but my calling is to be a wife and a partner to your father. I accepted it without question."

Holt met her gaze. "I never knew that."

"I saw no reason to mention it," Jessie Belle stated. "I'd made my decision the day I married your father."

"Any regrets?" Holt inquired.

Jessie Belle shook her head. "I have no regrets."

"I was so close to a record deal, Mother. I guess God closed that door to get me here."

Jessie Belle smiled and hugged him. "I'm so proud of you, sweetie."

"I thought you'd want to know. Now, don't go and spoil it by telling Father. I want to be the one to tell him."

"Okay. I won't say a word."

A dark-skinned full-figured young woman with braids and a brightly colored pantsuit walked into the foyer.

"Who in the world is that?" Jessie Belle asked. "Son, is this a friend of yours?"

"Yes," Holt responded. "She's a close friend."

He gestured for the girl to join them. The two embraced, and then he introduced her. "Mother, this is Frankie."

Jessie Belle saw the tender look he gave her and knew they were more than friends.

"My name is Francis, Mrs. Deveraux. But everyone calls me Frankie."

"Why?" Jessie Belle wanted to know.

"Mother . . ."

Frankie laughed. "It's okay. I was a tomboy growing up and I wanted to play basketball. None of the boys wanted to play with a girl, so I put on one of my brother's caps and pretended to be a boy. I guess the name stuck."

"Interesting," Jessie Belle murmured.

Mary Ellen joined them. "Hi, you must be Frankie. It's so nice to finally meet you."

Jessie Belle surveyed her son's friend while Mary Ellen engaged her in conversation. Frankie was tall—around five six—and dark-skinned, and looked like she hadn't missed a meal ever in life. She had a brightly hued scarf wrapped around hundreds of thin braids.

Jessie Belle caught Holt watching her and pasted on a polite smile. "Honey, you should go over and introduce Frankie to your father."

She glanced over at Mary Ellen. "Holt told you about her?" Jessie Belle questioned when they were alone.

Nodding, her friend responded, "She and Holt have been dating for two years now, I believe."

"Where did he meet her?"

"They met when he was in Los Angeles. They were just friends up until a couple of years ago."

"I can't believe he's dating her," Jessie Belle whispered. "She's nothing like the type of woman I thought he'd pick. And she goes around calling herself Frankie. What kind of name is that?"

"It's a nice name," Mary Ellen uttered. "Jessie Belle, why don't you like her? What's wrong with her?"

"Just look at her, Mary Ellen. She's got braids and that scarf wrapped all around her head. She looks so ethnic."

"I think she looks cute."

"Hopefully this phase in my son's life will pass."

"And if it doesn't? What then?" Mary Ellen questioned. "Are you going to try and pay her off?"

Jessie Belle sent her a sharp look. "I can't believe you said that to me."

"Why not? It's definitely your MO."

"There's no need to keep bringing up the past. If you were in my shoes, Mary Ellen—I believe you'd do the exact same thing."

"I'd like to think that I wouldn't interfere in my child's life. I'd trust him or her to make their own decisions. Or anybody's life, period." Mary Ellen finished up her lemonade. "Jessie Belle, I never told you this, but Richard told me that you knew about Amelia and the baby. I didn't believe him back then because I couldn't accept that a person who was supposed to be my best friend would keep an enormous secret like that from me. *But you did.*"

"Are you asking me or telling me?" Jessie Belle replied calmly.

"I knew you were very manipulative—I'd seen it with Atkinson, with Traynor, and even with Holt, but I never thought that you'd do it to me." She shook her head sadly. "What was I thinking?"

She'd never seen her friend look so angry. Mary Ellen's eyes glittered with fury and her mouth took on an unpleasant twist.

"Mary Ellen, I—"

"I really don't want to hear it, Jessie Belle. And before you fire me, I brought a copy of my resignation letter with me. I'm leaving Raleigh."

"You don't have to do this, Mary Ellen."

"Actually, I do," she retorted. "I'm not about to let you drag me down with your schemes. If you pull this kind of mess with your family—there's no telling what you'd do to someone who crosses you."

"Where are you going? Do you have another job lined up?"

"I'd rather not say. I've seen the damage you can do." Mary Ellen's eyes traveled over to where Traynor was standing. "You have such a wonderful family, Jessie Belle. Why can't you just stop trying to control them?"

"I've always known you were jealous of me, Mary Ellen. You want my life, but you can't have it. *Or my family.* You've tried to turn Holt against

me—don't think I'm not aware of what you're doing. You're just as manipulative as I am, trying to steal my son from me. You love throwing it
up in my face how much he confides in you."

"You're crazy, Jessie Belle. I don't want your life."

"It's time for you to leave, Mary Ellen."

"No, it's long past time for me to leave. I was just too blind to see
it."

"I really thought of you as my friend."

"I guess I should consider myself one of the lucky ones, then. But
then I see how you treat your own family. I feel sorry for you, Jessie Belle.
I really do."

"I don't need your pity."

Mary Ellen gave her a tiny smile. "But you have it anyway."

"Where did Mary Ellen run off to?" Traynor inquired.

"I'm not really sure," Jessie Belle responded. "She didn't say."

"You look upset. Did you two have an argument?"

"I'll tell you everything after our guests leave. I don't want to put a
damper on the evening. We'll talk later."

"Did you meet Holt's girlfriend? She's a lovely girl."

"He told me she was just a friend."

Traynor looked surprised. "They've been dating for almost two and a
half years, from what I understand."

"He didn't tell me that," she insisted. "He introduced her simply as a
friend. That's very telling, if you ask me."

"Relax, Jessie Belle. You won't lose your son."

Her heart started to race. "Are they talking about getting married?"

Traynor laughed. "No, I just wanted to see what your reaction would
be."

"When is she going back to Los Angeles?" Jessie Belle wanted to
know.

"I think she's going to be here for a couple of weeks. Frankie's looking
for a job in this area."

"Why?"

"She and Holt want to be together." Traynor put an arm around her.
"He loves her, Jessie Belle."

"It's not love," she countered. "Holt doesn't know anything about love. He's never really dated anyone seriously. I'm sure he likes her as a good friend, but I don't think we should call it love. This is just a phase."

"Jessie Belle, don't do this. Don't interfere in our son's life."

She glared at him for a moment before saying, "You know, I really thought you'd forgiven me, Traynor. But I guess you haven't."

"I forgave you a long time ago, but, sweetheart, I know how you are about your son. You've got to let Holt live his life on his own terms. If you don't, you'll lose him."

"She's not the one for him, Traynor. I'm sorry, but that's just the way I feel about it. That Frankie girl will never be his wife."

Traynor and Jessie Belle had a dinner invitation to John Winters's house. He'd called the day before, inviting them over.

"Have you talked to Mary Ellen?" Traynor questioned as he zipped up Jessie Belle's black dress. "We really need her back at the station. I haven't found anyone as capable as she is."

Jessie Belle shook her head no. "Traynor, we need to get used to the fact that our season with Mary Ellen is over. To be honest, I just think she couldn't get past her resentment that her marriage didn't last and ours did. She was jealous of my life."

"I never saw that in her."

"You're a man," Jessie Belle teased. "Women know women."

She picked up her purse and said, "I'm ready. We don't want to be late."

They walked out to the car and got inside.

Traynor pulled out of the driveway, saying, "I'm still wondering why John Winters invited us for dinner. It's not like we've ever been friends."

"I guess he's decided to change that," she murmured. Jessie Belle was excited at the prospect of a relationship with John Winters. She'd spoken with his late wife on several occasions in the past, but they never became confidantes.

John greeted them at the front door.

Jessie Belle noticed a young woman standing a few yards away and inquired, "Is this your lovely daughter?"

"Yes, it is. This is Natalia."

She eyed the brown-eyed beauty and smiled. *This is the type of girl I envisioned for my son.*

Traynor and John were over by the fireplace, talking.

Jessie Belle moved around the room, looking at the various family photographs. She pointed to one. "When did you graduate from college?"

"I just graduated law school. I'm taking the bar exam in a month."

"Good for you. Your mother told me a few years back that you wanted to go to law school."

Natalia smiled. "I've been talking about being a lawyer since I was a little girl. I love law.

"I met your son, Holt," she told Jessie Belle. "He's a very nice man and a wonderful preacher. I heard him over at Mount Olive Baptist a couple of weeks ago."

"Really?"

Natalia nodded. "He preached on true holiness. The message really spoke to me. I went up and introduced myself to him."

"So tell me, Natalia. What do you really think of my son?"

"I find him incredibly sexy, handsome and intelligent. Mrs. Deveraux, I have a strong feeling he's going places." Her gaze met Jessie Belle's. "Holt is exactly the kind of man my father would approve of."

Natalia glanced over her shoulder to where her father and Traynor stood before she continued. "I've been telling my father that it would be advantageous to both our families if we were to merge the two churches together."

Jessie Belle's eyebrows rose in surprise, but she remained quiet. She wanted to hear what Natalia had to say.

"Think about it. Your church is growing in leaps and bounds. You don't have any more space and our church is huge, but on Sunday, there are a lot of empty pews. The truth of the matter is that a lot of our members left to join New Salem Baptist Church."

"And you want them back?" Jessie Belle responded.

"As I said, it would be mutually beneficial to both families. You-all need a bigger church and we need more members. It's a marriage made in heaven."

"How does my husband fit into this?"

"He and my father would be copastors of the new Mount Vernon Baptist Church."

"And Holt?"

"A marriage made in heaven," Natalia murmured. "If Holt and I were to marry, my father would be more inclined to consider the merger."

Smiling, Jessie Belle said, "I see I was right about you."

"And I about you," Natalia shot back. "Mrs. Deveraux, I don't see anything wrong with going after what you want in life."

"You'd be very good for my Holt. I think that a marriage between our families would unite our churches and make ours one of the most powerful ministries available."

"I think my father would be pleased—this has always been a dream of his."

"That dream will be a reality if I have anything to do with it."

Natalia smiled. "I can tell we're going to be good friends."

Two weeks later, Jessie Belle held a dinner party to celebrate Traynor's birthday. John Winters and his daughter were in attendance.

Jessie Belle pointed Natalia out to Holt. "She's beautiful, isn't she?"

He agreed but didn't look that interested in meeting her. Jessie Belle wasn't ready to give up, so she said, "Her name is Natalia Winters."

"I met her when I spoke at Mount Olive."

"She seems like a lovely girl."

"She's nice." Holt glanced over at his mother. "I hope you're not trying to set me up. I already have a girlfriend. You do remember Frankie, don't you?"

"She's a nice girl, but I have to be honest with you. I'm just not sure Frankie is your soul mate, son."

"It's not your decision, Mother. Frankie and I have been together for almost three years—I love her."

"Sometimes it's best to be with someone that loves you—instead of someone you love."

"So you're saying I shouldn't marry for love?"

"Holt, a marriage between you and Natalia would unite our churches. John and your father are considering a merger."

"Why?"

"Well, we see the blending of the two church bodies as an opportunity for each. We need more space and they need members to fill the sanctuary. Uniting with Mount Vernon will help us both."

"It makes sense," Holt stated. "Pretty much we match theologically and in things like preaching style and stability."

"And you know that we're kind of landlocked where we are. There's no room to build a new sanctuary."

"You've got to present the idea to the congregations," Holt said. "A group of representatives from both churches could come together to form some type of study committee and look into it. But what would we do with our church?"

"I'm sure we could sell it to a ministry looking for a bigger place of worship." Jessie Belle pulled her son over by the huge picture window in the dining room. "Holt, if you and Natalia were to get together . . . well, people from both churches would embrace the idea of the merger totally."

He gave her a look of pure astonishment.

"You'd be doing it for your father. And Natalia, she's stunning and intelligent. You two would make a beautiful couple. She already adores you, Holt. She told me so."

"Mother, I don't know what to say to you," he uttered.

"Churches split all the time, Holt, but rarely do two ever come together like this. It's a rare opportunity. You just have to look at the big picture."

"So what you're saying is that I'm the deal breaker. Is that it?"

Holt was angry. She could hear it in his tone.

"I wouldn't exactly say it like that," Jessie Belle responded.

"Mother, you're trying to pimp me, and to be honest, I resent it. I am in love with Frankie and she's the woman I want to be with."

"All I'm asking is that you give Natalia a chance. That's all. Just spend some time with her."

"Drop it, Mother."

A few guests standing nearby glanced in their direction, prompting Jessie Belle to tell him, "Keep your voice down, Holt."

"I wish you much success on your venture, Mother. I'm going to say goodbye to my father and I'm going home."

"Holt, don't you dare embarrass me. I've supported you through everything you've done and wanted to do. I'm just asking you to spend some time with Natalia and just see what happens. Frankie's in Los Angeles and you're here. What's it going to hurt? Besides, how do you know for sure what you're feeling for Frankie is real? Has that love been tested?"

Holt didn't respond.

"I didn't think so. You won't know unless you test the waters some."

Traynor walked over to them. "You two look intense. Is everything okay?"

Jessie Belle eyed her son. "I was just explaining to Holt that I feel he should see other women socially—just to be sure Frankie is really the one he wants."

"Frankie actually said the same thing to me last night."

"She's being smart, Holt."

"I'll think about it, Mother."

Jessie Belle smiled. "That's all I ask, sweetie."

Holt walked across the room to where Natalia was standing. Soon the two were in deep conversation.

"You're trying to fix him up with Winters's daughter," Traynor accused.

"What kind of mother would I be if I didn't try to set him up with someone? It's a part of the job."

He chuckled. "You just can't help yourself, can you?"

"Traynor, I just want our son to be sure that what he's feeling is love. Frankie's getting ready to pack up her belongings and move across the country. Don't you think they both need to be sure?"

"I agree with you, Jessie Belle. It's just your tactics I'm not very comfortable with."

"I didn't say he had to marry Natalia. Just get to know her a little bit."

Jessie Belle didn't add that she hoped that Holt's dating Natalia would speed up the merger. She didn't want Traynor thinking she was pimping her son.

CHAPTER THIRTY-FIVE

Holt met his mother for lunch.

"So, how are things going with you and Natalia?" Jessie Belle asked as soon as they were seated in a booth near the huge picture window.

"She's a nice girl," he responded with a slight shrug. "And we have a lot in common." Holt picked up his menu and scanned it.

"See . . ."

"But she's just a friend, Mother," Holt quickly interjected. "I think she's beautiful, intelligent and funny. We have fun together, but I like her just as a friend."

The waiter came over.

Jessie Belle ordered lemonade and Holt ordered iced tea.

"That's too bad," she said after the waiter walked away. "I think she's more suited to you."

Shrugging in nonchalance, Holt replied, "I can't help the way I feel, Mother."

After bringing their drinks, the waiter pulled out a pad and pen to write down their entrées.

"I'll get the fried catfish, macaroni and cheese, turnip greens and corn bread." Jessie Belle handed him the menu.

Holt placed his order next.

The waiter left.

"Mother, you need to stop eating all that fried food. It's not good for you. Father told me that your cholesterol levels were high."

"I grew up on fried food, and so did you."

"Just cut back," Holt advised.

Jessie Belle smiled. "I love how you take care of me. You're such a good son."

"And you're a great mom when you're not trying to control my life." Holt sipped his iced tea. "Oh, I forgot to tell you—Frankie's coming to town tomorrow. She's got a second interview with IBM."

"Really?"

He nodded. "I think she's going to get the job. We've been praying about it, but if not, then it's not the one God has for her. I can't wait to have her here in Raleigh permanently. Being on different coasts is hard on a relationship."

"Does she know anything about Natalia?"

"I told her that we were friends."

"How did she take it?"

"She was okay with it. Natalia and I weren't dating or anything. Frankie's best friend is a male. One of the things I love about her is that she doesn't freak out over stuff like that. She's a very secure woman. I love that about her."

"I can see that," Jessie Belle murmured. She had to find a way to break up Holt and Frankie permanently.

The next day, she felt like fate had intervened when she ran into Frankie at the mall.

Jessie Belle tapped her on the shoulder. "Frankie, dear, how are you?"

She turned around. "I'm fine, Mrs. Deveraux. And you?"

"Blessed and highly favored," Jessie Belle responded. "So what brings you way over here this afternoon?"

"Holt and I had lunch together. I just dropped him off at the church. Since I was so close to the mall, I thought I'd come pick up a few things."

"I see." Switching her Louis Vuitton from one shoulder to the other, Jessie Belle added, "With you looking for a job, you might want to save money."

Frankie stiffened. "I'm not planning on buying anything I can't afford."

They stood there staring at each other in tense silence.

Frankie spoke up first. "Mrs. Deveraux, is there something you want to say to me? It doesn't take a brain scientist to see that you're not exactly fond of me."

"Frankie, I just don't want you to get hurt in all this. You're a sweet girl, but, dear, I have to be honest. You are not the one for my son."

"Does Holt feel this way?"

"Of course he does," Jessie Belle lied. "As you are aware, Holt's met a lovely young woman and they've been seeing each other socially."

"Holt's always been very honest with me. He told me about Natalia. They're just friends, Mrs. Deveraux. He'd tell me if it was something more."

"Frankie, he doesn't want to hurt you. He thinks of you as a very dear friend and he knows how much you care for him."

"Holt loves me," Frankie stated. "Mrs. Deveraux, he even told me that he wants to marry me."

"That will never happen."

"Mrs. Deveraux, I don't mean to be disrespectful, but I've had enough of this conversation. If Holt wants to break up with me—he'll have to be the one to do it." Placing her hands on her full hips, she added, "Not send his mama to do it for him."

"Holt feels something for you, Frankie. I won't deny that, but you are just not the woman for him."

"How can you say that? You don't even know me. Not once have you ever tried to get to know me."

"I didn't see any point, as you weren't a permanent fixture in my son's life," Jessie Belle responded.

Frankie walked away without another word.

Humming to herself, Jessie Belle strolled through the department store.

She spent the afternoon just going from store to store browsing. Jessie Belle left the mall around three thirty and headed home.

Traynor requested lasagna for dinner, so she went through her kitchen, pulling out the ingredients and the lasagna pan.

Jessie Belle had just stuck the casserole into the oven when the doorbell sounded.

"What did you say to Frankie?" Holt demanded when Jessie Belle opened the front door.

She stepped back to let him enter the house. "Hello to you, too."

He brushed past his mother. "What did you tell Frankie? She was very upset when I spoke to her earlier."

"I simply told her the truth—that she's not the woman for you."

"Frankie is the woman I love."

"That doesn't mean she's the one for you," Jessie Belle insisted. "The poor thing should really consider losing some weight. If she looks like that now—what do you think age and childbearing will do to her body?"

"I love her spirit, Mother. I love her heart—she's beautiful to me and it doesn't matter that she's not a size two."

"Natalia is stunning. Her honey-colored complexion, those soft brown eyes and that long beautiful hair coupled with your handsome features—my grandchildren will be beautiful."

Holt sighed in exasperation. "I'm not interested in Natalia, Mother. I told you that from the beginning. My heart belongs to Frankie. I'm sorry if you can't accept that."

"Why is it you don't know what's good for you?" Jessie Belle demanded.

"No, it's you who doesn't have a clue," he countered. "I know what I want. It's Frankie."

"So what about Natalia?"

"What about her?"

"Have you told her that you're not interested?"

"I've been very honest with her, Mother." Holt took Jessie Belle's hand. "I know how much you and Father want the merger and I believe it's going to happen whether Natalia and I are together or not. Everyone seems very excited about it. You don't have anything to worry about."

Jessie Belle sighed in resignation. "You may be right, son. I'm sorry for the way I've been acting."

"Frankie's my girlfriend. I'd like for you to treat her nice. Mother, can you please do that for me?"

She nodded. "Of course. In fact, I'd like to host a dinner in her honor tomorrow night."

His eyebrows rose in surprise. "Really? You'd do that for Frankie?"

Jessie Belle nodded. "Tomorrow night at seven. Don't be late."

Holt gave her a hug. "Thank you, Mother."

"I'm only doing this for you."

"I know." Holt kissed her cheek. "I'll see you tomorrow night."

When Holt drove away, Jessie Belle picked up the telephone and dialed.

"Natalia, how would you like to join us for dinner tomorrow night? I need you to be here at six thirty sharp."

Jessie Belle stopped by Traynor's office on her way to Bible study.

"How long are you planning to work tonight?" she inquired.

"I'm finishing up now. I'm going to sit in on Bible study tonight. Why?"

"I just wanted to know if you'd be going home with me. I thought we could have a late but very romantic dinner. Lasagna. We're having oysters as an appetizer."

Traynor surveyed her face. "What are you up to?"

She grinned. "It's not obvious? I'm trying to seduce my handsome husband. Humph. I must be losing my touch."

Pushing away from his desk, Traynor stood up. "Sweetheart, it's a date."

They walked down to the room where Bible study was held.

Jessie Belle sat down beside Traynor. She could barely think about Paul or what he had to say—her mind filled with fantasies of what she wanted her husband to do to her. Traynor still turned her on.

He apparently felt the same way because as soon as they walked inside the house, they tore off each other's clothes. Traynor made love to his wife on the floor in the living room and then again in the family room.

Jessie Belle groaned as she tried to sit up. "My bones never ached this much when I was younger."

Traynor laughed. "My knees are killing me."

"This is what I don't like about getting older. I'm still feeling a little adventurous, but my body . . ."

"Think you can make it to the Jacuzzi tub?" Traynor asked.

"Only if you carry me. I'm a little weak at the knees."

Jessie Belle made her way to the downstairs bathroom to shower while Traynor heated up their dinner. When she returned, Jessie Belle saw that he'd lit some candles and had music playing softly in the background.

"Oh, I invited Holt and Frankie over for dinner tomorrow," Jessie

Belle announced. "I thought it would be nice to try and get to know her in a less formal setting."

"That's really sweet of you, Jessie Belle."

"I'm going to give this girl a chance like you suggested. I'm not making any promises, though."

Traynor reached over and grabbed her hand. "Thank you, sweetheart. I know Holt appreciates you making the effort."

Jessie Belle broke into a smile. "I hope so."

The next day, Natalia arrived at six fifteen. She looked stunning in a bright green pantsuit with her midlength hair pulled back into a ponytail.

"Do you really think this is going to work?" Natalia asked.

"I don't know," Jessie Belle responded. "It's really up to you. Frankie has to see how well you and Holt mesh. The foolish girl still believes that she and Holt belong together."

Traynor came downstairs, putting an end to their plotting.

He was clearly surprised to see Natalia.

"Honey, Natalia came by to pick up some copies of the programs I did for Women's Day," Jessie Belle lied. "She wants to try and plan something similar. Since she's here, I invited her to stay for dinner."

Traynor didn't respond.

Jessie Belle could tell that he was upset with her. When he left the room, she turned to Natalia and whispered, "Don't you tell him I invited you over here before now."

"I won't," she promised. "Just make sure to give me a couple of the programs you mentioned."

Jessie Belle escorted Natalia to the family room, where Traynor was sitting. "You make yourself comfortable. I'll go get the programs and be right back."

"Thank you, Mrs. Deveraux," Natalia replied.

Traynor got up and followed Jessie Belle to the office.

"What are you up to, Jessie Belle?"

"Nothing," she mumbled while pretending to look for the program. "Natalia was supposed to come by earlier today, but for whatever reason, she didn't."

"So why invite her to dinner when you know Holt and Frankie are coming over?"

Jessie Belle gazed at her husband. "What is the big deal, Traynor? She might as well get used to seeing them together."

He folded his arms across his chest. "So you're saying that you have no ulterior motives?"

Waving a piece of paper in the air, she said, "Just this program."

Jessie Belle brushed past him, walking quickly.

"Did he buy it?" Natalia whispered when she entered the family room.

Nodding, Jessie Belle handed her the program.

Five minutes past seven, Holt and Frankie arrived.

Holt was shocked to see Natalia.

"Mother, what are you doing?" Holt asked in a low whisper. "Why is Natalia here? I thought this was supposed to be a dinner for Frankie. I can't believe you did this," he whispered.

"Be nice," she responded. "Natalia came here to pick up something and I invited her to stay. She needs to see you and Frankie together. So relax. It's only dinner."

Natalia was witty and a wonderful conversationalist. She was able to effectively shut Frankie out each time Holt tried to include her.

Smiling, Jessie Belle turned her eyes to Traynor.

He didn't look amused at all.

Frankie surprised Jessie Belle by not showing emotion. She didn't appear jealous or the least bit insecure. She laughed and grinned as if she didn't have a care in the world.

She's a lot stronger than I thought.

Jessie Belle eyed her son. Holt was polite, but beneath his blank expression, she could tell he wasn't happy either.

Like Traynor, he would blame her for trying to ruin his life, but Jessie Belle would continue to plead innocence. It wasn't like they could prove otherwise.

After their guests had gone, Traynor and Jessie Belle retired to their master bedroom.

She was up to her old tricks again.

Traynor knew it and Jessie Belle was aware that he knew it, too. She'd been trying to placate him throughout the evening.

"You were pretty quiet during dinner."

Traynor undid his tie and took it off, laying it on the dresser. "I didn't want to add to the tension that was already in the room."

Jessie Belle turned around to face him. "You thought there was a lot of tension? Hmmm . . . I thought everything went nicely."

Traynor sat down in one of the overstuffed chairs near the doors leading to the balcony. Removing his shoes, he stated, "Jessie Belle, our son's made it clear how he feels about Frankie. I think you should respect his feelings."

"He's young," she replied. "Holt doesn't have a clue what he really wants. But as I've already said, Natalia came here to pick up a program. Yes, I invited her to stay for dinner, but I thought it would be good for her to see Holt with Frankie."

"We were younger than Holt is now when we got married."

"Times were different then," Jessie Belle countered.

He began unbuttoning his shirt. "You told me that you wouldn't interfere."

"I haven't, Traynor. Holt and Natalia have become friends. If his relationship with Frankie is so secure, what's wrong with having dinner with a friend? Should they hide their friendship? Holt told me himself that Frankie's best friend is male. They go out to dinner all the time."

Jessie Belle removed the pins from her hair, letting it fall all around her face. She ran her fingers through the curling tendrils. "I don't see where I did anything wrong. I like Natalia and I feel like I should be able to invite her over whenever I want—this is my house."

Traynor loved seeing Jessie Belle with her hair down. He had a feeling she was trying to distract him. "If you push Holt, be prepared for him to push back, Jessie Belle."

She eyed his reflection in the mirror.

"I won't deny that I would love to have Natalia for a daughter-in-law. She's more suited to our son. Traynor, the merger would be guaranteed to go through if Holt and Natalia married. It would truly unite the churches."

"Is this why you're trying to push them together? Because of the merger?"

"I'm not trying to do anything, Traynor," Jessie Belle snapped in anger. "Stop blaming me for everything."

"The feedback from both churches has been positive, Jessie Belle. I don't think Holt needs to marry Natalia for the merger to go through. So leave them alone. I'm warning you. . . . If you try to manipulate your son, you're going to lose him." Traynor met her gaze. "And you'll lose me, too. I won't stand for your schemes this time around."

CHAPTER THIRTY-SIX

Jessie Belle tried to reach Holt the next day, but he wouldn't return her phone calls. She worried that Traynor was right—she'd pushed him too hard.

When the weekend came and went without a word from her son, Jessie Belle became really concerned.

"Honey, have you talked to Holt?" she asked Traynor.

"Not since he was over at the house for dinner. Why?"

"He wasn't at church this morning and we haven't heard anything from him. Do you think we should go over to his apartment? Make sure he's okay?"

Traynor shook his head no. "I'm sure he's fine. He and Frankie probably went out of town."

"I guess, but he could've told us that he was going away"—Jessie Belle began pacing the floor of her bedroom—"instead of leaving us to worry like this. I don't know where my son is and I'm beginning to get scared."

"Sweetheart, I'm sure Holt's fine."

Jessie Belle wasn't sure of anything.

She called his apartment once more.

"Holt will call you, Jessie Belle. Just come to bed and stop worrying. If anything was wrong, I think we'd feel it in our spirits."

She sighed in resignation. "Maybe you're right."

Holt was angry and probably wasn't speaking to her. Traynor didn't know about the argument they'd had, so Jessie Belle didn't mention it. She didn't want him upset with her, too.

That night, Traynor and Jessie Belle jumped up at the sound of the doorbell.

She glanced over at the clock. "Who in the world could be knocking on our door at this hour?"

Traynor got out of bed. "You stay up here."

"No, I'm going down with you," Jessie Belle replied.

She swung her legs out of bed and stood up.

Jessie Belle slipped on her robe and rushed out of the room to catch up with Traynor, who was halfway down the stairs.

They were surprised to see Holt and Frankie on the porch.

"Is everything okay?" Traynor inquired.

"We just needed to talk to you and Mother," Holt responded.

Traynor moved to the side to let them enter.

Jessie Belle surveyed her son, trying to discern if something was wrong. It couldn't be life-threatening because he seemed very happy—almost giddy. She felt sick in the pit of her stomach.

They gathered in the living room.

"I know it's late, but Frankie and I couldn't wait to share our news," Holt stated with a grin.

Jessie Belle frowned. *"What news?"*

"We're so sorry for coming by so late, but Holt insisted that this just couldn't wait," Frankie stated.

Jessie Belle's heart started to race and she gripped Traynor's arm. Surely her son didn't run out and . . . she couldn't even think about it.

"We eloped," Holt announced. "Frankie and I are married."

"What in the world were you thinking?" Jessie Belle asked. "How could you do such a foolish thing?" She could hardly contain her fury. "I thought you were more responsible than this."

"Honey, they love each other," Traynor interjected.

She glanced over at her son. "How could you do this to me?"

"This was never about you, Mother," Holt replied, looking her straight in the eye. "I love Frankie, and I wanted her to be my wife. She is the other half of me. She's my soul mate."

Jessie Belle grunted. "She'll be the ruin of you, that's for sure."

Frankie gasped. "Excuse me?"

Before Jessie Belle could utter a response, Holt jumped to his wife's defense.

"Mother, I won't have you saying things like that about my wife.

Frankie and I love each other and we'd been thinking about getting married for a while now but waited until we were sure."

"Your *wife*. Humph."

"Give it up, Jessie Belle," Traynor urged. "Frankie is a part of our family now. Accept it."

Natalia called Jessie Belle the next day and invited her to lunch.

She tried to get out of it, but Natalia wouldn't let up. "We really need to talk about your son."

"Around one," Jessie Belle suggested. Natalia was going to find out sooner or later, so she might as well be the one to tell her about Holt's marriage.

After deciding on a place, they ended the call.

Three hours later, Jessie Belle headed out to meet Natalia.

"I haven't heard from Holt," she complained when they were seated. "I thought he'd call me before now. My daddy told me to tell you that you're going to need to light a fire under that boy of yours. Holt can't possibly be interested in that girl that was at your house." Turning up her nose, Natalia added, "She's not cute at all."

Jessie Belle took a sip of her tea. "Natalia, I'm afraid there's been a change of plans where Holt is concerned."

"What are you talking about?"

"Holt did something really stupid last night. I didn't know anything about it until afterwards." Jessie Belle took a deep breath and exhaled slowly. "Natalia, my son went off and married Frankie."

A horrified expression took over Natalia's face. "He what?"

Jessie Belle reached over, covering Natalia's hand with her own. "I'm so sorry, dear. I had no idea he'd act so reckless."

"How could you let that happen?" she demanded, snatching her hand away. "You basically told me that Holt would be mine. Do you have any idea how long I've been after him? I've wanted him since he moved back from Los Angeles."

"Obviously, you didn't try hard enough," Jessie Belle accused, settling back in her chair. "I did everything I could—the rest was up to you, Natalia."

Arms folded across her chest, Natalia uttered, "Oh, so it's my fault."

"Well, it's certainly not mine."

"So what are we going to do now?" Natalia questioned. "I can't believe he married that fat cow."

"How do you feel about breaking up a marriage?" Jessie Belle asked. "Frankie is not the woman for him, but you've got to convince him of it. She's left for California this morning and won't be back for a few days." Pulling a key out of her purse, she continued. "Here is a key to his apartment. I'm sure you have an idea of what to do next."

Natalia took the key from Jessie Belle. "And what will you be doing?"

"Playing the dutiful wife and noninterfering mother-in-law. I'm not going to chance losing my husband or my son."

Jessie Belle stopped by the church to see Traynor.

"I saw Natalia not too long ago. She was distraught when I told her that Holt and Frankie eloped. Traynor, I don't think I've ever seen anyone so devastated."

"They were never in a relationship," he responded. "She couldn't be that distraught."

"She had deep feelings for our son."

"Jessie Belle, our son is a married man now. Natalia needs to move on with her life. I'm sure she'll find a nice young man to love."

"I'm well aware that Holt went off and got married. You don't need to keep throwing it in my face."

"I don't want you plotting with Natalia to break up his marriage."

"I wouldn't do that," Jessie Belle stated. "I resent the fact that you think that I would."

"I'm not going to argue with you, Jessie Belle. I just don't want you interfering in our son's life. He and Frankie are married. She's family."

"I can't believe you're blaming me for what happened all those years ago."

"You've manipulated me for years, Jessie Belle. You just don't know how to leave well enough alone."

"I guess I know how you see me."

"I'm only speaking the truth," Traynor stated. "I'm not as dumb as you might think I am."

Their conversation was interrupted by Holt. He strode into the office, closing the door behind him.

"Mother, I can't believe the lengths you'll go to just to get what you want."

She turned around to face her son. "What is your problem? You know, I'm tired of being blamed for everything that goes on around here."

"Frankie and I went home and guess what we found in my bed? Natalia. She was under the impression that Frankie was leaving this morning. The only way she could've known that was from you."

"I didn't send her over there to seduce you."

"How did she get into the apartment?" Traynor asked.

Holt glared at his mother. "She had a key."

Traynor looked at Jessie Belle. "You didn't . . ."

Shaking her head, Jessie Belle uttered, "No. I wouldn't do something like that."

"I don't believe you," Holt stated.

Jessie Belle's chest began to hurt. Rubbing it, she asked Holt, "Did it ever occur to you that maybe Natalia came up with this on her own? Maybe she did it because she believes that you two belong together? Who knows? Maybe you jumped the gun by marrying Frankie."

"It's no use talking to you," Holt stated with a sigh of frustration. "I need to get home to my wife."

Jessie Belle grabbed him by the arm. "Holt, I don't deserve this attitude of yours."

"And I deserve better from you," he shot back.

"You can't blame me simply because Natalia's not giving up without a fight. It's not my problem." The pain in her chest seemed to be getting worse and it was getting a little difficult to breathe.

It angered Jessie Belle that Traynor didn't step up to her defense.

"Well, aren't you gonna say something to your son?" she wanted to know. "I'll not be disrespected like this."

Jessie Belle felt sick to her stomach and experienced a moment of light-headedness. "I'm not gonna stay here and listen to this mess. You and your father can believe whatever you want—I really don't care."

Suddenly, a sharp knifelike pain ripped through her chest, bringing her to her knees. Jessie Belle groaned in agony.

Traynor and Holt were instantly at her side.

"Sweetheart . . ."

"Mother, what's wrong?"

"My ch-chest . . . ," was all she could manage. Jessie Belle struggled to keep the edges of darkness from consuming her.

"I think she's having a heart attack," she heard Holt say. "Call 911."

Jessie Belle surrendered to the dark void.

CHAPTER THIRTY-SEVEN

Jessie Belle was released from the hospital ten days after suffering a mild heart attack.

Holt walked through the double doors of her bedroom carrying a bouquet of mixed flowers. "Father tells me that you're being a little hardheaded."

Jessie Belle broke into a grin. "Hello, son."

He put the flowers on the dresser so that she could get a good look at them before he bent over to kiss her cheek. "You have to take care of yourself, Mother. Follow doctor's orders . . . eat healthier—that kind of thing."

"I'm trying to be a good girl."

"I love you, Mother, and I don't want to lose you. You really scared me the other night."

"I certainly didn't mean to," she responded with a smile. "Holt, I'm following the doctor's orders. Don't worry baby. I intend to be around for a very long time."

Jessie Belle reached over, placing her hand on Holt's cheek. "I'm sorry about our argument. I love you—maybe a little too much, but I just want you to be happy. Really, that's all I want."

Holt interrupted her. "It's forgotten, Mother. I just want you to concentrate on getting stronger."

Traynor walked into the bedroom.

"Hey, beautiful. Are you hungry?"

Jessie Belle shook her head no. "Not yet."

He sat down on the edge of the bed. "I'm meeting with John today to discuss and finalize the proposal for the merger."

She smiled. "That's wonderful. I'll be glad when it's all over and done with. I was worried that he'd change his mind."

Traynor rose to his feet. "I won't be gone long, sweetheart. Holt's going to stay here with you until I get back."

Jessie Belle propped up her pillows. "Where's Frankie?"

"She's at home," he responded. "Frankie thought it would be best if she stayed at the apartment, considering how you feel about her."

"It's going to take some time, Holt. But I am trying."

"Try harder," Holt stated firmly. "Mother, there's something I want you to know."

"This sounds serious."

"I love you and I love Frankie. She is my wife and I want her treated as such. Mother, I . . . Frankie and I are trying to have a baby. We're ready to have a family."

"But you two just got married."

"What's wrong with that?" he asked.

Jessie Belle decided to just back down. She didn't want to get into another argument with Holt and especially after all she'd been through healthwise.

"Nothing. I just thought you two might want to take some time and just enjoy each other before bringing a child into the world."

"Frankie and I want kids and we're ready for them."

Holt was grinning from ear to ear. "Hopefully in the next couple of months, we'll be announcing that we're pregnant."

Jessie Belle forced a smile. "Honey, I'm thrilled for you and Frankie. Congratulations."

"How do you feel about being a grandmother?"

She swallowed hard. "I'm looking forward to it."

"Frankie's a wonderful woman, Mother. Just give her a chance."

"I really don't have much choice now, do I? She'll be giving me my first grandchild."

Deep down, Jessie Belle was heartsick but was powerless to do anything. She consoled herself with the fact that John Winters was still interested in moving forward with the merger.

Apparently, he didn't hold a grudge against them for the way Holt rejected Natalia.

John had hoped for a marriage between his daughter and Holt as well. But, then, he really couldn't blame her or Traynor. Natalia wasn't the woman Jessie Belle had assumed. The twit didn't know how to snag a man.

Traynor didn't look happy when he returned home.

"What happened?" Jessie Belle inquired.

"I think John's changing his mind about the merger." He sat down on the edge of the bed.

"What?" Jessie Belle and Holt asked in unison.

"Did he say that exactly?" Jessie Belle wanted to know.

Traynor shook his head no. "He kind of alluded to it."

"What was his reasoning?" Holt questioned.

"You know why? You rejected his daughter," Jessie Belle stated. She clenched her fist in anger. "John wanted you and Natalia together just as much as I did."

Traynor shrugged in nonchalance. "There's nothing we can do about that. If Winters wants to pull out, so be it." His eyes traveled to Jessie Belle. "Sweetheart, you just got out of the hospital. Don't get upset about this—everything will be okay."

Jessie Belle folded her arms across her chest.

"I know that look on your face. What are you thinking about?" he asked her.

"I think it's wrong. We had an agreement."

He knew Jessie Belle was disappointed, but Traynor felt a small pinch of relief. Maybe it was all for the best.

Traynor surveyed his wife's face. He could almost see her mind busy working. He suspected she was trying to figure out a way to make the merger happen. Traynor resisted the urge to tell her to let it go. He didn't want to upset her.

Holt stayed another hour before going home to Frankie.

"They're trying to get pregnant," Jessie Belle announced.

"You're going to make a very beautiful grandmother," Traynor told her, bringing a smile to Jessie Belle's lips.

"Traynor, I think they're moving way too fast."

"It's not your decision, sweetheart."

He was surprised when she agreed with him and left it at that.

"Put on your pajamas and get into bed with me," Jessie Belle said. "Let's watch a movie together. I don't want to talk about the merger, Holt, babies—nothing. I just want to spend some quality time with you."

Traynor sent up a quick prayer of thanks. He prayed for Jessie Belle on a daily basis, asking God to change her heart and put an end to her manipulative ways. He was finally seeing it come to pass.

Thank You, God.

Two weeks later, while Traynor was at the church for a meeting, Jessie Belle called and asked Natalia to come over.

"Why did you want to see me?"

"Your father's thinking of backing out of the merger," Jessie Belle stated. "Did you know that?"

"I hadn't heard anything." Natalia's eyes scanned her face. "How are you feeling since your heart attack?"

"I'm blessed to be alive."

"You're looking wonderful," Natalia complimented.

"I need you to talk to your father," Jessie Belle stated. "We need the merger to go as planned."

"And what do I get in return?"

"Natalia, my son is married now. There's nothing I can do about that."

"Then I'm afraid I can't help you, Mrs. Deveraux."

"I held up my end of the bargain, Natalia."

Glancing down at her left hand, she responded, "I'm not the one with a wedding ring. The way I see it, when Holt rejected me—our deal was rendered null and void." Natalia turned and walked toward the door. "I'm glad to see you're doing so much better."

"You're making a mistake, Natalia," Jessie Belle warned. "You and your father will regret this for the rest of your lives."

The front door opened and closed.

Natalia was gone.

"This is far from over," Jessie Belle whispered.

CHAPTER THIRTY-EIGHT

"Thank you once again for such thorough work," Jessie Belle told the private detective. "I threw in a bonus."

She got up and left the table wearing a big smile. She'd initially worried that Gee wouldn't find anything on John Winters, and she'd never expected the explosive tidbit in her hands. Not only was the merger going to go through, but John was also going to step down and hand over the reins to Traynor.

"I've got you right where I want you, John Winters," she whispered.

Jessie Belle reached into her purse and pulled out her cell phone. "Hello, John. It's Jessie Belle. I'm in the area and wondered if I could stop by. . . . Wonderful. I'll see you in a few minutes."

She navigated to her car and got in.

Ten minutes later, Jessie Belle pulled into the parking lot of Mount Vernon Baptist Church.

She walked into his office without knocking.

John looked up in surprise. "Jessie Belle . . ."

Closing the door behind her, she said, "We need privacy for what I'm about to say."

"If this is about the merger, you can—"

Jessie Belle cut him off by saying, "This is definitely about the merger and you need to hear me out, John."

"Natalia told me how your son used her. I'm disappointed by his behavior."

She frowned. "What exactly did she say happened?"

"Holt slept with my daughter and then dumped her."

"That's a lie," Jessie Belle uttered. "My son would never do something like that. They never had sex."

"How do you know?" he questioned. "You weren't with them twenty-four hours a day. Natalia was a virgin."

Jessie Belle laughed. "You've got to be kidding me. That girl hasn't been a virgin in a long time. I'd bet my life on that."

He looked offended. "What are you trying to say about my daughter?"

"That she's a manipulative little liar." Jessie Belle sank down in one of the visitor chairs. "But that's neither here nor there. John, the merger is beneficial to your church and mine. I want it to proceed and I think it's time you retired."

"Excuse me?"

"A man of your lifestyle should not be leading a church," she stated. "I don't know how you can stand in the pulpit on Sunday and preach. You or Rick." Shaking her head, she uttered, "It's such a shame."

John's face grew ashen. "Jessie Belle, what are you talking about?"

She pulled out a photograph and slid it across the desk.

"Wh-Where did y-you get th-this?"

Jessie Belle gave a slight shrug. "It doesn't really matter, does it?"

"What do you intend to do with this?"

"It depends on whether or not the merger goes forth," she responded. "And you step down as senior pastor."

John picked up a legal-looking document. "You'd destroy my reputation and further humiliate my daughter for this?"

"John, you can't turn this around on me. You're the one sleeping with your assistant pastor. Homosexuality is a sin."

"So is what you're doing, Jessie Belle."

She gave him a look of disgust. "You and Rick have no right to be in a pulpit. This church needs a true man of God in leadership."

"And I suppose the church needs a Jezebel like you?"

"What's it gonna be, John?"

He glared at her before signing the papers. "I want those pictures."

Jessie Belle shook her head. "I'm afraid that wasn't part of the deal. Now, I also need you to tell Traynor that you've decided to step down as pastor and that you want him to take your place."

When she left Mount Vernon Baptist Church, Jessie Belle felt like she'd conquered the world.

––––––

Traynor surprised her with a trip to Hawaii for her forty-fifth birthday. Jessie Belle fell in love with the island of Maui.

"I'm not sure I ever want to go back home," Jessie Belle said with a laugh. "It's beautiful here."

"It *is* nice," he murmured against her ear.

She enjoyed their long walks at sunset, their frolics in the water and their romantic nights.

Twenty-six years of marriage, and their passion was still going strong.

Holt called to wish her a happy birthday.

"Mother, please ask Father to pick up the other extension. We have something to tell you."

"Holt wants you to get the other phone," she told Traynor.

When they were all on the line, Holt said, "Frankie and I are pregnant. We're going to have a baby."

"Honey, that's wonderful," Jessie Belle uttered. "Congratulations to you both."

Jessie Belle resigned herself to the fact that now, with Frankie pregnant, she had to accept the girl into her family.

"When we get home, I'm going to get with Frankie and see what kind of theme she's thinking of going with. I need to get an early start on the baby shower."

"Jessie Belle, I'm so proud of you. Now, this is the woman that I know and love."

"I've put you through so much, Traynor. I'm so grateful you didn't leave me."

"You're my wife, Jessie Belle. We made a vow to one another and I don't take it lightly."

"We're going to be grandparents. Traynor, we've got to think of cute names for the baby to call us. I'm still too young to be called Grandma."

He laughed. "Honey, we have time for all this."

"It's never too early to get started," Jessie Belle insisted.

Traynor and Jessie Belle returned home to the news that Pastor John Winters had committed suicide.

"Oh my goodness," she uttered. "I can't believe it."

"He hasn't seemed like himself for the past couple of weeks or so," Traynor stated. "I tried to get him to open up, but he wouldn't. This is a shame. Winters was a good man."

She didn't respond. John had had everyone fooled, including his late wife and his daughter.

"I guess that's why he insisted on stepping down as pastor. He was planning to die soon."

Jessie Belle nodded in agreement.

The next day, she paid a visit to Natalia to offer her condolences in person. She was surprised to find Mary Ellen there.

"Where's Natalia?"

"She's getting dressed. She'll be down shortly."

It was clear from the thick cloud of tension in the air that their friendship was over. Jessie Belle couldn't believe Mary Ellen was being so petty.

"When did you get back in town?"

"This morning," Mary Ellen responded. "I flew in and came straight here. John was a friend of mine and I thought I should be here for Natalia."

"I wasn't aware that you two were friends. I didn't think you knew each other that well."

"There's a lot you don't know about me, Jessie Belle."

Natalia came downstairs.

Jessie Belle met her halfway. "Honey, I just heard about your father. I'm so sorry."

"Why would he do this?" Natalia whispered, her face streaked with tears. "It just doesn't make sense."

Jessie Belle embraced her. "Was something bothering him?"

"Yeah, but he wouldn't tell me what it was." Natalia glanced over at Mary Ellen and asked, "Did he say anything to you?"

"No, but I sensed he was troubled by the merger."

Jessie Belle met Mary Ellen's gaze. "John wanted this just as much as Traynor and I did."

Shaking her head in confusion, Natalia said, "I never could get him to tell me why he changed his mind about the merger. He was adamant about pulling out after Holt and I didn't get together."

"I guess after he really thought it over—John decided it was the best decision for his church. His ministry meant the world to him."

Natalia agreed. "I guess so. He was always a good businessman."

"I still think it's a bit odd, though," Mary Ellen blurted. "Like Natalia said, John was adamant about pulling out of the merger, so what could've made him change his mind?"

"I guess we'll never know," Jessie Belle murmured.

CHAPTER THIRTY-NINE

January 1997

Holt Junior was born two weeks early on the fourteenth day of January.

Jessie Belle and Traynor went to the hospital to visit with Frankie and meet their first grandchild. She spotted Holt near the nurses' station when they stepped off the elevator.

"Holt, why didn't you call us? We could've come out here and stayed with you."

"Mother, I didn't want to keep you up all night."

"We could've handled it," she responded with a laugh. "We're not that old."

"How's Frankie and the baby doing?" Traynor inquired.

"They're doing well," he responded. "Y'all can go on in the room."

Traynor rapped lightly on the door before walking inside.

"Come in," they heard her say.

"Hello, Frankie," Jessie Belle greeted. "How are you feeling?"

"Just a little tired. I'm glad you and Mr. Deveraux could come. I've been telling Holt Junior all about his grandparents."

"Really?"

"Yes and he's very excited to meet you."

Jessie Belle glanced over at the little bundle in the see-through bassinet. All she could really see was a head full of black curls.

"You can pick him up if you'd like," Frankie told her.

"Let me go wash my hands first."

"He's so beautiful," Jessie Belle murmured as she stared down at her grandson.

"He looks like Holt."

She agreed. "He sure does."

A knock on the door drew their attention from the baby.

Mary Ellen stuck her head inside.

"Come on in," Frankie gushed. "I can't believe you're here."

"I told you I wasn't about to miss the blessed event."

"You were too busy to join us for the baby shower," Jessie Belle blurted.

"Which is why I made it my business to be here now," Mary Ellen responded. "Your grandson is beautiful, Jessie Belle."

"I think so, too. Wash your hands and I'll let you hold him," she said. Jessie Belle was tired of the tension between them.

Mary Ellen glanced over at Frankie. "Is that okay with you?"

She nodded. "Sure is."

Jessie Belle turned to her daughter-in-law. "I'm sorry. I didn't mean to overstep my boundaries."

Frankie's expression indicated that she didn't believe Jessie Belle. "It's fine."

After Mary Ellen, Traynor and Holt went down to the cafeteria to have lunch and spend quality time together, Jessie Belle decided to have a heart-to-heart with Frankie.

"I never hid my dislike of you, Frankie, but I want you to know that's all in the past now."

"I really don't think it is," she responded. "You have no choice but to accept me because I'm married to your son and I just gave birth to your grandson. You don't want to risk losing them. But if Holt knew who you really are—he wouldn't have anything to do with you."

Jessie Belle was taken aback by her words. "Excuse me?"

"I know what you did to him," Frankie stated. "I know all about the way you coerced the record companies into not signing him by threatening to take airtime away from their artists. He was devastated, Mrs. Deveraux."

"You don't know what you're talking about. I can't believe Mary Ellen would tell you something like that. I know she hates me, but to do this—it's cruel. I sat in here today trying to make peace with her and she's stabbing me in the back. I should've known better."

"Miss Mary Ellen has nothing to do with this," Frankie countered. "She never betrayed you and she wouldn't try to turn Holt against you. She didn't have to open her mouth. I know about it because I worked for

Peace Records. I never told Holt what you'd done—it would hurt him too much."

"Are you trying to blackmail me?"

"I would never sink to your level, Mrs. Deveraux. I simply want it understood that I know who you really are. As long as you respect my position in this family, you will have a place in my son's life. However, I won't let you use him as a pawn. Not the way you've done with your husband and Holt."

"Understood," Jessie Belle responded.

She rose to her feet. "I guess I'll let you get some rest."

Traynor decided to spend the day clearing out the office he and Jessie Belle shared. He couldn't stand the clutter any longer.

Jessie Belle was over at Holt's. Since the baby was born, she was trying to build a solid relationship with Frankie. It pleased him that she was making strides to not interfere in their marriage.

He thanked God once more for the positive changes his wife had made. Jessie Belle was a different woman now and Traynor was proud of her.

Singing softly, he walked over to the file cabinet to put away some files lying around on her desk.

Inside the cabinet were several stacks of yellow envelopes. There was one with Elton Newman's name on it, which Traynor assumed had to do with the radio station. His eyes strayed to a thick envelope with John Winters's name written on it.

Curious, he picked it up and looked inside.

When he eyed the contents, Traynor suddenly felt sick to his stomach. He went back and grabbed the one with Elton's name on it. He then saw other names he recognized. Charles Maxwell and several other deacons in their church. The pastors he ran against briefly for ECC president.

Charles and the other deacons suddenly changing their minds about the mandatory tithe increase all those years ago; Elton agreeing to give him a radio show—Traynor was sick at heart.

He could scarcely believe how deep her deceit went. Most of it was in the past—all except John Winters. She was up to her old schemes.

He heard the front door open and close. Jessie Belle was back.

"Traynor, honey, I'm home . . . ," she called out. "Where are you?"

"In the office," he yelled out.

She came running in, holding up the digital camera in one hand. "I got some great shots of Junior. Honey, he's getting so big."

Jessie Belle's eyes traveled down to the thick envelope in Traynor's hand. "What are you doing with that? Were you going through my personal things?"

"I thought you told me . . ." He rose to his feet. "No, you promised me that you wouldn't resort to blackmail anymore. And I see that you've got bank accounts—accounts I knew nothing about. I don't know who you are."

"Every woman has or should have their own bank account. It's not a big deal, Traynor. As for that stuff, I never did anything with the information."

"I guess you think I'm stupid," he uttered. "You went to John, and that's the reason he suddenly did a complete turnaround on the merger. Winters died because of this information."

"I don't like your tone."

"I really don't care," Traynor shot back. "You might as well have put the gun in his mouth yourself."

"How dare you talk to me like this?" Jessie Belle stammered. "I had nothing to do with John's death. I considered him a friend."

Traynor held up the envelope. "This is how you treat your friends? I told you I would not tolerate this type of goings-on."

"John Winters is dead because he was a coward. He killed himself, Traynor. It had nothing to do with me."

"I need to know, Jessie Belle. Did you go see him about this file?"

She chewed on her bottom lip, trying to decide what to tell Traynor. He was furious with her right now. Jessie Belle knew that he was probably going to leave her this time.

"Well . . . ," Traynor prompted. "And I want the truth."

"Honey, I was concerned—," she began.

Traynor stopped her. "I said the truth, Jessie Belle. You're not as good a liar as you think."

"John was a closet homosexual. He was involved with his assistant pastor. Doesn't that bother you?"

"Who are you to judge anyone?"

"I simply suggested to John that he consider handing the reins over to you once the merger was completed." Jessie Belle quickly went on to say, "I didn't threaten him, but I confronted him with the truth."

Traynor looked completely disgusted with her. "Holt once said that you manipulated me through our entire marriage. He's right, but no more. It ends now."

"What do you mean by that?"

"Just what I said."

"I made you," Jessie Belle stated. "Traynor, you didn't get here all by yourself. I made sure you were successful. *I made you.*"

"I can walk away from it all, Jessie Belle. You wanted all this. I never did. Oh, I went along with the ride, but I shouldn't have. My spirit was trying to tell me, but I ignored it. You have information on Elton Newman. . . . That's why he gave me the radio show, isn't it?"

"Yes."

"You did all this talking about how you had so much faith in me—it was all a big lie, wasn't it?" Traynor demanded. "Because if you had any faith in me at all—you wouldn't have gone around blackmailing people."

"Traynor, I do believe in you," she snapped in anger. "That's why I did it all. *I did this for you.*"

"You hung around that man's widow until you convinced her to sell you the radio station. Then you dropped her faster than a hot potato. And there's Mary Ellen—your own best friend. You even tried to manipulate her life. She told me how you kept Richard's affair from her."

Jessie Belle didn't respond.

"Why didn't you just trust God?"

She didn't have an answer for him.

"I can't be around you right now." Traynor tossed the envelopes on her desk. "I have to get out of here."

Jessie Belle found her voice. "Traynor . . ."

"There's nothing else to be said. It's over, Jessie Belle. *We're over.*"

"You can't mean that. Traynor, you promised to stay with me until death. I expect you to honor your vows."

He released a harsh laugh. "*You* want to talk about keeping promises." Traynor shook his head.

"Please don't leave," Jessie Belle pleaded. "I love you, Traynor."

He walked out of the office and headed upstairs.

She followed him.

Traynor pulled out a suitcase and began to pack. He couldn't stand to be near his own wife.

Traynor was an idiot! An ungrateful idiot.

He should be thanking her for all her hard work, Jessie Belle thought to herself. After all, everything she'd done was to propel his career forward.

I did all this for you.

Traynor's mad at me now, but he'll get over it. He always does.

He has to get over this and come back to me.

Jessie Belle's eyes filled with tears. Traynor had actually walked out on her.

Deep down, she knew there was no reason to be angry with Traynor. All of this was her own doing. If she'd just stopped going behind his back, scheming and manipulating others to get what she wanted, Jessie Belle wouldn't be in this mess.

How do I get him to come home? Lord, what do I do now?

She paced back and forth for nearly an hour.

Jessie Belle tried calling Traynor, but he wouldn't return her call. She called Holt, but there wasn't an answer over there either. She burst into another round of tears.

All cried out, Jessie Belle slowly headed back up to her bedroom and took off her clothes. She wanted to wash away the nervous tension in her body in a hot bubble bath.

She felt a little better afterward.

After slipping on a black silk nightgown and matching robe, Jessie Belle paced back and forth in her bedroom, praying for another chance with Traynor.

"I don't want to lose my husband," she whispered. "Please let him forgive me. I only wanted to help Traynor. It's not my fault that John took his own life. He couldn't live with his own shame."

Jessie Belle kept checking the clock, hoping that Traynor would eventually walk through the front door.

The telephone rang.

She answered it on the first ring.

It was Holt.

"Have you talked to your father?" Jessie Belle asked.

"He's fine, Mother. The reason I'm calling is to let you know that he's staying with us."

"Holt, tell your father that he needs to come home. We can't work out our differences if he's over there with you."

"He doesn't want to come home. Mother, he told me everything. I have to be honest: I feel as if I don't know you."

"He had no right."

"He had every right," Holt countered. "Mother, you need help. What you're doing is wrong. I have to be honest with you—I love you, but I don't like you. I don't want my son around a person who does the stuff you've done."

Jessie Belle's eyes filled with more tears. "So now everyone is against me."

"We're not against you, Mother. We are concerned about you and we're praying for your soul. You need to get right with God."

She didn't respond.

"We love you, but we have to love you from a distance right now. Father can't be around you and neither can I. I'm sorry, but you are just not the woman I thought you were."

"I don't want to lose you or your father," Jessie Belle blurted. "Please help me. I don't know why I do the things that I've done. I don't want to be this way, Holt. I really don't."

She could hardly talk for the sobs in her throat. "I'm so sorry for what I've done. Oh God . . ."

"Mother, calm down."

"Please help me," she pleaded, her spirit broken. "I don't have anybody. God, please help me. Please forgive me."

Jessie Belle dropped the telephone as she fell to her knees. "Father God, I come before You broken. I am a horrible person, but I don't want to be. Lord, You didn't make me this way, so please help me. I repent of my sins and I ask Your forgiveness. I need You, God. I need You. . . ."

She lay on the floor crying out to the Lord. For once in her life, Jessie Belle didn't care about anything else. She continued to seek after God.

Jessie Belle was barely aware of Holt's presence in the room. She had no idea how much time passed as she lay curled up in the fetal position, her eyes closed and her mouth moving as she continued to pray.

He called to her gently. "Mother . . ."

She opened her eyes.

Holt pulled her into his arms. "You're going to be alright. God heard your prayers."

"Please forgive me," she murmured.

"Mother, I love you and I forgive you."

Jessie Belle held on to her son for dear life. She felt like her entire world had crashed and for once, didn't know what to do about it. Except call out to God.

"Father, please help me . . . ," she pleaded. "I can't make it without You. I can't do it."

Holt stroked her arm. "Just give it to Him. Thank You, Father . . . ," he repeated over and over. "Thank You, God. . . ."

Jessie Belle must have fallen asleep in her son's arms, because she didn't remember when he left. She woke up early the next morning on the bed with a throw covering her.

Her head hurt and her eyes were swollen from crying. Her heart ached because she knew that Traynor was gone.

He's not coming back this time.

Jessie Belle felt like all her strength had been sapped out. She had no energy to do anything—even bathe.

Looking around the room, Jessie Belle felt her heart break all over again. There were so many happy memories created in this room that she wasn't sure she could ever sleep in there again.

It would hurt too much.

CHAPTER FORTY

Jessie Belle sat in her usual seat at church on Sunday. Traynor had been gone for three days and they hadn't spoken during his absence.

Frankie surprised her when she sat down beside her. "How are you doing, Mrs. Deveraux?"

"As well as can be expected, I guess. How's my husband?"

"He misses you, but he's very hurt."

Jessie Belle's eyes filled with tears. "I don't deserve your kindness, Frankie. I know what you must really think of me. If it matters any to you—I don't like the person I've become either. I don't really blame Traynor for leaving me."

"Mrs. Deveraux, you are my husband's mother and the grandmother of my son." She took Jessie Belle's hand in her own. "While I hate what you've done—I love you as a person because that's what the good Lord expects of us."

"Hate the sin but love the sinner," Jessie Belle murmured. "How many times have I heard Traynor say that?" She met Frankie's gaze. "I actually believed that you can love someone into submission. . . ."

She paused a heartbeat before continuing. "I was wrong about you. Frankie, I'm so sorry for the things I said and did to you."

"It's all in the past, Mrs. Deveraux." She smiled. "You're a new creature in Christ."

"I've lost so much." She wiped away the lone tear rolling down her face. "I shouldn't have come here today. I'm not ready."

"It's going to be okay, Mrs. Deveraux. I'm right here beside you."

"My son is very lucky to have you, Frankie." Jessie Belle gave her a tiny smile. "I hope that one day you'll be able to call me Mom. I'd be honored."

Frankie embraced her. "Thank you, Mom."

They talked about the baby for a few minutes until it was time for service to begin.

Traynor looked genuinely surprised to see her when he stepped into the pulpit. Normally, he would have a secret smile for her, but not this time. Jessie Belle hadn't expected it and wasn't disappointed.

When it was time for the sermon, Traynor stood up and said, "Today I'm going to tell you about a Phoenician princess, the daughter of the priest-king of Sidon. Her name was Jezebel."

Traynor's eyes strayed briefly to where Jessie Belle was sitting, but quickly moved on. Heat spread through her body and outward, causing her to fan herself with her hand.

Frankie signaled for one of the ushers to bring a fan.

Jessie Belle returned her attention to Traynor. She knew that he was talking to her and she wanted to hear his sermon.

"Jezebel was a religious woman. She was also powerful, cunning and arrogant. She actively opposed the Lord and worshipped idols. That was her character. Her triumph was using manipulation to gain power at the expense of others. Her tragedy was that her arrogance, plotting and scheming all led to a shameless death. There was no redemption for Jezebel. Just think how different her story could have been had she harnessed her power, her drive and her devotion. Imagine the mighty ways God could've used her."

Jessie Belle felt the sting of tears. She blinked rapidly.

Traynor continued with his sermon, discussing the life and times of Jezebel. He drew to a close by saying, "Ours is a society that worships sports heroes, movie stars, money, sex and power. Each of us has more power than we realize—did you know that? God wants us to use it for godly purposes, but what we do with it is our choice. . . ."

Jessie Belle felt the heat of his gaze and looked up.

" . . . God is always willing to forgive and show His mercy even to the worst kind of sinner. King Ahab, the worst king Israel ever had, comes to his senses and repents of his evildoing, so God forgives him. God gives unlimited second chances. But for Jezebel, there was no redemption. She was arrogant to the end and never repented."

When Traynor did the altar call, Jessie Belle was one of the first ones down to the front. She fell to her knees in prayer. Before, she would never let any of the members see her raw emotions, but Jessie Belle no longer cared. She yearned to return to the arms of Jesus.

Traynor hadn't been as convinced as his son that Jessie Belle wanted to change her life. He initially assumed that it was just another form of manipulation. But now after he'd seen her in church—it was something about her demeanor. Jessie Belle didn't seem herself.

After the sermon, she came up with several other church members seeking prayer. Frankie came up and prayed with her.

She was never prone to public displays of emotion, but today, she was on her knees crying out to the Lord.

Traynor half expected her to come to his office when services ended, but she didn't. When he walked out to his car—Jessie Belle's car wasn't in the parking lot.

She didn't attempt to come speak to him. Deep down, he felt a thread of disappointment.

Experiencing mixed emotions, Traynor drove to his son's house.

Frankie was in the kitchen cooking when he entered the house.

"How is Jessie Belle doing?" he asked his daughter-in-law. "She didn't seem quite like herself at church."

"She's dealing with everything she's done in the past. Your wife really feels bad about the pain she's caused people."

"She told you that?"

"Not in so many words." Frankie stuck a roast into the oven.

"Do you believe she's sincere?" Traynor wanted to know. Frankie had good instincts when it came to reading people.

"I do, Dad. I think your leaving her forced her to really look inside herself. I think she'd made you her god and I believe she needs this time away from you so that she can focus on the true God."

"I'd never thought of it that way," Traynor responded.

"She loves you more than anything, Dad. She definitely loves Holt to death. She worships you both. She's materialistic. She loves jewelry, cars, money and being in control, but losing you and her son—that's what brought Mom to her knees."

Traynor didn't say it aloud, but he was worried about Jessie Belle. She invaded his thoughts most of the afternoon. He couldn't think about much else, so after dinner, he drove over to the house to check on her.

He let himself in with his key.

Traynor ventured straight through the house to the family room, but she wasn't in there. He went upstairs looking for Jessie Belle.

He found her in their bedroom on her knees with her head bowed.

She's praying.

Traynor had seen his wife pray many times over the years, so he wasn't surprised by this picture.

He eased away from the doorway and tiptoed down the stairs. Traynor gloried in the knowledge that God was really dealing with Jessie Belle and he didn't want to get in the way.

He left the house.

"Have Your way, God," Traynor whispered. "Just have Your way with her. . . ."

Jessie Belle read the entire books of 1 and 2 Kings. She wanted to read more about Jezebel and her daughter, Athaliah, who was a lot like her mother.

When she was done, she closed the Bible and bent her head in prayer. She was using this time to get right with God.

Jessie Belle could see her life so much clearer now. She'd allowed her love for power and money to consume her. She'd made Traynor and Holt more important to her than God. She wasn't sure when the last time was that God had first place in her life. Jessie Belle couldn't truly say if He ever was a priority to her.

"This is not the life that I want, Lord," she whispered. "I want to serve You. And if it's Your will—I'd like my husband back. I love Traynor, but I will not put him before You ever again. I will keep You first place in my life from this moment forward. Father God, I will accept Your will for my life."

Jessie Belle felt like a new person.

She went out and purchased a piano, suddenly wanting to play again after all these years.

Traynor used to love to listen to me play. He once told me I could be a concert pianist—I was that good.

Jessie Belle forced her mind to the present. There wasn't much point in living in the past—especially when that past was so ugly. But her future didn't look any better.

Her husband was still angry with her and Jessie Belle was pretty sure they were headed for divorce court. Before last Sunday, she couldn't think of Traynor without bursting into tears, and while she grieved for him, Jessie Belle knew that she needed to focus on her relationship with the Lord. She had to trust Him with her marriage.

Not an easy task.

If given another chance, Jessie Belle vowed to be the wife she should have been from the moment she said her vows. But if her marriage was truly over, then she prayed that God would grant her the strength to accept it and that He would give her peace of mind and heal her hurting heart.

But mostly, Jessie Belle prayed for Traynor. She prayed for God to show her husband exactly who he was as a man of God. She had always believed in Traynor, but she didn't let go and let God. Instead Jessie Belle tried to use manipulation to get ahead and failed miserably.

It was wrong and she knew that now.

Unfortunately, there were no do-overs in life. Jessie Belle couldn't go back and rewrite history—she simply had to accept the consequences. She was encouraged, however. She knew that whatever happened—God would be by her side.

CHAPTER FORTY-ONE

Two weeks later, Jessie Belle stared at the telephone long after the call from Traynor ended. He wanted to see her.

But why? Is he going to ask me for a divorce?

She vowed that she wouldn't throw a tantrum if he announced that the marriage was over. Jessie Belle continued to pray for God's help in accepting the truth. If Traynor no longer wanted her, she would set him free. She owed him that much.

"I need Your strength, Lord."

Jessie Belle strolled into the huge walk-in closet in search of something to wear. The old her would've slipped on something skimpy with the intent of seducing her husband home, but she had no desire to play those games. She found a simple silk sheath and slipped into it.

She pulled her hair up into a bun and decided against any makeup. Jessie Belle walked through her house, making sure everything was in its place. She didn't want Traynor coming home to a mess.

Rosa was on vacation this week and Jessie Belle hadn't bothered to do much cleaning. She'd spent most of her time in her bedroom, so the place was in good shape.

If Traynor wants a divorce, we're going to have to sell this house. I don't want to live here alone. He never really wanted this house in the first place. He bought it just to make me happy.

Jessie Belle sat down at the piano and began to play "Blessed Assurance" as she waited for her husband to arrive. Traynor was always prompt and she expected him within the hour. She sang along softly.

A tear slipped from her eye as she thought of the man who'd been her husband since she was eighteen years old.

Only she didn't know if he would still be her husband when he left.

Traynor wasn't sure what he was going to say to Jessie Belle, but he knew that it was time for them to have a serious talk about their marriage. Rumors were starting to circulate around the church, but not only that—he needed to find some closure.

He pulled into the driveway and parked the car.

Jessie Belle opened the front door just as he walked up to the porch.

"Hey," she murmured in greeting.

He embraced her, holding her tight. Traynor sucked in the light floral scent of her favorite perfume.

They stepped away from each other.

"It's time we made some decisions about our marriage," Traynor blurted. "That's why I'm here."

Jessie Belle nodded.

"I was thinking that we should file for a legal separation."

Her head snapped up. "I've made some horrible mistakes, Traynor—I can't deny that. I just want you to know that I'm truly sorry for everything. I hope that one day you'll find it in your heart to forgive me." Jessie Belle paused for a moment before continuing. "I love you so much, Traynor. I want our marriage even if I don't deserve it."

Traynor believed her. "I love you, too, Jessie Belle. Sweetheart, I never stopped loving you. I just don't know if we can still have a marriage. So much has happened. . . . I honestly don't know."

She sighed in resignation. "Traynor, I won't fight you on anything. If you want the separation—that's what we'll do. I don't want one, but . . ." Jessie Belle began to cry. "I'm sorry. I said I wasn't going to do this."

He hugged her. "I hate to see you so sad. I don't want to hurt you, Jessie Belle."

She placed a finger to his lips. "I did this, Traynor. All of this is my fault."

Traynor surprised himself when he kissed her.

Jessie Belle responded by kissing him back passionately.

Desire ignited in the pit of his belly, the flames growing. Traynor wanted to take Jessie Belle upstairs and make love to her, but to do so would only hurt her more.

She must have sensed his withdrawal, because Jessie Belle moved away from him. "Traynor, if you think that getting a legal separation is soften-ing the blow for me—it's not. If what you really want is a divorce, then I'd rather you be honest and say so."

"Is that what you want?" he asked.

Jessie Belle shook her head no. "I want you home so that we can try to salvage our marriage, but I have to face the truth that it may be beyond repair."

"I have to be able to trust you, Jessie Belle."

"I know my telling you that you can trust me won't convince you. All I can say is that I want you to pray about us—the marriage, everything."

"That's all I've been doing, Jessie Belle. I want my marriage," Traynor replied. "I just don't know if we can get back what we lost."

"We never lost our love—the kiss proved that. I know I've said it before, but I truly mean it this time. I will work hard to earn your trust back. Traynor, you were talking to me when you preached on Jezebel. I can admit that now. I was delivered of that spirit the night you walked out on me, even though I couldn't put a name to it then. It wasn't until I heard you preach on Sunday that I understood what happened. I went home that day and read the entire books of 1 and 2 Kings. Queen Jeze-bel used her power to encourage her husband to worship false gods and to practice ritual prostitution. Because of the close bond of marriage, spouses are influenced by each other. That's when the realization hit me full force, Traynor."

Jessie Belle paused a moment before saying, "This is why God doesn't want believers to be married to unbelievers. That type of union would produce different agendas and goals in life, rather than the couple being dedicated and committed to serving the Lord and bringing Him glory. See, I failed to realize that what matters most in life had nothing to do with climbing the ladders of success or all the luxuries we acquired over the years—our relationship with each other and our relationship with God is what should have been the priority."

I am just as guilty as she is, Traynor silently acknowledged. "I have to ac-cept my part in it, sweetheart. I allowed the spirit of Jezebel to infiltrate my house and my church."

"I see everything so much more clearly now. Knowledge is power be-cause now that I know the truth—the spirit can't take over like it did before. I'm delivered by the grace of God."

Traynor had never heard her talk that way in all the years he'd known her. "I thank God for your deliverance."

"I've been thanking Him and praising Him nonstop. I see life so differently now. Just before you arrived, I was thinking that we should sell this place. Especially if you're not coming home."

"You love this house."

"It's not the same without you, Traynor. I don't need something so big."

"Would you feel that way about it if I told you that I was coming home?"

Jessie Belle met his gaze. "You never wanted this house. You bought it to make me happy. Even if you were to come back—I still think we should sell. I'd be happy with you anywhere."

Traynor broke into a smile. "I looked at a nice little two-bedroom condo. It's about two thousand square feet."

"Are you thinking about buying it?"

"I considered it. But then I realized that I'd miss living here with you. Jessie Belle, I want to blame you for everything that happened, but God showed me that I had to accept my part in it, too."

"What do you mean?"

"I could've said no to you, but I didn't. Why? Because I enjoyed the benefits. I loved driving that Mercedes just as much as you did." His eyes traveled the length of the room. "I love this house."

"I went behind your back and while you could've fought me on some stuff, I don't think it really would have mattered, Traynor."

"Jessie Belle, what do we do?"

"I want to fight for our marriage. I'd like to do it without a separation, but no matter what—*I want us.*" Jessie Belle held out her hand and said, "I'd like for us to pray for the restoration of our marriage."

Traynor helped her down to the floor and he sat on his knees beside her. When they were done, he assisted her up.

"I like the piano," he told her. "I used to love to hear you play."

"I never realized just how much I missed it," Jessie Belle stated. "Would you like me to play something for you?"

He smiled. "I'd love it."

Jessie Belle played a couple of his favorite hymns and then she stopped because she couldn't contain her tears any longer.

Traynor comforted her. After a moment, he said, "Don't cry, sweetheart. We'll figure this out. Why don't we start with a date? I'll come pick you up tomorrow night and we'll have dinner together."

Jessie Belle wiped her face with the back of her hand. "I'd really like that, Traynor."

"We'll hold off on the legal separation and we'll pray about selling this house. Maybe it would do us good to start fresh in someplace new."

Pulling her closer to him, Traynor covered her lips with his, kissing her hungrily. "You still take my breath away, sweetheart," he whispered.

Traynor had barely walked out the front door when Jessie Belle broke into a praise dance. She then walked over to the piano and played while singing praises to the Lord, giving thanks. There was still a lot to be settled between her and Traynor, but Jessie Belle believed that their marriage would be restored.

God has given me another chance and so has Traynor.

She could hardly sleep that night because she was excited about her date with her husband.

Jessie Belle was up early the next morning. She and Frankie had lunch before her hair and nail appointment to prepare for her date with Traynor. She also wrote Mary Ellen a letter apologizing for her actions, which she'd given to her daughter-in-law to mail. Jessie Belle didn't have the address.

After her appointment, she stopped at a florist to send flowers to Minnie Newman. Jessie Belle had heard she was in the hospital. She even tried to reach Natalia, hoping to invite her over for dinner one night—the poor girl was all alone now and after all that Jessie Belle had done, she owed Natalia and she wanted to try to make amends.

When she returned home two hours later, Jessie Belle read her Bible and wrote in the prayer journal she'd started after Traynor moved out. She'd begun a habit of recording the many ways God blessed her, as well as noting the dates God answered her prayer requests.

I have so much to be thankful for, she noted silently.

That evening, Jessie Belle took her time getting ready for her date. Dressed and waiting for Traynor to arrive, she strolled through the French doors leading to the balcony.

Jessie Belle used to come out there to admire her estate and all that she'd acquired, but now she was standing there admiring the beauty of God's handiwork. He was the ultimate artist.

Jessie Belle heard a sound and turned, assuming that it was Traynor.

Instead, she found herself face-to-face with someone covered in black from head to toe. A scream caught in Jessie Belle's throat.

Before she could recover from the fear that paralyzed her, Jessie Belle felt the breath knocked out of her as she was pushed backward. She could feel her body falling in slow motion.

This time the scream erupted, echoing through the night air.

For a split second, Jessie Belle felt the pain from her fall, then nothing. Blackness surrounded her.

CHAPTER FORTY-TWO

As he drove to the house, Traynor thought back to the first time he ever saw Jessie Belle. She was so beautiful. For him, it had been love at first sight and he married her quickly because he feared losing her if they waited.

But the Jessie Belle he'd seen yesterday no longer possessed an ugly soul. She was a very different person from the woman he'd married. He prayed that God would continue to work within her.

And in me, he added silently. *Help me to completely forgive my wife.*

Traynor knew he would never forget all she'd done, but he didn't want to throw Jessie Belle's wrongdoing in her face. Doing so would mean he had not truly forgiven her.

He'd been looking forward to their date all day. Traynor had always enjoyed Jessie Belle's company and he missed seeing her every day.

His heart began to race as he turned on the street leading to his house and noticed the police cars parked in front of it. Traynor could see flashing lights and hear sirens in the distance. His heart dropped.

Oh Lord . . . what did she do this time? he wondered.

As he neared his house, Traynor spotted a team of police gathered in his yard, while paramedics appeared to be working on someone lying beneath the balcony outside his bedroom. He climbed out of his car and began walking toward the house, his pace rushed and steady.

Traynor recognized his son's car parked in the circular driveway. The pace of his footsteps quickened and he sprinted across the lawn.

A uniformed policeman stepped into his path. "Sir, I'm sorry, but you can't come up here—"

"This is my house," Traynor interjected. "I demand to know what happened here." As an afterthought, he quickly added, "I'm Pastor Traynor Deveraux. Who is that lying over there? Is that my son?"

"Father . . ."

Traynor turned in the direction that the voice came from. "Holt . . . thank the Lord. You're okay."

"It's Mom. Somebody pushed her over the balcony."

Traynor stared at his son in disbelief.

"Somebody tried to kill her. I just came by here to check on her." Holt's eyes filled with tears. "I found her lying out here. I don't know how long . . . how long she's been out here."

The world came to a crashing halt for Traynor. "Is she . . . ?"

Holt shook his head. "I don't know. They're working on her and they won't tell me anything. She was still alive, I think. Dad . . ."

Traynor began to pray. He and Jessie Belle both would need the strength of the Lord to get them through this.

Jessie Belle swam in and out of consciousness.

There were times she felt intense pain and other times when she felt like she was floating above the clouds.

Through the haze she heard voices, low and indistinguishable. Jessie Belle tried to follow the one voice she did know.

Her husband's.

Traynor's voice ebbed in and out of the darkness. In her more lucid moments, she tried to call out for him, but no sound would spill from her lips.

She slipped back into the unknown.

Jessie Belle was in a coma.

The doctors had done everything they could to save her, but told Traynor that they weren't sure she would regain consciousness, as her blood oxygen levels were too low to sustain life.

Traynor sat at her bedside and held her hand, praying that God would give her the strength to survive.

They'd rushed her to surgery two days ago, hoping to repair the three broken vertebrae, and she'd had to endure a second surgery this morning. The doctors informed him that she would probably be fully paralyzed.

Traynor's eyes filled with unshed tears.

For every action, there is a consequence. Jessie Belle's lies and manipulations led her here.

The police still had no leads on the person responsible for the attempt on his wife's life. Nothing had been stolen, so it was personal. Traynor couldn't deny that Jessie Belle had made a lot of enemies over the years.

But he didn't tell the police that.

Together, he and Holt had decided to burn the contents of the second drawer in the file cabinet to protect her life or her memory.

The door to the hospital room opened.

Holt and Frankie walked inside.

"How is she doing today, Father?"

Traynor wiped his eyes. "They don't think she's going to make it through the night."

Holt placed a reassuring hand on his shoulder and said, "We need to ask God what He has to say about this."

Traynor stood on one side of the bed holding Jessie Belle's hand, while Holt and Frankie were on the other side.

They prayed for her strength and her courage. They prayed for God to lay His healing hands on Jessie Belle.

Traynor told her, "In my heart, you are still the beautiful angel I met all those years ago in Mayville, Georgia. I am still your husband, Jessie Belle, and I'm not going to just let you die. I know you're tired, sweetheart, but don't give up. Fight, baby. Come back to me. I need you, Jessie Belle."

"Mother, I still need you," Holt stated. "We are not going to let you just leave us. You have always been stubborn and a fighter. Well, we need you to fight your way back to us now."

As she lay there in deep coma, Traynor continued talking to her. "God's Word is real, Jessie Belle. The Bible is God's Word and is a true account of God's dealings with man. I want you to remember that God loves you so much and once you leave this earth—it's too late to build a relationship with Jesus. God has pressed on my spirit that He's not going to let you die. He's not done with you yet, sweetheart."

"Did you hear that, Mother? God is not ready for you to leave us. You need to wake up."

Frankie wiped away her tears.

Traynor placed his hand on Jessie Belle's forehead and began praying once more. He wasn't asking Jesus to heal her but declaring it already done and giving God the praise.

He soon felt a blessed sense of peace and wholeness overtake him. Traynor sat down. "Thank You, Father, for Your grace and Your mercy. Thank You, God. Thank You."

Still holding on to her hand, Holt began singing softly.

The next day, Jessie Belle's blood oxygen levels had returned to normal, surprising the medical staff, who'd just lost someone else with the same condition.

Traynor, Holt and Frankie continued praying for her. By the evening of the next day, Jessie Belle had been disconnected from all life-support machinery except for an apparatus to assist her breathing.

Jessie Belle began responding to their voices.

It was a miracle!

Traynor couldn't stop praising God for all He'd done. Jessie Belle still had a heavy burden to bear, but at least she was alive.

That evening, Mary Ellen came to the hospital. "I jumped on a plane as soon as I heard," she told Traynor. "I had to be here for Jessie Belle. We've been through some craziness, but I still love her."

Traynor embraced her. "Thank you for coming, Mary Ellen. She's really missed you over the years. And she's changed—she's not the same person you knew."

"Praise God," Mary Ellen murmured. "I've been praying for her."

An hour later, they received more good news. Jessie Belle was now opening one eye from time to time.

"Thank You, God," Traynor uttered. He continued to believe in her healing.

Frankie persuaded Traynor to go home and get some sleep in a real bed for the night. "You and Holt have been here around the clock. I'll stay with her tonight."

"Who has the baby?"

"My sister's here. She knew that I'd want to be here to help you and Holt." Steering him toward the door, Frankie said, "I'll call you if anything comes up."

"I'll be back first thing in the morning."

"Take your time."

He embraced her. "Thank you, Frankie. I appreciate it."

"We're family."

He nodded and left, but Traynor was back at the hospital bright and early the next day. Holt and Mary Ellen arrived a few minutes later.

Shortly after Frankie left, Jessie Belle regained complete consciousness.

All Traynor could say was, "Praise the Lord!"

No matter how hard she tried, Jessie Belle couldn't move. She glanced up at the nurse, who said, "The doctor will be here in a few minutes."

Traynor, Holt and Mary Ellen walked into the room.

"I'm so glad to see those beautiful eyes of yours," Traynor said, planting a kiss on her forehead. "Welcome back, sweetheart."

"Can't m-move," Jessie Belle wanted to say but couldn't because of the ventilator.

The doctor entered the room before Traynor could say more.

Holt and Mary Ellen left the room so that he could examine Jessie Belle, who continued to watch Traynor. She tried to reach out to him, but couldn't lift her arms.

She soon found out why.

The doctor gave her the news that she had three broken vertebrae and had undergone two surgeries—one a tracheotomy. When he told her that she was left fully paralyzed and not able to breathe on her own due to the head and neck injuries in the fifteen-foot fall off the second-story balcony of her home, Jessie Belle felt like she would lose her mind.

She was nothing more than a vegetable. Death would've been better than this.

Traynor dried her tears and told her over and over how much he loved her. Jessie Belle turned away from him. She didn't want his pity.

He didn't leave her side.

Holt and Mary Ellen joined him and they continued to speak life over her. But Jessie Belle didn't want to live. She had nothing left to offer anyone.

HER REDEMPTION

CHAPTER FORTY-THREE

Jessie Belle returned home in early October from a rehabilitation center at Rex Hospital, where she'd been undergoing therapy since mid-June after spending over a month in the intensive care unit.

Whenever Jessie Belle got upset over her situation, Traynor would mention what a blessing it was that her spinal cord had not been severed during the fall. He felt she should be thankful for that.

I've had to endure two surgeries—a tracheotomy and the repair of three broken vertebrae. I'm confined to a wheelchair that I can only move by blowing into a straw and I'm on a ventilator. For this, I should be grateful?

Jessie Belle was angry. She'd repented of her sins and changed her life for the better. God's judgment of her was cruel and harsh.

Surely death would have been a better punishment. *What kind of life is this?*

Although Traynor was trying to keep his voice low, Jessie Belle could hear him talking to someone on the telephone.

"She's doing well," he was saying. "I just thank God. . . . Her mind is perfect. Her voice wasn't affected much and there's nothing really physically wrong with her aside from the paralysis. I truly believe she survived all of this just to be a testimony to all of us."

Jessie Belle's eyes filled with tears.

"She's going to continue to receive therapy at home. The doctors will be working to wean her off the ventilator and get Jessie Belle moving on her own again. I'm still praying for a miracle that she'll get the feeling back in her arms and legs and walk again. I need to check on her, but thanks so much for calling, Deacon Daniels. I know Jessie Belle appreciates all the flowers, cards and expressions of love she's received from the church members."

Traynor hung up the telephone, then walked over to the bed. "Hey. I thought you were in here sleeping. I just spoke to Deacon Daniels. He wanted to let you know that he and his wife are thinking of you. Mary Ellen called earlier. She's going to try to fly down here this weekend to see you."

Mary Ellen had visited her several times over the past months. She sent her cards and notes of inspiration almost weekly. Despite all Jessie Belle had done, her friend was there when she needed her the most.

"Are you in any discomfort?" Traynor inquired. He felt like a heel for asking her something like that. She was paralyzed—Jessie Belle didn't feel anything from the chest down.

"No," she whispered.

Jessie Belle couldn't talk very loud, so he moved close enough to hear her words.

Traynor sat down on the edge of the bed. "Sweetheart, I have to tell you . . . I'm overwhelmed with the support we've both received throughout this entire experience," he stated. "Everyone has really reached out to help us in any way they can. Jessie Belle, it's wonderful. People all over the world have been helping and praying for you. Their compassion and love have been unbelievable."

"It's so nice," she murmured. "I appreciate it."

"We have had a bunch of people volunteer to make the necessary renovations to make the house handicapped-accessible for you."

Jessie Belle's eyes teared up a second time.

"Sweetheart, you're not alone in this," Traynor said as he gently dabbed at her eyes.

"You're injured, but life will go on, Jessie Belle. We've hit some rough spots in our lives before, and through the grace of God, we made it through. We'll work together to get through this, too. You're still the same woman I married twenty-seven years ago."

Traynor grinned before adding, "You never liked dancing much anyway."

He was trying so hard to be happy, but Jessie Belle knew this was challenging for him as well. He still loved her—she saw it every time Traynor looked at her. He deserved so much more, but he was all she had. She couldn't just go on with her own life. Jessie Belle was helpless.

She wished that God had allowed her to die.

Traynor prayed for a way to rid Jessie Belle of her depression.

He couldn't imagine what she was going through, but it pained him to see her so sad.

My heart bleeds for her.

She had aged considerably since the fall. Her hair had grayed, giving it a dull brown appearance. Nonetheless, he still found her attractive. Jessie Belle was still the love of his life, even though she tried to push him away at times, even to the point of asking him to put her in a home and seek a divorce.

But Traynor refused to abandon her. He reminded her that he married her for better or worse. He was still committed to his marriage and devoted to being her rock.

Traynor continued to lift her up in prayer, asking for Jessie Belle's strength and for the spirit of depression to leave her body.

He kept his emotions in check until he was downstairs alone. Traynor wiped the water from his eyes. "God, I know that You will be glorified in this somehow and someway. I may not see it right now, but You will have the victory."

Traynor took a deep breath and released it slowly. "I have to believe it because Your word says so. I have to believe it."

On her good days, Traynor took Jessie Belle outside for a ride around the neighborhood, hoping just being outdoors would remind her of how much she loved admiring the beauty of God's handiwork.

Jessie Belle could feel herself falling into the black abyss. She opened her mouth to scream, but no sound would come out.

She came awake with a start.

Eight months passed since the attempt on her life, and the police still had no leads. The killer was still out there and his identity a secret.

Jessie Belle heard a noise.

Traynor was away at the church and she had no idea where the nurse was.

It's Cathy, she kept telling herself. *It's just the nurse.*

Her fear dissipating, Jessie Belle sighed in relief when Cathy entered the bedroom carrying a large poinsettia.

"Mrs. Deveraux, how are you doing this morning?" she asked, opening the curtains.

"Fine," she answered. "Is Traynor still here?"

"No, ma'am. He left about five minutes ago. I bought you some poinsettias for your room."

Jessie Belle smiled in gratitude. "Christmas used to be my favorite time of year. I looked forward to decorating the house and the tree. I always went overboard, you know."

Cathy agreed. "I'm the same way. If you'd like—just tell me where you want everything to go and we'll get it decorated just the way you like it, Mrs. Deveraux."

"Thank you," Jessie Belle murmured.

The nurse prepared to give Jessie Belle her bath.

She was so humiliated over having to have a complete stranger live in her home to care for her.

The ordeal over and Jessie Belle in a jogging suit, Cathy put her in the wheelchair and pushed her out of the room.

Traynor had had an elevator installed in the home.

They took it down to the first floor and navigated to the kitchen, where Cathy had breakfast ready for Jessie Belle.

She sat down at the table to feed her because Jessie Belle was unable to do it herself.

After breakfast, Cathy gave Jessie Belle her medicine and then took her on a stroll around the neighborhood.

I deserve this, I know, but Lord . . .

Jessie Belle fought back her tears. She was trapped inside a useless body. "I can't live like this."

It was a moment before she realized she'd actually said the words out loud.

Cathy rubbed her shoulders. "Honey, just take it one day at a time."

She wiped away the lone tear that escaped Jessie Belle's right eye.

"There's this part of me inside shouting that I'm alive, but I can't move. I can't do anything for myself. I've always taken care of me, Cathy."

She gave an understanding nod. "Mr. Deveraux told me that you were very independent."

"I'm being punished for my sins."

"Mrs. Deveraux, God isn't like that. He loves us."

"He isn't being unfair," Jessie Belle stated. "I deserve this and more. I wasn't a nice person before the fall. That's why someone tried to kill me."

Cathy gave her a hug.

"Mrs. Deveraux, once we admit our shortcomings, we have to relinquish all of them to God. Then we reach out and accept His cleansing forgiveness. Honey, God is always willing to forgive us. He's waiting and ready to embrace us. Even the worst kind of sinner can walk into His open arms. No matter how wrong our actions, the Lord will always forgive and restore us if we are sincere and humble ourselves."

Traynor had said those same words in many of his sermons over the years. So had her father. Despite having been in church her entire life, Jessie Belle felt like she was hearing them for the first time. *After everything I've done, God welcomed me back with open arms. He also allowed me to suffer the consequences of my actions.*

Galations 6:7 came to Jessie Belle's mind. *Do not be deceived: God cannot be mocked. A man reaps what he sows.* She knew well enough through her experiences in a farming community that no seed can produce except after its own kind. Jessie Belle knew from Traynor's sermons that one cannot sow to the flesh and reap from the Spirit.

It just never hit home until now.

CHAPTER FORTY-FOUR

"I turned in my resignation before I left the church," Traynor announced shortly after he arrived home. "I've been praying about this ever since the attempt on your life and I think it's time we withdrew from the public eye. I thought that it might be a good idea if we move after the New Year. Start somewhere fresh."

Jessie Belle agreed wholeheartedly. She didn't know who wanted her dead, so moving away sounded good to her.

"Your daddy's church is in need of a pastor and they've asked me to consider being preacher there. If I accept, that means we'd be moving back to Mayville. I know you never wanted to go back there to live."

"What did you tell them?" Jessie Belle asked.

"I told them I would take the job if you agreed. However, I hope you'll say yes. I really feel it's the right thing to do for us."

"Sounds like you've made up your mind."

"Are you okay with my decision?"

"I am," she whispered.

The fear she once had of living and dying in Mayville was becoming true, but strangely enough, Jessie Belle was at peace with it.

"I feel like it's where all this started," she began. "Maybe this is my chance to start over for real. To get it right."

Traynor sat down beside her. "It's our second chance. We will get through this together, Jessie Belle. No more separate agendas."

She nodded in agreement.

He reached over and took her hand.

Jessie Belle couldn't feel Traynor's touch, but she could still feel his love for her. "I thank God for you every single day of my life. Wherever you go, Traynor—I will go with you. I wanted to die when I came out of that coma. I couldn't see how I'd make it another day, but your love and your strength saved me. Your faith kept me pushing through."

She paused for a moment, resting her voice. "It's not easy for me being like this, but I know that God will work this out for my good. I'm holding on to that, Traynor. I'd lose my mind if I didn't."

Jessie Belle asked him to get her prayer journal. She had him start from the beginning and read what she called her praise reports. Together they sat there rejoicing in the many ways God showed Himself to her.

Thinking of His goodness filled Jessie Belle with something she couldn't define. Traynor turned on the radio to the gospel station—their radio station.

She looked at him and asked, "What are you going to do with the station?"

"I've been thinking about that," Traynor responded. "You have any ideas?"

"What if we checked with Mary Ellen—see if she's interested in buying it? She's always wanted her own station."

Traynor nodded in agreement. "I think that's a good idea."

At Holt's house, they celebrated the birth of Jesus, and because Holt was also born on December twenty-fifth, they celebrated his birthday as well.

Jessie Belle enjoyed spending Christmas with her son and his family. Her grandson was old enough to unwrap his presents, and she received pleasure in watching his excitement.

She was going to miss him dearly. She and Traynor would be moving to Brookhaven, a small town located ten miles outside of Mayville.

Traynor found a lovely little house for them, and Jessie Belle couldn't wait to see it in person.

Mary Ellen walked over and sat down on the sofa. "Thank you," she said. "Traynor told me that it was your idea to sell the station to me."

"It was *our* idea. I know you're exactly what that station needs, Mary Ellen."

"I'm so happy to see how well you're doing, Jessie Belle. I'm so proud of you and how far you've come."

"You have been a far better friend than I've ever been to you and I'm sorry about that."

"I love you, Jessie Belle. You are my dearest friend. Now, we're not going to keep looking behind us—if we do, we'll never see what's ahead of us. Okay?"

"Okay." Jessie Belle gave a tiny smile. "I love you, too."

One month later, Traynor wheeled Jessie Belle into a modest one-story home.

"This house is nice," she whispered to him. "You did good."

The brick ranch-style house paled in comparison with the Raleigh mansion they used to live in, but Jessie Belle no longer cared. She just wanted to feel safe again. It didn't even bother her that Traynor's salary was meager compared with what he was leaving behind.

They had some money in the bank from the proceeds of selling their house—her medical bills had wiped out much of their savings. They were together and happy.

Jessie Belle missed her son terribly. If only Holt had agreed to leave with them . . . She partly blamed Frankie. He probably would've come if he weren't married to her.

Convicted for what she was feeling, Jessie Belle raised her eyes heavenward and prayed. "Father God, I'm sorry. I know I shouldn't be feeling this way about Frankie. She is Holt's wife, and I need to respect those boundaries. I know that I was wrong about her. Frankie's been nothing less than a wonderful wife to my son. I'm trying to do better now even though I slip from time to time. I'm trying, but I can't do this alone. Please take those feelings away from me."

Traynor couldn't explain it, but he was happier than he'd been in a long time. He finally felt like he and Jessie Belle were back on track, despite her disability.

It took going through all of this to get my wife back.

Jessie Belle was adjusting well to living in Brookhaven, and she seemed to sleep better, no longer plagued by nightmares of someone trying to kill her. He knew that she really missed Holt.

Traynor hadn't told her, but Holt, Frankie and their son were coming for a weekend visit. He wanted to surprise her.

Her nurse, Helen, came into the room where he was watching television and said, "Mrs. Deveraux is asking for you, Pastor."

Traynor jumped to his feet and rushed to the bedroom. "What's wrong, Jessie Belle?"

She gave him a bewildered look. "Nothing, honey. I was feeling lonely and so I had Helen get you. I just wanted to know if you'd read some to me from the Bible. I have the audio Bible, but I love listening to you read the Word."

Traynor broke into a smile. "It would be my pleasure."

It pleased him that she hungered so much for the Word of God. God would continue to give her strength if Jessie Belle drew closer to Him.

Traynor sat on the bed beside her and read from the book of Job until she fell asleep.

Watching her, he recalled all the happy memories they'd created together. Some of the worst moments in their marriage popped up, threatening to ignite bitter feelings, but Traynor fought to keep them at bay.

In forgiving Jessie Belle, he had to change his way of thinking, which meant he couldn't allow those memories to take over. He then had to accept Jessie Belle. Traynor had to deal with the damage that had been done to their relationship, but now he was experiencing the healing—the restoration of their marriage.

Glory to God.

CHAPTER FORTY-FIVE.

For the past couple of months, Jessie Belle hadn't panicked at every strange sound in the house. She was finally comfortable with being home alone for a short time while Traynor was at church. Her nurse went to pick up a couple of prescriptions for Jessie Belle and would be gone for at least twenty minutes.

She occupied herself by watching television.

A weird sensation washed over Jessie Belle.

"Is someone here?" she said as loud as she could manage. Her words still came out in a raspy whisper, although her voice was a little stronger now.

Jessie Belle could feel a presence in her room and knew she was not alone.

She spied the thin form of a woman out of the corner of her eye and turned her head. "Natalia . . . what are you doing here?"

"I came to see you, Jessie Belle," she replied, her tone cold and exact. "I remember how you came to visit me as soon as you heard my father was dead, however insincere it was. Well, I thought I'd repay the favor."

"But how—"

Natalia cut her off. "I ran into Holt and his wife—what he sees in that cow, I have no idea. . . . Anyway, I told him just how concerned I was about you and how much I missed talking to you. Holt gave me your address."

Jessie Belle didn't know why, but she was bothered by Natalia's tone. She knew the young woman was bitter, but there was something more going on.

Natalia sat down in a nearby chair. "So how's life treating you these days? Getting around much?"

"Excuse me?"

She broke into a little laugh. "Oops, I'm sorry. That was pretty cruel of me, wasn't it?"

"Have you been drinking?"

"Of course not," Natalia responded. "I don't drink, Jessie Belle. You know that."

"What are you doing here? I tried to call you before the accident. I wanted to get together with you. I—"

Natalia interrupted her by saying, "You know, I'm truly surprised you survived that nasty fall. I expected you to die. I guess you really are blessed and highly favored. That is what you're so fond of saying, isn't it?"

Jessie Belle didn't respond.

"You know, I keep going back to how you were so sweet to me after my daddy died. Back then, I thought to myself that you must really care about me."

"I do care about you."

"*Really?* Is that why you forced my daddy to agree to the merger? Is that why you forced him—no, blackmailed him—into stepping down as pastor? Before he killed himself, my father wrote me a letter. For whatever reason, it ended up under the cabinet in his office. I found it when I decided to take your advice and redecorate. I realized that day that you never cared about me at all. I wanted to make you pay."

Jessie Belle's heart started to race as the realization dawned on her.

It was Natalia who pushed her. "You . . ."

She smiled. "You were always a smart woman."

Opening her purse, Natalia pulled out a knife.

"Please don't kill me . . . ," Jessie Belle Deveraux pleaded, fear knotting inside her. "I'm begging you. . . ."

A satanic smile spread across Natalia's thin lips. "Why should I let you live? Did my father plead with you to keep his secret? Did he beg you not to destroy my impression of him? *Did he?*"

"I was wrong for the way that I treated you and your family, but I'm not the same person I used to be—I've changed. Being like this . . . and in this wheelchair . . . Natalia, I'm so sorry for the pain that I caused you."

"You'd say just about anything with a knife wielded at you—I'm not stupid."

"You don't have to do this," Jessie Belle replied in a small, frightened voice. "Don't end up like me. Natalia, you still have a chance to have a normal life. *A real life.* You don't want to spend it in prison."

"Me in prison . . . now, that's a laugh. Prison is exactly where *you* belong."

Natalia's laugh had a hint of insanity to it, the shrill sound of it chilling Jessie Belle's useless bones.

"You'd be amazed how things can change in an instant," Jessie Belle stated. "One minute you're on the top of the world and then . . . then you're paralyzed. You may not think so, but I'm paying for my sins. Natalia, I don't want you to travel down the same road I traveled. I made a lot of mistakes."

"*Made mistakes.* Humph. You ruined lives. My father . . . he committed suicide because of you. My family's ruined. You haven't paid enough."

Jessie Belle tried to keep her fragile control. "I know that. Natalia, you can't know just how sorry I am. For the past year I've had to relive all the horrible choices I made."

Tears rolled down her cheeks, blinding her, but Jessie Belle was unable to wipe them away, her arms laden with lead.

"I'm so s-sorry."

"Your tears don't sway me, Jessie Belle. You've taken everything away from me that I ever cared about. It's time for you to pay."

Jessie Belle breathed in shallow, quick gasps. Her chest felt as if it would burst.

"Look at me," she uttered, her voice raspy. "You don't think I've paid for my crimes . . . my sins. I've paid and I'm still paying. . . . Every single day I wake up in this useless body." Jessie Belle closed her eyes and began to pray. Not for herself but for Natalia, who was getting ready to take her life.

A chill black silence enveloped the room, surrounding them.

"You deserve to be in that wheelchair and more," Natalia hissed. "For all the horrible things you've done—you should live out the rest of your life in pain and suffering. The once-great Jessie Belle Deveraux has fallen. *Just like Jezebel.*"

The nurse returned, much to Jessie Belle's relief.

"How did you get in here?" Helen asked, looking from Jessie Belle to Natalia.

"The door wasn't locked," Natalia replied, sticking the knife back inside her purse. "It's okay. I'm a close friend of the family. *Right, Jessie Belle?*"

She forced a smile.

"Well, I must be going," Natalia said. "It was good to see you again."

"Be safe," Jessie Belle whispered.

"Give my love to Pastor."

"I clearly remember locking that door behind me," Helen stated when Natalia left.

"It's okay," Jessie Belle uttered. "I'm just glad that you're back. I'd like to listen to my audio Bible. Could you turn it on for me, please?"

"I sure will," she replied. "I'll do it right now for you, Mrs. Deveraux."

When Helen returned, Jessie Belle was sobbing.

"What's wrong, Mrs. Deveraux?"

Jessie Belle bared her soul to Helen, who sat in stunned silence. When she finished talking, the nurse said, "Mrs. Deveraux, when you accepted the gift of salvation—all that stuff washed away. That's not who you are now, so we'll have no more living in the past."

"It's not that easy to just shed the old skin, Helen. Sometimes the past has a way of catching up to you. As painful as it can be at times, I'm trying hard to make peace with everything."

Natalia was still prominent on her mind so much that Jessie Belle didn't even hear Traynor enter the bedroom.

He took one look at her face and asked, "Jessie Belle, what's wrong? You look like you've seen a ghost. Sweetheart, what happened?"

"I had a visitor," she told him.

Traynor sat down in a nearby chair. "Who was it?"

"Natalia Winters."

Traynor was surprised. "Really? She came all the way to Georgia to see you? That's sweet of her to do that."

Jessie Belle decided to be truthful about Natalia's visit. "It wasn't really a friendly visit. Natalia had a lot of stuff she needed to get off her chest."

His expression changed to one of concern. "What did she say to you, Jessie Belle?"

"Natalia just made me take a long hard look at myself."

"I'm afraid I don't really understand."

"I hadn't really accepted my part in John's death until today," Jessie Belle confessed. "She made me face the fact that I did something terrible, and it led to her father killing himself."

A lone tear rolled down her cheek.

Traynor wiped it away.

"Sweetheart, you don't have to keep rehashing your past. You've repented of your sins—it's in the past."

"She's right, you know. She said what I've been feeling all along. I'm in this chair because of what I did to Natalia, what I did to Mary Ellen—you and Holt," Jessie Belle blurted. "I deserve this."

"Sweetheart, I've seen the way you've turned your life around. . . . It started long before the fall. You're not the same person."

"I just feel like it's not enough. Natalia tried to kill me, but I don't want her sent to jail—I want to find a way to help her."

"It is more than enough, Jessie Belle. You saw the errors of your ways and your heart is willing—God sees the heart."

"I wish I could have a do-over," Jessie Belle whispered.

"There are no do-overs in life, sweetheart."

"I hated seeing so much pain in Natalia's eyes. I'm really worried about her."

"Did she threaten you, Jessie Belle?"

"Honey, Natalia could've killed me if she wanted to, but she didn't. I just pray that she'll find some peace and happiness in her life. She has a chance to get it right. I just hope she does before it's too late."

"Every day you wake up gives you one more chance to make a change," Traynor stated. "As for Natalia, she needs help, sweetheart. The kind of help we can't give her."

"Traynor, we can't prove a thing. It would be my word against hers. Let's pray for her. God can do more for Natalia than any doctor. She reacted in the heat of the moment. That day, she'd just found a letter that her father left. In it, he said I'd blackmailed him into proceeding with the merger and stepping down as senior pastor. *It's true.*"

"But she tried to kill you, Jessie Belle. Are you sure you want her roaming free? What if she comes back here?"

"She won't," she assured him. "Natalia said my being in this chair is punishment enough. Besides, a lot of people had motive to want me dead. I've made a lot of enemies over the years. She might have just said it was her to shake me. We'll never know for sure, but if it was Natalia, then I forgive her, Traynor. I pray that one day she'll be able to find it in her heart to forgive me."

The months were passing in such a blur that Traynor felt like life was fleeing. He didn't want to waste another moment thinking about what would never be; instead he wanted to enjoy every moment he had left with his wife.

Since the accident, Jessie Belle seemed to have good and bad days. Although she never complained, he could tell her body was failing her, but even in her weakened state, she refused to miss a single Sunday of hearing him preach. She kept telling him that hearing his sermons gave her great joy.

The Sunday before Thanksgiving, Traynor Deveraux stood in the pulpit of Mayville Baptist Church. Jessie Belle was seated in her wheelchair beside the first pew. His eyes traveled to her and he smiled briefly before moving on.

They spent a lot of time together just discussing the Bible and Jessie Belle offered him insight and several points when he worked on his sermons. They were still a team, but this time they were both on the same path.

After church, Traynor drove home.

"Honey, you did a wonderful job this morning," she told him. "I'm so glad you preached on King David. I'm encouraged every time I hear his story."

Jessie Belle tired more easily these days, so as soon as they arrived home, the nurse and Traynor assisted her into bed for a nap.

He noted that her naps were lasting longer. This time Jessie Belle slept until six p.m. Her health was failing, but there was nothing they could do about it.

Traynor had dinner with Jessie Belle and readied her for bed. While she listened to the audio Bible, he went to the family room to make a few phone calls.

He returned twenty minutes later and cut off the CD player. "I'll finish reading the passage to you," he told Jessie Belle.

Lying in the hospital bed, she replied, "I'd like that."

"You okay?" Traynor inquired.

She nodded. "I just miss Holt. I'd sure like to see my baby. Holidays aren't the same without him."

Traynor kissed her cheek.

"Maybe he'll surprise us and come up for Thanksgiving." Taking a seat in the chair he kept beside her bed, Traynor began to read from the Bible.

When she fell asleep, he allowed his tears to fall.

The next day, Jessie Belle woke up to a wonderful sight.

Holt and Frankie had arrived with four-year-old Holt Junior, surprising her with their visit and lifting her spirits. Jessie Belle felt better than she had in weeks just seeing them.

"Oh my goodness," she exclaimed. "What are y'all doing here?"

Holt planted a kiss on her cheek. "We came to see you and spend the holiday with you. Father said you were demanding that the family come together for Thanksgiving. Well, I told Frankie we had to come because you'd given us our marching orders."

"Funny . . . funny," Jessie Belle managed.

Frankie gave her a hug. "You're looking as beautiful as ever, Mom," she murmured.

"Thank you, sweetheart. You're looking pretty cute yourself." Jessie Belle eyed her. "Are you . . . ?"

Frankie nodded. "We're pregnant again. And we're having identical twin girls."

Jessie Belle beamed with pleasure. "Oh my goodness. *Twins?* Congratulations."

A thread of sadness dampened her happiness. She wouldn't be around to meet her granddaughters.

Traynor walked into the room and announced that she had another visitor.

Before she could respond, her best friend walked through the door.

"Mary Ellen . . ."

"Jessie Belle, it's so good to see you."

"Come sit here," Jessie Belle told her. "I have missed you so much."

Traynor cleared his throat and said, "I'm taking Holt, Frankie and Junior with me to pick up some food. We'll be back shortly."

Jessie Belle smiled at him in gratitude. He instinctively knew that she'd want some time alone with her friend. There was so much she wanted to say to Mary Ellen.

"Mary Ellen, I'm so glad that you're here. Traynor is going to need a friend."

"Honey, what are you talking about?"

"I . . . I'm dying, Mary Ellen. I can feel it."

"I don't want to hear you talking that way."

"Don't cry," Jessie Belle told her. "No tears, Mary Ellen. I can't . . . no, I won't have you crying. Remember, I can't even wipe my own face."

"That's not funny."

Jessie Belle smiled. "We have today. We have this moment. Let's not squander it by shedding tears. God gave me another chance to get it right, and I didn't waste it. We should be rejoicing. Right?"

Wiping her eyes with the back of her hand, Mary Ellen nodded. "You're right. You know, I never did thank you for writing me that letter."

"You are my dearest friend and I thank you for loving me—the good and the not so good. I love you even more for telling me the truth even when it hurt."

Mary Ellen kissed her cheek before saying, "We're supposed to be rejoicing, girl."

They were soon caught up in happier memories.

When Traynor returned, Jessie Belle was sleeping and Mary Ellen was in the family room watching television.

"How does she seem to you?" he asked.

"She tires easily." Mary Ellen's eyes filled with tears. "She told me that she can feel her life slipping away." She wiped away a tear. "I'm sorry, Traynor. It's just that it breaks my heart to see Jessie Belle lying in there like that. She was such a beautiful and vibrant young girl—that's the way I see her in my mind."

He gave an understanding nod. "I know. I see her the same way."

Sighing softly, Traynor sat down on the love seat. "The strange thing is that she's so much more of a woman now than she ever was. Jessie Belle is the woman I always knew she could be, but now I'm losing her."

"We're not going to think that way, Traynor. The way I see it—your wife has been in some pretty tough situations and she's come out on top. This is no different. But if she leaves us—at least we know that we'll see her again. There are two types of healing. This side and on the other side."

"This may be the toughest battle of her life. I have to admit that she seems at peace, though. Jessie Belle is more concerned about me."

"Even with everything she's done, Traynor, Jessie Belle never lied about loving you. She has always adored you."

"I feel the same way about her. There was a time when I wasn't sure I even liked her anymore, but when I came home and saw her lying on the ground—I knew that I would love her for the rest of my life."

Holt and Frankie joined them in the family room.

"Junior's taking a nap," Frankie said. "He was getting cranky."

"The food's ready," Holt told them. "Frankie sat everything out on the counter. Is Mother up to joining us?"

"She was sleeping, but she might be up now," Mary Ellen said. "The nurse is in there sitting with her."

Just as they were preparing to eat, Helen rushed out of the room, saying, "Mr. Deveraux, I just checked on your wife. I'm sorry, sir. She slipped away quietly. She's gone."

They followed her to the master bedroom.

While Helen was on the phone making the necessary calls, Traynor went over to his wife. Holt, Frankie and Mary Ellen said their goodbyes, and then left Traynor alone in the room with Jessie Belle.

She looked so beautiful and peaceful; she still took his breath away.

"I've never met anyone like you," he whispered. "Your character questionable, your triumphs led to tragedy, but before you left this earth, your redemption was complete. It was my honor to have loved you. Goodbye, my sweet Jessie Belle."

AUTHOR'S NOTE

I hope you have enjoyed *Jezebel*. I wanted to share some more thoughts on this particular character in the Bible found in 1 and 2 Kings.

In Hebrew the name "Jezebel" literally translated means "without cohabitation." Simply put, Jezebel will not dwell with anyone unless she's able to dominate the relationship. In cases where she's submissive, she's actually lying in wait to gain the upper hand. She will not allow anyone to control her.

A woman under the influence of Jezebel will use her feminine wiles; however, she won't use physical contact if a seductive glance of her eyes will allow her to gain control.

I think it's noteworthy to mention that while Jezebel is often referred to as a woman, this spirit is without gender.

Had Jezebel thought more about her inevitable end, her story may have had a different ending. Although we don't like to think of our own demise, we should. Doing so humbles us. It strips away any illusions and serves as a reminder that we have to answer to God.

I challenge you to take a few minutes and just imagine your last day on earth. What kinds of memories do you want to leave behind? Pray and ask God to show you what in your life can be celebrated and what in your life needs to be changed. You can overcome the haughtiness of Jezebel by seeking the meekness of Christ.

JEZEBEL

JACQUELIN THOMAS

A CONVERSATION WITH JACQUELIN THOMAS

Q. When did you know in your life that you wanted to be a writer?

A. I was painfully shy as a child, and so writing was therapy for me. I wrote my first story in the third grade, and my teacher, Mrs. Appling, encouraged me to pursue creative writing. By the time I was sixteen, writing had become my passion.

Q. How do you feel writing has changed your life?

A. I wouldn't say it's changed my life, but it has definitely added to my life. Through writing Christian fiction, I've developed a closer relationship with God, and I've learned so much more about the Bible. God has used my own novels to minister to me—He's awesome like that.

Q. When you sat down to write Jezebel, *was there a specific message you were hoping to impart to the reader?*

A. I wanted readers to understand just how powerful the Jezebel spirit can be and how easily we can get caught up. It's important to stay prayed up and ask God for a discerning spirit.

Q. Do you have a theme in mind for your next book?

A. I'm really excited about my current work-in-progress. It's a modern-day adaption of Queen Vashti's story in the book of Esther and is titled *Trophy Wife*. Several themes are woven throughout the story, including submission to your husband and sexuality—what's considered moral and immoral when it comes to the marriage bed.

QUESTIONS
FOR DISCUSSION

1. Jessie Belle's mother had no problem flirting or using her looks to get the butcher to give her a better cut of beef or to get a few yards of extra fabric. What message do you think she sent to her daughter?

2. People have made both wise and foolish choices when it comes to marriage. Did Traynor make a wise or foolish choice in marrying Jessie Belle? How important was his choice in a wife? Explain your answer.

3. Jessie Belle was never satisfied. The more she got, the more she wanted. How do we fight jealousy and greed? How do we fight discontentment?

4. What kinds of negative influences surrounded Jessie Belle? What could she have done to negate those influences?

5. Do you believe that Jessie Belle truly loved her husband? Why or why not? How did she go about achieving her dreams of enlarging Traynor's ministry?

6. How did Traynor let his wife get so out of control? Do you think he was blinded by love, or pleased with the fact that his ministry was growing and he was achieving the level of success Jessie Belle predicted?

7. What level of guilt does Traynor have for Jessie Belle's actions? To what degree, if any, are we responsible for the sins of our spouses?

8. What level of guilt does Jessie Belle have for her actions? To what degree is she responsible for Natalia's quest for revenge?

Photo by Glamour Shots

Jacquelin Thomas is the *Essence* bestselling author of *The Prodigal Husband,* *Defining Moments,* and *Redemption.* She lives in North Carolina with her husband and children. Visit her Web site at www.jacquelinthomas.com.